COME FROM AWAY:

The Plot to Assassinate Churchill

1941

An Historical Novel

J. F. Leahy

ISBN-10: 061566962X
ISBN-13: 9780615669625

LCCN: 2012956335
Naval Writers Group Annapolis, Newport, San Diego

DEDICATION

For Terry and Dennis, hunters extraordinaire,
who joined me in exploring the Cape Shore
and the rest of the Avalon Peninsula
over forty years ago, and for Mary,
who has supported us and cheered
us on these many years.

CONTENTS

ACKNOWLEDGMENTS

Although writing has been described as the loneliest
of professions, no book is solely the work of the author
listed on the cover. I am grateful for the collaboration and
expertise of associates of the Naval Writers Group
and others in helping to bring this work to fruition:

Ms. Amanda Lee Waluzak who served as the primary editor of this volume, and who dealt skillfully with unfamiliar naval jargon of the period, and quickly came to appreciate the lilting speech patterns of the people of the southern coast of Newfoundland. It is said that no man is a hero to his valet; neither is an author to his editor, especially an author with as tentative a grasp of the rule of punctuation as I. Thanks, Amanda!

Dr. Anne K. Dellinger of Saint Paul's College. A friend and colleague for over forty years, now retired to Brataslava, Dr. Annie conducted valuable research including countless hours spent uncovering primary documents in Germany, France, Canada, and the United Kingdom.

Ms. Amanda Renee Eldridge, who served as primary editor for my previous book *Lost at Sea, an Enlisted Woman's Journey* and who kindly agreed to generate the charts and graphs which appear in this volume, and who contributed her skill as a photojournalist in the selection and inclusion of the graphic elements of this work.

Mr. Jim Lynch of St. John's, retired educator and member of the board of directors of the Royal Newfoundland Constabulary's Historical Society, for providing clarification on the jurisdiction of the various local and Allied law enforcement personnel operating in Newfoundland during World War II.

And a very special word of gratitude to **Deputy Chief (Ret.)Gary Browne M.O.M.** of the Royal Newfoundland Constabulary for his kindness and assistance provided in personal emails at critical points in the development of this narrative. Gary, as author of the seminal work on the subject: *To Serve and Protect: The Newfoundland Constabulary on the Home Front World War Two* (ISBN 0-9783434-9-2 273 pages DRC Publishing, St. John's,) knows well the challenges of "getting it right" when exposed to conflicting interpretations discovered in the historical record. *As loved our fathers, so we love, where once they stood, we stand.* Thanks, Chief.

WINSTON CHURCHILL AT SHIP HARBOUR (NAVAL OPERATING BASE, ARGENTIA),
Placentia Bay, Newfoundland on 10 August 1941

AUTHOR'S NOTES

1. This is a work of fiction: Much of this narrative relates events precisely as they are recorded by contemporaneous accounts or in scholarly research. Other parts of this narrative are products of the author's imagination. It is often said that truth is stranger than fiction. I leave it to the wisdom of the reader to discern between the two.

2. Come-From-Away: An individual, not island born, who as a resident or visitor abides on the island of Newfoundland.

3. Glossary: A glossary of unfamiliar words, terms and usages unique to the navies of the United States, Canada, Britain, Germany and to the people of Newfoundland and Labrador may be found in the rear of this volume.

4. Newfoundland: Rarely has any place name been subject to as many variations in pronunciation. Local speakers place emphasis on the last syllable, i.e. Newfound**land** (rhyming with "Understand"). During the time of this narrative, the island was properly 'The Dominion of Newfoundland'. After Confederation in 1949, it is properly referred to as the 'Province of Newfoundland and Labrador.'

5. Newfie: One unfortunate by-product of World War II in the North Atlantic was the proliferation of the offensive term *Newfie* by outsiders to refer to the people of Newfoundland. Out of respect and affection for my many friends at Placentia Bay and elsewhere in the province, this pejorative appears nowhere in this narrative.

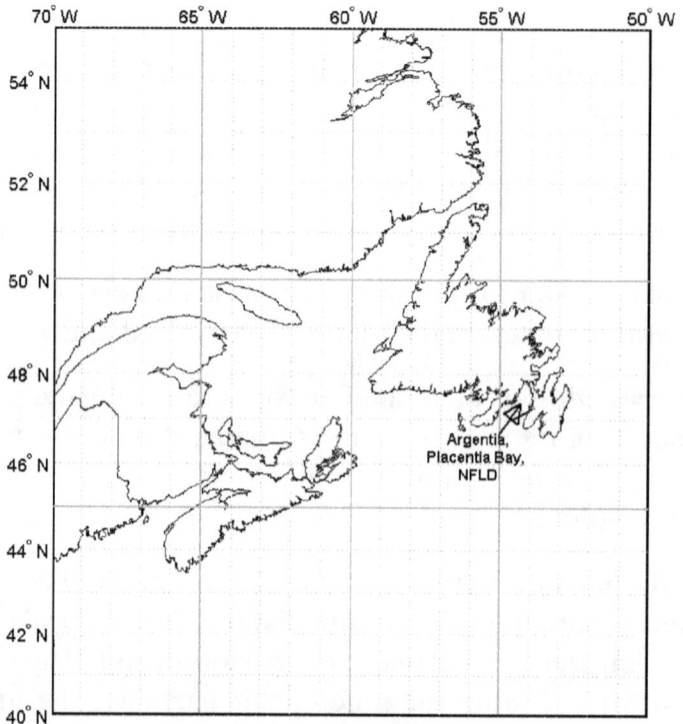

THE DOMINION OF NEWFOUNDLAND
AND THE CANADIAN MARITIMES – 1941
(Chart – A.R.E)

PROLOGUE

20 December 1999
St. Colm's Parish Rectory
Placentia Bay, Newfoundland
12:30 PM NST

The radio on the windowsill played merrily, and Father Michael Cashin hummed quietly to himself. Every Saturday morning, station VOCM in St. John's played a selection of jigs, reels and ballads, long forgotten everywhere except in the remote fishing villages of Newfoundland. And St. Colm's Parish was certainly that. The small wooden church and attached rectory stood lonely vigil at Black Point, Placentia Bay, just north of the small fishing village of Little Barasway. The signal from St. John's was pleasingly strong. "They must have a repeater around here, somewhere; maybe up north near the Trans-Canada Highway," Father Cashin thought to himself. "It's what? Nearly eighty miles to the city, I'd guess."

Outside the window, snow fell steadily, driven by a brisk westerly wind. It was a week before Christmas, and so far the winter had brought several feet of snow to the Avalon Peninsula. "Worst winter in living history," he heard Carl Wells say on the CBC weather report the evening before. "Living history...," Father Cashin thought to himself, "What an appropriate phrase for today. That's what brought me here, all right. Today I'm recording the history of the living and of the dead, may they rest in peace."

He sighed, and turned again to the stacks of paper on his desk. "I'll say this about old Monsignor Jeremiah O'Donovan McHugh – the man certainly was organized. He's kept every piece of paper that had anything to do with St. Colm's for the last fifty years, it appears." The parish registers in the priest's flawless handwriting recorded births, confirmations, marriages and deaths for every Catholic family along this section of the bay. Recently, though, the proportion of deaths recorded greatly outweighed all other transactions. Father Cashin sighed. Emigration was the curse of Newfoundland.

Sadly, Christmas Eve Mass would be the last at St. Colm's. Emigration, an aging population, and a critical shortage of priests meant that the parish would close within the week. Father Cashin, vice-chancellor of the Archdiocese, had been sent to wind up parish affairs. A Cape Breton native, he knew well the impact that the steady decline of the fishery had on small villages all through-out Atlantic Canada. "Kids graduate from high school – if they're lucky – and the next morning they're on the ferry to the main-land," he thought. "Take a walk up The Danforth in Toronto – or any road in the tar sands up by Fort McMurray – and you'll hear the gentle Irish-tinted lilt of Newfoundlanders, most pining for the simple, decent lives they left behind."

The Archbishop had wanted to close St. Colm's for years. It really didn't make any economic sense to keep it open – the parish-ioners, those few that were left – could easily attend Mass at Sacred Heart in Placentia, just a few miles up the shore. Father Cashin chuckled to himself. "I remember the time that the Archbishop first presented that idea to old Jerry McHugh – the language we heard through the heavy oaken doors was more suited to the pubs of his native West Belfast than the Episcopal study." The Archbishop raised the subject a few more times, but finally conceded that

St. Colm's might as well remain open so long as Father McHugh was able to look after his dwindling flock. In declining health for years, the old priest, over ninety, had passed away at the Health Sciences Center in St. John's just a few weeks before.

"Ah, he must have been a terror in his day," Father Cashin thought. All those old Irishmen were, back then. He was a Maynooth man, was Jerry McHugh, trained in the great ancient seminary in County Kildare. It didn't matter where they wound up – be it Newcastle, Nevada or Nairobi – they ruled with an iron hand. It was no different here on the south coast of Newfoundland. The population was overwhelmingly Catholic and had been for countless generations. Many families could track their roots back to a distant ancestor that arrived with the fishing fleets in the sixteenth or seventeenth centuries. Many of them escaped from the fishing admirals and settled in these outports along the bay, Father Cashin remembered. They called themselves the "Masterless Men" – but there was usually one master that they respected, and loved, and even feared. And that was the master in the tattered black cassock, frayed biretta and plain white collar.

Father Cashin moved a stack of papers, and turned to Father McHugh's worn black breviary. Like all priests of his generation, Father McHugh had spent hours in contemplation and meditation, reciting the Latin psalms, hymns and reflections in the tattered prayer book. He flipped it open to the imprimatur on the first page. Beneath it was an inscription in elegant cursive script. "Holy Redeemer Monastery, Clonard, Belfast 1936," he read. It might have been a gift from his mother when he was ordained, he thought.

He shuffled aimlessly through the pages, admiring the illuminated letters that opened each paragraph. The book was full of prayer cards, funeral notices and old yellowed clippings used as bookmarks. As he turned the pages, two small black-and-white photographs fell to the desk. Father Cashin looked at them in turn. One was a family photograph – a father, mother and two small daughters, with another young woman, perhaps a servant or a boarder, standing to one side. On the reverse, he read in Father McHugh's precise handwriting the phrase "Come from Away."

The second picture piqued Father Cashin's curiosity. It showed a horizontal stone grave marker, covering what was obviously a newly closed grave. Father Cashin studied the photograph closely. The form of the crucifix was one that he had never seen anywhere else in Atlantic Canada – it showed a traditional Latin Cross, but with a second, diagonal line closer to the base. He recognized the cross as a form often seen in the Orthodox Church, but rarely, if ever, in the Roman Church. There was no legible inscription on the grave marker, but below the crucifix was a horizontal line, deeply etched into the stone surface. A series of short vertical lines, some above, some below, and some crossing the horizontal line, was clearly visible in the photograph. On the back – again in Father McHugh's impeccable handwriting – was the phrase "Came to Stay."

Father Cashin pondered the photograph for a long moment, turning to look out the window. "Come From Away – Came to Stay. Now, I wonder what that's all about?"

The snow had stopped for the moment, and there was a bit of clearing off to the west. Holding the photograph in his hand, and comparing objects with the view from the window, it was clear that the photograph had been taken in St. Colm's parish burial ground. Aligning the dark shape of Gibraltar Rock in the image with the rock itself farther up the bay, he could see the approximate spot where the grave must be. He rose and retrieved his scarf and coat from the wooden stand in the corner. He left the warmth of the worn wooden rectory, and started down the hill toward Placentia Bay.

He stopped from time to time to get his bearings. It did not take him long to find the approximate area, and, clearing the snow and ice with a gloved hand, soon found the mysterious gravestone. It was covered now by wild oats and sea grasses, dormant in the winter, but with just a bit of effort he could now faintly discern the crudely chiseled strokes, now long weathered, which had been so clear in the photograph taken when the stone was first laid down. Blessing himself, he recited "Eternal Rest grant unto them, O Lord...," and completing the prayer, turned and walked slowly uphill to the rectory and church beside.

He entered the welcoming kitchen. He was greeted by the warm, steamy smell of fish and brewis – a traditional Newfoundland "scoff." Annie McGrath, long the housekeeper at St. Colm's was busily tending the boiling pot of water-soaked hard bread, pork fat, and salt cod. "Father McHugh always loved a feed of fish and brewis of a Saturday noon," she said. "He said it used to remind him of the bread puddings his own mother made, back before he left Ireland. Now, there's some townies, I suppose, that use a bit of butter in place of the pork fat, but Father was some particular, was he. He'd be some cross if there wasn't enough scrunchions in his meal."

Father Cashin breathed deeply and laughed.

"Aye, he was a man of regular habits, was our Father McHugh," she continued. "A nice roast of beef for his Sunday's dinner, and Jig's dinner with good salt beef and any vegetables I was able to round up for Monday. Nearly twenty-five years I cooked for the old Father, and I had no need of a calendar, or a watch, either. Every night at six, to the minute, he'd ring the Angelus, and then come sit down to his supper. You could tell by the plate what night it was, so you could."

"Twenty five years, indeed, Mrs. McGrath. Tell me, did he ever mention these photographs to you, by any chance?"

Mrs. McGrath dried her hands on her apron, and sat at the plain deal kitchen table. She studied the family photograph closely. "Ah, sure, now, that's a bit before my time – but I'd be almost certain that's John and Maggie Duffy's family, there. Now as for the other lass, I'm not sure – but there's no mistaking Mr. Duffy. He must be six foot three if he's an inch, and he weighed nearly sixteen stone when he was a young man, so people say. He was the policeman up in Placentia town for, oh, nearly forty years. He was a gladiator, so he was. Why, there's not a Frenchie from over in St. Pierre that he wouldn't take on, gladly, if things got out of hand on a Saturday night."

"Is he still on the go?"

"Aye, he is that, although he himself must be near ninety, now. His was one of the families that were moved from Argentia, when the Yanks came during the war to build their base, just up the bay a bit. The Duffys, the Powers, the Clearys and hundreds more besides, all had to move their houses and fishing gear when the Americans came. It was hard on the Argentia people, then. They even had to move their graveyard, and Holy Rosary parish church and everything. But that base meant plenty of good work and prosperity after the hard times of the depression. Our Father McHugh had just come out from Ireland about then; he and Father Dee, the Pastor at Holy Rosary protested the moving of the people from Argentia. It was all sorted out in the end and the families settled all around this side of the bay. Mr. Duffy and several others moved out to Freshwater, and he's there to this day."

"Do you think he'd mind if I dropped in?" Father Cashin asked as Mrs. McGrath ladled out the steaming dinner. "Mind? He'd not mind at all, I don't think! He and Father McHugh were the best of friends – he'd come down here to help around the church, sometimes, and Father would drive out there of a summer's evening and they'd sit and talk of old times. His eyesight isn't as good as it was, nor his knees, from all those years in the Newfoundland Constabulary, traipsing up and down the countryside, but he's still as sharp as a pin, is old Mr. Duffy. He'd be delighted to see you, I'm sure."

After dinner, Father Cashin drove the short distance to Freshwater. It was easy to find the Duffy home – as Mrs. McGrath had told him, it was the last house till the road gave out into the bush. "As befits an old Constable," the priest thought as he parked his car and walked up toward the porch. "Those fellows were part game warden, part magistrate, part policeman, and everything else out here in the outports, back in the days before Newfoundland joined Canada in 1949." Or, as many of the baymen gleefully told the Nova Scotian – "when Canada finally got wise, and joined Newfoundland."

He knocked, and the door was opened by a young woman – not much younger, Father Cashin guessed, than the adults in the family photograph. "Is Mr. Duffy in?" he asked. Before the girl could speak, came the booming reply from within, "I am, that, by the grace of God! Kristin – don't stand there mute like a tomcod – show Father in and make us a cup of tea, for God's sake!"

The girl smiled as if to say "Well, that's himself at his best." She showed Father Cashin into the modest parlor, warmed by a wood-burning heater, glowing dull red. "He gets cold of an evening" she said, smiling, "you'll roast with that coat, Father, give it to me and I'll hang it by the door, just." The heady aroma of pipe tobacco filled the room.

"Three Nuns, begging your pardon, Father, Three Nuns! I've smoked it since I was a lad, so I have, and it's done me no harm at all! Three Nuns – none today, none tomorrow and none the day after – that's what the old lads used to say, back in the depression days. Surely, there's no harm in a bit of a smoke, now and again, is there?"

"Far be it from me to judge, Mr. Duffy!" Father Cashin introduced himself, and sat across from the old man.

"Kristin, did ye go off to Toronto for the tea, God love you? Father is perishing with the cold, so he is." Turning to Father Cashin, he explained, "Kristin is my granddaughter, home here for a visit from upalong in Ontario. Her mother Mary is one of my twin daughters. They were our first, back in 1940. She lives in Florida now, down by Clearwater, with all the other Newfoundlanders escaping the winter. Her twin sister Regina lives in Texas now, married to a tool pusher on the oil rigs. They're down there with all them other fellas from the "oil patch" as they call it. Salt water cowboys is what we Newfoundlanders became, ever since the wells out on the Hibernia Bank in the gulf hit oil in '76. Changed everything for folks on the south coast, so it did. The Lord himself only knows what our people see in Florida or Texas. They haven't a moose to shoot nor a codfish to catch for miles around, but that's where the money is, I suppose. I'm content meself to sit here, and look out into the woods of a winter's evening – did you know we've got moose that will come right up to the front door, bold as you please, like they were looking for a handout?"

Father Cashin smiled. "So you've lived here all your life, then?"

"Ever since we moved from Argentia in 1941," the old fellow replied. "Built this house with my own hands, with a lot of help from my neighbors. Every fisherman had his winter trade, back in those days. Some were good with wood or fixing engines; others with electricity. Me, I put in the heating stoves for people, mostly. My memory isn't as good as it used to be, but, then, for a lad my age, I suppose it's a wonder that I can remember anything at all, isn't it?" he laughed.

Father Cashin explained the purpose of the visit. "I'm finishing up the records at St. Colm's, and there are one or two things that I can't seem to find in the parish register. Is this your family, perchance?" He handed Mr. Duffy the photograph.

"Aye, it is indeed," he replied. "That's me and my Margaret, God love her. Gone now these twenty years or more, Father, so she is. She was a wonderful woman, my ….gave me six good kids, she did, and we had a happy life together. That's the twins; there's Mary on the left, and Regina. Four more came after them, and, do you know, Father, there's not one of 'em left here in Newfoundland. All upalong now, although they all come home from time to time to see how I'm getting on."

"And the other young woman? Who might she be, Mr. Duffy? And do you know anything about this other photograph? They seem to have been taken around the same time."

Duffy shifted in his chair and put down his pipe. He looked closely at the photograph, and slowly closed his eyes. He remained silent for a long moment. Opening his eyes again, he looked at the photographs, first one, then the other, as the visiting priest waited expectantly.

He sighed. "These were Father McHugh's, I suppose, eh?" The priest explained. "In his breviary they were, clearly they must have meant something to him." Duffy nodded.

"I thought I'd go to my grave and not hear nor speak a word about what happened that day," he said. "Many's the night I lay here, listening to the wind howling in the trees, and think of that day nearly sixty years ago. For a long time it burned inside me, but I dare not speak a word. I suppose now I'm the only one left that knows the whole story – not even Father McHugh knew all the details, and I've little enough time left to set the record straight. Sit comfortably, Father. There's a story behind those photographs, and someone beside myself ought to know."

COMMISSIONING OF N.O.B ARGENTIA – JULY 1941
(Official USN photo)

1 WASHINGTON - I

08 July 1941
The White House,
Washington D.C.
0950 EDST

Missy Lehand, the President's long-time secretary knocked softly on the door to the Oval Office. Not awaiting an answer – she knew that the President was alone – she entered and crossed to the massive desk, where the President was reading the overnight collection of dispatches provided by the State Department. "Your regular 10 o'clock visitors have arrived, Mr. President. Shall I escort them in?"

Franklin Deleno Roosevelt nodded. The thirty-second president, recently reelected for an unprecedented third term, was tired – more tired than he had been in his life. At fifty-nine, after eight years in office, and suffering from the additional burden of paralysis for the past twenty years, he had hoped to be at his summer home at Warm Springs, Georgia by now. Events in Europe made that unlikely as Britain and her allies neared the second anniversary of the invasion of Poland and the beginning of World War II in September, 1939.

"Send them in Missy and bring your stenography pad. I'd like you to make a full transcript of this meeting, if you would. Mark it 'Top Secret,' of course."

Roosevelt sighed, as he re-arranged his chair, trying to find some comfort in the oppressive heat. It was a hot summer day already, and it was becoming clear that the remainder of the season would be even more uncomfortable than usual in the Nation's Capital.

Henry L. Stimson, Secretary of War; General George Marshall, Army Chief of Staff; Admiral Harold Stark, Chief of Naval Operations; Captain John Beardall, Naval Aide to the President; and Harry Hopkins, his closest advisor, seated themselves in the comfortable leather-bound chairs facing the President. All were silent, allowing the President to open their bi-weekly meeting.

"We'll keep this short today. General Marshall – what's the status with the Russians this morning?"

"Not good, Mr. President – not good at all. We've received word, and have pretty much confirmed, that Hitler's Army Group Center – that's Guderian's group, and Hoth's Third Panzers – pretty much have Smolensk encircled. Captain Beardall reached into the leather map case which he had brought to the meeting. In addition to being the president's immediate connection to the Navy Department, Beardall was responsible for providing the President with the necessary charts and maps so that he might fully grasp the strategic situation in a single glance. He unrolled a small copy of the larger map of the European front which he kept in his office. General Marshall continued, "Here's Smolensk – it's right on the Dieneper, about 225 miles southwest of Moscow. Napoleon came through here in 1812, as you may recall, sir. The Soviets are putting up strong resistance, but it doesn't look good for them at all. Stalin's throwing everything he's got to try to fill the breach, Timoshenko, Zhukov, and Yeremenko are pinned down, and are taking very heavy losses. The Germans continue to move quickly on a very broad front, and it's doubtful that the Soviets have the resources to stop this attack, at least not until the weather turns colder. If they can clear Smolensk, they'll no doubt turn left and make for the southern approaches to the capital. It looks like Hitler may succeed where Napoleon had failed, after all."

The others nodded. Hopkins spoke first. "The world may never fully comprehend why Hitler and Stalin agreed to their non-aggression pact two years ago, and I certainly don't understand why Hitler chose to violate it three weeks ago. Does that make any sense to you?"

Roosevelt chuckled. "Well, I don't know if the world will fully comprehend, but it's certain that Henry Luce over at *Time* doesn't understand. Hitler shot the legs right out from under him on this little surprise, I suppose. But it makes about as much sense as anything else Hitler does." he replied. "It was certainly in both of their best interests in '39 to send Von Ribentroff and Molitov to declare hands-off each other, at least from Hitler's perspective then. He figured he could knock the British out of the game and clean up Western Europe before turning his attentions east in his search for open spaces – for *Lebensraum*. And as far as old Uncle Joe was concerned, it bought him time. Having decimated his officer corps out of his paranoid fear of coups and uprisings, he needed time to get things back together, knowing that eventually he'd be at center stage for whatever assaults Adolph had planned for his Eastern Front. But I think all of us were surprised with Hitler's June decision to march on the Soviet Union. He might have been better positioned if he could wait until early next spring – that would give him an additional three or four months before the weather turned on him. Nevertheless, he's made his move, and there's no turning back for Hitler. What was it that Winston said in Parliament the other day? 'If Hitler invaded Hell I would make at least a favorable reference to the Devil in the House of Commons.' The others nodded and smiled.

The President turned to Admiral Stark. "Well, Betty," calling him by a nickname first bestowed upon him at the Naval Academy in the waning months of the previous century, "How are things going for the convoys?"

"They've improved somewhat, Mr. President, but it's still very much touch and go for the Allies. Our fifty destroyers which we exchanged for bases up and down the Atlantic Coast are at last beginning to make a difference. Ernie King was pretty sore about losing his mothball fleet – and angrier about the newspapers using the phrase 'over-aged destroyers', particularly since a good number of these were Clemson class destroyers, and Ernie still has a number of ships of that class active in our Atlantic Fleet today. The tin cans were divided mainly between the Canadians and the British themselves, although one or two are manned by Free French or Norwegian crews. They did free up a good number of British and Canadian Corvettes for mid-ocean duty, though . . . although I'd rather not take one of those old whale catchers out into force ten winds in the North Atlantic, myself, if I could avoid it. Meanwhile, the British just lost the troop transport *Anselm* about 300 miles north of the Azores. We believe that they were able to rescue most of the troops onboard, but perhaps as many as 250 were lost before the rescue could be completed. They were mostly RAF personnel enroute to West Africa, I believe. And they just got involved in an extended engagement in the north Atlantic about ten days ago. . . a fast convoy from Halifax (HX-133) and a slower convoy from Sydney, N.S. (SL 78) got tangled up with several U-boats between Cape Race and Cape Farwell, Greenland, and lost a total of ten ships – most with essential war materials onboard – before additional escort forces could reach them. It's a sad situation really – we're gearing up to provide whatever materi-als we can under Lend-Lease, but it doesn't do much good if they wind up at the bottom of the ocean before they can be of any help to Churchill, I'm afraid."

"Speaking of Churchill – Harry, you've spoken to the Prime Minister most recently – how's he holding up?"

"Well, no surprises here, Mr. President – he's glad for all the support we give him, but I know his fondest wish is for us to get into the war, completely. And, by the way, Mr. President, even though we've been communicating with him through our Embassy in London and privately through their diplomatic pouch via their embassy here, I still don't think he's totally comfortable with his level of access directly to you. We've been talking to Winston directly since he took over as First Sea Lord again in March of '39, and even more so since King George asked him to lead the gov-ernment last May, but I know he wants more access to the White House directly."

Roosevelt sighed. "He's been barraging me with cables and let-ters, and, while we finally got Lend-Lease through the Congress for him, I'm still not at all sure that he really understands what we're up against politically here. I'm getting it from all sides: I've got Wheeler in the Senate, Hamilton Fish in the house, Lindbergh and the America First Crowd stomping all over the country, McCormick and his crowd out there in Chicago – and yet I'm cer-tain that 80% of the American people back us and understand that we can't wait until Hitler is three miles offshore before we act in our own defense. And, to be sure, I'm not all that certain how the world looks to Winston – there's only so much we can say by diplomatic cable, and, quite frankly, I'm still very cautious using the overseas telephone link we've established to the Cabinet War

Rooms in London. He chuckled as he glanced toward General Marshall: I don't care what those Signal Corps fellows tell you, General – I'm half afraid that the Germans are listening in every time we use the damn thing." What I really need to do is to sit down with Winston, man to man, and get a feel for the fellow and how our relationship can best proceed."

Secretary Stimson spoke, "I think he'll jump at the opportunity, Mr. President. He's the kind of fellow who likes grand gestures. If we suggest this to him, we ought to phrase it in terms which make it look like it was his idea originally. Just as we have political pressures on this side of the Atlantic, so does he. He still has a fair amount of 'appeasers' among his press, that much is certain. Even if nothing is said overtly, they certainly will get the impression that we are actively considering how we can further help Britain in this war."

Harry Hopkins interjected, "Well, if I understand Mr. Churchill, he'll probably be writing his press releases touting the results of 'Our successful meeting,' even before he leaves London for the trip. I read the other day that his personal secretary, Brendan Bracken was quoted in one of the London papers as saying 'The problem with Winston is that he awakes every morning with ten audacious ideas, nine of which are totally impracticable, and one of which is pure genius. The problem, though, is that no one, including Winston knows which is which." Everyone, including the President, chuckled.

"Harry, draft a message to Ambassador Winnant and have him approach Winston directly and suggest that we meet sometime this summer. I feel a heck of a lot more comfortable with John there than I ever did with old Joe Kennedy. At least John will relay messages without editing or adding defeatist comments

6

to them. I suspect that Winston will welcome the idea…he's been hinting at a meeting for the last several months, now. I'm not sure where the best place to do it is, nor the best way to go about it, but General Marshall – you and Admiral Stark work out the details. In fact, Harry, why don't you fly over there and work with Churchill and his people to get things moving smoothly from that end. We're going to need to keep this secret, of course – if the Germans get wind of the fact that Winston is on the sea, they'll throw everything they can at him. We'll need to keep it secret for our own good as well. We'll spread the story that I need a break from this terrible heat and humidity, and that I'm going to spend a week or so on the yacht *Potomac*. We can go out of Charleston, if we decide to meet in the Bahamas, or perhaps in Bermuda, or we can take it up the New England coast if we decide to do it on the Saint Lawrence River. We'll need to transfer from the *Potomac* to one of your capital ships if we're going to leave U.S. waters, Admiral. I certainly enjoyed the cruise on the *Augusta* that last time – we might want to use her if we go to sea to meet Winston. If we organize this properly, neither Winston nor I need be away from our offices for more than two weeks." The president pushed back his chair in a signal to all that the meeting was concluded.

As the others rose to leave, Missy Lehand caught the President's eye. The president nodded, and she lingered behind for a moment. More than a private secretary, she often served as a sounding board for the president, to whom she was fiercely loyal. "Are you sure you want to consider meeting Churchill in the Bahamas? I know it's the closest British Colony to the coast, and you could get over and back from Florida within a couple hours – but you remember that they finally shipped off the Duke of Windsor to be the governor there. And he has *that woman* with him, of course. I'm not at all certain that a visit there would be seen in the best light, either here or in Britain, and certainly not among our own friends who know and despise Wallace Simpson."

"They don't know the half of it," Roosevelt replied. "They had to get him out of France where he washed up after the abdication. He was palling around with Nazis and collaborators, and Churchill finally decided that he could do the least damage over in Nassau. But you're certainly right – I'll get a note off to Admiral Stark and we'll see if we can find a more appropriate place, most likely Bermuda, I suppose. I'll brief Harry if the meeting with Winston looks like it might come to pass."

2 NEW YORK CITY

14 July 1941
AT&T Long Lines,
24 Walker Street, New York City
0830 EDST

Bob Nelson was furious. Once again, a perfectly good morning had been thrown into turmoil. Upon arriving at his office on the eighth floor of AT&T's command center in downtown New York City, he learned that over the weekend, Chesapeake and Potomac Telephone, the Bell system operating company serving the Washington D.C. area, had forwarded an urgent order activating the secure radio circuits linking Washington with London. They were needed early the next morning, Tuesday, July 15th, and the expected duration was listed as "unknown." Some idiot had placed the order for the circuit in his in-basket on Friday evening, and, eager to begin his weekend, no doubt, had departed without notifying anyone. "Those C+P guys must think we can do this with ten minutes notice," he growled to himself. "They're down there in the sticks, and they don't have a single clue as to what needs to be done to get this circuit up and running." He pressed the call button on his intercom. "Get all the wire chiefs in here in the next five minutes – we've got an urgent circuit order, and we're already behind the eight-ball." As he released the call button, he could hear his secretary's voice on the intercom, calling each of the four supervisors to their boss's office. If his day was starting badly, he thought to himself, theirs is about to get worse, and fast.

One by one, they filed into the office. The usual banter was absent; it was rare enough for one to be summoned by the PA speakers, and very unusual for all four duty supervisors to be summoned simultaneously. Bob Bruna arrived first, followed by Stan Kaplan. Denny Barley and Jerry Hann arrived a few seconds later. This was obviously an operational issue, and no one took a seat.

"This is the third or fourth time this has happened," Nelson began. "I'm not sure what irritates me most about this – the C+P guys who keep springing these little surprises on us, or the second-shift idiots who drop things in my inbox without letting anyone know. We've got a super-special on for tomorrow morning, and we've got less than 24 hours to make things right. It looks like it will be a scrambled call to London – I wouldn't be surprised if it's FDR himself – so we'll need to be sure that the A3 is up and running properly. Stan, get on the order-wire with C+P and have them test things on a local loop between here and there. Have them get the Signal Corps guys at whatever location that originates the call to local-loop with them, too. Bob, you get on the hook with RCA, and tell them we have a hot one coming through to them. The order indicates that Washington will begin with long-count tests at 0730 tomorrow and go with live traffic at 0800. That's midafternoon in London, but that's not our worry. Our worry is to make sure that this circuit is as solid as we can make it, and the voices from our end don't sound like the buzzing Green Hornet when whoever is on the other end picks up the receiver. One of these days, those pointy heads over at Bell Labs will figure out a way to run voice over the undersea cables, but until that happens, we're stuck with these shaky HF radio signals from Long Island to the UK. OK, guys, we've been doing this long enough that each of you knows what needs to be done. Let me know if you need me to run interference for any of you. We'll check back here around lunch time and see how thing are coming along."

The four wire chiefs scattered back to their own private fief-doms on "the floor" – the hub of AT&T's nationwide, and increas-ingly world-wide, activity. Stan Kaplan had the longest trip – the Bell Labs Model A3 scrambling equipment took up most of a locked, glass walled room at the far end of the work area. The A3 was invented at Murray Hill NJ, the site of many of the world's most important advances in telecommunication, just a few months earlier. These sets consisted of electronics that could mix two sig-nals: one from the telephone set on the "A" side of a circuit, and a random noise generator contained in the encryption set. A syn-chronization signal was sent as a separate component of the total signal, and the process was reversed at the "B" end of the circuit so that the distant user was both audible and intelligible to the user at the other end. In theory at least, eavesdroppers would hear only the noisy signal, and would be unable to understand the voice inside.

Meanwhile, Bob Bruna was on the order-wire with his oppo-site number at RCA's Radio Central. The huge facility in Suffolk County's Long Island Pine Barrens near the village of Rocky Point contained the high powered transmitters and gigantic antennas which made up the transmitting portion of the nation's only trans-atlantic telephone circuits. Linked by cable to its receiver site at Holton, Maine, the station was in constant contact with its UK equivalent located near Fife, Scotland. The operations supervi-sor at Radio Central reported that no problems had been noted in the past forty eight hours, although radio propagation condi-tions were experiencing their usual summer atmospheric distur-bances. Bruna noted these comments on the service order, and walked back across the floor to inform Nelson that at least one thing was going in their favor this morning. As he passed by Jerry Hann's station, he noticed the empty chair behind his colleague's desk. "Probably gone off to the can," Bruna thought to himself.

"A morning like this is enough to make anyone nervous, even if Jerry and his people are not directly involved in this call setup."

Hann was not in the restroom, or indeed, even in the building. Immediately after leaving Nelson's office, he had entered an elevator bound for the ground floor lobby, and crossing Sixth Avenue, walked into Whelan's drug store, just a few steps from the AT&T building. Hann, born Gerhard Höen in 1914 in the German province of Alsace was brought to the United States in 1919 by his widowed mother. His father, whom he barely remembered, died at the Somme in July, 1916. Through the benevolence of her eldest brother, who had emigrated to New York early in the 20th century, he received a fine technical education, and secured a much coveted place with AT&T during the darkest days of the depression. Quiet, and thought by many of his peers and subordinates to be moody and distant, he nevertheless was an excellent telephone engineer, and was admired if not particularly well liked by those with whom he worked.

He walked purposefully to the row of pay telephones at the rear of the store. None were occupied, and he entered the most distant booth of the row. It was immediately adjacent to the wall; excellent for the type of business Hann had come to complete. From memory, he dialed a number in the Atwater 9 exchange. Like most telephone professionals, he recognized the exchange as serving the Upper East Side. More importantly for his purposes of the moment, he immediately recognized the gruff male voice who answered on the first ring. It belonged to Richard Eichenlaub, a member of the espionage ring led by Fritz Duquesne, and the owner of the Little Casino Restaurant in the Yorkville Section of the city. It was while dining at the Little Casino in 1937 that Eichenlaub had recruited Hann and others as German agents. Hann, like many German emigrants of the time, had blamed internal subversion within Imperial Germany for their humiliation, not on the battle-field but at the negotiation table after the armistice. Hann coughed twice, paused, and coughed again. Eichenlaub said nothing, but coughed once. Hann simply said "7:30 tomorrow morning," and waited for the cough, which indicated that his message had been received and understood. Hanging up the telephone, he retraced his steps, and returned to work on the eighth floor.

The message passed quickly from one German agent to another. A "ham" radio transmission from an agent in Brooklyn was received at the German Embassy in Mexico City. The message was swiftly encoded, and retransmitted to a receiving station of the German *Beobachtungsdienst*, or *B-deinst*, the communications arm responsible for intercepts, codes, and ciphers. By late evening, *B-deinst* had alerted monitoring stations at Borkum and Hilversum in the Netherlands, who were alert to the potentially critical intelligence about to be transmitted. Everything that Roosevelt or Churchill would discuss in the morning would soon be in the hands of German Intelligence, and of Adolph Hitler himself.

July 15, 1941
Deutsche Reichspost Abhörstelle
Noorwijk, Occupied Netherlands
1405 MET

The first weeks of July were unseasonably warm and dry at the German Deutsche Reichspost's extensive wireless monitoring station (Abhörstelle) at Noorwijk in occupied Netherlands. Located in a disused boy's camp in the province of South Holland, about forty kilometers south of Amsterdam, the main camp buildings had been connected by covered walkways, and additional structures built to accommodate the large number of collection, recording, and analysis staff manning this critical intercept facility. Among other responsibilities, Noorwijk was the primary monitoring point for "Schaltung Anton," the German designation for the RCA-GPO transatlantic voice circuits.

Based on Hann's telephone message, an urgent 'Action Alert' had been transmitted from Berlin late the previous evening, indicating that critical traffic could be expected by mid-afternoon. *B-dienst* specialists attached to the facility were responsible for the descrambling equipment, which defeated the American and British attempt to conceal the content of high-level communications between continents. Both the *B-dienst* and Reichpost's best specialists were ready when the call-up message tape from Long Island began shortly before 1400, Middle European Time (MET). The very clear and strong signal through RCA Long Island began:

"1-2-3-4-5 5-4-3-2-1 This is a test transmission for circuit adjustment purposes from a station of the American Telephone and Telegraph Company. This station is located near New York City. 1-2-3-4-5 5-4-3-2-1."

The transmission repeated several times, as the intercept operators, realizing the gravity of the conversations which were the target of their intercept station, continued to fine tune their Telefunken E52 receivers – by far the most sensitive High Frequency receivers in the German arsenal of radio equipment. Conditions at the fifty and thirty-eight meter wavelengths were good, and when the synchronization signal was received shortly after the hour, there was little buzz or distortion in the voice of the American technician:

ACTUNG! Streng Geheim

(Most Secret)

[Transcript of Schaltung Anton Intercepts at Noorijk beginning at 1403 Hours, July, 1941]

Unknown Technician: You are through to your party, Sir. You may begin speaking at any time.

ROOSEVELT: Good morning, Winston. . .or, rather should I say Good Afternoon. It's still morning here, of course.

CHURCHILL: Good day to you, Franklin. Perhaps our old fashioned way of greeting friends is best. If one stays up until the early hours of morning, as I am wont to do, it saves a great deal of embarrassment until one finds a clock to confirm the time of day.

ROOSEVELT: I am quite sorry to disturb you with everything that is happening, Winston, but matters of [atmospheric interference] and I think you will find it useful were I to convey them to you immediately.

CHURCHILL: That's perfectly all right, Franklin. I'm certain that your estimation of the urgency of matters is measured and justified, as it always is.

ROOSEVELT: You've spoken to Harry, then?[1]

CHURCHILL: Yes, he was by to see me today, and he presented me with the outline for this call. I need not say how happy I am to see that we are of the same mind about all of this.

ROOSEVELT: Indeed, I believe that we are. I met with Harry, as well as the Chiefs of the Army and Navy staffs and all of us are in agreement about the basic plan of action. There are some matters of logistics to be resolved, as there always will be, but I think the underlying idea is sound, and will be helpful to both of us if we implement this without further delay.

CHURCHILL: Yes, your assessment is sound, Franklin. I have here an aide-memoire which Harry kindly prepared for me. I trust you have an identical copy?

ROOSEVELT: Yes, he prepared it before he left for London. Shall we start with item ONE?

CHURCHILL: Indeed. I agree with you that doing this sooner rather than later is the best course of action. I am increasingly worried that things are not going well for the Soviets at all. Once Guderian makes his turn to the left, Stalin will have a very short time of it until he'll hear the Horst Wessel sung in Red Square. I know he had contingency plans east of the Urals, but time is of the essence, I should think.

ROOSEVELT: His situation is grave, there's no doubt of it. Do you think we can plan on early next month?

CHURCHILL: It is certainly feasible, and I think desirable, Franklin. Much will depend on Item TWO, of course.

ROOSEVELT: Yes, that one is a bit stickier. I'm getting conflicting views from my advisors.

CHURCHILL: Well, let's look at the first option in Item TWO. Have you objections to visiting that lovely area along the river as I first suggested?

ROOSEVELT: I'm afraid I do, Winston, although "objection" may be too strong a word. I'm not certain there is an advantage to the river keeper being privy to our plans, at least not at this stage of our discussions. Sumner [Wells] suggested I go to my summer home, which as you know is just a few miles from our friend's property, but I'm not certain that you'd want to come to visit me here at this stage of development, Winston. [2]

CHURCHILL: [Pause] I suppose you're quite correct about that, Franklin. There may be political considerations, which would over-ride that choice, although our mutual friend may find his nose out of joint if it appears that we are ignoring him. He's been most coopera-tive, at some risk to his own political position, in what we've done collectively heretofore, and I rather feel now that we'd be best served if we stay out of his backyard, both physically and politically, at least for the moment.

ROOSEVELT: We see things the same way. He does have a rather large minority who have take exception to his involvement dating back all the way to 1939, Winston.

CHURCHILL: Indeed. Harry also suggested in point b. of Item TWO that we consider the blacksmith's daughter of whom Lord Nelson was so enamored. [3] I spoke with Pound just a few moments before coming down here to the telephone, and he was lukewarm at best about that consideration. He's concerned that it would add at least a day of risk from this side, and he's already quite nervous about the audacity of doing this when things are by no means under control on our western approaches. He asked if you could make the journey here, but after the briefest consideration, he recognized the impracticality of that. . .

ROOSEVELT: *I'm afraid that is totally impractical, indeed, Winston. The little dogs which yap at my heels would never stand for that, and it would certainly cast a pall over their willingness to assist us in our endeavors should conditions worsen. Totally impractical, I'm afraid.*

CHURCHILL: *That's what I told Pound. That leaves us with the third option under Item TWO, doesn't it? Pound thinks that that is the safer option; your neighbor will not be offended, since we can argue that since it is ours and not his he has no standing in the matter, and I understand your arrangements there are progressing nicely. How do Stark and King feel about it from their perspective?*

ROOSEVELT: *Stark is fine with the idea, and King, for a change, didn't raise any serious objections. I actually think he sees political advantage in his own circles. With our buildup in the Pacific, and the very sparse resources that Admiral King has to flex muscles in the Atlantic – and he's still disappointed by my choice of "Betty" for the top [atmospheric interference] – he thought it should be his.*

CHURCHILL: *(Laughter can be heard) Betty! Well. At least your naval fellows are open about things.*

ROOSEVELT: *(More Laughter) It's not what you think, Winston. I know your famous comment about 'Rum, Sodomy and the Lash,' but that's not it with Stark at all. Apparently there was a famous performer named Betty Stark when he was at the Naval Academy,* *and some upperclassmen tagged him with the name. Since he became Chief of Naval Operations, I suspect they are all still admirals, but commanding garbage scows in the backwaters of the Brooklyn Navy yard again. But, to conclude this conversation, let's plan on sometime around the 10th, in proximity to the new silver mines we find so attractive. Does that suit your needs, Winston? [4]*

CHURCHILL: *I suspect that it will. It should be lovely to be at sea again, now that high summer is upon us.*

ROOSEVELT: *As it will for me. Those were most enjoyable days when we were younger men, weren't they?*

CHURCHILL: *Some of the best, Franklin. . .some of the best. Do give my regards to your fine lady, Mr. President.*

ROOSEVELT: *And mine to your lovely Clementine, Mr. Prime Minister. Good day and God bless all of you.*

The Reichspost and *B-dienst* analysts, one fluent in British English and one in Transatlantic English, conferred and added these comments before the document was forwarded under the highest priority to the *Ausland/Abwehr im Oberkommando der Wehrmacht* (Abwehr), the leading intelligence agency in Nazi Germany, as well as to their respective headquarters in Berlin:

[1] May be <u>Mr. Harry Hopkins</u>, an associate of President Roosevelt, based on previously noted references.

[2] We have records of telephone calls originating at the President's family home in New York, and his summer retreat in Maine, quite near the Canadian border. In context, the "neighbor"

may be the Prime Minister of Canada, Mr. McKenzie King. Canada's French-speaking minority has long been divided in loyalty, particularly after our quick success in France.

[3] We have no records to compare where this usage is found. In context, this seems to refer to a location, and not a person, however. Again, in context, this seems to suggest an imminent meeting somewhere at sea.

[4] The reference to "silver mines" is obscure. It may point to a location at least one day's voyage closer to England.

The annotated transcript was immediately encrypted using the Enigma M3 machine, the most secure available, with Steckerbrett modifications, and transmitted with the highest precedence of *UU- Unverzügliche Übermittlung (operationally urgent)* via secured cables to Berlin. Indeed, by the time President Roosevelt had left his office for lunch, and Prime Minister Churchill had left for his evening tea, the message was in the hands of the German intelligence services, and by breakfast the next morning, in the hands of the Abwehr Director, Admiral William Canaris.

3 BERLIN - I

16 July 1941
Abwehr Headquarters,
76 Tirpitzufer, Berlin
0715 MET

Admiral Wilhelm Canaris arrived in his Berlin office at 76 Tirpitzufer promptly at 0700. His deputy, General Hans Oster was waiting for him in the foyer. "We have something very important to discuss, Herr Admiral. I believe we should retire to your office immediately." Canaris nodded silently.

The Abwehr headquarters, adjacent to the High Command of the Armed Forces (*Oberkommando der Wehrmacht,* or OKW) was one of the most highly guarded and secure buildings in Berlin. Nevertheless, upon entering Canaris' office, General Oster turned and locked the door behind them. True to his training in intelligence, he remained silent. Oster opened his locked briefcase, and removed a metal folio, which he also unlocked. He handed the document inside to his boss and mentor, and sat silently. Canaris studied the two-page transcript carefully.

"Well, it's good to see that the Reichspostministerium is capable of something other than just issuing postage stamps graced with the image of our beloved Führer" he commented, without a trace of irony in his voice. This time it was Oster who nodded. One link which joined them was their discontent with Adolph Hitler and National Socialism in general; a discontent which would link them both in death at Flossenbürg concentration camp after the failure of the 20 July 1944 plot against Hitler.

"What do you make of it, Hans? It certainly seems that Churchill and Roosevelt are planning a face-to-face meeting, and rather soon, if the conversation here is accurate."

"I think it is, Herr Admiral. We're certain that neither the British nor the Americans are aware that we can descramble their trans-Atlantic telephone calls, and the rather clumsy attempt at disguising the meaning of their words. I'm not an expert at codes or ciphers, but it appears that they have great faith in the scrambling abilities of their transatlantic circuit. Fortunately, one of our other friends at their vaulted Bell Laboratories in New Jersey provided the schematics which were brought over to us by a steward on the Norddeutscher Lloyd liner *Bremen* a year or so ago. Their attempt at concealment of their intent, though, could be decoded by a first week trainee at our academy at Seibersdorf."

Oster continued, "Immediately upon receiving this. I had the analysis groups working on the 'blacksmith's daughter reference, and it took them about five minutes to identify that as Lady Hamilton, Horatio Nelson's mistress before his death at Trafalgar. The *B-Dienst* field notes rightly estimate that the references are to a place and not a person, and I doubt seriously that Churchill and Roosevelt are planning to meet off the coast of Spain at Trafalgar, unless they want to engage the entire Kriegsmarine in their conversations. The researchers identified two potential locations though: Hamilton, a Canadian city on Lake Ontario, and Hamilton, the capital of Bermuda. If we interpret the comments about summer homes and river keepers, it's obvious that for their own political reasons, Canada appears to them to be unsuitable. But, reading along further, it appears that Bermuda is considered unacceptable, as well. This leaves us with 'The Silvermine' wherever that might be."

Canaris rose from his desk, and moved to his map board. He flipped to Quadratkare Nr. 3401 – the Kriegsmarine U-boat operational map of the North Atlantic. "Ah, let me see. Yes, here we are, Hans. Going against anyone's concept of neutrality, including a sizable minority within their own country, the Ami's have recently negotiated rights to a major base in Newfoundland. It's well along in its construction now, as it required their naval construction forces to level a small fishing village called Argentia. Argentia . . . that's Latin for Silver, isn't it? It's situated on the western side of the Avalon Peninsula, about two thirds of the way up Placentia Bay, a deep water fjord with excellent access to the shipping lanes between the United Kingdom and Canada. Newfoundland is a British dominion; that would account for the comments about the Canadian's not having much say in the matter, of course."

General Oster nodded. "I think we should contact Herr Doktor Ohnesorge immediately, and thank him profusely for his contribution to the war effort. I'll do it if you like. I'll lay it on thickly – I know that he's has felt that the Reichspostministerium has been ignored recently, and that others felt that his monitoring services should be incorporated into a unit more closely connected to the High Command, probably as a part of *B-Dienst*. This will put a feather in his cap, I should think."

"That's an excellent idea, Hans. With a dozen or more organizations feeding intelligence on various topics to the High Command he is generally treated as rather small beer most of the time. Until this point, perhaps his most valuable contribution has been intercepting, opening and copying international messages carried by regular post, although it was his group which assisted us with the development and deployment of microdot methods among our agents. Hiding the dot under the postage stamp, and strengthening the adhesive so that we could detect tampering was his idea, if I recall correctly."

"Tell him, too, that we'll give him full credit with the Führer when we brief him. I won't remind the Führer that it was one of our agents in America that recruited the Bell Laboratories engineer who participated in the development of the scrambling system. We'll let the Doctor bask in his glory for a while."

"While you are doing that, Hans, I'll contact Großadmiral Raeder immediately, and through him, we'll be certain that the OKW and the Chancellor's office are fully informed. I know that Hitler has been very firm with Raeder that the Americans were to be off limits to Dönitz's U-boats. The last thing the Führer needs now is to have the Americans come into the war, now that we're involved in battles on both the western and eastern fronts. Even so, I suspect that we can make a compelling case that stopping, or at least disrupting, any meeting between Churchill and Roosevelt will defer, if not deter, the Americans from coming in on the side of the British. Roosevelt is under tremendous pressure from the "America First" lobby and other isolationists at home, and the latest intelligence from Britain seems to indicate dissatisfaction with Churchill, especially from people in the slum areas of the docklands of London, Liverpool and elsewhere. But this decision is ultimately the Führer's and, if he decides to follow up on this, OKW will have to move quickly to get things organized. I don't think Göring has any assets which would be useful under these circumstances; he has no long range bombing aircraft to speak of, and it's certain that there will be an impenetrable air cover, out to their maximum flying range, for both the British and American aircraft. This one looks like it will involve Dönitz, and if Raeder agrees, I'll ask him to have Dönitz fly up here from Lorient to begin the operational planning without delay, perhaps as early as tomorrow morning. Don't say anything to Ohnsorge that would lead him to believe that he'll be involved in the planning as it goes forward, but do ask him to be extra vigilant should other information come his way. And let's plan on meeting again during the early afternoon. By that time, I think we'll better know how we are going to proceed."

Both men left the office together: Oster to the communications center located in the basement to make a secure telephone call to Doktor Ohnesorge, and Canaris via a heavily guarded underground passageway to the adjacent OKW headquarters. Großadmiral Raeder was absent for a monthly meeting at his operations center at OKM (Kriegsmarine) headquarters, codenamed *Koralle* (Coral), located near Bernau, about 30 kilometers north of Berlin. Admiral Canaris persuaded Raeder's flag lieutenant to clear the Großadmiral's calendar for the following afternoon, and to include Admiral Karl Dönitz as a participant at the critical meeting.

Admiral Canaris & General Oster
(DLArchiv)

17 July 1941
Secure Conference Room "A"
Oberkommando der Wehrmacht,
Tirpitzufer, Berlin
1300 MET

The invited participants met in a secure conference room at OKW headquarters. Befitting his rank and status, Großadmiral Erich Rader entered the room last. All rose, saluted, and resumed their seats at the mahogany conference table. Present were Admiral Canaris, General Oster, and Admiral Karl Dönitz, Commander of the U-Boat service, *Befehlshaber der U-Boote* (*BdU*). By coincidence, Dönitz had attended the OKM monthly high command meeting at Koralle the previous day, and had delayed his return to Lorient upon Raeder's orders.

Raeder had reviewed a copy of the telephone-intercept upon his return to OKW the previous evening. Dönitz had read Canaris' copy shortly after entering the conference room. All were aware of the content and significance of the critical intelligence and the importance of the meeting.

"Well," began Raeder, "it does appear that the 'Former Naval Person' (using the thinly disguised nome-de-plume which Churchill used in transatlantic cables to Roosevelt – many of which were read by the Germans, often before being seen at the White House) is again about to go to sea. Could it be that Göring has made things too warm for him in London, perhaps?"

The others smiled ruefully, for each knew that Göring had been unable to overcome the spirited air defenses which had ultimately forced the postponement of *Unternehmen Seelöwe* – Operation Sea Lion, the invasion of Britain. It had been planned for the previous summer, but had been cancelled in September. Out of deference to General Oster, none of the naval men present expressed their secret relief that Göring had taken the blame for the delay, relieving them of the onus of having prepared too few landing craft on the seacoast for the planned invasion.

"I believe he is more emboldened by his recent success manipulating his new friends in the White House, Herr Großadmiral, than with his temporary setbacks to the Luftwaffe," remarked Dönitz, "although we've seen little impact of the fifty destroyers he was able to extort from the Americans. Churchill, always a master manipulator, succeeded in convincing Roosevelt that if we were successful with Sea Lion he might have to surrender the remnants of his fleet, or to scuttle them, rather than let them fall into our hands. He promised Roosevelt that he'd sortie every ship still under his command, with the hope that some or all would reach the Canadians, and live to fight another day. But the presence of the transferred destroyers just adds a layer of confusion in the North Atlantic at the moment, and I don't expect that situation to change. The real impact may well come from the bases – spread from Newfoundland to Barbados – rather than the four-stack destroyers."

Raeder nodded, "Why don't you repeat to our colleagues from the Abwehr the highlights of your briefing to the OKM high command yesterday, Admiral Dönitz?"

Dönitz unlocked his locked dispatch box and brought out his briefing notes from the previous day's meeting.

"Since the beginning of June, there have been 541 ships in fourteen convoys departing North America for Britain. Of those, five were slow convoys dispatched from Cape Breton, and nine were so-called 'Fast' convoys from Halifax. In June, we attached

76 enemy vessels, and sank 61. In the first ten days of July we attacked eight and destroyed six. We had thirty-three boats at sea during June, and roughly the same number at sea during the first fifteen days of July. As you may know, however, The Führer had ordered us to deploy as many boats as possible to the Norwegian coastline, to interdict war material shipments to Russia via Murmansk and Archangel. This has required us to transfer a score of more boats from Lorient to more northern ports, and has reduced our ability to control enemy shipping in the Northwest Atlantic. We have reason to believe that since 01 June, we've accounted for over 450,000 tons of war or war-supporting materials. We believe that we continue to destroy allied shipping at a greater rate than it can be replaced, but I regret to report to you today that U-651 commanded by Kapitänleutnant Peter Lohmeyer has been lost. Information has come to us that he was able to scuttle the boat, but that he and his entire crew are reported to be in the custody of the British."

The room went silent for a moment. While all were valiant war-fighters, none save Dönitz knew of the sheer terror, which could overcome a man when the conning tower went awash, and nothing but the bitter depths stood between himself and death.

Dönitz resumed his briefing, "As of this moment, we have thirty-one available boats (on patrol) and sixteen more preparing to depart within the next ten days. We have five boats undergoing repair, and thirty-eight in various stages of construction or pre-deployment training. We can easily establish picket lines at any point in the North Atlantic, although there would be great danger if we sailed much closer than the 600-fathom curve, either west of Britain or east of Canada. If we attempt to intercept and destroy a capital ship – and I am assuming that would be our target – then by far the best place to attempt it would be in the 'Happy Zone' – that area of the mid-Atlantic gap where Allied air attack is not possible. It gives us about a six-hundred mile gap, along the major convoy routes, where air protection from Newfoundland, Greenland or Iceland is not yet available."

"Well," interjected Raeder, "were I making a mad dash across the North Atlantic, I'd prefer to do it when the moon is dark. I have checked the almanac: The moon is new on July 24 and full on 07 August. I'd prefer to be out there during the early part of the waxing moon, or the later part of the waning moon. It seems though, from the comments in this intercept, that Churchill, 'Former Naval Person' that he might be, has little skill as a navigator or seaman, does he?"

"He was never a mariner himself, Herr Großadmiral," reported Dönitz. "He was First Lord of the Admiralty, true enough, but that's a parliamentary position. He was expected to rely on the First Sea Lord for practical guidance. Although a new cadet from Kiel might know more than he does about the practical side of things." Raeder laughed dryly.

"So then, how will we know when the fox is out of his den? If I can persuade the Führer that this is a golden opportunity to strike a serious blow at the Allies – and it's by no means certain that he will share our optimism about it – he would never permit a lengthy redeployment of the U-boat forces which he wants deployed along the Norwegian coastline. We'll need something more definite that 'sometime soon' if we wish to convince him."

General Oster spoke for the first time. Turning to Canaris he asked, "With your permission, Herr Admiral?" Canaris nodded, and sat back in his chair.

"As you all may know, the Abwehr has been deploying assets throughout North America for the past five or six years. We've been aided in this task, of course, by our loyal German comrades in the *Amerikadeutscher Volksbund*, led by Fritz Kuhn as Bundesführer. He is an *Alter Kämpfer* (long term member) of the party, and fought with the Bavarians on the Western Front in the last war. He makes a great deal of noise, and organizes parades and rallies, particularly in those cities with large Germanic populations such as New York, but perhaps his greatest contribution is to cast a very large shadow under which other, more subtle and skilled individuals can operate. The Führer directed Kuhn to tone down his propagandizing about two and a half years ago, but he still is useful when we need to draw attention away from other activities, which the Abwehr is conducting in that theatre. But it is not Kuhn about which I am encouraged." he continued, "At present we have about fifty active assets, mostly along the east coast of the United States, and another sixty or seventy in reserve in other areas, mostly industrial, spread through the USA. We have about a dozen active in industrial areas in Canada, and of course, our embassy in Mexico serves as a critical communications relay for urgent information in both directions. Routine or less time sensitive information makes its way to the Embassy in Washington, where it's sent via diplomatic pouch to Berlin. We are using a variety of protection methods, of which you are all aware, such as microdot photography, encryption by Enigma and other mechanical means, but we are by no means certain that our diplomatic or other mail from the region remains inviolate. The British are known to intercept mail destined for Europe while in transit at Bermuda. However, our agents, who are in communication with Mexico City, use one-time pads for encryption, and those are the most secure tools available to prevent compromise. That is our greatest advantage – that and having as our main adversary the American Federal Bureau of Investigation, which is the least professional, least prepared and least successful counter intelligence organization, which we have ever faced. Even their self-promoting leader, John Edgar Hoover would not last one week – perhaps not even one day! – in Herr Himmler's *Geheime Staatspolizei*, (Gestapo) or the *Sicherheitsdienst*, (Security Service). Indeed, I rather think he would be removed were he the policeman directing traffic outside their offices on Prinz-Albrecht-Straße!"

Canaris interrupted, "You can see that the good General has little regard for our opponents. I don't have a great regard for them myself, but I do respect the threat that they present to us, and to an operation such as we are discussing now. But every challenge is an opportunity. It thus seems to me, given the openness of American society and particularly their newspapers and other journals, that it would be difficult for the Americans to keep Roosevelt's absence from Washington secret for a very long time. He does not, shall we say, exhibit the usual characteristics of the 'man in the street,' to use the American idiom. He is taller than average at 188 centimeters (about 6'2") weights about 85 kilos (188 pounds), and must use leg braces because of his Poliomyelitis. Of course, as is very well known throughout the world, he must use a bathchair for transportation by his valet and bodyguards when outside the public eye. He even has issued orders that, when riding on trains, they proceed at less than 85 kilometers per hour (55 mph) to lessen the pain of his legs. While it may be difficult to deduce just where he is going, it should not be difficult to determine when he is on the move."

"A second point to consider is that we have established a net-work of coast-watchers along the eastern seaboard of Canada. This network, which we have named *Die Stadtverbunden* (the city network), consists of stations monitoring the ports of Montreal, Quebec, Halifax, Sydney and, most recently, Argentia, Newfoundland. Each uses a short town name in *Die Heimat* (our homeland) as identification. The Americans have not yet silenced the amateur radio service; they still have over 50,000 'radio hams' transmitting innocuous personal information on a variety of wavelengths. Many of our stations 'hide in plain sight' among these chatters, and, since our messages are so short, attract no significant attention. They transmit on the forty-meter wavelength during the evenings, and all can be received clearly at the control station in Mexico. If necessary, we have additional stations in the Midwestern United States which can relay messages, adding just a few minutes to the total transmission time from the agent to our receiver sites at Hilversum and Coxhaven."

Großadmiral Raeder reviewed his notes. "Very well, then, I shall ask for an immediate appointment with the Führer, and I will inform you of his decision forthwith. I think it is prudent for us to do two things now, in anticipation of a positive response. Admiral Dönitz, establish an intercept plan, using whatever U-boats are operating in the area now, or those scheduled to depart shortly. Moreover, select your most appropriate U-boat, and hold it in immediate readiness, to be dispatched with twelve hours notice. While you do so, I will contact Reichsführer-SS Himmler and seek his advice and assistance about what additional personnel might be necessary, should we not be able to effect an interception at sea and be forced to enter into Placentia Bay." A brief cloud of discomfort passed, almost imperceptibly, across Dönitz's face. "Don't be dismayed, Admiral," Raeder continued, I can sense what you are thinking. I'd like to relive Prien's audacity in getting into and out of Scapa Flow, and sinking *Royal Oak* right under the British Navy's eyes in 1939. But the geography here is totally different.

Placentia Bay is a long wide fjord, with only one exit to the sea. Prien had a few options, unpleasant as they might have been, but a U-boat entering Placentia Bay will have to exit the way he came in. This is one of those rare cases when calling upon Himmler might be to our distinct advantage. We'll have some demolition specialists and perhaps sharpshooters along for the ride . . . just in case. Select a U-boat with great care for this special assignment; a Type IX boat, with the ability to remain quietly on station for some time would be ideal.

The answer was not long in coming. By Monday 22 July, the Führer had approved the plan in principle. The *City Net* coast watcher network was alerted; a hand-picked SS team was enroute to Lorient, and *B-Dienst, Abwher and Reichtspost* monitoring stations were on high alert. The farmer intended to be ready when the fox left his den and began his travels to the hen house.

Admirals Raeder and Dönitz
(DL Archives)

4 NAVAL OPERATING BASE ARGENTIA - I

15 July 1941
U.S. Naval Operating Base
Argentia, Newfoundland
1300 NST

Lt. Tom Carpentier had arrived at Placentia Bay, Newfoundland aboard *USS Niblack* with the advanced party of Marines escorting the *SS Richard Peck* to Argentia in mid-January. Carpentier was a French-Canadian native of Oquossoc, Maine, thirty miles from the rugged boarder with Quebec. From the moment he stepped ashore, he had worked diligently with Third Provisional Company, earning the trust and respect of Major Dunkelberger, the detachment's skipper. A football standout in high school, he earned a scholarship to the Maine Maritime Academy in Castine, forty miles "downeast" of Bangor. A standout fullback for the Mariners, he had graduated with an engineering degree in the top quarter of his class. He had planned on a career in the merchant marine, but times were hard in 1937, and jobs on the waterfront almost non-existent. He was happy to accept a commission in the Naval Reserve, and served first as a watch officer on *USS Niblack*, before being assigned as beachmaster with the advanced party overseeing construction of the new naval base at Argentia. As beachmaster, he was essentially the "traffic cop" for all materials being unloaded from ships or rail, and during the early summer months, eighteen-hour workdays were not uncommon. But the morning of

15 July 1941 marked a significant milestone; at ceremonies that morning the base was officially placed into commission and Tom had learned that he'd been reassigned as Officer-in-Charge of Naval Radio Station NWP, newly constructed along the shoreline at Point Moffett. The news reenergized him; Newfoundland bore striking resemblance to his native Maine and the potential for a long-time assignment in a land rich in hunting and fishing pleased him greatly. He even looked forward toward hearing again the language of his childhood; just a short boat ride would bring him to the colonial French islands of Saint-Pierre-et-Miquelon, just south of the Burin Peninsula on the west side of the bay. It would be interesting to see how life had changed for the 5,000 or so inhabitants of these two small islands. When France fell to the German onslaught in 1940, France's colonial dependencies worldwide had fallen under the control of the puppet government at Vichy.

As he started back to his quarters after the commissioning ceremony, he reflected on what he had learned about Newfoundland during the round of short speeches from local dignitaries. For nearly four hundred years European fishing boats, attracted by the teeming Grand Banks, had fished along the east and southern coasts of Newfoundland. Sir Humphrey Gilbert landed in St John's in August 1583, and formally took possession of the island in the name of the English queen. Ruled originally from London, the British Government permitted limited local government in 1854, but the island retained its colonial status until, as with Canada, Australia and New Zealand, each became a separate Dominion in 1907. In the postwar period, however, things deteriorated to the point where the Attorney General actually arrested the Prime Minister, Sir Richard Squires, on charges of corruption. Political tumult continued until the Great Depression, which because of reliance on the export of a few natural resources was particularly hard on the island's people. Finally, after pressure from London, the local government voted itself out of existence at the end of 1933. In early 1934, a Commission of Government took control, with final decision-making residing in London. Newfoundland remained a Dominion, but in name only. After serious consideration, even before the bases-for-destroyer agreement, Britain granted the United States the use of part of the Avalon Peninsula "in perpetuity" for the development of an operating base in the North Atlantic. Agreement came in the form of a note to the U.S. Secretary of State, Cordell Hull, stating, "His Majesty's Government will secure the grant freely, and without consideration of the lease, for entrance thereto, and the operation and protection thereof on the Avalon Peninsula and on the Southern Coast of Newfoundland."

"So that's how we wound up here," Carpenter thought, as he changed from his dress white uniform into working khakis. Going outside to the still muddy road, he flagged down a passing truck and asked to be dropped off at the radio station. It was foggy in Placentia Bay that Thursday afternoon. Fog was not unusual at any time of the year; high summer came usually in late August and early September, and even then morning overcasts or light rain were not unlikely. Newcomers were greeted with the old canard, "It's either windy enough to blow a man right over or it's foggy enough that you can't see the hand in front of your face. If you don't like how it is right now, just wait ten minutes – it's sure to change." Argentia was on the windward side of the Avalon Peninsula, and it was not unusual to experience complete "pea soup fog," while St. John's, the capital city only seventy miles away by rail, was sunny and dry. Placentia Bay, however, was generally ice free, one of the compelling reasons that the region had been chosen for the operating base. Argentia, on the eastern side of the bay, was about seventy kilometers upstream from Cape St. Mary, which marked the southern opening of the fjord-like waterway. One of the ten most important fishing settlements on the island, it was regrettable that over 700 structures had to be destroyed in order to level the necessary land for the airfield and other military needs, and nearly 900 residents were relocated to neighboring communities, many receiving what they considered inadequate compensation for their loss. For a time, tensions between the Newfoundlanders and their uninvited "guests" were high. By the time of commissioning, however, all but a very few began to realize that the benefits, including steady year-round employment for many previously seasonal fishermen, would in time outweigh the dislocation in their lives.

Arriving at Point Moffett, Lt. Carpentier thanked the driver, a former resident of Argentia, now living a few miles away in Freshwater, and walked up to the newly constructed radio station. He noticed that a chain link fence had been installed since he last passed by the location, and that crews, both Navy and civilian, were continuing work on the concrete-block and wooden building. The gate-guard immediately came to attention and saluted, then pressed a button inside the guardhouse to open the gate. As Carpentier approached the Radio Station's front door, he heard a buzzer sound, as the gate-guard unlocked the steel windowless door for him. He entered the 10,000 square foot building, and found himself in a short, wide passageway leading to the operations area.

To his left was a small two-roomed office, with a two-line nameplate "Jack D. McCroy, Chief Radioman" newly installed on the door. He turned and entered.

"Attention on Deck!" A seaman working in the outer office snapped to attention and sounded the traditional alert that an officer had entered the workspace. "At ease, sailor," replied

Lt. Carpentier, pleased by his first impression of his new command. "Is Chief McCroy onboard?"

"He's in the operations area, Sir. Shall I ask him to come out to greet you?"

"If you would, yes. Please inform him that Lt. Carpentier has reported aboard." Carpentier, wise in the way of the Navy, knew that his name, and probably all of his vital statistics, would have been known to Chief McCroy within minutes after Admiral Bristol had asked his chief yeoman to cut a set of orders detaching him from Niblack and assigning him to "RadSta Argentia." Chiefs looked out for each other, and radio was not the only form of communication available to Navy CPOs!

Within seconds of the seaman/yeoman entering the operations area, the door opened again, and this time a tall, well built sailor, in the khaki uniform of Chief Petty Officer, exited the operations room. His uniform was immaculate, and Lt. Carpentier recalled seeing him at the commissioning ceremony a few hours before. He also recalled thinking to himself that the division, which this man led appeared particularly sharp and squared away.

The men exchanged salutes. "Good afternoon, sir. I'm Chief Jack McCroy. Welcome to Radio Argentia. Would you care for a cup of coffee? We can sit in my office and I'll update you on your new command, and what we have here." Lt. Carpentier nodded, and noticed that the seaman/yeoman was already enroute to the coffee mess, with two large mugs in hand. "This IS a squared away operation," he thought cheerfully to himself as he seated himself beside Chief McCroy's desk.

The two sailors exchanged pleasantries while drinking the extremely strong and hot coffee.

"Do I detect a hint of chicory in the 'Joe?'" asked Carpentier. McCroy smiled.

"Good pickup on that, Mr. Carpentier. I learned how to make coffee the right way when I was a boot seaman on the battleship *Louisiana*, back in 1918. I always figure that if sailors learn how to do things the right way the first time they cross the quarter-deck, they'll be good for as long as they stay in. Most of the chiefs you'll meet around the base served during the last war, of course."

"Well, if first impressions are any indication, you've carried that over to this command, as well. It looks squared away, Chief, at least as far as the front passageway."

"Thank you sir. It's newly constructed, of course, but so far, I'm very impressed with the quality of the electronics that the Bureau of Yards and Docks has provided, not only here at this building, which we're using as the receiver site and message center, but also at the transmitter site up on the north end of the base. I suppose you know that we always try to keep the transmitters and receivers as far separated as we can, so that we don't interfere with our own reception, don't you, sir?"

Lt. Carpentier noticed Chief McCroy glancing toward his right hand. He smiled. "I'm not a ring-knocker, Chief, if that's what you're wondering. The only time I've set foot inside the Naval Academy is when I stopped by the ship's store there once to pick up new gloves to replace ones that had become so tattered that they were a disgrace to the uniform."

"You're not a mustang either, then, are you, Sir? You seem a bit young to have been formerly enlisted."

"Nope, I'm a mariner – MMA, as you can probably tell from my accent, but I accepted a commission four years ago. You couldn't even get a job as third mate on a tugboat back then. Things are getting better on the waterfront now, but I like where I am and what I'm doing. I had been on *Niblack* for four years, and was the Operations officer when we came up here. The communications division was part of my department when I had that slot, and I suppose that's why I got tapped for the OIC slot here at the RadSta."

Chief McCroy smiled. "*Niblack* — your call sign was NACV, wasn't it?"

"No, it was NAVC, chief."

McCroy – who knew the call sign of every ship in the North Atlantic as well as he knew his own name, smiled and thought to himself, "This guy may be all right after all. Maybe we really *did* get lucky and actually picked up an OIC that knew which end of a radio the sound comes from."

He continued, "*Niblack* has a pretty good radio gang. We handle their traffic when they are out on neutrality patrol."

Lt. Carpentier laughed ruefully. "Neutrality patrol, my eye. There's a shooting war out there in everything but name only and I'm not sure when we're going to be into this thing all the way, but I'm betting that it won't be long. Every month there are more and more U-boats out there right in our backyard. Somebody is going to slip up one of these days, and American sailors are going to get hurt or killed, and then we'll be in it up to our eyeballs. But, say, let's go take a look at the operations area and let me start getting a feel for what you – er, <u>we</u>, – have here, shall we?"

Both men rose, and, returning to the central passageway, turned left. Passing through a set of double doors, they entered a large rectangular room, stretching before them. Teletype machines, with associated radio receivers, lined the wall to their left, while six radio operator wearing earphones, each using a specially modified typewriter equipped with capital letters only, monitored the active radio circuits to their right. Each operator had two receivers positioned at eye level, and each had a J-38 telegraph key mounted comfortably by his right hand. Two desks were located in the center of the room, one facing the Teletype machines and one facing the radio operators.

The watch supervisor, RM1 Bobby Ray, spotting khaki, was about to call the radio gang to attention, but Chief McCroy quickly intervened. "Belay that, Ray. This is Lt. Carpentier, our new OIC." Ray remained at attention until told to carry on with his duties.

"I've spent most of my time at sea," Chief McCroy continued as they walked around the operations area, "but I recently spent one tour at Cubi Point, in the Philippines, and, to tell the truth, Sir, I think the gear here is better than what we had there, back in '37. These National RAO-2 and Hamerlund BC779 receivers are the best I've ever seen, and those Hallicrafters SX-28 commercial receivers are so new that the Bureau hasn't yet gotten around to assigning them a Navy designator. They were shipped to us directly from the factory in Chicago. We've got one each at the CW positions – I'm sorry sir, that's CW for 'Continuous Wave' — it's what radiomen call Morse code. We've got a couple of hot-spares set up on the workbenches in the back of the shack. And you also "own" the transmitter site too, Mr. Carpentier. Up there, we have six large TNA transmitters, running 6,000 watts each, several smaller transmitters for local use and all are connected to those rhombic, 'bird cage' and dipole antennas you can see from the road. What ever happens, I think we're going to be in pretty good shape."

Lt Carpentier continued to be impressed. He walked along behind the radiomen operating the CW circuits. Most had their headphones pushed forward of their ears; old-timers swore that the vibration through their temples went directly to their brain, and made it easier to copy faster keying. Other held that moving the "cans" forward helped prevent hearing loss. But one certain side effect was that those standing close by could listen in to the rhythmic notes of high-speed Morse without the need for loudspeakers.

"This first position is covering the 500 kcs. distress frequency," Chief McCroy noted. "In peacetime, there's usually not much happening on 500 – just ships making initial contact with their shore stations and then shifting off to a working frequency. But, since I've been up here, I've heard more distress traffic on 500 than I've heard in 23 years in the Navy. We're perfectly located to copy everything in the North Atlantic, and you can certainly imagine how busy the distress frequencies have been. There's a convoy out of Halifax that passed Cape Race yesterday, and the U-boats are hitting them pretty badly right now. We try to broadcast the U-boat locations whenever we can, to assist other ships to maneuver their way around them." Both sailors were silent for a minute, imagining the terrors that others faced, just a few dozen miles offshore.

McCroy continued as they walked aft. "This second position copies the Navy's FOX broadcast . . . that's continuous traffic from Washington, relayed via multiple transmitters around the world."

He glanced briefly at the receiver dial. "He is copying NSS at Annapolis right now. They're always strong around this time of day. Generally, radiomen will type out only those messages which contain their ship or station's call sign, but to give these fellows practice, I have them record all traffic coming in on the broadcast. At 22 words-per-minute, it soon helps them become experts in reading Morse code. All of the other positions are used on an as-needed basis, depending on which ships are operating in our area, and what their communications needs may be."

Chief McCroy glanced briefly at the large clock on the far wall. "We're just about to relieve this section in about thirty minutes, sir, so things are going to get a bit squirrely for awhile. We're operating in four sections now after the last draft got here a few weeks ago. I've got the watch, quarter and station bill set up in a 3-3-3-72 rotation. Each section stands three eight-hour evening watches, three day-watches and three midnight-watches and then is off watch for 72 hours. I allow the leading radioman of each section to set his own "tricks"; a man usually works for two hours on a particular circuit, and then rotates to another assignment. And off-watch doesn't mean off duty, either. You'll see off-duty watch standers in here at all hours, wielding paintbrushes, or installing equipment or what have you. There's not a lot to do on liberty at Argentia, and most of the local islanders are working just as hard as we are to get things up and shipshape. But it's a good crew – at least most of 'em are – and I think you'll be happy with your new command, sir."

"Very well, Chief, and thanks for the quick tour. I'm quite impressed by what you've done in the short time the station has been active. I'll be onboard for morning quarters tomorrow, and every day there after. I noticed an empty office next to yours. That's mine, I suppose?"

"It is, sir, and we'll have it squared away for you when you arrive. And, if you like, sir, I'm about to send the station truck back to the barracks area to pick up the oncoming watch section. You can hop on board, and I'll have Seaman Doyle, our acting yeoman, drop you back at your quarters."

Chief McCroy escorted Lt. Carpentier to the front door, saluted, and saw him on his way.

July 15, 1941
Naval Operating Base
Argentia, Newfoundland
14:30 NST

Seaman Doyle dropped Lt. Carpentier at his quarters, and swung by the row of newly constructed enlisted barracks near the airfield. It had begun to rain, and Doyle was careful to park the "bread truck" on the newly laid gravel, keeping as clear as he could of the ever changing, ever expanding mud puddles surrounding the barracks. It was the least he could do to help the ongoing watch standers keep their "boondockers" clean, if not particularly dry, before they faced the meticulous Chief McCroy at the beginning of their eight-hour evening watch.

RM1 Ashford Holden, known universally to his shipmates as "Ash Hole," was first to arrive at the truck. Befitting his position as leading petty officer of watch section three, he claimed the passenger's seat. The remainder of the crew quickly exited the barracks and, dodging the rain, opened the back doors of the van, and scrambled onto the jury-rigged benches, which lined both sides of the enclosed vehicle.

Holden turned for a quick head count. "Where's Hannigan? Gawdammit! Where is *Hannigan?* "We're five minutes late already. Doyle . . . go see if he is coming, or does he plan to walk over to the station in the rain?" Doyle did as he was ordered, and returned after several long moments with the straggler. "Hannigan . . . I swear to Gawd . . . if you screw up one more thing this week, I'm going to cold cock you and shanghai you right back on that tin-can that dumped you on us. Now get into this gawdamn truck and let's move it. Chief is gonna be pissed off at us as it is. Doyle, what the hell took you so long getting over here? We've been waiting for you for the last ten minutes."

As the truck jolted down the unpaved, rutted roadway, Doyle explained, "The new OIC showed up this afternoon, and the chief was walking him around the station. I had to wait, and then take him by the BOQ before I got you guys."

"So, what's he like? Another one of these ninety-day wonders?"

"Naw, he's an older guy. At least he ain't a butter-bar ensign. His name is Carp-Carp-something or other. He's some kind of Frenchie. He's off the *Niblack,* he says. I've seen him around the base before in a hard hat and safety vest. Some kinda mustang or something, I guess."

"Frenchie!" exclaimed RM2 Boudreaux from the back of the van. "Cajun? We're finally getting another Cajun except me into this radio station? Outstanding!

"Ain't no Cajun, Frenchy. Says he's from Maine or somewhere. Big fugger, too . . . I heard him say he played football before he came in." Doyle, whose seat in the outer office permitted him to overhear all conversations and at least one side of every telephone call, was a treasure trove of scuttlebutt, much of it wrong, about everything which affected the radio gang.

The radio crew debated the news. A tin can sailor was better than some guy right out of ROTC somewhere, or, heaven forbid, someone from the Naval Academy. Any academy graduate who found himself beached at Radio Station Argentia was sure to have screwed up somewhere, big time. "Stow that chatter," Holden finally ordered. "We'll find out soon enough as is."

The crew arrived at the Radio Station. "Hannigan . . . get out of the truck, have the gate guard hold open the gate, and you hold open the main station door. No sense all of us getting drenched on the way in. Your shirt is wrinkled already; it looks like you slept in your dungarees and gawdammit, Hannigan! *Where's your cover?* Somebody loan Hannigan a white hat, before he drowns on the way into work, or before the chief catches one of my crew out of uniform. Whoever loans him the white hat, go camp out in the head until we tell you the coast is clear. I'd have Hannigan camp out in there, but he might get lost on the way back. Now, *move* it, Hannigan!"

The crew hightailed it into the radio station and five sailors in pressed chambray shirts, creased dungarees and shined shoes – and RM3 Timothy (Hambone) Hannigan, who sported none of these – presented themselves in the operations' area. After a brief conversation between RM1 Ray and RM1 Holden, the crew fanned out and stood behind the watchstander who had manned their operating position throughout the day. Each picked up a spare pair of earphones, and began monitoring the circuit for which they'd be responsible for the first "trick" of the evening watch. After "getting the picture" for a few moments, and briefly conferring with their opposite number, they uttered the usual Navy formalities "I relieve you," while the off-going sailor replied, "I stand relieved."

Everyone knew the wording, drilled into sailors since their first day of boot camp, and which hadn't changed since the Republic was young – everyone, that is, except Hannigan. "Go relieve yourself," he shouted to the 500 kcs. position operator, sitting not two feet in front of him. "You don't have to shout, Hambone," the off-going crewman growled, "I ain't deaf yet." Shaking his head, more in frustration than anger, the off-going operator unplugged his headset, and joined the rest of section two as they made to the front door for a few hours of on-station liberty. Within a few minutes section three had matters under control, and settled in for their evening duty.

48

Chief McCroy stayed out of the radio shack until the change-over was complete and things had settled into the usual routine. He had full confidence in his leading radiomen, and generally allowed them to organize their watch sections as they saw fit. After a few minutes had passed, he entered. Holden and Boudreaux were at the farthermost operating position, tuning a pair of receivers to the main Canadian escort operating frequency. Seeing McCroy enter, Holden returned to his desk and took the seat opposite his boss. Both were "lifers" – long term sailors who had survived the depression on Navy chow, and each had a great deal of respect for the other. McCroy looked around the radio shack.

"What are you and Boudreaux setting up?" he asked.

Holden replied, "We've got two Canadian corvettes down the bay. . .I heard them talking to Cape St. Mary a couple minutes ago. They're heading this way, and I'm getting ready for the usual 'Canuck-kerchunk' – you know how it is with the Canadians. They usually key the bridge microphone a couple times before announcing their arrival. I'm not certain why, exactly. Maybe it alerts their docking crews and makes the line handlers look that much sharper to their officers. Just another courtesy among our Canadian friends, I suppose."

"Good sailors for such a small Navy, which really didn't exist until this war started for them in '39," the Chief replied. "Squared away, every one of 'em I've ever met. Speaking of which: tell Hannigan to get a haircut before his next watch. And to change out that shirt – I wouldn't be surprised if it got up and walked away without him. Are you having any luck with the kid yet?"

"Not much, but we're trying. It's the craziest damn thing I've ever seen, Chief. He is, by far, the best CW operator we've got in the section. Except for maybe one or two of the other senior radiomen, he's probably the best we have at the entire station right now, if all you are looking at are technical skills. As a junior petty officer though . . . hell, just as a *human being* . . . he's about as drifty as they get. He is one weird dude, that boy is." Holden refrained from mentioning that he knew that Chief McCroy had taken him off the hands of an old shipmate on the *USS Plunkett* when it passed through Argentia, mostly to keep his fellow chief radioman from certain homicide, or to prevent the rest of their radio gang from chucking the kid over the side as soon as *Plunkett* left port. The scuttlebutt was that Chief McCroy got Hannigan for two cartons of Lucky Strikes, but as with most scuttlebutt, it was wide of the mark. The chief on the tin can, which had just left the Brooklyn Navy yard, had given *McCroy* a carton in gratitude. McCroy scowled at the memory.

"I read his service record after I got him. I should've read it first. He's been a royal screw up since he hit the fleet. Chief Zabrinski said when he first reported aboard *Plunkett* at Brooklyn, he tried to rearrange the radio shack all by himself. Didn't tell anyone – just thought it would work better his way. He can't chip paint without taking gouges out of the bulkheads, he can't paint without leaving streaks, and before they left, they had to rescue him during swim call off Coney Island. When they finally got out of the yards, he was seasick, even before they cleared New York Bay. He barfed his way up here, and 'Ski used to find half of his receivers tuned to civilian radio stations and whatnot. 'Ski would have dumped him himself, but it appears that Hannigan's old man was a sailor – a warrant boatswain on the old four-stacker *USS Higgs*. *Higgs* was the first ship to go to the aid of the S-4 off Cape Cod when the submarine was rammed by that Coast Guard cutter, back in, oh, '27 or '28 or thereabouts. Hannigan's old man was in charge of the deck gang, and got fouled in a rescue line trying to save one of their divers who got into trouble and was suffocating. He got pulled to the bottom and tangled up in the sub's wreckage, and they never recovered the body. 'Ski knew the guy, and had heard the story around the waterfront at Newport. No one ever found the Higgs bos'n, though they thought they had at one point, but it was just a problem with the cable. But 'Ski figured he should look after a shipmate's son, who had a pretty tough time after his old man died. Apparently, the kid's mom couldn't handle him and his three older sisters, so she packed the girls off to relatives, while he wound up in an orphanage in Philly and she disappeared back to the coal regions in upstate Pennsylvania. He was there till he graduated from high school, but nobody ever came to visit the poor kid, or even ask about him. Pretty sad story, really. But it seems that one of the Catholic brothers at the orphanage was a ham-radio operator and got Hannigan interested, so by the time he left he was a pretty good technician and an even better operator. He got a job at the RCA plant across the river in Camden, and, when the V3 program offered to take radio technicians directly into the Navy at RM3, he signed up. He lasted about three days down at radioman school at Bainbridge; he was faster on a speed-key than most of the instructors, so they sent him to Brooklyn, and you know the rest. Now that it looks like we're gonna get into a shooting war, the fleet is taking just about anybody who can walk, talk and chew gum, or any two out of three. He landed on *Plunkett* and now he's here. How's he doing on 500 kcs?"

"He's unbelievable, Chief. The first day I got him, he was walking around, fiddling with dials, and asking for a chance to operate the gear. I stuck him on 500 kcs when it was slow just to check him out, and had Frenchy sit with him to make sure we didn't miss anything. In about an hour, Frenchy unplugged and told me the kid didn't need him anymore. And Frenchy's been pounding brass since Marconi was a mess cook. The kid's got ears like a rabbit; if it's out there, he can hear it, and his fist is just about perfect; I've never heard him mash a letter. He's got that banana boat swing when he's using a straight key – now that I know he was a ham operator that accounts for it – they all do that. One mid-watch last week when things were slow, I loaned him my Vibroplex speed key and the kid took off like it grew outta his arm. He was working some Brit at about 40 wpm before I made him stop. And the only reason I did that was because none of us was fast enough to know what the hell he was saying."

McCroy shook his head. "Craziest damn thing I ever saw. Well, I'm gonna head back to the CPO barracks and get ready for chow. Get one of your guys to drive me and Doyle back, and bring the truck back so that your guys can go fetch chow later. Do you want Hannigan to drive? I could get a little informal windshield time with him and get to know him better that way."

"Not if you want to arrive alive, Chief. Apparently he never got out of the orphanage much, and he said that one of the brothers tried to teach him to drive, but the guy got so frustrated that he put in his papers and went off to the missions in Africa or someplace. He gave up on Hannigan and made him take the streetcar wherever he needed to go from then on. He's been like this for a while, it seems." McCroy just shook his head in amazement, and, after checking that everything was in order, left for the evening.

The watch continued, and at 1700 local time, two hours after the watch began, Houlton substituted two other sailors on the 500-kilocycle distress frequency and Fox circuits. He called Hannigan over to the desk.

"Hey, Hambone. I hear you're good with receivers. How about going back to the test bench and fire up that SX-28 back there and see if you can get us some baseball scores, OK? Pipe it into the speaker here on my desk, and I'll keep the gain low so that it doesn't disturb anyone. Think you can handle that?"

"Sure, Ass H . . . er, sure, Holton. No problem."

Hannigan walked back to the test bench at the far end of the radio shack. Within seconds, he not only had baseball scores, but he had picked up a transmission of the Philadelphia Athletics and Detroit Tigers game, live from Briggs stadium in Detroit. Holton and the other watchstanders not on critical circuits listened, as the Tigers took the lead 3-2 in the bottom of the seventh inning, and never looked back. "Looks like Bobo Newsome got another one," Holton commented to no one in particular as the game ended. "Damn . . . I thought Lum Harris had that one for a while. Hey, Hambone! Come over here for a minute. Where'd you find the game, huh?"

"WCAU in Philly has a short wave transmitter, WCAB, on 9590 kcs. I used to tune to it all the time back when I was on the *Plunkett.*"

"Yeah, so I've heard." replied Holton, "I betcha they loved that. But don't come with that salty 'back when I was on the Plunkett' crap with us, boot. We know you were on there for, what, two weeks?"

"Three weeks, Chief – er, Holton. Three weeks."

"Regular Popeye, ain't he guys?"

"Ah, don't bust his chops, Ash . . . he got us the game, didn't he?"

"Yeah, but what was that strong carrier sitting on top of the announcer anyway, Hannigan? I couldn't hear By Saam half the time calling the plays."

"I dunno, Holton, but it was really really close. Is there a 9-Meg transmitter somewhere around here, do you think? Next time I'll try to figure out what it is, OK?"

"Shouldn't be, kid. Let me check." Holton hit the key on the intercom, and spoke with the technician manning the transmitter site on the north end of the base. "Are you guys up on 9-megacycles with anything?"

"Not us, Holton. We've never been near 9megs, as far as I can see in the logs here. That's not a frequency that anybody's Navy uses, as far as I know; not us, nor the Canadians nor the British. Sorry, pal."

Holton shrugged.

Hannigan returned to his 500 kcs distress circuit for an otherwise uneventful evening, happy that he had at least impressed the other guys in the section for once.

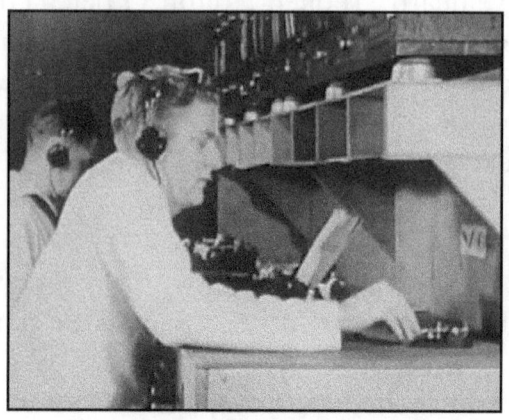

**RADIOMEN OPERATING POSITIONS 1 AND 2
500 KCS DISTRESS AND NAVY 'FOX' BROADCASTS**
(Official USN photo)

5 LORIENT - I

22 July 1941
BdU Command Headquarters
Chateau Kerneval, Lorient
Brittany, France

Nine experienced U-boat captains met at the shore-side entrance of Keroman 2. They stood together chatting beside three highly fortified and vigorously defended submarine pens at Lorient, the U-boat base on the Bay of Biscay. When all had assembled, they walked together and boarded a launch to carry them across the River Scorff to Chateau Kerneval, the forward operating headquarters of U-boat command. The weather was warm and the short trip pleasant, and after debarking, they walked up the cobbled roadway and through the imposing wrought iron gate, past the saluting guards and into the impressive marbled foyer of the confiscated chateau. Turning right they descended a small stairway to the basement, and walking a few meters more, ascended a plain metal staircase to the fully enclosed, windowless and strongly constructed bunker adjacent to the chateau. They gathered in the large conference room on the first floor, a room familiar to them all.

"I've often spotted '*Onkle Karl*' on the roof of this bunker, spyglass in hand, when coming up to the pens from a combat patrol," one remarked to no one in particular. "I don't think he ever misses a returning boat, at least not during the hours of daylight. I always see him there."

"He's there at night, too, I know," remarked another. "I've come in well before dawn when the tide requires it, and I've seen him there, backlit against the loom of light from fifteen or twenty miles inland, waiting, just waiting, until he knows we're safely moored. I've never known a commander who cares so much about his men or his ships. I doubt that anyone does."

There was a murmur of assent as they took their places around the conference table. A side table held flasks of strong coffee, tea, cold water, and platters of pastries, while good Kriegsmarine silver utensils completed the array. No one wanted to be the first to disturb this modest display, which seemed unbelievably lavish to men who routinely spent weeks at sea with sparse provisions. All sat quietly until Admiral Dönitz entered a moment or two later. They rose and greeted the BdU commander with traditional naval salutes. Among the elite of the U-boat service, party salutes were reserved for "outsiders." Dönitz returned their salute, and brought the meeting to order. His flag lieutenant quietly entered and took up his position at another small table near the door.

"Gentlemen, to help Oberlieutenant Eichs, who is new to the position, so that he might maintain an accurate log, please be so good as to identify yourselves to him beginning on my left." Going clockwise around the table, they replied:

Oberleutnant zur See	Harald Gelhaus	U-143, First Flotilla- Brest
Kapitänleutnant	Hans-Heinz Linder	U-202, First Flotilla- Brest
Kapitänleutnant	Walter Kell	U-204, First Flotilla- Brest
Kapitänleutnant	Josef Moll	U-115, Second Flotilla-Lorient
Kapitänleutnant	Günther Krech	U-558, First Flotilla-Brest
Oberleutnant zur See	Reinhard Suhren	U-564, First Flotilla-Brest
Oberleutnant zur See	Albert Schnee	U-201 First Flotilla-Brest

| Kapitänleutnant | Georg Zimmermann U-112, Second Flotilla-Lorient |
| Kapitänleutnant | Paul Schröder | U-114, Second Flotilla-Lorient |

"Thank you, gentlemen, and, as always it is good to see each one of you. I've spoken with each of you as your last patrol had ended, and I trust that you have enjoyed this short respite ashore before you and your crew goes again in dangerous waters. I do not have to tell you how much your service and sacrifice mean to the Führer, to our homeland and to me, personally."

"We have some critical news from our good shore-bound colleague Admiral Canaris. Ah, – alas for poor Wilhelm – his duty is to practice *Abwehr* all day, while we get to practice *Angriff,* is it not?" The U-boat commanders smiled. Dönitz, not a man known for his sense of humor, had made a slightly irreverent pun on the words for *defense* and *offense.* "But this time, the Abwehr has presented us with a gift, which, if we treat it properly, will be the greatest gift of the war – indeed, perhaps the greatest gift of our generation to us. "Eichs – be so good as to pull back the curtains on my Atlantic Ocean wall chart, would you?" Turning to the assembled officers he remarked "Eichs has some recent personal experience in those waters, don't you Eichs? At least the top three feet or so, eh, Joachim?"

He explained that Oberleutnant Eichs was most recently third navigator on the battleship *Bismarck* and was but one of a handful of survivors pulled from the sea nearly thirty hours later by the weather trawler *Sachsenwald.* "Since he was off the coast at Brest at the time, I offered him a place here at Lorient. Slide open those curtains widely, so all can see the entire area. Thanks."

The map was clean of any ship positions, but showed arcs extending out from the North of Ireland, Iceland, Greenland,

Newfoundland and the Azores marking the range of allied aircraft flown from those bases. There were at least thirty U-boats and a dozen or more allied conveys at sea, but Dönitz had directed that a clear board be prepared overnight. He wanted no distractions to the information he was about to deliver to his U-boat captains.

"Through the efforts of the *Abwehr* and the *B-dienst* and even other more obscure practitioners of the intelligence trade, we have come into information – and it appears to be well documented, as I have seen the original dispatches myself – which indicates that Churchill, the British Prime Minister, has taken a longing for a sea voyage, and has invited his new best friend, President Roosevelt to share the well-known benefits of the good sea air. Perhaps we might add a whiff of diesel exhaust for them, shall we? While we are lacking as much operational detail as we would like to have, intelligence received from agents in Russia indicates that Roosevelt's confident Harry Hopkins, who has been visiting with Stalin, is moving heaven and earth to be certain that he is back in London not later than August 1, one week from Friday. Other intelligence seems to indicate that the two leaders intend to meet at a base now under construction on the south coast of the island of Newfoundland, off the Canadian coast, as is well known to you. Canaris' best estimate is that the meeting will occur sometime during the second or third week of August, and the Führer has given us his permission, indeed, his most enthusiastic approval, to demonstrate our 'interest' in their meeting. You can imagine the impact on the war if we are successful in disrupting this little discussion of theirs, I presume?"

"Before we go any further, gentlemen . . . I have a personal question for each of you. Have any of you played Fußball in your youth?" All laughed, and raised their hands. Well, gentlemen we are about to play for the *Europameisterschaft* (European championship), and we are going to be the Home team. Churchill, and whoever he has to accompany him, will be the Visitors and, just like in the game we know so well, our task is to prevent the visitors from scoring. And, since you all claim to be excellent footballers, I shall open this meeting to your frank impressions of what strategy our opponent may choose to implement, and how best we can stymie him at his own game. I've named this opportunity as *Operation Fußball* by the way. Now, which of you would like to begin?" They shuffled in their seats, but gradually the meeting began to open up.

'**Kaleunt Linder**: I would certainly keep under the air umbrella for as long as possible on both sides of the Ocean. That goes without saying, yes?

Oblt zS. Suhren: I would use the fastest and heaviest capital ship at my disposal. In this case, I'd have his party embarked on either *HMS King George V* or *HMS Prince of Wales.*

'**Kaleunt Schröder:** Ah, you were out and about during that recent dust-up, weren't you, Reinhardt? *Prinz Eugen* damaged *HMS Prince of Wales* seriously below the water line. He is undergoing repairs even now, I think.

Admiral Dönitz: Yes, at Rosyth, on the Firth of Forth. He suffered major damage to the bridge and forecastle as well, but Luftwaffe photograph reconnaissance shows that they are working vigorously to have her ready for sea quickly. I would not count *Prince of Wales* out quite yet.

'**Kaleunt Georg Zimmermann:** With all due respect to my comrades, and to you, Herr Admiral, I take a different view.

Were I planning this voyage, I'd be certain that my "gift" was hidden in plain sight. I'd place Churchill and his party on a small, insignificant vessel. One of those devilish corvettes should suit him fine! I'd let him pitch and roll and yaw his way across the Atlantic. It's what the drunkard deserves, isn't it? He'd be in fine fettle when he meets Roosevelt, yes? Perhaps Roosevelt can make him a "lend lease" of his bath chair to get around, do you think?

The others laughed. In their heart of hearts, though, perhaps they had a moment of sympathy for their fellow seaman of the Royal Navy, for the hardships they endured on the makeshift corvettes, those small converted whaling ships ill suited for the arduous job of escorting convoys across the North Atlantic.

Georg Zimmermann: Or, perhaps, he can ride over on one of those four funnel destroyers that Roosevelt pawned off on the drunkard not long ago. They must have found them at a *Flohmarkt* (flea market), yes?

Oblt zS. Suhren: If he doesn't take Georg's advice, I would certainly look for at least a squadron of escorts, which is a tactic the British use always. It is rare to find one of them all alone on the high seas.

The others had begun to confer among themselves, and Dönitz, ever the schoolmaster, quieted them with a single look of disapproval. "Very well, let's see where that leaves us. Eichs, draw a rhumb line between Britain and Newfoundland, please. We don't know where they may depart, so broaden the eastern end into two forks . . . one departing from, let us say, Rockall bank in the North, and the other from South of the Hebrides. I don't think the British would chance being trapped in the Irish or North Seas on an occasion such as this. Extend the western end to Cape Race. By that point he'll be well under air cover, and every ship within 1000 km will no doubt sortie to give him protection." Eichs did as ordered.

"Now, Eichs, draw a box, let us say, 150 km on either side of this line, staying out of the danger cones where we could encounter air cover. Read out the coordinates to us, Eichs."

"I make the coordinates as 25 to 35 West, and 50 to 54 North, Sir."

"You learned well on *Bismarck*, Lieutenant. Thank you. Now, kindly consult BdU chart 3401 and present these gentlemen with coordinates with which they can communicate among themselves and with us here, please."

Eichs did as ordered. "It would be a course which enters at AK66 and leaves at AK87, Herr Admiral."

"The killing ground, gentlemen," Dönitz declared. "That's where we'll find Churchill if he is foolish enough to cross the sea. So there you are – That's our Fußball pitch, then. We know where we'll meet; we just do not yet know the fixture – the date of our contest. Each of you is to return immediately to your crews, and prepare for sea as quickly as possible. It is necessary that we be on the pitch to welcome our visitors. We shall divide into two separate forces, thus:

"Linder you will lead the First Flotilla Boats: your own U-202, and U-143, U-204,U-558, and U-564. You will patrol a line from 49 N to 53 North, along latitude 25-28 West."

"Zimmermann, you and your U-112 shall be in charge of the 'backfield' With you will be Schröder in U114 and Schnee in U-201. Neumann in U372 is just coming into Brest this evening. Linder, you are to brief Neumann as soon as possible, and report to me when that has been accomplished. Zimmermann, you and your element will patrol along a line from 54 to 58 North along latitude 29-31 West. This disposition gives us the best chance to intercept the vessel or vessels carrying Churchill and his party, even if weather, seas state or time of day are not in our favor. As soon as you are ready in all respects for sea, you are to signal this command, and we will release you in such a way so as not to draw too much attention while crossing the Bay of Biscay. You are to avoid contact with the enemy at all costs – this is not a patrol where maximum tonnage is the goal. It's quality, not quantity of the target, which will determine your success. When contact is made, signal immediately with coordinates, course and speed, but do not send the usual homing signals. We will plot the battle from here, and transmit coordinates and instructions for both lines to meet up and attack. Have you any questions?"

All were silent, although Moll, a short and stocky former wrestler from the Pfälzerwald appeared uncomfortable, as his name and the U-115 had not been mentioned. Dönitz, sensing his discomfort remarked, "Have no fear, Josef, I have not left you out. Stay behind a moment when your comrades leave, please."

"Very well, gentlemen. Before you go, a final thought. I am reminded of two times in European history — once when 300 men changed the fate of the world at Thermopylae, and much later when Horatius and two comrades saved Rome at Pons Sublicius. History has been kind to those valiant warriors, and history may yet add ten more glorious names to join them: not of those who fought beside or above the water, as did they, but those who fought below. Go now, and good luck to you all."

The others departed, and Dönitz and Moll were alone. "Well, Josef, I suppose you are wondering what your role in all of this is to be, perhaps?" Moll remained silent. "You were with Prien on U-47 at Scapa Flow, weren't you?" Moll nodded. "We've lost a most exceptional captain when we lost Günter," Dönitz continued, sadly. " I was stricken when I heard the news in March – he had accomplished so much – not only by his audacity in destroying the battleship *HMS Royal Oak* at Scapa Flow, but also by preventing over 200,000 tonnes of war materials from reaching the enemy's ports. You were, what, an *Oberfähnrich zur See* (sub-lieutenant)?"

" Yes, Herr Admiral, and I share your grief for our loss. He was like a father to me."

"I have followed your progress these last two years, Moll. You commissioned the U-115, and your last two patrols have been splendid. Your crew is excellent – well trained and well disciplined, and I don't mind telling you, Josef, that they have the greatest respect for you as a tactician and as their leader. You may yet have a chance to honor Prien's memory yet, Josef. To continue our analogy, you'll be the goaltender in our little sporting event here. I want you to depart as soon as possible, and, in absolute stealth, take up a position about 350 km south and west of Cape Race. I don't expect that you will be able to do what Günter did at Scapa Flow. Placentia Bay is a much deeper and longer fjord, there is a wide opening to the sea from the south, just west of Cape St. Mary, but there is no outlet to the north. There are certainly blockade ships and underwater nets guarding the entrance. But if Churchill makes it that far, you are our last hope of preventing him from meeting with Roosevelt and bringing the Americans in on the side of the British."

"But be absolutely clear on one thing, Moll. The Führer has given direct orders that no one is to harm the American President. The last thing we need now is to have them come into the conflict before we are ready to take them on. Indeed, if disaster befalls Churchill, the Führer feels that it will strengthen the arguments of Roosevelt's domestic opponents, and help keep the Americans out of the war until we are able to complete our mission against Russia. At the Führer's order, you will have some passengers, I am told. I had no say in this, and I would gladly have it otherwise, but three 'specialists' from the Schutzstaffel will join you shortly. The ultimate success of the mission is yours, and yours alone, but you are to give due consideration to whatever "suggestions" their officer might give to you. Because of your passengers, I suggest you detach three men from your crew, and leave them behind here in Lorient." Dönitz paused for a long moment, and continued somberly. "And, Josef, were it I who was forced to make such a selection, I would chose to leave behind married men with children." Moll nodded, understanding perfectly.

"Three hundred men and three men" those were brave and valiant men, Moll, as I know that you and your men will be. Go now, and come back to us safely. Moll stood to depart as he raised his hand in the Naval salute. Dönitz rose, but rather than salute, extended his hand and grasped the hand of Moll. *Grüß Gott* (God bless you) the admiral murmured softly, using the traditional farewell once used in the Pfälzerwald and Bavaria, but now forbidden by the Nazi regime. *"Grüß Gott, Moll."*

6 NAVAL OPERATING BASE ARGENTIA II

20 July 1941
Naval Operating Base
Argentia Newfoundland
0730 NST

"Yo Hambone! Come on. Get up. You wanted me to wake you so you could go to church this morning, right?"

Hannigan had made few friends among his shipmates, but RM2 Boudreaux had taken him under his wing and protected him from the wrath of Chief McCroy, Holden, and assorted masters-at-arms and shore patrolmen with whom Hambone had run afoul. Francis Xavier Boudreaux – who, like every Cajun who ever entered the U.S. Navy immediately became known as Frenchy – was, like Hannigan, a practicing Roman Catholic. And, like Hannigan, he participated more out of fear of an angry God than any theological conviction. Early education among nuns and priests had seen to that; Hannigan at St. Joseph's Orphanage and Boudreaux along Bayou Lafourche near Thibodaux, Louisiana. Besides, as Frenchy knew, and Hannigan was quickly learning, church was a great place to meet girls.

Sailors had first attended Mass at Holy Rosary Church in Argentia, but, when it was demolished in April to make way for new runways, Mass shifted to the base galley, the only space large enough to hold all the congregants. A dining hall was not the ideal venue for church services, but in the early stages of base construction it served alternately as an assembly hall, chapel, movie theater, and gymnasium. Catholics Mass started at 0800 sharp; Protestant services at 0930 and by noon, sailors were lining up for chipped beef on toast, or other culinary delicacies served from hatches that lined the left side of the room.

Hannigan scurried to get ready, and by 0755, both sailors were at the galley door, presentable in their undress summer white uniform. Hannigan found the Latin of Mass comforting, but the prospect of meeting some of Frenchy's many lady friends much more enticing. There was this one tall, young brunette that Hannigan worshiped from afar for the past few weeks. He spotted her again as Mass began and sighed. Maybe today he'd work up the courage to say hello.

"We really catch a break," he thought to himself. True, church-call came earlier than for others, but Mass was open to military, contractors and local residents alike, and Argentia and the Cape Shore were overwhelmingly Catholic. And Irish, too, Hannigan thought to himself; the area was full of Duffys and Mulligans, McGraths, Murphys and dozens of other Irish names besides. He wasn't sure about Father Dee – that didn't sound like an Irish name, but he felt sorry for the poor parish priest of Argentia who was forced to close his parish church when the military arrived and move with his congregation to Freshwater, just outside the gate. He was glad that Father Dee would say Mass today, and not one of the other priests who visited the base. Father O'Reilly, the curate, was as slow as molasses, and Father McHugh, who'd come up from below Point Verde on occasion to help out, reminded him of the stiff grouchy priests who came by the orphanage to say Mass and cage a free meal. And Hannigan didn't need anyone to remind him about those days.

He turned slightly and saw her on his right. Her name was Kathy, according to Boudreaux, and she was twenty-three. He smiled at her, and she smiled back. Women, or people in general, didn't smile at Hambone much. He was tall, and thin, and at 21, occasionally showed signs of his adolescent acne. Regardless of how much he tried, he could not control his shock of red hair. When he first appeared at Radio Station Argentia, RM1 Holden looked him up and down, and said "Stick out your tongue, boy, and turn sideways." Assuming this was some sort of medical examination, Hambone did as required. "You're so skinny I can see the bumps in your spine. Dufus, you look just like a zipper. Now, get moving and go grab a swab and clean up the mud you just tracked in." It was as kind as anything his watch supervisor ever said to him.

Father Dee, true to form, was quick. His sermon lasted just a few minutes. He spoke about Good Samaritans, and, while no one in the Argentia community had ever anticipated the arrival of the Americans, they bore an obligation under God to be as kind and openhearted to them as they would to any other visitors. Hambone took a surreptitious glance at his watch. Father Dee recited the final prayer at precisely 0847. "Not bad," thought Hannigan. Not bad at all.

As the congregants filed out of the makeshift chapel, he spotted Boudreaux, who, true to form, was chatting with several young women. "Hey, Hambone," he called out, "Come on over here for a second. I want you to meet someone." He introduced his shipmate to two girls in the crowd. "This is Violet Maloney – she and I are dating, aren't we, sweetheart?" Violet, pleasingly plump, blushed deeply. "And this is her friend, Kathy. Violet and Kathy are nurses at the Cottage Hospital out in Placentia, ain't you, girls?" Kathy grimaced at the mangled grammar, and smiled at Hannigan once more.

"You're the Yank that I've seen every week in church, aren't you?" she asked. "But your real name can't be Hambone, can it? What's your real name?"

Stammering, he replied: "Well, it's Timothy, but people call me Tim, except in the Navy where they call me Hambone. I guess that's because I was a ham-radio operator when I was a kid."

She laughed. "I know how lonely it must be for all of you up here," she continued. "I'm a stranger here myself. My real name is Katherine French, but everyone just calls me Kathy. I'm not Catholic myself, but Violet here is, and I come to church to keep her company. I'm Canadian and I've only been here a short time, too. Violet and I are going to stay behind and go berry picking up by the old silver mine with Frenchy. Want to come along?" Out of sight of the young ladies, Frenchy winked broadly at Hannigan.

Hambone readily agreed and squeezed between Kathy and Violet in the back of the truck which Frenchy had cumshawed from a Cajun buddy in the motor pool. "Violet is new too, Tim," Kathy continued. "Because of all the construction and folks working on the base, Placentia asked for volunteers to come from other hospitals to help out. Violet is from the east end of St. John's. She and I became friends at the Grace Hospital there and decided to come over here together."

Violet protested, "Now wait a minute. I'm not some uppity girl from the East End. I'm a good Irish girl from the Outer Battery, thank you very much, and proud of it. That Italian feller, Marconi, used to come by our house for a good feed, so me mum tells me, when he was fooling around with his wireless, up there on Signal Hill. I don't know why he called it wireless though; he had miles

of wire strung all over Cabot tower. Me mum said you'd be in fear
of your life if you ever went courting up on the hill after dark, for
all his perishin' wires. Not that it stopped her and me da, I don't
expect. Nor me either . . ."

"That's enough about us," Kathy quickly interjected. "Tim, tell
us something about yourself, eh?"

Hambone, who was pleased that someone would actually call
him Tim again, stammered out the brief outline of his life, and
how he happened to be in Newfoundland. Fortunately, the truck
stopped on the dirt road adjacent to a scrubland of bushes, shrubs
and stunted trees, before he could anesthetize the nurses with the
esoterics of radio transmission and reception. The view over the
water to the ships lying off shore was stunning on this rare clear
and warm Newfoundland day.

Violet had the foresight to bring along small sacks and bas-
kets. Kathy remarked, "We're after bakeapples today, Tim – do you
know what those look like?" He shook his head. He knew what
baked apples looked like – they served them at the Orphanage on
special occasions – but he thought it unlikely that they'd grow wild
on bushes. Kathy took him by the hand. "Here, silly! See these red
berries with the funny skin that looks like little warts? They almost
look like miniature red pumpkins. See? They're good! They taste
like, well . . . it's hard to explain, but it's kind of like an apricot covered with honey, but they are really, really good. Newfoundlanders
make them into jam, and there's nothing better than some bakeapples on fresh churned ice cream. Come on, have one!" And she
popped one right into his mouth.

Hannigan could have been eating road apples, for all he cared.
He was falling in love – a condition about which he knew little,

other than he liked it a lot. He didn't know much about women; he had been too young to really know his mom or his sisters, and the orphanage was all male. Indeed, the only people Hannigan knew were sailors, and, while sailors talked about women every waking moment, and dreamt about them the rest of the time, well, given that they were sailors, they just wouldn't understand something so pure, so blissful, as wonderful as love, or the attraction of bakeapples, either, for that matter.

Boudreaux and his one-true-love *(summer-1941 edition)*, Violet, wandered off farther into the bushes, and when Tim started to follow, Kathy held him by the arm. "I, uh, think they would like to be alone, Timmy." Hannigan blushed, not so much from the revelation, but from someone calling him Timmy. He hadn't heard that since he was little. He and Kathy wandered around the scrub trees and grasslands, and talked about everything and nothing. They talked about the bitter cold of Manitoba, where she had grown up, and he talked about, well, everything he could think of about Philadelphia. In addition to radio, he was fascinated by trolley cars, and told her about his exploits in riding around the city on one fare and a lot of transfers, and how the motormen on the Route 60 streetcars, which passed the orphanage on Allegheny Avenue, knew him by name. The time passed all too quickly, and when the disheveled Boudreaux, with Violet in tow, reappeared, they realized it was time to return the truck to the motor pool. Kathy solicitously brushed stray twigs and grass from Violet's hair as they hopped aboard for the return trip.

"Say, er, Kathy, can I come and see you sometime? You can tell me more about bakeapples and Newfoundland, and I can tell you all about . . ."

"About what, Tim?"

"Er, about, well . . . I know a little bit about radios, I guess."

"Oh, how wonderful," she replied, without a trace of sarcasm. "I stay with the Duffys in Freshwater . . . just beyond the main road where it turns to go down to Jerseyside and Placentia. Mr. Duffy just got a great new radio from the Constabulary. It picks up everything, and Mr. Duffy said they paid nearly sixty dollars for it. Would you like to come by to see it next Sunday after Mass? I'll ask Mrs. Duffy if we could make some ice cream, and we'll save some of the bakeapples for a topping. I'll see you at church next week. Frenchy and Violet can come along too. Promise me you'll come, Timmy?" Speechless for once in his short life, Hannigan just nodded wordlessly. "Good bye, Yank!" she said, as Frenchy dropped off the girls at the gate for the short walk back to Freshwater. She looked at Timmy expectantly, pursing her lips, but, as rarely happened with Hannigan, sadly, this time the radioman missed the message. Frenchy looked at him and shook his head.

Hambone floated around the barracks until it was time to get ready for work. He grabbed a quick shower, changed into his good working uniform and hustled outside so as to not keep Holden and the others waiting. He was first aboard, being prudent enough not to claim the shotgun seat, and thus start the watch on the wrong foot with his leading Petty Officer. The rest of the crew quickly climbed aboard, and they were actually about five minutes early for changeover, which went quickly. "Everything is better when you are in love," thought Hannigan, while he waited for Holden to assign him to his first trick.

"I'm going to swap things around to give everybody a shot at the hot seats," Holden remarked, checking his clipboard. "Morris, you're on 500 kcs; Rebonich, you're on the Fox broadcast; Boudreaux, you take the locals, and keep an eye on Morris and

71

Rebonich; and Hambone, you handle the teletypes for a while. It's usually slow on Sunday and you can get some experience working with the routing slips so that every department on base gets their right messages. I don't want a screw-up like Section 4 had last week . . . the admiral in Norfolk sent a highly personal message to the skipper, critical of his performance, and one of those idiots in 4 routed it as 'All hands.' They were running around the base retrieving messages from inboxes and from under doors, trying to get all the copies back before someone noticed, but some of them got loose. They busted one guy, and I think they are going to bust the RM1. Frenchy, If you ever get your act together and get qualified as a watch supervisor, you've got a chance to take over that crew. I bet you they bust Pirelli, their RM1, for that screw-up."

Hambone smiled, and was going to make some wise-guy comment, but thought better of it. There, but for the grace of God, went he. Holden continued, "Hambone, while the teletypes are all quiet, why not go back and use your magic ears to find us another ball game, eh? It's just a little after 1500 here; that makes it about 1330 or 1:30 PM back on the east coast, if I figure it right. I'll never understand how this gawd-forsaken place has a time zone of its own, and one that is an hour and a half ahead of civilization. Go to it, boy!"

Gladly, Hambone did as ordered. While there were a fair number of east coast stations with shortwave outlets, he was partial to the Philadelphia teams. After energizing the SX-28 receiver he tuned around, and shouted back to Holton, "I've got Detroit and the Athletics again; the White Sox at the Yankees are coming in strong; and the Braves are at St Louis, but there's lots of static on that one. Which game do you want?

Boudreaux intervened, "Well, I ain't no fan of anything having to do with Yankees, seeing as grandpa spent four years shooting at 'em whenever he saw one coming after his regiment, but I like the White Sox. Go ahead and leave that one on." The others, except for those wearing headphones, chimed in and agreed.

Hambone retuned his receiver to the game, relayed on WGY, Schenectady's transmitter on the 31-meter band. "Tiny Bonham is pitching right now for the 'Sox . . . I don't know who is in for New York – ah, wait a minute, he just closed out the top of the third. It's 5 to 3, Sox are ahead, and Thornton Lee is heading out to the mound."

Boudreaux continued, this time addressing Holden. "Hey, Ash . . . you may want to keep the volume down. I looked at the Plan of the Day before I left the barracks and Lt. Carpentier is the Command Duty Officer. He probably will wander in here some-time this afternoon, if he hasn't already. Let Hambone sit back there by the receiver, and have him flip back to a Navy frequency if he shows up here. I'll go out and tell the gate-guard to give us a heads up if he appears, OK?"

Holton nodded, and the crew settled contently into the rou-tine of an evening watch. "Life is always better on the weekends," Holton thought to himself, "No chiefs or officers around to screw things up for otherwise decent honest radiomen." He busied him-self with paperwork as the White Sox continued to stomp on the Yankees. "Stay alert back there, Hannigan, and if you see the boss come in, jump off the game, ASAP. Got that?" Hannigan nodded.

"Life is good," Hambone thought to himself. "First Kathy and now this." The signal was strong and clear, but Hannigan was an inveterate fiddler, and could never leave the dials of a radio alone. Glancing toward the front of the radio shack, he noticed that everyone was busy, and so he began slowly rocking the tuning knobs of the SX-28 receiver to see if he could improve reception even more. He tried each of the five filter positions, from extra narrow to extra wide, changed the AF and RF gains, adjusted the automatic noise control and the antenna trimmer, and generally fiddled with the receiver as if it were still hiding out at the ham station in the attic of the orphanage. He pulled down a pair of earphones and plugged them in. "Those guys up front are listening to this on a standard Navy communication speaker," he thought to himself. "They might as well be listening to it on a tin-can telephone. As long as they can hear the scores, they'll be happy." Contented, he continued to tune the signal, as no one seemed to mind or notice.

While he had the filters set to their widest setting, he heard a CW signal off to the side of WGY. It was not particularly strong, but it had the watery, wavering note that suggested a ground wave transmission from a station not far away. Instinctively, he began to copy the code in his head. *VVV KOELN KOELN K.* (Station KOELN Testing, Reply). After a few minutes the transmission repeated itself, and did so again for a third time. Apparently, the distant station with which he was communicating answered, because the operator began to send, slowly but accurately, a message consisting of random five letter groups. Having neither paper nor pencil handy, Hambone listened for a few minutes until the operator concluded *KOELN SK,* (end of transmission) and left the air. "That's interesting," thought Hannigan, "I wonder who that was?" He removed his headphones, and walked up to the desk facing Holden, and removed manuals ACP-100A and ACP-100B, the large loose-leaf binders containing the radio call signs identifying Navy and Merchant ships. "I'll be right back with these," he explained to Holden, who just shrugged. Returning to his receiver, he began to idly thumb through the thick volumes. Navy call signs all began with the letter "N," he knew, so it obviously wasn't an

American naval ship. He found the listings for all worldwide merchant shipping, and quickly deduced that, while many American merchant ships' call signs began with the letter K, they consisted of four letters and not five.

As he thumbed through the books, the unidentified station began calling once again. *VVV DE KOELN KOELN K.* Hambone's curiosity was peaked; he'd never stumbled across a station whose call letters he could not identify. Not only that, but there was something strange about the operator's keying; he was very precise and sent perfect code, albeit quite slowly, except for the letters O and E in his call sign, which he tended to run together. He did it every time, so it was not likely a slip of his key. Hannigan idly thumbed through the appendices of the commercial call sign book. At the back, under special characters he found what he was looking for. By just the slightest change in spacing – perhaps a quarter of a second, the English letters O and E could be transmitted as the German letter Ö. He listened again as the station transmitted its call up endlessly. "That's not KOELN," Hannigan thought to himself – "that's *KÖLN!* That's a German station!"

Just then, there was a commotion in the front of the radio shack. Lt. Carpentier entered, but waved to the crew to carry on with their work. Hambone immediately shifted the receiver's frequency from the ballgame and set the filters to receive only the unknown station. Holton escorted Carpentier as they toured the various operating positions, and observed each operator perform his duties. They reached the last position, and, spotting the various documents spread around the table, Carpentier asked Hannigan which station he was monitoring. "We've got a German spy, right here on the base! I mean, not on the base, but close to the base!" He handed the Lieutenant his earphones, but, as luck would have it, the mystery station had gone silent. "I know it's German, sir;

he's got umlauts and everything . . ." Carpentier looked at Holden, Holden looked at Hannigan, and Hannigan, in his haste to show his boss what he had just discovered, knocked the loose leaf binders on the floor, sheets from which came lose and floated everywhere. Holden and Carpentier retreated to the front of the radio shack.

"Is he like this often, Holden?"

"He's a great radioman, sir, but he's as flakey as a wet aspirin."

Carpentier nodded. "I'll have a chat with Chief McCroy in the morning. I suppose we really ought to see what this is all about."

28 July 1941
Navy Radio NWP, Argentia
0800 Local time.

Chief McCroy and Lt. Carpentier met in the Lieutenant's office after morning quarters. "So that's what he said, Chief. He thinks there are German spies lurking around Argentia." Chief McCroy – who, at the moment was seriously considering sending Hannigan to join the fishies in the deep blue sea– kept his composure with the Officer-in-Charge. Like all good Chief Petty Officers, he defended his men, even when they were accused of heinous crimes afloat or ashore. And this, in the overall scheme of things, was not a big deal.

"Let me see if I've got this straight. He said he heard German CW signals, and they sounded close to the base. Tell me again why he thought they were German?"

Carpentier replied, "Something about umlauts."

"*Omelets!*" roared Chief McCroy. "*Omelets!* What the hell does that have do with anything?"

"I didn't understand, either, till Hannigan explained it to me. *Umlauts.* Those are the little dots that go over some vowels in German – he said that there are special Morse characters and that the station he heard was using them. Ever hear of anything like that, Chief?"

"Not on this side of the world, Sir. Now the Japs – er the *Japanese* – use special characters, but their alphabet is not like ours. And the Russians have some weird ones, I know; we used to listen to Vladivostok when I was on the China Station back in '32 and '33. I'm not sure about the Germans, but I'll find out quick enough, Sir."

"Good idea, Chief. Personally, I don't see how it might be possible, but we probably don't want to take chances. It's probably the kid's imagination, but still . . ." It went unsaid that covering one's posterior was a good Navy policy whenever anything even vaguely unusual was on the go. "He may be right. He seems to be some sort of idiot-savant, doesn't he?"

"I don't know about that, sir – I don't know what that is. But an idiot, yes; that part I can agree with."

Later that morning, when the things had stabilized, Chief McCroy called Holton and Hannigan into his office. Both started to sputter explanations, but McCroy, ever the Chief Petty Officer, bellowed, "Belay that crap! Hannigan, this is exactly the sort of thing that 'Ski over on the *Plunkett* warned me about. What part of 'squared away' don't you understand, anyway? And if I ever – if I EVER hear anything about you from topside – if you go running to the Lieutenant or any other officer on this base without going through the chain-of-command, and your chain of command is ME, sailor, I guarantee you you'll be on the way to *Bluie*. Do you know where station *Bluie West* is, Hannigan? It's in *Greenland*, dipshit, and if you think Newfoundland is in the boondocks, just wait till I send your dumb ass up there. One more screw-up Hannigan and your ass is grass, and I'm the lawnmower. Now get back to work. Move it!! Holden . . . stand fast!"

After Hannigan beat a hasty retreat, Chief McCroy sat behind his desk, and motioned Holton to sit in the guest chair to the side. "You think there is anything to this, Ash?" the Chief asked in much more reasonable tones than he had just used with Hannigan.

"I dunno, Chief, honest I don't. I didn't say anything to the Lieutenant, but we were listening to the ball game, and I had primed Hannigan to "Ixnay the amegay" whenever he was around. Where this cock-n-bull story about Germans and spies and pig's snouts or umlauts or whatever the hell he's talking about is coming from is beyond me."

"The kid can really pull 'em in on that SX-28, can't he?"

"He's unreal, Chief. He's got ears like a rabbit, and a fist like a code machine. I set up the code-training machine one night when we were on the midwatch, and had a burn-out between Frenchy, the kid and me, and he creamed both of us. He was still going strong at 40 words per minute. Solid. And that's as fast as that old machine can go. He's amazing."

"Well, for gawds-sake, Ash, keep him on a short leash, will ya? And don't let me hear about anyone listening to the ball games on watch, either. Got that, Holden?"

"Yep, Chief, I do. No more ball games on watch."

"Who won, Ash?"

" Chicago 7-3"

"If you, er, get any good scores anywhere, Holden, let me know, would ya? Understand what I'm saying, shipmate?"

"Perfectly, chief."

Holden left the Chief's office. "He'll make a damn good chief one of these days," McCroy thought to himself. "And with war coming on, the way things look now; it won't be long, either. That's the difference between being a good radioman, which

Hannigan might well be, and a good Navy Petty Officer, which Holden certainly was. If only I could melt 'em together, I'd have this job knocked," Chief McCroy thought, as he turned to address the never-ending pile of paperwork on his desk.

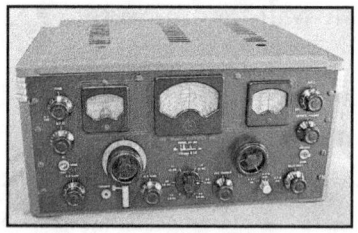

HALLICRAFTERS SX-28 COMMUNICATIONS RECEIVER 1941
(author's collection)

7 LORIENT - II

Kapitänleutnant Josef Moll stood at the top of slipway *Anton,* inside the submarine pen on the Keroman peninsula. The first built at Lorient, the structure was designed to withstand direct bomb hits from the heaviest British aircraft. At places, the reinforced concrete roof, of a honeycombed design, was 3.5 to 7.1 meters thick. Surprisingly, there was little water inside the structure; U-boats were hauled out of the river on a trolley-like platform, and pulled by fixed and mobile engines into the heart of the secure building, which served as both a shelter and a dry dock for several u-boats concurrently.

U-115 was in the last stages of provisioning before departure. Moll looked at the boat – his boat – with a practiced eye. Laid down and completed at the massive shipyards Aktien-Gesellschaft Weser at Bremen, she had completed two missions in the North Atlantic since arriving at Lorient late in the previous year. She was a successful boat – her crew called her the "lucky boat" and, aside from the wear and tear of constant service in the turbulent North Atlantic, she had sustained no serious damage, and no damage at all from enemy action. She was unique among the ten boats selected for the mission; the others were type VII-C boats, the

81

workhorses of the campaign against allied shipping; U-115 was a newer and larger type IX-B U-boat, with greater range and the ability for much longer time-on-station.

Moll, who had spent several weeks at the shipyard and supervised the boat's fitting out, knew her specifications by heart. With an overall length of 76.5 meters, she was double-hulled, and the internal pressure hull extended nearly 59 meters, making U-115 and her classmates a bit less claustrophobic for the crew. Her total external beam of seven meters also added to her bulk. She was just under 10 meters in height, keel to conning tower, and could lie fully submerged in less than fifty feet of water. Surfaced, her 4400 h.p. diesel engines could propel her at speeds over eighteen knots, and, even submerged, U-115 could reach speeds of seven knots, faster than many of the merchant ships sailing in the slower SC convoys from Cape Breton to the United Kingdom. She could cruse for 12,000 miles (two round trips from Europe to North America), and carried twenty-two torpedoes, serving four bow and two stern tubes. Her maximum depth was officially published as 230 meters, but other boats of the class, under active attack, had approached 300 meters and lived to tell about it. She carried a 105 mm deck gun, and normally carried 110 rounds of explosive ammunition. She usually sailed with a crew of 52, but Moll, following Dönitz's strong recommendation, had detached three crewmen to make room for the expected passengers. One crewman had lost his home and several family members to Allied bombing in the Berlin area; one had requested leave to marry and another had proved generally unsuitable for life aboard a wartime submarine. Moll, as he boarded the boat, wondered how suited to cramped, dark, foul-smelling and, at times, terrifying life the passengers might be.

The deck watchman, *Matrosen-Gefreiter* (Able Seaman) Gottfried Ziegler, of Minden in Westphelia saluted and greeted his commander. Moll, by no means a martinet, returned the salute, and stopped for a moment's conversation. "Have they completed the offloading of the extra torpedoes, Gotti?"

"They have, Herr Kapitän. They pulled the last of them around 0500 this morning. We have now only eight onboard. That leaves us only with enough 'fish' for the tubes, and one spare at each end. Bootsman Wulff was stomping and swearing all night long. "First we load them, then we unload them! Who's in charge of this lunacy, anyway?' It's a good thing only U-boat men were listening as old Wulfie ranted on, Herr Kapitän, ja?"

Moll laughed. "Don't be so certain of that, Gotti. *Wie man in den Wald hineinruft, so schallt es heraus, eh?* (What you shout in the forest sometimes echoes back).

The watchman laughed. "I knew an old woodsman from the Pfälzerwald like you, Herr Kapitän, would know that old saying." Moll smiled, and went below.

He spotted "Smutje," the ship's cook, Willi Scherer, a Brandenburger, as he passed through the control room. "Ask the officers to gather in my cabin in five minutes time, would you, Scherer?" The cook nodded, and went off to find the officers. Moll entered the small space, more an alcove than a cabin, and isolated from the busy passageway only by a dark curtain. "It's good there are but a handful of officers or we'd never all fit," he thought to himself. "I wonder how many officers will be amongst our passengers?" Quickly, the small space filled as the officers, all of whom had been recalled to the ship and had remained onboard for the past twenty-four hours, entered. Moll looked about the room. Nearest the curtain that divided the room from the passageway stood his First Officer, Oberleutnant zur See Jürgen Fleischer 26, a native of Rauenberg. It was only a matter of time until Fleischer left the U-115 for a command of his own. He was audacious, and, with a little bit more seasoning, would make a good commander, Moll reflected. To his left stood the Engineer, Oberleutnant zur See Ulf Strebel, from a small farming village in Schleswig-Holstein. At 37, he was the oldest of the ship's officers, and was the subject of much friendly banter about his accent, which seemed to be more Danish than German.

"Well, back home, they say that my Danish sounds more like German, too, so I suppose it all works out equally – but my engineers don't care. They can't hear me back there, anyway." The young Second Officer Leutnant zur See Theodor Mueller 23, a Bavarian, squeezed in the farthest corner. Called "Tiny" because of his bulk, the most recent patrol was his first, and he had acquitted himself well. His less than successful attempts to grow a bushy red beard, though, had been the source of much levity among his shipmates throughout the voyage.

"Let's have a quick update on where we are. I understand that the spare torpedoes have been offloaded, right, Number One? What does that do to our total weight?"

"It takes it down considerably. All told, we save about twelve tons. That will be made up, at least in part, by the extra provisions, which should be arriving around 1000 this morning. Our maximum time on station, from a provision perspective only, will increase by about ten days. The supply officers of the 2nd Flotilla have told me that we're getting the best they have to offer, so our 'guests' should be happy, anyway. Do you know any more about them, Kapitän?"

"Only what I learned at the meeting with Admiral Dönitz last week. We'll have three or four – I don't think we'll know exactly until they show up on the gangway – Army types, and most likely Waffen SS. Has their material arrived yet?"

Fleicher replied, "Yes, we received three large crates for them. It's all very mysterious. The crates were painted flat black, and, aside from a small number stenciled on one side, there were no other markings. He consulted his clipboard. The total weight of all three together was 196 kilos. That hardly makes a difference in our weight and balance . . . hell, if Muller over there doesn't lose some of his baby fat soon, *he'll* start to influence our weight and balance. Do you have any idea, sir, what might be in those sealed crates?"

"None whatsoever, Number One. I'm in the dark about this as much as anyone. I do know that we're expected to go down the ways sometime in the late afternoon, so I suspect that they'll be on board by then. Otherwise, they'll have to come aboard on a dingy, and that's not the way to greet guests, is it? But tell me this – any of you – what's the crew saying about all of this? Any good rumors?"

"Oh plenty," volunteered Strebel. "One of my fellows claimed to have heard from someone in operations that we are going into the South Atlantic, around Cape Horn, and pick up the staff of the Embassy in Chile. Another one says that, no, we are going all the way to Japan to transport the Emperor back here for a conference with the Führer. 'Smutje' thinks we are going to go into the deep Artic, where there are some mysterious secret passages he read about in those adventure magazines he is always smuggling aboard, and wait there for heaven-knows-what. Unloading the torpedoes really did throw everyone into a tizzy, I'm afraid."

The skipper chuckled. "Well, if past experience is any guide, I can let them know more right after we sail – and we'll be going out as soon as possible after true dark. Since the moon is new on Thursday, there won't be much light and we should be out of here around 2300 at the latest. We'll fight the tide for a couple hours until we can get out in the Bay a little, and then down we go. We'll be submerged for a great deal of this trip, I think. We've got strict orders – and I mean strict! – that we're to avoid contact with anyone until we reach our operations area, and, even then, we'll be down more than we'll be up. Ulf, my friend, when we do get up to recharge batteries and to air out the boat, we need to be as fast as humanly possible. I'm toying with the idea of having one or two extra lookouts when we do surface. I'd use the radio operators, but they'll be busy receiving messages when we're surfaced, even though they will not be transmitting. By the way, Number One, be certain to disable the transmitters, and anything else that can radiate sound or wireless signals. I'm afraid the gramophone won't get quite as much use this trip as it has in the past, unfortunately."

"Can you tell us any more about this mission, Kapitän?" Muller asked.

"I would if I could, but until that sealed envelope shows up, and we get far enough offshore to open it, you pretty much know what I know. I suspect, though, that our passengers may know a bit about their role in all of this, and if they get here early enough, we may be able to anticipate what's in the sealed orders. But, till then, just assume that the cook is right. A nice quiet six weeks frolicking around the North Pole is just what we need to get away from the heat and humidity here on the Breton coast. Now off to work with all of you. We're going to have a busy day and a busier night, from the looks of it."

By 1300, a lorry had delivered an additional two hundred kilos of provisions. That, coupled with the longer range and "dwelling" ability of the type IX boats, would allow the U-115 to remain on station three weeks or longer, if necessary. By 1600, all hands were aboard, and all materials were securely stowed. Additional rumors continued to circulate; young *Matrose* (Ordinary Seaman) Noltan, who was only eighteen years of age, approached the first officer and asked, tentatively but hopefully, if it was true that the U-115 was sailing to French Polynesia, and if it was true about everything the other fellows were saying about the women there. First Officer Fleischer smiled, and said, honestly, "I don't know anymore than you do, but I'll take that suggestion to the skipper." They both laughed.

By 1700, the dock master had visited three times, and was becoming increasingly anxious that U-115 vacate the slipway to make way for an incoming boat, which had received significant damage while on patrol. Fortunately, the weather had turned overcast, lessening the dangers of being at the piers rather than safely under cover. Moll negotiated a compromise; if the visitors did not appear by 1800 sharp, the dock crew could begin the process of getting the boat back into the water. Moll was increasingly worried about their departure time and maximizing the limited darkness of an August night to insure a safe passage away into the deeper waters of the Bay of Biscay. When 1800 came, the yard workers began to roll the U-boat down the ramp, and by 1930 she was safely tied to the pier. The passengers had yet to appear.

Moll called his officers for a short meeting at 2000. "The absolute latest that I am willing to get underway is 2145. If they're not here, we sail without them. All that I know of them is that they are soldiers, and perhaps damaged roads or some other reasonable cause has delayed them. But we cannot wait here all evening for them. At 2145, we go."

As he was speaking, there was commotion topside. *Matrosen-Obergefreiter* (Leading Seaman) Kuefer, the duty watchstander, came sliding down the ladder into the control room. "Herr Kapitän, we have visitors who have just come across the gangway. I think you may wish to meet with them topside before bringing them into the boat, sir. They seem to be, well, somewhat incapacitated."

Moll did as suggested. When on the main deck, he was astounded to see three men struggling with the very slight incline of the gangway leading from pier side. One immediately snapped to attention, and gave the Party salute. "Heil Hitler!" Moll shrugged, and returned it with a rather casual naval salute. A second staggered to the lifelines, and loudly and with great effort, added to the biological contents of the water on the windward side of the deck. His heavy load of alcohol smelled worse coming up than it did going down.

The third visitor, attempted to hold his footing on the very gently bobbing surface of the main deck, but fell backwards, his head just missing the deck gun housing. Their officer announced, "I am SS-*Obersturmführer* (Lieutenant) Fritz Braun, and these men and I will assist you in the mission of which you have been informed." By now, his two associates had returned to their feet, and were standing at something approaching attention. "This is SS-*Unterscharführer* (Sergeant) Hirsch, and with him is SS-*Rodefører* (Corporal) Lars-Anders Fiskdal, of the Norwegian Nasjonal Samling, serving in the Germanske SS-Norge. I must apologize, Herr Kapitän, for our delay, but operational pressures of a most sensitive nature prevented us from coming sooner."

Right, thought Moll, something out in the beer halls and brothels of Lorient, no doubt. "Kuefer, show SS-Obersturmführer Fritz Braun to the former third officer's bunk, and take his two associates as far forward as you can until you find a space for them to berth. And, he added *soto voce* "place a bucket near each of their heads. I rather suspect that when we hit the open water they are going to need them."

"Bootsman," he called out loudly. "Set the special sea detail. Single up all lines, and prepare for departure. I want to get as far away from here as I possibly can before the sun comes up again. As soon as we're safely underwater out in the bay, I'll open the sealed orders which Unterscharführer Hirsch has brought along for our reading pleasure, and I'll let everyone know just exactly what we'll be up to over the next few weeks."

U-BOAT REPAIR AND PROTECTION PENS
KEROMAN I, LORIENT FRANCE
(Bibleo France)

8 NAVAL OPERATING BASE
ARGENTIA - III

22 July 1941
Naval Radio Station NWP
Naval Operating Base
Argentia, Newfoundland
0900 NST

Chief McCroy, like all Navy Chief Petty Officers, regardless of their rating, was incapable of error. If faced with a deteriorating situation of his own making, he simply changed course based on information newly received. "Officers may run the Navy, but Chiefs run the ship," was an adage repeated by wise sailors from the time of Noah onward. And God help the sailor who did not understand this simple concept.

McCroy, who had fought in one world war, two revolutions and innumerable bar fights from Stockholm to Subic Bay, knew that a strong offense was his best defense. After morning quarters on Monday, he announced a complete shakeup of the watch-quarter-and-station bill, the document which outlined the duties of everyone within the division. After the debacle with the misrouted message, section four was completely torn apart and Pirelli, the Section Chief, was "loaned" to base sanitation, never to be seen again. The traffic checker, who should have caught the message before it ever left the room, was given the opportunity to work with the cooks and bakers as a messman for ninety days. Handpicked sailors from the other sections were rotated to cover the vacancies in section four. RM1 Holton, as the best supervisor in the division, was brought over from section three as leading petty officer, and, most significantly, RM2 Boudreaux was "frocked" as a watch supervisor, replacing him in section three. Several green radioman "strikers" appeared on a transport from Norfolk, and, as a final tune-up, the watch rotation was changed from 3-3-3 and 72 hours off duty, to 2-2-2 and eighty hours off, compressing the workweek, but allowing slightly longer liberty at the end of a cycle. In the wilderness which was still Argentia in mid-July, this was greeted with shrugs. "If there ain't much to do on 72 hours off," grouched Boudreaux, "there sure as hell ain't anything to do for the extra eight hours. Except, of course," he thought to himself, "there's always Violet!"

Hannigan, though, was delighted in the change. Extra time off, even if it meant a tighter work schedule, made it easier to visit with Kathy. He hadn't been able to get outside the gate to Freshwater yet, though, mostly because he had no transportation. And that's where Boudreaux, the only shipmate that ever treated him politely, if not particularly kindly, was about to make a contribution.

"Hey Frenchy," Hannigan asked one afternoon, standing in the chow line,

"Don't you have a Cajun buddy down in the motor pool?"

"Sure 'nuff, Hambone, a guy named Guidry. He's the leading petty officer for the small vehicle pool – he don't mess around with the Caterpillars or the big rock haulers much. Why you askin?"

"Do you think he'll check out a truck to me if I ask him?"

"Well, he would, if you show him your government driver's license and a chit from someone. I could sign it, I guess. What do you want with a truck, anyway?"

"Well . . . er, well . . . you know . . ."

"Ah yeah, Hambone. Jeez, man, you don't waste no time, do you? You just met that babe on Sunday. You got a Navy driver's license? If you don't, all you gotta do is show 'em your state license and they'll issue one for your right there. No test or nuttin', and I'll put in a word for you. You got a license from Pennsylvania, or Jersey or wherever the hell in Yankee land you come from?"

"Er, no, Frenchy. I always rode the streetcar, and I never learned to drive."

"Let me get this straight, Hambone. You're what? Twenty-one or twenty-two? You want to cumshaw a truck from the 'pool' to go see your new squeeze out in Freshwater, but you don't even know how to drive? Boy . . . you are seriously screwed up, do you know that?"

"Would you teach me, Frenchy?"

"Teach you? Boy, if you don't know what to do when you get with a girl, there ain't nobody can teach you . . . I learned that with the neighbor girl, laying down in my daddy's pirogue when I was, like, twelve-years old."

Hambone looked at him wide-eyed. "What do Pierogis got to do with being with a girl? Those are Polish donuts, aren't they?" he asked, confused.

"No, boy, my daddy's *pirogue* – that's a flat bottom boat we use on the bayou. If you get to rockin' that thing just right . . .oh, wait, you ain't talking about *that* – you mean, teach you to drive a truck? Well, that's different . . . I guess so, man. The weather has finally gotten nice; it only rained three times yesterday. We can tell Guidry that we need you to drive the bread-wagon, now that the chief mixed up the WQS bill again. Not that I oughta complain, I guess. I'm a shoe-in for RM1 now that he gave me section three, provided you and those other bootcamp rejects don't get me fired, too. Meet me after watch this afternoon, and we'll see what he says, OK? And don't get my tits in a wringer over this, boy. I'm the only friend you got, and the chaplain ain't showed up yet!"

The newly reconstructed section three had the day watch, so there was no opportunity for Hambone and the others to boot-leg any of the ball games from stateside radio stations. For the last trick of the watch, Hambone worked the port-control voice circuits, which were particularly busy, with American, Canadian and British warships forming up into patrol groups to defend convoys passing from the Canadian coast to Britain. He heard the "Canadian Kerchunker," several times during his two-hour stretch on the voice circuits, and after a while, began to look for a pattern as to when the signals might appear. "Hey, Frenchy," he called out during a quiet moment, "Didn't you say that the Kerchunker is just a Canadian destroyer or corvette letting their line handlers know to get ready for them to turn the corner and come around the breakwater into the piers? So how come I hear kerchunkers, and never hear the ship report its arrival, huh?"

"Dammed if I know, boy. Just consider it a marvel of modern electronics, Hambone. Next time you are down by the piers, ask one of their wireless operators what it means. I'd ask 'em, but whatever those guys from Quebec are speaking, it don't sound like good Cajun French to me. I can hardly understand 'em. And, speaking of Quebec, anybody see the Lieutenant lately?"

"Doyle says he was in earlier, but didn't come into the operations room. He stayed holed up with the Chief, probably talking about which dog sled to take when the skipper sends both of 'em to the North Pole. Then he went over to the transmitter site to watch them install some new equipment."

"Well, speaking of Doyle, when he drops everyone off at the barracks, stay aboard, and you and I will go over to the motor pool and see what we can arrange, OK? You got a spare buck you can contribute to this little operation, Hambone? Newfoundland money is better for what we need to do, and all I've got are greenbacks."

Hambone reached into his sock and pulled out a small wad of cash, and peeled off a single blue one-dollar bill. "Jeez, Boudreaux, their money sure is colorful, isn't it?"

"Yeah, right, but if you keep carrying it around in your socks, Dufus, it's gonna go black with the mold." But Frenchy took the tattered note gingerly and stuffed it into his pocket.

When the watch was relieved, they piled into the "bread truck" and after dropping the rest of the crew, persuaded Doyle to drop them off at the motor pool. On the way, Boudreaux spotted a tall heavy-set civilian operating a road grader. Over the noise of the exhaust, Frenchy called out: *"Allons Jacques! Pouvez-vous me vendre une bouteille de bonnes choses?* (Got any of the good stuff?) The operator nodded, and reached into a gunnysack under his seat. Doyle stopped the truck, and Frenchy ran over, exchanging the tattered dollar bill for a mason jar of dark liquid. He climbed back into the truck.

"What the hell was that all about, Frenchy?" Doyle asked.

"Ah, he's a guy from over on Cape Breton. They are cousins to us Cajuns. That's where our people came from, back in the olden times. He makes Screech on the side; ever taste any? It's made out of rotgut rum that gets smuggled in from down in the Caribbean somewhere. Then the local good old boys run it through a still again. It's about 90-proof, and it's sort of like Newfoundland's very own bootleg. I never heard of it either, till Violet gave me some a while back. Take about two slugs of this stuff, and you'll know why they call it Screech right enough. It'll knock your socks off. Speaking of which, Hambone, change those stinky socks of yours before you come back on watch, will you? You've got about a thousand miles on 'em already."

In a few moments, clutching the precious jar of Screech, the two sailors disembarked at the motor pool and went to find Guidry, who was out on the line, inspecting his 'fleet.' Boudreaux greeted him in animated Cajun-French, with the occasional nod in the direction of Hannigan, who stood there, mouth agape. With a back slap and a laugh, the Mason jar was exchanged for the keys to a severely dilapidated pickup truck. Motioning to Hambone, Boudreaux hopped into the driver's seat, and after a couple tries, got the truck started. After a moment, it was running smoothly, although when they got it on to the gravel roadway, it was clear that it had seen better days.

"What you just saw there, boy, is what civilized people call a *lagniappe*. It's a little sumthin' to make business run smoother, not that you Yankees would ever know nothin' about that. Guidry says that some idiot ran this off the end of the runway and it fell down the berm and busted a spring, but other than that, it's OK. Just runs a little wobbly, so we gotta keep it slow. He says nobody is liable to come looking for it for a while; he replaced it with a new one that just came off the freighter." Boudreaux turned slightly and looked into the bed of the truck. "Nice roll of co-axial cable we've inherited back there. Looks like RG8/U. Might come in useful some day."

There were relatively few paved roads on the base as of yet, but Frenchy found a stretch of fresh laid gravel, and pulled the truck over to the side. "OK Hambone. Your turn. Slide on over." Boudreaux hopped out of the truck, went around the back and climbed into the passenger seat. "Now the first thing to remember is where the clutch is, and where the gears are. The clutch is under your left foot. The gears are on the gearshift. This ain't brain surgery, Hambone. If Doyle can do it, anybody can. See that little diagram on the knob of the gearshift? They make the Ford people paint that on there. It makes it sailor-proof. Even you can remember 1-2-3-R, can't you, boy? Now, push the clutch all the way in, set the gear to 1, that's the lowest gear, and slowly . . . slowly, DAMMIT! . . . let the clutch out. Now slowly, hit the gas, and drive. There you go, boy! Keep your eye on the road, and stop wiggling all over the place, Hambone. Jeez, you drive like my uncle Teeboon, coming up the bayou in his shrimping boat with half-a-load on. That's it, boy! The good thing about these gravel and dirt roads up here is if you get your tires in the tracks, the truck will pretty much steer itself. Now that you've got some speed, shift it into second. There was a crash of gears. "NO, idiot! First the Clutch! THEN the gears. Man, you ARE drifty, ain't you?"

The driving lesson continued for several hours, and was repeated over the next few days. Hambone soon got the hang of listening to the engine, and knowing when to shift from one gear to another. Aside from a slight encounter with a stunted pine tree ("Tell Guidry it jumped out in front of us," Boudreaux suggested) after the third or fourth lesson, Hambone was ready to try driving in "civilization," or at least what passed for it on the half-completed Navy base.

Driving back to the motor pool, elbow resting on the driver's side window frame, a cigarette dangling from his lip, Hambone, who was beginning to look, if not act, like a real sailor, approached Frenchy with an idea. "Why don't we head down to the piers, and see if we can find any Canadian radiomen, and ask 'em about the 'Canuck Kerchunk' huh?"

"Well, first off, Hambone, I wouldn't call 'em Canucks, unless you want to loan some guy a fistful of your teeth. When I was growing up, before I left school in the sixth grade, I never knew there was a country north of Yankee land. I though y'all were as bad as it gets. But those Canadian fellas are all right, I guess. Why don't we do this. See that roll of wire that's still in the back of the truck? I've got a bunch of papers on my clipboard; why don't you and I go have a little 'working party' down on the docks, eh? You carry the wire, I'll carry the clipboard. It'll look better that way, since I outrank you, anyway. If we see any Canadians, we can ask 'em where their communications guys are, and make like we're delivering the wire, only we'll find out it's for the wrong ship, and take the wire back with us. No harm, no foul. But we can strike up a conversation with 'em anyway, and see what they say, OK? I don't know what a Canadian radioman's rating badge looks like, except it probably has a lightning bolt on it somewhere. Any radioman I've ever seen in anybody's Navy has something like that on his badge. That's why they call us 'sparks,' I reckon."

They found a place to park the truck, just north of the base piers. They joined in the general hustle and bustle, Hambone with the spool of coaxial cable, and Frenchy with his clipboard, till they came to the first ship flying the Canadian white ensign. "Hey, mate," Frenchy called out, "which ship is this?"

"K-177" came the reply.

"Hmmm," Frenchy whispered to Hannigan "I'm not sure these Canadians even name their ships – I see the 179, the 173 and the 175 all lined up there in a nest. Let's go over and see what we can find out, eh?" He heard bits of French – with a distinct Quebecois accent. Hambone, wandering around with his mouth ajar, found himself in the bight of a hawser being pulled back aboard a departing destroyer.

"Tabernac! Sortez de la route. Rousse fou! sortir de mes cordes! Vous âne stupide! Les marins américains stupides! Idiot!! (Quebecois sailor talk for, well, English sailor talk.)

Frenchy grabbed Hannigan just before he was about to be caught up by the hawser and pulled overboard. "For God's sake, Hambone, did you just sneak into the Navy on the last midwatch? Watch yourself, boy!" Hannigan shrugged.

"What was that guy saying to us, anyway, Frenchy?"

"You wouldn't want to know, Hannigan, but it ain't nice . . . "

"Can I help you guys?" A sailor, wearing the wristband of the regulating branch walked over to where they were standing.

Frenchy, thinking fast said, "Er, we've got some cable for the K-175. Do you know who their radioman is?"

"Radioman? Oh, you're Yanks; you must mean our wireless telegraphist. That'd be McKenzie . . . ah, there he is, right there by the fantail. Go on board and give him his cable. We need every-thing we can get; we're going out in about four hours on the next high tide. No telling when we'll be back."

They crossed the brow and went aft. "Are you McKenzie? That Shore Patrol on the dock said you're the leading telegraphist. We're from NWP, the Naval Radio Station here. We've got a roll of cable for you guys on the (looking at his clipboard), the K-179. That you?"

"Naw, mate, we're the K-175, *HMCS Wetaskiwin*.

"Wet Ass Queen?" asked Hannigan, unfamiliar with the names of Canadian warships, and unsure of the "foreign accent." The Canadian, whose "foreign accent" was the result of growing up in Windsor, Ontario, just across the river from Detroit, laughed. "Hey, that's a good one, I gotta remember that. No, this is the *HMCS Wetaskiwin*; it's named after a town in Alberta. You want our sister ship over there, *HMCS Buctouche*, the K-179, pointing in the direction from which they just came.

Hambone though he heard "Butt-Touch" but before he could respond, Frenchy replied, "Thanks, buddy. Say, didn't we work you guys on 2716 kcs when you were coming into port the other day?"

"Yep, probably. We usually break radio silence once we get up abeam the breakwater."

"Don't you key your transmitter when you're down the bay to let your line handlers know you're coming?" asked Hannigan.

"Why would we do that? We let them know when we clear the submarine nets. Besides, our wireless school at St. Hyacinthe always teaches never to key the transmitter repeatedly. It runs the risk of blowing out the rectifiers. And there sure as hell ain't no place to get spares when you're out in the North Atlantic. Naw, the first time you'll hear from us is on 2716 when we're within view and almost at the docks."

Frenchy thanked the guy, and tossed him a pack of Lucky Strikes.

"Thanks, mate," the Canadian replied. 'We've been away from Halifax for weeks, and we're running short of smokes. If we get into Iceland we might be able to pick up some. English, if we're lucky. Otherwise, we're stuck with the Icelandic cigarettes, which I think they make out of whale meat or something. See you around."

"Be safe, shipmate," Frenchy replied as he turned and saluted the Canadian white ensign flying on the fantail.

As he turned to leave, Hannigan questioned him, "Why did you salute their flag? I thought we were only supposed to salute the Stars and Stripes when we're on duty."

Boudreaux looked at him, sadly. "Don't you know there's a war on, Hambone? A real, honest-to-God shooting war. And these guys are fighting it, while you and I go screwing around the base chasing your goofy ghost signals. If it wasn't for those guys, and their British cousins chasing around out there in Force Ten gales in these little converted sardine cans, Hambone, one of these days the Andrews Sisters are gonna be singing in German on the Hit Parade. I'll salute them, or their flag, or their ugly mother-in-law any day, kid."

FRENCHY INSPECTING THE PICKUP
(Official USN photo)

**NAVAL OPERATING BASE, ARGENTIA, 1941
(BARRACKS LOWER RIGHT — RADIO NWF
OUT OF FRAME UPPER LEFT)**
(Official USN photo)

9 WASHINGTON - II

President Roosevelt looked up from the stamp collection spread over his desk in the Oval Office. It was another very warm day, but the president kept the door to the Rose Garden closed. He didn't want any stray breeze, if such a thing existed in midsummer in the nation's capital, to disturb his prized collection. It was the only hobby which had held his interest from boyhood through his near-fatal bout of polio and the difficult rehabilitation which followed, and the strain of nine years as president. A buzzer sounded, and the president reached under the lip of his desk and pressed a small black button. The door to the office opened, and Chief Usher Harold Crim entered.

"Miss Lehand is away today, Mr. President. I suppose everyone should take some time away from this heat and humidity, if they can, Sir. I believe she's gone to Ocean City for the weekend, Mr. President. Anyway, your guests are here. Shall I show them in?"

"Indeed, Mr. Crim, indeed. Just give me a moment to straighten up, please. I'll buzz you again when I'm ready."

The usher left and the president stacked the stamp albums neatly in one corner of his desk. He took a special sheet, and placed it in a folder in the center of this desk. He buzzed again, and his visitors trooped in: Steve Early, his press secretary; Mike Reilly, the head of his secret service detail; senior military aides General Edwin M.(Pa) Watson and Navy Captain John R. Beardall. They remained standing until the president, with a wave of his ever-present cigarette holder, directed them to sit on the comfortable couches surrounding a coffee table off to his right. Taking the folder, he turned and wheeled himself over to join them in conversation.

"Well, boys, it looks like we're definitely going to go through with it. Crazy as it may sound at first blush, I've just received a cable that Winston will be on the move by tomorrow morning, and Admiral King tells me that our planning is pretty much complete. But how do things look from your individual perspectives?"

General Watson spoke first. "The logistics look good, Mr. President. We have a special train laid on for late tomorrow morning, and the governor of Connecticut, as well as the Commandant of the Coast Guard Academy have been placed on standby. We didn't inform them of anything other than your plan to arrive at New London around 1900 hours tomorrow. All that they know is that you'll use New London as a transfer point to the yacht, which is it quite logical, sir. And – owning to world conditions, I've notified the Zone of the Interior to have armed sentries at all bridges, tunnels and major crossings along the way. The Pennsylvania railroad will undertake to inform ZI command of the progress of the train along the route we've laid out."

"Good work, Pa," the president replied, using General Watson's nickname. "I hate having all those fellows standing out in the heat, but if you work it so than no man is out there for more than sixty minutes or so, I suppose it's the best we can do. Captain Beardall – how are things from your end?"

"Complicated, Mr. President, but we've simplified things as best we can. As General Watson noted, you'll do a quick meet-and-greet when you detrain, and then we'll get you on board *Potomac* as quickly as possible. On Monday, you'll have guests aboard *Potomac* with you, and we'll meet with the other ships involved late Monday evening. Tuesday morning, if we stay on schedule, we'll head north with an ETA at our destination about noon on Thursday. We have several contingency plans for the return trip, but I won't go into details now, as we're not certain what the circumstances will be early in the following week."

The president nodded. "Steve, how are we looking with the press corps? Do you see any indication that our ink-stained friends are getting suspicious?"

"Not that I've heard, Mr. President. It all seems logical to them; they live in Washington, too. Anyone who can get away for a week or ten days, sail around the New England coast, get in some big-game fishing, and generally get away from the stress of this office for a while is a pretty lucky fellow, in their estimation. The biggest problem I've had so far is convincing them that we don't have a lot of room on the train, and nothing on the yacht, so as far as they are concerned, New London is the end of the line for them. Some of them are going to hang around Swampscott, Mass. for a while – that's the transfer point for the return trip to Washington – on the odd chance that something happens to cause you to return earlier than scheduled. I'm going to bird dog them when they're there, and if things begin to leak, I'll step in with the pre-planned materials we have already developed to explain the trip."

"Good, good," replied the president. "Who is coming along for the rail portion of the trip? Do you know yet?"

"I told the press corps that this was all routine. I also gave them a deadline of 8AM this morning to let me know. Right now, we've the *Los Angeles Times*, the *New Haven Journal Courier*, the *Philadelphia Evening Bulletin* and the *Philadelphia Ledger*, the *Washington Post*, the *New York Times* and the *New York Post*. Neither the Philly guys nor the New York fellows let each other out of their sight, even if this were just a trip out to the Rose Garden. And they know that there's no room for them on any of the other escort ships, per Admiral Ernie King. Not that any of them would be pleased with being cooped up with the Admiral for a week or two."

"Now, now." The President admonished. "Let's be kind to Admiral King. We're going to be in his good hands for a while, and we don't want him agitated more than he normally is."

"Did you see what Walter Winchell said about him a while ago? He interviewed King's daughters – he has six, you know – and told them that everyone says that he has a bad temper. One kid replied: 'He is the most even-tempered man in the Navy. He is always in a rage!'"

"Hmmm . . . six daughters, six weddings to pay for . . . I can see why he's a bit grouchy at times . . . but nonetheless, I suspect that he's still disappointed that I passed over him to give Betty Stark a chance as CNO. Captain Beardall, how are we doing getting my two boys to Argentia for a quick visit with their old man?"

"No problem, Mr. President. Franklin Junior's ship, USS *Mayrant,* will be docked in Argentia later this evening, and Elliott has received orders to fly down from Gander Bay airbase early in the week. Both should be there in time to act as your aides de camp for the visit."

The president nodded. "No one let them in on our little secret, did they?"

"No sir. We are most definitely playing this one close to the vest, Mr. President."

"Fine. Reilly, how are things going with your dumb Irishmen in the Secret Service?"

"You've got to be dumb to want a job like this, Mr. President." Everyone laughed, since they know that any of Mike Reilly's men would give his own life in a heartbeat for this or any other president. "Things seem to be shaping up. I have packed up a shipment of special material, which will be useful to you." To avoid a moment of awkwardness, he didn't identify the President's special leg braces, wheelchairs, and other mobility equipment specifically. "It is en route right now to that new Navy base on the Newfoundland coast. A destroyer will pick up several crates at the Brooklyn Navy Yard, and the tin-can should arrive at Argentia a day or two before we show up. And as for the diversion we discussed Mr. President – and if this works, I'll buy you a new hat! – Captain Beardall tells me that the skipper, LCDR George Leahy, has identified at least two crewmen on *Potomac* who approximate your general body type, height and weight. We'll use one of them as a stand-in or decoy when we're far enough off shore that no one will get a clear facial photograph, if it comes to that. The Coast Guard, as usual, will have patrol and picket boats deployed around the *Potomac*, so that no one will be able to get too close for comfort. And we'll have the decoys wear the same hat and jacket that you'll be seen wearing on Monday, before we slip away. I actually feel better about the diversion than I do about the gallivanting around New England the day before, truth to tell. Admiral King can defend you against battlewagons with 16-inch guns; I worry about the Wilkes-Booths, Czolgoszs or Guiteaus carrying a pocket pistol more than anything. But we are as well planned as we can make it on this, Sir. I've asked the Boston field office to give me some additional agents for the 'public' part of this show. I'm confident we've done all we can to make this run smoothly."

All were silent for a moment, awaiting the president's confirmation of their plans. Roosevelt, however, slid out the sheet of postage stamps, all of which had been issued by the Dominion of Newfoundland, and passed it around the small group. "I want to share these with you fellows. Winston gave these to Hopkins a few days ago, and Harry sent it over in the diplomatic bag. I trust that Churchill's kindness doesn't come back to haunt us, although there has never been any indication of tampering with our diplomatic pouches, at least of which I am aware. But, in any event this series of postage stamps was issued in 1919, just after the last war. General, I'll put you on the spot. Do you see the inscriptions under the picture of the caribou? The print is very small, and each denomination is different. Can you read those to us?" He handed the General his magnifying glass, and the others all chuckled.

"Hmm . . . Suvla Bay . . . Gudecourt . . . Monchy . . . Steenbeck . . . Beaumont Hamel. Those were all battlefields in the last war, weren't they, Mr. President? Beaumont Hamel is on the Somme — sixty thousand men lost their lives on that one day, July 1, 1916, and many more were wounded. What's the connection, if I might ask, Sir?"

"Apparently, Newfoundland raised a regiment as soon as war was declared. It's not a very big place, Newfoundland. The island itself is large but the population is very small. Churchill's note accompanying this gift tells me that the Newfoundland Regiment, called the Blue Puttees from the color of the leggings they wore, were attached to the British 29th Division and were all but annihilated in the first attack across no-man's land. 'The pride of the island's manhood,' is the way he described it. The loss set the island back for a generation or more. You know, fellows, I thought back then that we'd finally learned our lesson about war and death and famine and destruction, those four horsemen of the Apocalypse. The 'war to end all wars,' as my predecessor President Wilson called it. And here we go again, it seems. Perhaps we'll never learn, will we?" The men sat in silence for a long moment.

Sighing, the president signaled that the meeting was completed. As they rose, he addressed General Watson again. "Pa . . . make sure that Frank Jr. and Elliot are there when we arrive, would you? I haven't seen them in ages, and heaven knows when we'll be able to get together again, Do that for me, would you?" As the others left, he wheeled himself back to his desk, and opened yet another stamp album.

Sunday, 03 August 1941

In one of those turns of fate which are sometimes inexplicable, Sunday morning dawned much cooler and with much lower humidity that the previous weeks in Washington. The president commented to Ivan (Mac) McDuffie, his valet that it was a bit like planning a trip to Warm Springs, his Georgia retreat where the volatility of the weather had been a standing joke among the staff. To be safe, McDuffie suggested some last minute changes in the wardrobe for the trip, suggesting a few warmer sweaters to prevent the president becoming chilled while on the water. FDR, knowing that he would soon be on the coast of Newfoundland, yet unable to bring Mac into his confidence, appreciated the added insurance the warmer clothing provided.

A large limousine pulled into the South Portico promptly at 10:30 AM. The President, with his personal physician Admiral Ross T. McIntyre; Pa Watson and Captain Beardall entered for the short drive to Union Station. To avoid undue attention, the car entered a non-descript portal leading to the lower concourse, and stopped directly before the special Pullman car which the president had used during his election campaigns. Pullman porters, who had traveled extensively with the president on previous trips, quickly assisted Secret Service agents in assisting the president to board the car and made him as comfortable as possible, given his disability, on a specially installed chair which helped isolate him from the shocks and bumps of the roadbed. The train departed precisely at 11:00 AM, meeting the schedule, which had been finalized after Saturday morning's short meeting.

The President heaved a sigh of relief. Although years of therapy had made his upper body stronger than most men and certainly stronger then most men of his age, exertion, such as transferring from the automobile to the Pullman car, was tiring. "I'm glad we're getting out of town, even if the weather seems to have broken," he remarked to Steve Early. " Let me rest here for a few minutes, and then you can go up a couple cars, and let the press contingent know that I'll be happy to speak with them before long. Let's tell them that we'll do it right after lunch, and that we ought to be around Philadelphia by then. That should make the Bulletin and Leger fellows happy – they can toss their stories out the window as we pass through 30th Street Station."

"Especially the Bulletin fellow," Early replied. "Their offices are right next door to the station. The Public Ledger guys are going to think we're playing favorites."

"And if I did, that's exactly the way I'd play them," the President laughed, considering the Ledger's opposition to everything his administration stood for. Early went forward to make the notifications.

After a light lunch, the press gathered in the president's car. Both Early and the President kept to the cover story; the president was taking ten days away from the White House, but not away from his duties. He'd be in constant contact with Vice President Henry Wallace, who remained at his residence aboard the Naval Observatory on Massachusetts Avenue NW. When asked why no press would accompany him at sea, the president laughed. "I'm trying to get away from all the stress and strain, and, off the record boys, YOU are part of the strain. Besides, I can't fit everyone on *Potomac*, and Admiral King won't loan me any more of his destroyers since I sent fifty of them to the British and Canadians." After drinks from the well stocked bar, and polite meaningless small talk from the president, the press retreated forward, and the President settled in for a quick snooze as the train made its way along the Delaware River and into New Jersey.

By the time he had awakened, the train had passed through Penn Station in New York City, and had crossed into Connecticut. On schedule, the train arrived at New London promptly at 8:15 PM, and after shunting back and forth for a few moments, backed to within 300 feet of the brow leading to *USS Potomac (AG-23)*. Built as a revenue cutter in Wisconsin, the 165-foot vessel had been modified specifically to meet President Roosevelt's needs in 1936. After greeting the dignitaries and military officers who had awaited his arrival, the president boarded the yacht, and greeted its skipper, LCDR Leahy, whom the president held in high regard. *Potomac* departed promptly and steamed along Long Island Sound to Point Judith, R.I, about fifty miles eastward, where it berthed for the night. The Coast Guard Cutter *Calypso*, which had escorted the *Potomac*, kept watch on the outer harbor, insuring that no alarm would disturb the President's first night at sea.

Monday, 04 August 1941
At Sea
0630 EST

The president had left instructions to be awakened not later than 0630. Mike Reilly knocked firmly on the president's stateroom door, and when he was certain that the president was awake, turned and signaled to the yacht's chief steward, who had sailed on several previous occasions with the president. "He's ready for you, Chief," the Irishman said softly. "When he's dressed and has completed his morning ablutions, signal the galley and they'll send up his usual breakfast. A man of set routine, the President usually started the day with grapefruit juice, strong Navy coffee with fresh cream, crisp toast and scrambled eggs and fruit. The eggs were a family tradition, which the Roosevelts had brought with them to the White House. On *Potomac,* they were prepared according to a recipe which Mrs. Roosevelt had left with the stewards after their first trip aboard in 1936. Using a liberal amount of butter, they cracked half a dozen eggs and added four ounces of sweet cream and salt and pepper for the President's breakfast. On his tray the stewards placed a copy of the Washington Post, and the president chuckled to himself as he read a story posted at noon on Sunday, which echoed the cover story perfectly.

By 0800, the President was presentable, and with assistance of his secret service detail, proceeded to the bridge to greet Captain Leahy and his officers. Dressed in a blue three-button blazer, open white shirt and white cotton trousers, he watched from a specially placed chair as the crew navigated the yacht across the mouths of Narragansett and Buzzard's Bays and dropped anchor at 0930 off the New Bedford yacht club in South Dartmouth, Mass. The president was discretely lowered into a Chris Craft speedboat provided by the club commodore, and taking the controls himself, "roared up to the dock," according to one observer, shortly before 10 AM.

Waiting for the president were state department officials, and a party of Norwegian royalty now in exile. The Norwegian royal family, fleeing the German invasions of 1940, had sought refuge in the United States. Among the group on the dock were Crown Princess Märtha and her two young daughters, Princess Ragnhild, aged 10, and her younger sister Princess Astrid, aged 9. After brief formalities and desultory conversation, the President surprised everyone by offering the three royal princesses a ride in the speedboat, which he himself would drive. In front of newsmen's flashing cameras, and no doubt some very nervous Norwegian and State Department security officers, the president and his very cheery and photogenic young guests departed for a short but exciting tour of Apponagansett Bay. Returning to the *Potomac* shortly before eleven, FDR and the entire diplomatic party, who had been ferried out by the Captain's gig, departed for a fishing excursion in Buzzard's Bay. By presidential order, neither the Navy nor Coast Guard interfered with the ad-hoc flotilla of private boats trailing in the yacht's wake (the President nicknamed them "Hooligan's Navy"), many of which had been chartered by the media, and which relished numerous photo opportunities. The president remained on deck as much as possible, chatting with his guests, fishing for bluefish and occasionally waving to the onlookers. As evening approached, *Potomac* returned to the dock and after a final speedboat ride for the Royal Princesses, FDR bid farewell to his guests and departed seaward.

When out of sight of land, *Potomac* again escorted by the cutter *Calypso*, changed course for Vineyard Sound. Arriving shortly before midnight, both vessels dropped anchor in a sheltered area. By 0600, as the sun was rising, Potomac went alongside *USS Augusta, (CA-31),* which had spent the previous evening anchored off Smithtown, L.I. before joining with *USS Tuscaloosa (CA-37)* during the hours of darkness. Awaiting them between the Elizabeth Islands and Martha's Vineyard, off the southeastern coast of Massachusetts, was a flotilla of ships from the Navy's Atlantic Fleet. At 0617 EDST, the President left the *Potomac* and embarked on the *Augusta.* By 0640 local time, the Augusta was underway and, convoyed by Tuscaloosa and the screening destroyers *Madison, Moffett, Sampson, Winslow* and *McDougal,* set out for their ultimate and most secret destination – the naval base at Argentia, Newfoundland.

Before departing *Potomac,* Roosevelt had left behind several suits of clothes, and one of the spare sweaters so hurriedly packed before leaving the White House. His Presidential flag remained at the masthead, and Captain Leahy quickly dressed one of his selected seamen in the president's garb, complete with a long-billed fishing cap, which helped disguise his appearance. Gesturing with a cigarette holder in a pose made famous by FDR, the sailor spent what was, perhaps, the most entertaining and leisurely days of his enlistment. *Potomac,* escorted by *Calypso,* with the "president" visible on the fishing platform, returned to the inshore waters of New England, where it was seen and photographed by press and public alike. Mike Reilly, who had also embarked on the *Potomac,* made certain that his ruse continued for the next several days.

Joining the Presidential party on *Augusta* and *Tuscaloosa* were General Marshall, Admiral Stark, General "Hap" Arnold of the Army Air force and Admiral Ernie King. King – who, as Commander in Chief, Atlantic Fleet, had orchestrated much of the operation with his typical thoroughness – soon passed a single message by blinker light from *Tuscaloosa* to the President "Churchill is at sea." Stark and Marshall would travel on *Augusta* with the President; the other members of the party would remain on *Tuscaloosa*. Heading east past the Nantucket Shoals lightship until they were far outside the shallows in which mines might be laid, "Task Force One" was 280 miles offshore by Tuesday morning. Wartime precautions went into effect when the president came on board. When an anti-mine paravane fouled, Admiral King had the cable cut, refusing to allow *Augusta* to slow down, even for the short time needed to retrieve it.

The president was fond of the *USS Augusta*, and had sailed on her on previous occasions. *Augusta* was of the Northampton class, launched in February 1930. She displaced 9,050 tons, was 569 feet long, with a compliment of 795 officers and men. With a top speed of nearly 33 knots, *Augusta* was armed with nine 8-inch guns, eight 5-inch antiaircraft guns and assorted weapons of smaller caliber. *Tuscaloosa*, though of the later Minneapolis class of heavy cruisers, had similar dimensions, speed and ordnance. These vessels, built during the moratorium on battleship construction were roomy and comfortable; visitors, particularly the senior Army officers aboard, marveled at their luxuriousness.

By the pre-dawn hours of Thursday, August 7th, "Task Force One" was approaching the coast of Newfoundland. At 0845 NST the flotilla, which during the previous night had been joined by the battleship *Arkansas*, passed Cape Saint Mary Light at the southeastern extreme of Placentia Bay. At 0924 local time, *Augusta* dropped anchor in Berth No.2, Ship Harbour, Placentia Bay, Newfoundland.

The executive officer of *USS Mayrant*, Ensign Franklin Roosevelt Jr. soon came aboard by motor launch. General Arnold had arranged for Lieutenant Elliott Roosevelt to fly down from

116

Gander Bay the next morning. Roosevelt borrowed what he mock-ingly called the "gold spinach" (aiguillettes) from the ship's offi-cers, and commissioned Franklin, Jr. and Elliott as junior aides for the occasion. They enjoyed the reunion – the first in several months – and it would be years before they had the opportunity once again. But, save for the family reunion, there was little to do but wait. The presidential party fished – not an easy task from the decks of a heavy cruiser – and they cruised along the shoreline, viewing the progress of construction on the new base. Although still in early stages of development, underwater nets and submarine detectors were already in operation, protecting British, Canadian and American ships present in the extensive harbor. An additional capital ship, bearing a very important passenger, would soon arrive for what everyone hoped would be a safe but historic occasion.

FDR IN THE OVAL OFFICE AUGUST,1941
(National Archives)

THE PRESIDENTIAL YACHT POTOMAC – 1941
(Official USN photo)

USS AUGUSTA (CA-31) – 1941
(Official USN photo)

FDR AT SEA – AUGUST, 1941
(Official USN photo)

10 NEWFOUNDLAND - IV

02 August 1941
Radio Station NWP
Naval Operating Base
Argentia, Newfoundland
1215 NET

The last watch of section three's cycle fell, fortunately, on Saturday. While it didn't provide a full liberty weekend for the crew, at least on Saturday there was much less chance of the OIC or the Chief Radioman wandering into the radio station and disrupting the routine. Indeed, most sailors considered the day as a "rope-yarn Sunday" – a day when the iron men on the wooden ships of yester-year took care of minor personal needs – mending clothes, spinning yarns, or winding the dog-watch. At least, that's what they told Hambone, who, until tipped off by Frenchy, didn't know the difference between the dog watch and the dog house. Except he only had the dog watch from 1400 to 1600Z. He was in the dog house more often than that.

Traffic was light on most of the circuits, although a very long encrypted message arrived on the Fox broadcast, addressed to the commanding officer of the naval station. Alarm bells went off in Boudreaux's head; mishandled messages to the skipper were the reason why section four was now scattered to the winds. He quickly called Hannigan to the operating position, and sliding Morris - still occupying his rolling chair - out of the way, made space for

119

Hambone to take over without missing a character. Like many important messages, it was encrypted, but since the precedence in the call-up line was "Routine," he decided to delay calling Lt. Carpentier to decode it until after noon chow. "There's no sense ruining his dinner unnecessarily," he though to himself.

Hambone had guarded the 500 kcs distress frequency for much of the morning. While there were no SOS, (ship in distress) XXXX (person in distress, i.e. survivors), SSSS signals (submarine sighted) or RRRR (surface raider) signals, the channel was nevertheless busy much of the day. When the duty driver returned with the box lunches for the noon meal, the operators made quick rotations among the operating positions, a beloved evolution universally called a Chinese fire drill, so that each sailor got at least a few minutes to consume his baloney sandwich, banana, cupcake, and pint of milk in relative peace. Three cigarettes, of brand and vintage unknown to anyone under the age of sixty, completed the "com-rats" for the day.

Frenchy looked around his new section. While the old hands were generally qualified on all positions, he discovered that the newly arrived 'strikers', non-rated seamen who had shown at least some aptitude for the radioman rating, were still shaky. They had attended but a brief introductory course at one of the new training centers which were springing up all over the country to take some of the load off the stations at Great Lakes and Bainbridge, Md. Returning Morris to the Fox broadcast, he directed Hannigan to set up a code practice oscillator on the back benches of the station. It would be good if Lt. Carpentier, when he arrived to decode the inbound message, saw all-hands productively occupied, rather than salivating over the *Police Gazette*, copies of which Frenchy collected from the various operators and stowed safely out of sight in a bottom drawer.

While Boudreaux dialed the Bachelor Officer's Quarters, and had the duty watchstander alert Mr. Carpentier to the incoming message, Hambone did as directed, and gathered the three new strikers around the bench. After listening to each send code for a minute or two, he took the key and began to instruct his new ship-mates in the right way to send Morse code.

"Now listen up, you guys. You know the old saying, right? There's the right way, the wrong way, and the Navy way, remember? I'm going to show you guys the right way to handle a telegraph key. It may not be the way that they taught you at school, but if you try doing it this way, your arm will get less tired, your keying will be more crisp, and, most importantly, all the ships that we work will think that NWP, Radio Station Argentia, is really squared away. So listen up."

Hambone, facing away from the main part of the operations room, did not see Frenchy and Lt. Carpentier approach the back of the group. Frenchy was about to call "Attention on Deck," but Mr. Carpentier touched him gently on the arm, and shook his head. He was interested in what Hannigan had to say to these junior sailors.

"Now, down at the orientation classes, I bet that they taught you to hold the key with a death grip – to hold the knob tightly so that you had good control of the character spacing, right? That's the Navy way, and it's good if you're out on a rolling destroyer or minesweeper or somewhere, I guess. But here ashore, it's better if you just place your thumb against the left edge of the key knob; the first finger on top of the knob at the rear and lapping over the rear edge just a bit; and the second finger against the right edge of the knob, about in the center or slightly to the rear of center. Some old railroad telegraph guys like to put their thumb against

121

the left edge but then place their first and second fingers to rest directly atop of the knob. The important thing is for the thumb to be on the side of the key. Just make a loose fist with your other fingers, OK? Don't hold them so tight that your fingernails bite into your palms. Keep your fingers, hand and wrist relaxed at all times. That's the way the old-time ham operators do it, and that's they way I learned it. If you do that, you can send thirty or thirty-five words per minute all day long, and not get as tired as a guy sending fifteen words per minute holding the key the other way. Sit up straight, don't hunch over the table, stay relaxed, and keep your spring tension on the key just tight enough that your key doesn't chatter and bounce. In no time, you'll be the best operators around, and sailors will be talking about the sharp operators at Argentia all the way from here to China. Go on and practice for a while – I'll put on a set of "cans" and listen while you guys take turns sending to each other."

Frenchy and Lt. Carpentier stepped back a few feet, and turned and entered into the crypto vault. They chatted as Boudreaux loaded the HW-6 "Caesar" system with the proper keys. "Hannigan seems to be a pretty good instructor," Carpentier noted. "He seems to understand how to break things down into pieces, and he makes the new men seem comfortable. What do you think?"

"Well, sir, there's no doubt that he's the best technical radio-man at the station. I've heard him send long complicated messages – like the six hour weather forecasts which are full of numbers, letters, symbols and odd characters all mixed up – and never make a mistake. And if you give him a pair of earphones, he can copy code all day long, every day, and get it just about perfect. It doesn't matter if there's static, thunderstorms, or other stations right on top of his target station. He's good."

"Chief McCroy seems to think that he's really – what is the word you guys use? Drifty?"

"Oh, he's drifty all right. Most of the time he's drifting like a 'gator in the sunshine. But the 'gator at least has a one-track mind. He wants to invite you to lunch, and you'll be the main course. But Hambone, er, sorry sir, I mean RM3 Hannigan bounces from one thing to another like a flea on a griddle. Can I tell you something, man to man, sir?"

The Lieutenant nodded. "He may be on to something, sir. When I first got here, back with the very first detachment to come to Newfoundland, I was told that the Canadian ships always alert their line handlers that they're coming 'round the breakwater by keying their TBS voice-circuit microphones once or twice. We never thought much about it; it was just what they did. But Hambone. . .er, I've got to stop that! I mean Hannigan, sir! Hannigan and I went down to the piers and talked to a senior radio guy from one of their ships – don't ask me the name of it, 'cause I can't pronounce it – and he said that not only don't they do that, but their rules prohibit them from keying a dead carrier signal. And that makes sense – you can blow out a tube or two that way. So, where's the signal coming from? I've heard it, the Chief has heard it, and there's probably not a guy in any of the four sections that hasn't heard it. On the last mid watch, I had Hannigan hook up an oscilloscope to the signal, and it's got that watery look like it's a low power signal from fairly close by. But yet it's strong enough that we have all heard it. I just don't get it, sir."

"Sounds like a ground-wave, then, maybe?" Boudreaux looked at the Lieutenant with some surprise. "Don't be startled, Boudreaux. They taught us a couple things down there at the Maine Maritime Academy. I listened enough to earn my engineering degree, not that I get much chance to use it these days. But what about his other mystery signals?"

"Well, that's another kettle of fish, sir. I don't know what to make out of that one, and Chief McCroy promised to shanghai the next guy that brings up the topic, especially to any of the officers. That's why it's better for me, at least, if we keep this conversation on the QT. Otherwise, instead of running a watch section and being on the verge of making RM1, I'll be following some dog team up there in the Arctic. And about right 'cheer is about as far north as a good Cajun boy wants to go, sir."

As they prepared to decode the encrypted message for the Captain, Hannigan knocked briskly on the crypto vault's steel door. "Excuse me, sir, but I have something that both you and the watch supervisor ought to hear. Can you step out for just a moment?"

They walked the few steps back to the test bench. Hambone had set up the SX-28 receiver again, and had tuned it to the frequency where the 'Kerchunker' was known to operate. After they stood there for a moment listening to the static, the signal came through again. "Now listen," Hannigan said, "listen *real* close. Hear that talking in the background? It's only there when the signal is present. It's like someone talking or maybe a radio playing in the background as the operator keys the microphone. He may not even know that the background voices are being picked up.

Look. . .watch this oscilloscope the next time it hits. I'll turn up the volume so you can hear it too."

They stood around, chatting about things both significant and not, until the signal appeared again. "Hear that?" Hannigan exclaimed excitedly. "Look at the O'scope while you listen, it helps. Listen!" They strained to listen, and it was clear that there was voice, perhaps an AM radio playing faintly in the background. . . *Le Président de la France, le maréchal Pétain, a (static)note de félicitations à l'Führer (static) la 11e armée allemande autour de 20 divisions russes à Oeman,(static) au sud de Moscou. . . .*

"Now, what do you make of that?" Hannigan asked. "I can see it on the O'scope. . .it's definitely sound being retransmitted over the Kerchunker's radio, wherever he is."

"Well, wherever he is, his French is perfect," Lt. Carpentier noted, his interest in the entire matter now being peaked. "That sounds like a Parisian accent, and upper class at that."

Frenchy nodded. "Yes sir, even I can understand it. It sounds like the Ursuline nuns we had in school. They were after us about how bad our Cajun accents were. But my momma would have whipped my butt if I started talking like I was putting on airs. So what gives here, anyway?"

Lt. Carpentier thought for a long moment. "It's not Quebecois, either, unless it's the Archbishop of Quebec, Cardinal Villeneuve himself, and even he sounds like a shoemaker's kid from Montreal most of the time, which I believe he is." He closed his eyes for a second in deep thought.

"Boudreaux, how far are we from St. Pierre?" Frenchy hustled up to the front of the station, and returned with a local area chart. "About eighty miles as I make it. but I'm not a quartermaster, sir. Here, take a look at the chart yourself and check it out."

Carpentier measured the distance with his thumb and forefinger. "More like ninety or ninety five, I'd make it. Hannigan, how far will a ground wave travel at 9 mcs, do you think? Up to a hundred miles, maybe?"

"That's roughly Philadelphia to New York, sir. I'm certain it would carry that far, especially over water. But why is someone sitting on the Steel Pier and keying his transmitter without saying anything for weeks on end, sir?"

"It's *St. Pierre*, Hannigan, not the *Steel Pier!* St Pierre is off the coast, the Steel Pier is in Atlantic City," Boudreaux replied, shaking his head sadly. Out of respect for the officer present, he didn't add the expletives that would usually accompany a response to one of Hambone's non-sequiturs.

"You've asked a good question, and one we need to have answered quickly. Boudreaux, come with me back into the vault again, please. I need to get that message decoded and down to the Captain's office, but we need to talk, too."

Once inside the bank-like vault, the OIC continued. "I'm not going to tell the Chief that you and I have had this little conversation, nor experienced what we just experienced, at least not yet, Boudreaux. But do this. Let Hannigan tune around when you can spare him, and make sure he keeps a good log – dates, times, frequencies and what kind of traffic he's hearing. Pass those logs to me as he gets them. In fact, if he can copy the traffic itself, all the better. The *USS Arkansas* is scheduled to be in here in a couple days, and, if there's something that needs to be looked into, their Communications Officer is a full commander, and not a piss-ant little reservist like me. *Arkansas* is an old WW-I battleship, mostly used for training nowadays, but they've got more resources than we do. But remember – make sure he documents everything. It's probably nothing, or something easily explained, but we don't want to be the ones holding the bag if it's something we ought to be worried about. Get the message, *Mon ami?*"

"Got it, Mr. Carpentier. *Laissez les bon temps rouler! OK* ? "

"Now, get outta here, Boudreaux, or I'll never get this message decoded!"

Hannigan spent the remaining two-hour trick of the last watch of the cycle encamped before his much-loved SX-28 receiver. He tuned all the likely places where he might hear the mysterious signal, but it was nearly at the end of the watch when he picked up the distinctly slow but accurate keying near 9590 kcs. The filtering on the Hallicrafters receiver was so good that he could clearly distinguish among signals only a kilocycle apart. He heard the call up again VVV KÖLN KÖLN KÖLN K repeated several times. This time, however, he was prepared and logged the exact starting time, how many times the call-up was repeated, and listened closely to either side of the mysterious transmission in an attempt to find the corresponding distant station. In this he was unsuccessful, but he was able to hear and record a penciled copy of the transmission, which started promptly at 1500 local time:

16198	16198	STRIYU	JYECY	HYWSH
AAMF	YRBVU	GIMUIO	SYRWS	SUMRH
TREVC	HUIKO	FGYUU	UBYRV	DFYBV
HIMOI	HIUTBV	GUGKJ	KARFG	BERTA

He passed the log and traffic to Boudreaux, who left it in a sealed envelope in Lt. Carpentier's mailbox. The watch was quickly relieved by section four, and Holden tossed the bread truck's keys to Frenchy, who promptly chucked them underhanded to Hannigan. Hambone dropped the keys, and stooped to retrieve them. "He's now your duty driver, Frenchy?" Holden asked incredulously.

"He ain't the duty driver yet, Ash, he's just working on a learner's permit. He's coming along, but it's a real grind, just like he does with the gears when he's driving," Boudreaux replied. Holden laughed. "You ought to stop at the chapel tomorrow, and have that priest give you guys the last rites. If he's driving, you guys are gonna need 'em!"

11 LONDON

03 August 1941
The Admiralty Citadel
Horse Guards Parade
London, England
1100 BDST

In many ways, it was easier for Churchill and his cabinet officers to preserve the secrecy of the upcoming Newfoundland meeting than it was for Roosevelt and his immediate advisors. While the trip was considerably more perilous, and the danger from enemy attack by U-boat or aircraft was more grave, everyone in the United Kingdom was by now conversant with the needs for strict operational security. "*Loose lips sink ships*" and other similar dictates were familiar to everyone, most especially Londoners as the second anniversary of the war approached on September third. Ten Downing Street continued to inform the press of the Prime Minister's schedule, maintaining the fiction that it would be business at usual for the next several days. Churchill, who as a parliamentarian relied more on his ministries than the President, was persuaded by his colleagues to include two journalists on the trip, however, which contravened an informal agreement that the two leaders had made earlier.

By late Sunday morning, the delegation implemented the hastily developed plan. Those traveling to Argentia, accompanied by various administrative and clerical staff who would travel only so far as Northern Scotland, began to gather near Horse Guard's parade, at a complex of three buildings housing the Royal Navy's senior command staff. The length of the journey required at least a week for travel to the conference, and an additional week for return to the UK. By noon, the group of thirty-plus conferees were sorted out into various automobiles and departed at staggered intervals, traveling by slightly different routes to Marylebone railroad station at Dorset Square W1. The boot of each car, and a separate lorry, were packed with both essential and contingent materials, since the relative brevity of the scheduled conference itself would preclude transfer of forgotten items.

Arriving at Marylebone shortly before noon, the travelers made their way to Platform 4, where a special twelve-car train awaited them. With steam up, the train was prepared for a timely departure, and precisely at 12:30 PM the engine driver released the brakes, and the train departed northward. It rolled smoothly thought the northern suburbs of the city, arriving at a local platform at Wendover in Buckinghamshire, quite close to Chequers, about an hour later.

Pacing to and fro on the platform impatiently was the Prime Minister, accompanied by a smaller group which had been overnight guests at his home. Churchill scarcely waited for the train to come to a full stop before bounding aboard. The Prime Minister, who could be depressed and withdrawn at times (he called his depression "the black dog" and against which he freely self-medicated with strong spirits,) was ebullient and puckish, energized by both the prospects of the journey by rail to the very tip of Scotland and the sea voyage across the perilous waters of the North Atlantic which would follow. With staff scurrying, and the Prime Minister shouting to get the train moving again, it was only good fortune which kept several members of the party from being left behind.

Churchill rode in his private carriage, accompanied by Admiral Dudley Pound, the First Sea Lord; General Sir John Dill, Chief of the Imperial General Staff; and Sir Alexander Cadogan, Permanent Under-Secretary of Sate for Foreign Affairs. After the Prime Minister and his chief advisors had settled down, other members of the party who had not been privy to discussions of the conference were brought in and informed by the Prime Minister himself of their ultimate destination. Those not going to Argentia were warned, in the strictest terms, of the danger to their colleagues and to the war effort if any word were to leak before the party had returned in two week's time. They learned for the first time that their immediate waypoint would be on Scotland's northern coast, at Thurso, in Caithness, which was the gateway to the Orkney Islands. After a bit of shuttling, they would board *HMS Prince of Wales* for the nearly one-hundred hour trip across the U-boat infested waters to North America.

Churchill dared not share with them the very reassuring news that the government was presently reading messages encrypted in the German Enigma system, and that these "Ultra" messages gave them a marked advantage in avoiding U-boats which might be operating along their path. The members of his inner circle: Pound, Dill and a few others all knew. Those not informed had no need to know, except perhaps for personal peace of mind. After a very good dinner and convivial conversation, the Prime Minister and his party retired, lulled to sleep by the rhythmic sound of wheels clacking over steel rails as the *London, Norfolk, and Eastern Railroad's* best rolling stock carried them ever closer to their highland destination.

The August sun rose early, particularly in these northern latitudes, and before 0500 it was possible to see the gorse-covered highlands. Regrettably, it was raining and windy when the train pulled into Thurso at 0930. "It will be a fine rehearsal for our time in Newfoundland," remarked Inspector Walter Thompson, Churchill's personal bodyguard to the Prime Minister's private secretary, Patrick Kinna. "It's just like bloody Ireland; raining so hard it's going sideways, and perishing cold for August Bank Holiday Monday."

"I thought it wasn't for two weeks or so, Inspector?" replied Kinna.

"The bloody Scots like to celebrate their Bank Holiday early, lad. They look forward to the fine weather, no doubt!"

"Ever been to Canada, Inspector?" Kinna asked, making the common mistake of lumping Newfoundland with its larger neighbor to the west.

"Not I, Patrick, nor did I ever think that I would. I'm for moving off to some nice warm spot when I'm done with this lot. They say there are parts of Australia and South Africa where it never rains. Maybe I can go back to being a village constable in Nevergetwet or some such place, then, eh?"

They laughed, and jogged, dripping, to the cars which would take them to the fishing village of Scrabster, where they'd board naval vessels for the trip through Scapa Flow to the *Prince of Wales*. The delegation was dismayed to learn that Scrabster harbor was too shallow for the destroyers to land at the dock, and that they would be forced to shuttle via lighters to the two camouflaged destroyers which would take them past South Ronaldsay and Hoy and then around Flota to the battleship's anchorage. Churchill and the senior military commanders embarked in *HMS Oribi;* the other members of the traveling contingent boarded *HMS Croome* for the passage through the submarine booms and narrow channels to Scapa water.

"Bloody spot where the Jerries sucker punched *Royal Oak*," Thompson remarked to Kinna.

"Don't remind me, Inspector, for heaven's sake let's have none of that! I'm terrified enough as is. I was a squadie when this all began in '39, like my father and his father before him, not a bleedin' sailor." Both men stood grimly at the rail, ignoring the falling rain, until *HMS Prince of Wales* came into view beyond Flota.

The passengers aboard *HMS Oribi* transferred first, and then those from *HMS Coome*. Churchill greeted Captain John (Jack) Leach RN, the battleship's commanding officer and his senior staff, and immediately re-embarked for a trip to *HMS King George V* to confer with Admiral John Tovey, Commander in Chief, Home Fleet. While he was absent, the other members of the traveling party were shown to their quarters. Although Leach had hoped to sail with the tide promptly at 1600 BDST (1400Z), cumulative delays and the inability of anyone, save perhaps his wife Clementine, to make Churchill move any faster than his lordship desired, forced the *Prince of Wales* to weigh anchor some twenty-five minutes behind schedule. While of no real consequence, the delay added to the estimated time for the crossing.

Prince of Wales was a fast ship. Of the *King George V* class, laid down at Cammell Laird and Company at Birkenhead in 1937 and launched shortly before hostilities began in 1939, she boasted a flank speed exceeding 30 knots, although recent damage in the battle with the German heavy cruiser *Prinz Eugen* limited her current speed to 24.8 knots. Displacing some 43,786 tons, with a length of 745 ft and a beam of 103 ft, her complement was slightly more than 1500 officers and other ranks of the Royal Navy, many of whom were landsmen, enrolled as "hostilities only" ratings. Astoundingly, giving the circumstances, her ship's motto was "*Ich Dine*" German for "I serve" which adorned the family crest of the Prince of Wales himself.

Escorted by the destroyers *HMS Croome, Oribi, Harvester, Havelock, and Hesperus*, the *Prince of Wales* exited Scapa Flow through the western passageway, passing abeam Graemsay Island shortly after 1530Z.

Immediately, the ship began to feel the effects of the open sea, which *Prince of Wales* and its destroyer escort experienced a few points off the port bow. The metrological office had provided *Prince of Wales* with the latest forecasts of weather en route, and the prospectus was not good. To avoid the two perils of ice and heavy weather, Captain Leach proceeded on a base heading of 270 degrees, swinging slowly to the southwest to avoid closing on the Hebridean coast, but still remaining well within the cone of protection provided by Scotland-based aircraft.

By 0300, abeam Rockall, he ordered a course change to his planned baseline course of 245 degrees. Unavoidably, this placed the heaviest swells and wind on his starboard quarter, and while the inherent size and stability of the battleship attenuated the effects on his passengers, it compounded the difficulty of the destroyer escorts maintaining station. The heavy weather was expected to blow itself out over the next forty eight hours, but the U.S. weather bureau was reporting an additional storm tracking up the Atlantic coast, which was expected to turn out to sea. It would be a very rough trip, at least through Wednesday evening and part of Thursday.

Churchill, though, was in his element. He had frolicked aboard the *Prince of Wales,* dressed in one of his signature "Siren suits" since returning from the *King George V.* He had scampered up and down ladders, explored passageways and various compartments, and stopped to chat with officers and other ranks wherever he encountered them. Colleagues had commented privately that, in his sixty-sixth year he was a bit long in the tooth for the role of Peter Pan, but nothing could stop the Prime Minister when in an ebullient mood. He had a special affinity for men of the lower decks, and frequently asked about their time of service, where they'd been, what they'd seen, and most especially, how their families were coping. He encountered a leading seaman, the killick of his mess, who had lived in South Africa, and Winston recounted his adventures there during the Boer War. But even he, as the weather worsened, was forced to curtail his adventures, and returned to the flag wardroom which had been sequestered for him and for the most senior members of his party.

Tuesday August 5, 1941
Aboard HMS Prince of Wales
Approaching 58.5W 14.0N

In the very early hours of Tuesday, weather conditions continued to worsen. By 0300Z, winds had reached Force 8 and continued to freshen. Forecasts compiled by stations in Greenland and Iceland predicted that the storm would continue to strengthen along the projected track to Newfoundland, and by 1800Z on Tuesday, Force 9 winds (50 mph or greater), and Sea State 6 (with wave heights of fifteen to twenty feet) were likely. Frequent wind gusts and rogue waves could be even more severe. Communication with the escorting destroyers was becoming increasingly difficult. All ships were maintaining complete radio silence, and the rolling, pitching and yawing made communication by semaphore, flag hoist or blinking light extremely difficult. After consulting with Admiral Pound, Leach reluctantly detached *Croome* and *Oribi* to return to Scapa, and by 0900 Tuesday he detached the remaining three destroyers to allow them to run for shelter. Completely blacked out, in total radio silence, and depending only on the wind and high seas for concealment from lurking U-boats, *Prince of Wales* continued across the stormy waters alone.

Midday Tuesday found *HMS Prince of Wales* about 450 miles southwest of Scapa Flow. The weather had continued to deteriorate throughout the morning, and as Tuesday wore on, the *PoW* was beset by a full-blown gale. The weather decks were secured to all but lookouts, and Captain Leach strongly suggested to the embarked delegation that they confine their movements to their staterooms and adjacent wardrooms, several of which had been reserved for their exclusive use. Churchill and his military staff retreated to the specially prepared war room, complete with maps, dispatch boxes and other materials of interest to those charged with the prosecution of the war.

The ship maintained strict radio silence. All radio transmitters, save one, were de-energized and that single transmitter was connected to a telegraph key which had a solid Bakelite "biscuit" screwed tightly down between the gold-plated contacts, to prevent even the possibility of "key chatter" activating the stand-by emergency transmitter. The receiver positions, on the other hand, were fully manned, and a constant stream of messages: political, administrative and, most importantly, operational, were plucked from the ether by experienced wireless telegraphists. Since departing Scapa Flow, Captain Leach had received several reports from Bletchley Park of U-boats lurking ahead, and he issued the order to begin zigzag diversions from his base course of 245 degrees true.

He directed his navigators and watch officers to execute Royal Navy Zigzag Plan 'Baker' (modified), which first required deviations from the base course with a 17 degree turn to port after 20 minutes, a 17 degree turn to starboard after an additional 20 minutes, a 25 degree turn to port 15 minutes later, and 25 degree turn to starboard again after 15 minutes. Each iteration substituted varying values and timings, making the task complex and very tiring for the navigator, but hopefully making it more difficult for a lurking enemy to achieve a firing solution before the target moved unpredictably. Fortunately, the departure of the destroyer screen back to port did provide the zigzagging warship with the unanticipated byproduct of being easier to implement, since only a single ship was now involved.

Churchill had retired early Monday evening and slept late on Tuesday morning, and arose to find that fixed mealtimes had been suspended, although stewards would strive diligently to keep him and his companions fed, and, most importantly well lubricated. The Royal Navy prided itself on being "wet," a privilege not shared by the Americans. He worked on replies to a number of messages from Atlee, who was acting in his stead, and consulted regularly with Admiral Pound and Captain B.B.Schofield, Director of the Trade Division as well as Commander M.G.Goodenough, of the Planning Departments of the Admiralty. Promptly at 1600 Z, twenty-four hours after the (scheduled) departure from Scapa, the Chief Yeoman of Signals knocked softly on the "war room" door, and handed Commander Goodenough a half-sheet, recording the ship's present position as 58N, 18.5W. In spite of the wind and weather, and ground lost to zigzagging, *Prince of Wales* had made approximately 650 miles since departing, and was essentially on schedule for a 0900 Friday arrival at Argentia.

Later that evening, as the delegation at last began to develop their sea legs, Churchill and his party gathered in the ship's largest wardroom, and enjoyed the first of several films which the Royal Navy had thoughtfully provided for the entertainment of their guests. Before the trip was complete, the travelers would view at least one current release each evening, with the Prime Minister providing his usual commentary after each showing.

Noticeably absent from the cinema was Captain Leach and his most senior watch standers. By sunset on Tuesday, the *Prince of Wales* was well within the most dangerous area of the trip. Air cover from Allied bases left a large gap outside the range of shore based aircraft, and weather conditions still made it impossible to launch or land float planes. The ship had to rely on speed and stealth to avoid confrontation with the enemy. Speed had been negatively impacted by the damages after its encounter with *Prinz Eugen* and the hurried repairs at Rosyth. One of its eight boilers had been secured, limiting its cruising speed to slightly under 26 knots. Stealth required a total blackout of the ship, and the Master-at-Arms and his regulating petty officers (colloquially known as the "crushers") roamed the ship. They made certain that not a glimmer of light, not even from the fag-end of a crewman's "snout," was visible on the weather decks. This requirement was made doubly difficult by the absence of escorts, who would normally report even the smallest light visible from a distance. Secrecy was aided by the constant stream of intelligence from the Admiralty, much of which originated from the code breakers at Bletchley Park. Leach stayed at his sea cabin just aft of the bridge and frequently visited the chart room, where his navigators integrated all information available about their situation and what might threaten them. As the evening progressed, the sea state worsened, and the period between rolling waves, now almost bow-on, shortened dramatically. Crew and passengers settled in for an even less comfortable, but still more perilous night's sleep.

Wednesday August 5, 1941
Aboard HMS Prince of Wales
Approaching 55.0 N 28.0 West

While the weather had attenuated during the early morning hours of Wednesday, dawn found the weather deteriorating yet again, but perhaps not as badly as the previous day. This was not unusual, particularly in August; smaller disturbances were apt to follow in the trail of larger storms, particularly those tracking east from the Gulf Stream. Churchill and his party were thankful for even the slightest improvement, which at least allowed meals to be served in a more orderly and convivial fashion. Although still prevented from exploring the weather decks, he made excursions below decks, visiting with everyone he met, and retelling stories of his days as First Lord of the Admiralty to anyone who would listen. And, since there was really no retreat from the PM, most especially in the middle of the North Atlantic, *everyone* listened. There was no question that Churchill was a beloved figure among the men and women of the Royal Navy. His first message, when resuming as First Lord of the Admiralty in 1939, "Winston is back," was received with glee throughout the fleet. Officers and men felt that, regardless of Churchill's class or political persuasion, he backed them all the way, and in general he did just that.

Affinity for Winston did not limit the growing anxiety felt by Leach and his staff. During the night, a steady stream of U-boat locations, most obtained by high-frequency direction finding ashore and afloat had reached the *Prince of Wales*. When plotted, they showed a curious "blank spot" ranging from about 30 to 35 degrees west longitude. There were concentrations on either side of that line, and HX and SC eastbound convoys had reported confirmed contacts, but it was curiously quiet in the mid-Atlantic. Pound and Leach were aware that the Germans

140

had pulled many boats out of the Atlantic to interdict shipping around the north cape of Norway in support of their Russian offensive, but it seemed curious indeed that no boats were transmitting from the areas directly before them. Leach discussed this with Admiral Pound, and Pound with the other Naval Officers in the traveling party, and all agreed that even more aggressive evasive action was warranted. With the weather improving slightly, Leach increased the number of lookouts topside. It was about the best they could do – the absence of howling does not preclude the presence of a wolf – but there was additional unease when their 1600 position showed them within fifty miles of 52 degrees north, 34.0 degrees west, well outside aircraft range, in the heart of the "killing zone", and a point surrounding which no HF/DF contacts with enemy U-boats had been recorded for several days.

Thursday, August 5, 1941
Aboard HMS Prince of Wales
Approaching 50.6N 39.3W

First light on Thursday morning brought sighs of relief to every-one onboard. While the skies were overcast, and long rolling swells continued, conditions on board were much better than they had been at any point of the trip. Most importantly, by 1300 hours, they would be at the extreme limits of air cover coming from the west, and, even more importantly, they could expect Canadian destroy-ers to meet them within the next several hours.

Promptly on schedule, *HMCS Ripley* and *HMCS Restigouche*, with *HMCS Assiniboine* trailing to provide protection from astern appeared on the western horizon. Given the speed of the destroy-ers and the speed of advance of *Prince of Wales*, it was not long until all three destroyers were abeam, and circling the larger ship like a pack of puppies welcoming their master home. The weather decks were declared passable, and Churchill and most of his party waved to the Canadians from the port side of *Prince of Wales*. After the greetings were completed, the Canadians pulled away, taking station at 3500 yards distance on the port and star-board quarter, and somewhat closer astern. Asdic from the 'side boys' swept in a cone leading the *Prince of Wales*, and the rear guard provided protection from abaft. For the destroyers, famil-iar with the weaving and bobbing needed to escort sometimes wayward merchantmen in convoy, this would be an easy and happy assignment.

Much of Thursday was spent preparing for an early morning arrival at Argentia the following morning. Although landfall at Cape Race on the southeastern coast of the island was not sched-uled until shortly after dawn on Friday, and arrival at their final anchorage off of Ship Harbour, Placentia Bay was scheduled for

0900 Newfoundland time, a sense of euphoria spread throughout the ship. Crew members had learned through the ever present scuttlebutt that the American sailors on *Augusta* and her escorts had prepared special gift packages for their fellow seafarers, with hard to find foodstuffs, including ripe oranges, not seen since the earliest days of the war. Members of the delegation reviewed position papers, and made last minute changes as directed by the Prime Minister.

Inspector Thompson and Patrick Kinna, who had barely known each other prior to boarding the special train at Marylebone, had become friends during the voyage. In order to perform their duties effectively, Thompson berthed immediately across the passageway from the Prime Minister, while Kinna's small stateroom (previously an anteroom) was abaft that of Churchill. In a very real sense, they represented the working class of Britain; both were south Londoners and felt more at home with the crew than with the "toffs" who made up most of the delegation.

On Thursday evening, they accepted a standing invitation to visit the Chief Petty Officer's mess. They made a strange pair; Thompson, at age 51 a "copper's copper", and Kinna, 28, a slight bespectacled fellow who looked more like a jockey than a member of the Army's Intelligence Corps, where he was assigned prior to being seconded to diplomatic service. They were welcomed by the Coxswain, the senior petty officer on the ship, and treated to a tot of Pusser's rum and some good sea stories as they sat in the smoky confines of the mess. "Do you know the difference between fairy tales and sea stories?" the Cox'n asked. Seeing the blank looks on their faces, he continued, "Fairy tales always start out, *Once upon a time. . .* Sea stories always start, *No shit, now, this really happened. . .*" Both laughed, and Thompson replied "Ah, me granddad told me that 'un when I was a nipper, growing up on the Isle of Dogs."

"So you'se is both from the Smoke, eh?" one grizzled CPO commented. "I'm Dusty Miller, Chief Engine Room Artificer, and this here's is Chalky White, Chief Mechanician. I'm from Bermondsey, and Chalky is from down by the El'fint and Castle, ain't ya, Chalk? Me and the Chalk will be your graft chinas; you stick close with us and you won't go far wrong, will they, mates? You'll be alright here in the Andrew if you just use your loaf, and keep your mince pies open, eh lads?"

"Ah, tune it up there, Dusty! We jocks nay kenn ya when you go nattering in Cockney!" grouched another sailor, who wore the Crown and three-bladed propeller of a Chief Stoker. "You'd think ye was in the boozer down the Ratcliffe Highway, the way yez goes on!"

"Speaking of the Ratcliffe Highway," another interjected, "I see where Winston went walkabout down the East End, giving encouragement to all the people who were bombed out. Did ya go with him, Mr. Thompson?"

"I did, and it was a sad sight. People wandering the streets, looking for their relatives, with glass and metal shards everywhere. It was awful." The men around the table sat silently for a moment. Many others were also Londoners, or had seen similar destruction in their own towns and cities.

C/PO Miller continued. "He's a right good 'un, isn't he, our Mr. Churchill? He warned Chamberlain and the others about Hitler, but none of 'em listened to him till it was too late, did they? I hope he's able to get the Americans in on our side. It's getting bleeding lonely since the Froggies gave in, and the Dutchies and all those other fellows. I wouldn't half mind seeing the streets of Portsmouth, or London even, filling up with those Yanks again, even if they go about bragging like they did in that last lot. We need all the help we can get, and that's dead cert." The others nodded, and soon, knowing they'd have an early morning, the gathering broke up, but it was clear that the forthcoming meeting would be critical, not only on the diplomatic front, but also to the common people of Britain as well.

After a restless night's sleep - this time from pleasant anticipation and not fear of disaster - the ship was greeted by an American destroyer escort off Cape St. Mary, the entrance to Placentia Bay. In a final manifestation of the fog of war, the British realized that they were ninety minutes early: Newfoundland was one and a half hours ahead of U.S. Eastern time, and someone had neglected to convert times properly to British Double Summer time before departing. Cutting donuts in the ocean, the ship made several circuits around the wide mouth of Placentia Bay before dropping anchor at Naval Operating Base's berth two at precisely 0900 NST. The two great leaders of the free world prepared to meet face to face for the first time to discuss the fate their nations and the fate of Europe and her people.

12 FRESHWATER, NEWFOUNDLAND

03 August 1941
Naval Operating Base
Argentia, Newfoundland
0715 NST

After four tries, and two more Mason jars of Screech to Guidry, Hannigan had earned his Navy driver's license. "Next time you get back home, Hambone, go out to your local driver's license bureau and show them your Navy license," Boudreaux suggested. "They'll accept it as proof that you can drive, and you won't have to take the test for your stateside license. On second thought, though, go there on the streetcar. It's not that I don't trust you, 'Bone, but just in case. . ."

This Sunday morning, though, Hambone did not need Boudreaux to awaken him for Mass. He had tossed and turned for half the night in excited anticipation of the planned events for the day. Frenchy had persuaded Guidry to let them keep the pickup truck over the weekend, under the guise of delivering another reel of coaxial cable, this time to *HMCS Dawson*, K-104. It would have been a long delivery however; *HMCS Dawson* was parked at the pier in Esquimalt, B.C. It was enough to convince Guidry, however, whose only knowledge of ships was his immense dislike for the possibility of being assigned to one. He rued the day when he visited the recruiters in Lake Charles. The Army guy was out to lunch, but the Navy recruiter was in. Through such small things, lives are changed forever. Boudreaux tossed in another Mason jar of Screech, to help soothe his friend's anxiety about waking up in a hammock on the mess decks of a battlewagon, miles from the nearest bootlegger.

Hannigan rose early, and paid particular attention to his hygiene as he showered and prepared himself for the 8:00 Mass. He noted with some satisfaction that his acne, long a problem, was disappearing quickly, replaced with a bit of tan, picked up no doubt while driving around the hills in the rare summer sunshine. He lathered on the Barbasol, shaved, and splashed on some Aqua Velva (borrowed from Morris on the understanding that Hannigan would cover an extra trick during their next watch cycle), and took a healthy gulp of Listerine before sauntering down to the lobby of the barracks. Frenchy arrived shortly after, and looked him over with a practiced eye. "You smell like a Storyville hooker, you know that?"

Hambone, who had no experience with either New Orleans's famed red light district, nor the ladies who dwelled there, just shrugged. "We're going out to town after church call, aren't we Frenchy?" "Good Lord willin'," Frenchy replied, as they started through the potholed parking lot to the truck. "Man, I don't want to get my boondockers muddy," Hannigan remarked, "I spent half the night trying to get them squared away." "You're a lifer in the making," Frenchy laughed, "I hope the Chief doesn't see you today; his heart won't take it." They pulled up in front of the galley/chapel shortly before 0800.

Hambone was disappointed that Father McHugh from the parish down the bay was celebrating Mass in place of Father Dee. He could hear the priest before he saw him; in his sharp Belfast accent he was berating the alter boys about one thing or another.

When he came out to the alter to begin Mass, it was clear that he'd rather be somewhere else; he gave the distinct impression that he considered his presence at this early hour an imposition. His sermon ignored the scripture readings; instead he railed on for several long minutes about the threat to the modesty and morality of the women of the parish by the "invasion" of the military on their peaceful island. "These Come-From-Aways will be the death of us yet, you just mark my words," he thundered. "Ye take their filthy money and ye allow them to take your homes and land – just mark my words, your daughters and your wives will be next. My own parish is far enough down the bay, thanks be to God, that we don't have that problem yet, but it's coming, and we'll be ready for it when it comes. None of our young maids will ever associate with anyone but good baymen, of that you can be certain."

Most of the local congregants were glassy eyed, having obviously heard similar rants before, while the handful of American and Canadian sailors squirmed uncomfortably. Hannigan dozed, having heard pretty much the same story about sexuality from the celibate clergy of Philadelphia, but Frenchy paid rapt attention, on the odd chance that he'd pick up some new ideas that he could try out on his forays into town. With a few additional words denigrating the heathens on the Burin Peninsula on the west side of the bay, the priest concluded in a huff and sped through the remainder of the service.

The girls were waiting for them outside the makeshift chapel. "Wow, what did you think about that?" Hannigan asked of no one in particular. "Ah, he's just a creepy guy who wears a black dress," Violet giggled. "What do you expect him to say, huh? I bet he was a real sheik, cuttin' up a rug dancing with all the altar boys in the seminary back in Ballykillcooties, or wherever he comes from."

"Aw, they're all the same, more or less wherever you go. In fact, it sounds worse in French," Boudreaux remarked, "being the language of love, and all. But what's this 'Come-from-away' stuff he was spouting, anyway?"

"That's what we Newfoundlanders call anyone from off the island," Violet, a proud daughter of the Outer Battery, remarked. "We're the oldest neighborhood in the oldest city founded by the English in North America, and we like things just the way they are. The old lads say it all the time. If you were born here, you're either a townie or a bayman. If you moved here, you're a 'Come from away.' But not that many people ever move out here to this poor god-forsaken island, at least not many that I know of, present company excluded." They laughed, and prepared to drive off through the main gate toward Freshwater, a mile or so away.

Kathy remarked, "Frenchy, why don't you drop Timmy and me off at Mr. Duffy's house, before you and Violet go off, would you? I promised Timmy that we'd make some fresh ice cream and I gave Mrs. Duffy the money for all the ingredients. It will take awhile – why don't you come back for us later this afternoon, OK? And their little twins both are getting their first teeth, so Mrs. Duffy didn't take them to church this morning – she'll probably go over to her mother's house on the Dunville road after a bit. Mr. Duffy is away. He's helping another policeman look for a dory that went missing over on Red Island. He's a member of the Newfoundland Constabulary, you know. So, maybe around two o'clock ought to be fine."

Frenchy looked at Violet, Violet looked at Frenchy, and both smiled. Hambone, though, missed the implication. His mind was preoccupied with thoughts of fresh ice cream. Frenchy tossed Hannigan the keys. "You drive, hotrod." Hambone was touched by this sign of confidence and his budding equality with his now bosom buddy, Frenchy. Frenchy, who realized that someone was going to have to double up on the seat of the pickup, was touched by something else altogether. Kathy jammed into the middle, and Violet gleefully leapt on Frenchy's lap. One more worldly or cynical than Hannigan might have sensed a hidden agenda at play.

The Duffys lived just off the track which led to North East Arm, an inlet of Placentia Bay. The house was painted canary yellow; it was the custom of outport families to paint their residences in bright colors, in such a way that fishermen coming back to port in foggy weather could better discern to which settlement they were navigating. Kathy and Hannigan both removed their shoes at the door as to not track mud into the plain, wooden foyer. Once again, Hannigan was glad he had a buddy like Frenchy. At his urging, he had changed his socks that very morning.

"Mrs. Duffy – this is the young fellow I was telling you about – this is Timmy. Timmy, this is Mrs. Duffy – her first name is Margaret, but I just call her Aunt Maggie. I call Mr. Duffy Uncle John, too. They've been like a family to me since I came out here to the hospital in Placentia – Uncle John gives me a ride down there in the Constabulary truck when sometimes I sleep-in and miss my regular ride. It's about a mile and a half down by the waterside – not too bad if you have to walk down, but you can hardly walk back – it's uphill all the way. And these little two little angels are Mary and Regina; they're twins, as you might have noticed. They're just coming up on their first birthday in September, and they're getting their teeth in. Uncle John says to put whisky on their gums, but out at the hospital where I trained in Winnipeg, they'd die if you suggested that. Of course, it's a Sally Ann hospital – just like the one in St. John's – so you'd expect them to say that, of course."

"Sally Ann?" Hambone asked in some confusion. "What kind of hospital is that?" "*Salvation Army*, silly!" Kathy replied. "You Americans sure are strange, you know that?" Hambone just grinned.

"Well, Kathy, I'm about to go down to me Mum's. John stopped off and got some ice from the processing plant for you before he left, as well as about four pounds of rock salt, and you'll find everything else you need there in the ice-box. Help me gather up those two magpies, and see if you can find their spare nappies, and I'll let you to your business. It's been nice meeting you, Yank!"

Kathy and Hannigan adjourned to the kitchen. "Now let's see, we used to make this back home in Winnipeg, Timmy. Except, for about ten months of the year, we didn't need to send out for ice. We just went and cut it from the pond at the end of our street. And in our two warm months, often enough it would fall in the form of hailstones, as big around as a robin's egg. But here's what we have to do." Kathy looked around the small kitchen, and gathered up four eggs, 5 cups of milk, 2 spoons of vanilla extract, 2-1/2 cups of sugar and four cups of whipping cream. She added just a pinch of salt and loaded the bottom of the ice cream churn, attaching the churning paddles and handles. "Now, as we start stirring that, every now and again, I'll check to see how it's going, and add some ice and salt to the mixture. It's going to get hard to stir as it gets thicker, but that's the fun of it all. Here, I'll take the first time till you get the hang of it."

As they churned the ice cream together, they began to share a bit of their lives with each other. Hannigan never guessed how easy it would be to talk with a woman. From the time his dad died, almost to the present, every girl or women he had ever talked to had been a relative, or a nun. But Kathy was a great listener, and he shared stories of the good days he had at St. Joseph's Home (relatively few), and how finding out about radio, and how a pair of

152

earphones and a telegraph key could take him away from the painful reality of his life, if only for a few hours on a weekend afternoon. He told her about Sundays, when he'd go up to the attic as soon as Mass ended, so that he wouldn't feel so left out when the other boys had visitors; no one had ever come to see him. He told her how awkward he felt in the Navy, and how Frenchy was really his only friend, even though he too sometimes joined in on the ragging when the other guys got started. He told her how lonely he was, and how he wished he could get away from the Navy and the other sailors and come out to Freshwater every day. He talked so much that, at times, he forgot to churn, and Kathy took his hand in hers and got it back to the monotonous task of making ice cream. The warm touch of her soft hand brought him back to the present. "But what about you, Kathy? I know you said you're from Winnipeg, but tell me more about yourself and your family, if you want."

"Nothing much to tell, Timmy. We grew up off Luxton Avenue in Scotia Heights. Dad was a machinist for the railroad, at least until he got hurt at the CNR yards in 1934. He'd been working overtime, and had been in the yard for nearly sixteen hours, when he missed the ladder on a rolling locomotive, and slipped and fell on his back. That was a terrible time to be crippled, and he's really never worked a day since. I've got three big brothers, and all of us pulled together to keep the family eating and warm with mom sick and dad off work. We'd go down late at night with gunny sacks and pick up the coal that fell off the trains coming into the yards. All three of my brothers are in the Winnipeg Rifles now; two are in England, and one is still in Canada. He'll be going over shortly, I guess. I am terribly afraid for all of them. I suppose that's one reason I trained as a nurse; if I can't help my brothers, maybe I can help someone else's brother sometime. And I guess that's why I offered to come down to Newfoundland, too. I mean, well, we read about the war every day in the Free Press, and we'd all listen to Lorne Greene read the news on the CBC, but we knew that the war was a long way away, and we on the prairie were safe from attack. But out here I felt like I am *part* of something, and when they asked for volunteers for Placentia, I knew that would bring me even closer to the fighting fellows. I suppose I have a secret hope that some day Ivan or Greg or Nick will walk down the gang plank and right out the gate and stand there in the doorway, just like you did a moment ago." She started to cry, softly, and once again, he took her hands into his.

"I've got an idea, Timmy. Let's listen to some happy music on the radio for a while, shall we? We have, oh, twenty or thirty minutes more to churn before the ice cream is ready to eat, and don't forget I saved some of those bakeapples to put on top. We'll save some, too, for Violet and Frenchy when they get back with the truck." She rose, and going into the parlor, returned hauling a bulky radio. "They say this is portable, but you'd have to be a horse to lug it around very much," she grunted, as she placed the battery powered radio atop a locked cabinet in the corner. "The Constabulary issued radios to all the men in the outports last winter so that they could monitor the revenue service boats and the Newfoundland Ranger's transmitter up at Whitbourne Junction. The Rangers look after most of the island, and all of Labrador, but the Constabulary looks after St. John's and the Avalon Peninsula. Sometimes, Uncle John lets us tune in VONF, VOWR or VOCM, the broadcast stations in St. John's, provided that we tune back to the Constabulary transmitter when we are done. He even made a tiny scratch with his pen knife to show where the radio ought to be tuned. I don't suppose he tells his sergeant, but in the evenings he likes to listen to that fellow Joe Smallwood on the *Barrelman* program, and in the winter he listens to Foster Hewitt broadcasting the hockey from Toronto. Many the night at home I listened to that fellow say 'Hello Canada, hello hockey fans in the states and in Newfoundland!' and never thought I'd be down here on the island someday. We can plug it into the electrical mains, although it has batteries so that he can take it along in the truck when he's out on a call and might need it. You can't send with it, though. When he's out there, he's pretty much on his own."

As excited as Hannigan was about being with Kathy (very!), and about turning the ice cream churn with her (not so much,) his first sight of a battery-operated portable shortwave receiver took his breath away. Imagine taking a short wave receiver along on a picnic, or even lying in the barracks after lights out, snuggly under the thick Navy blankets, listening through headphones to far-away stations! He stopped cranking the churn, and walked over to examine the radio more closely. "Hey! Timmy! Get back to work; the ice cream is going to get all soggy and not set properly if you don't keep turning that crank! We don't want to waste all the effort we've put into it so far! Crank, boy, Crank!"

Timmy did as ordered, although it took all his will power not to run over and start fiddling with the dials. Kathy tuned to VONF, the government station, which had a stronger signal than the others, and adjusted the extendable antenna for best reception. Dance music soon filled the air, both big band and swing. "I promise you, Timmy, as soon as we get this ice cream made, we can dance right here in the kitchen for a while, OK? Lots of times folks from all over the area come around for what they call 'kitchen parties,' and you ought to hear the old time fiddle and button box music then! It's better than anything you can hear on the radio, most days. All you hear are politicians or preachers going on and on about this and that, except when there's a good music program on."

Kathy came over and held his hand as he continued to turn the crank. The task became harder and harder, as the ice cream set up, and finally, after adding just a bit more ice and salt, Kathy pronounced it as ready-to-eat. She took down two small bowls (usually the much fought-over property of the twins), and spooned both ice cream and the bakeapples into each. "Open up, Timmy – you're just like one of the babies!" He opened his mouth, and she navigated the spoon so that not a drop spilled on the table. It was good – really good, and the bakeapples lent a special flavor to the concoction. He returned the favor, and spooned the ice cream into Kathy's mouth, and she licked her lips in delight. Timmy was in a level of ecstasy that he had never felt before. He looked into her eyes, and she into his, and he knew the opportunity was ideal, and might never come again. "Kathy," he stammered. "Kathy. . .Kathy. . .can I take a good look at that radio?" Kathy sighed, more in resignation than disappointment. "Violet keeps telling me that sailors have a one-track mind, Hannigan, but I thought it was going to be on something else. Sure, Tim," she sighed in resignation, "but don't break it, whatever you do."

Hambone leapt up, and took a good look at the radio. He had seen advertisements for this model before in QST, the ham-radio operator's magazine. It was a Sky Traveler S-29, and it was one of the very first completely portable all-wave radios. It weighed a whopping twenty-eight pounds with batteries installed and had a twenty-four inch extension antenna. Moreover, it completely covered the entire broadcast and short wave spectrums. Compared to the eighty pound rack-mounted radios Hannigan had used as a ham operator and Navy radioman, though, the little solid cube was a delight. He spun through the dial, switched bands, and, for several minutes was in a world of his own. A world which, unfortunately, ignored the young lady slowly eating ice cream by herself at the kitchen table.

"Uh, Tim, why don't you tune back to St. John's? There's good dance music, and it would be a shame to waste it, wouldn't it? Violet and Frenchy are going to be back here in about an hour, and I wouldn't be surprised if Aunt Maggie or Uncle John walked in, either. Let's Dance!"

Of the limited social skills Hannigan possessed, dancing was very low on the list. In fact, he had never danced with anyone. Kathy took him by the hand, led him through some very basic steps, and they danced – swayed would be a better verb – cheek to cheek through several medleys of Benny Goodman, Kay Keiser and Dorsey Brothers' hit numbers. "I'd teach you to jitterbug," Kathy laughed "but I don't think the furniture would stand it. Besides, it's time we clean up this mess we made with the ice cream machine, before we get into trouble. I like living with the Duffys, especially the babies, and I want them to like me, too." Once again, she looked into his eyes, and he into hers, and this time Hambone, crack communicator that he was, finally picked up on the message. They kissed chastely at first, but Kathy steered him toward the Chesterfield in the corner, and after a few seconds old Father McHugh, had he been there, would have certainly gathered enough material for a whole month of sermons.

CONSTABLE DUFFY'S NEW PORTABLE RADIO
(Author's Collection)

157

13 BERLIN - II

Dönitz had received an urgent message late the previous evening. While brief and deliberately vague, it suggested strongly that he return to Berlin at the earliest opportunity. An aircraft was quickly provided the next morning at Morbian Airdrome, the huge Luftwaffe base a few kilometers outside the city. The 1300 km flight took less than two hours, and a staff car quickly transported him to the Abwehr offices adjacent to OKW Headquarters. Admiral Canaris greeted him in an anteroom, and quickly escorted him into his private office. After the briefest of conversation, the two Admirals – colleagues, if not friends, since the earliest days of World War I, got down to business.

Canaris began "We've gotten firm information that Roosevelt is on the move, and Göring has a Focke-Wulf Condor reconnaissance flight over Scotland at this moment. If the weather improves, he'll attempt to detect any movement by the capital ships of the Royal Navy. We don't have many places to look – those that are in home waters are at Scapa Flow, and while we don't know if Churchill will be transported on the *King George V* or the *Prince of Wales*, if the Condor can get good aerial photographs, we should have some idea as to which is ready to sortie.

It's raining heavily now, and a major storm is approaching, so I'm not certain of the probability of success. Göring has not been informed as to why this information is critical, but he is cooperating, and there is, after all, some significant risk to his crew and aircraft which are undertaking this mission. Ever since Prien went in there with U-47 two years ago, they've become extremely sensitive about seeing a successor to *'Der Stier von Scapa Flow'* on their doorstep yet again."

Dönitz nodded. "Ah, you and I are old U-boat men, Willi. Can you imagine what it must have been like on the U-47 going in and coming out? We're old men now, and gray, but I tell you Willi, had it been me on the '47 – I'd have been gray that very evening. I had two boats in that war – the UC25 and the UB-68, and I know you had five – but then again, you're older than I, aren't you?" Both laughed.

"Yes, Karl, I am. By about four years, I think. I did command five, but my favorite was the UC-27. She was a sister boat to your UC-25, remember?"

Dönitz nodded and continued, "It's too bad about Günter, though. I shook hands with him and wished him Godspeed when he left Lorient for the last time in February. To this day we are not certain what happened to the U-47 – that was the only boat which he had ever commanded, and his crew loved him dearly. We're still not over the shock."

"Well, perhaps we can give the Tommies a bit of a shock, too. "Here, Karl, let me show you some of the information we've received regarding Roosevelt's recent movements. While no one has actually spotted him away from their inland waters, the Americans are so naïve and immature in their operational security that, as they say in English, 'there are smoking guns everywhere.' Look at these, Admiral."

Canaris handed Dönitz a sheaf of messages. "The first is from an associate of Fritz Duquesne, the senior Abwehr agent in New York. One of his frequent contacts, Felix Jahnke, a dock worker in Brooklyn had spotted several large wooden crates with White House markings being loaded aboard the Destroyer USS *McDougal.* Shortly thereafter, the destroyer departed upriver. Jahnke then got into his automobile, and spotted the destroyer as it passed under the Hells Gate Bridge, going into Long Island Sound. All of this happened on Saturday morning. Jahnke, by the way, has a short wave transmitter at his apartment, and the message was relayed to us by Mexico City, as usual. But, much more significantly, I think, is information developed that evening. The USS *Augusta,* a ship much favored by President Roosevelt, anchored off of Smithtown on the North Shore of Long Island that afternoon, as did USS *McDougal.* We suspect that the material was transferred from ship to ship there. More important than that is the fact that a number of her junior officers were invited to a dinner-dance at the Sand Point club, which is not far away. As often happens, the combination of liquor and junior officers is an intelligence officer's dream. You'll recall that it was an associate of Richard Eichenlaub, the cafe owner who alerted us to the telephone call between Roosevelt and Churchill. Yet another associate was working as a waiter at the Sand Point Club, and overhead conversations which he interpreted as plans for the president to come aboard somewhere farther out in Long Island Sound, perhaps off Block Island or Martha's Vineyard."

"Most of the major newspapers in the U.S. have Roosevelt spending a week or ten days on a fishing and boating holiday in that same area. Indeed, the matter has been given the widest publicity;

an unusual situation, even for the Americans who are still neutrals. But who can fish from a heavy cruiser, eh? It's a clear shot from the mouth of Long Island Sound, or the water surrounding those offshore islands to Cape Race, as well you know."

Dönitz smiled. "Well, for once, Willi, the gods of war seem to be nodding in our favor. After our last meeting, I convinced Großadmiral Raeder to allow me to "strip" the Western Approaches to Britain of every boat we could spare. He would not permit me to take any boat dedicated toward interdicting shipments around the North Cape to Russia; the Führer would never stand for that. But, counting the boats that I had in ports along the Bay of Biscay, at Brest, Lorient and at our newest base at St-Nazaire, I was able to assign ten to this mission. All are now briefed, as fully as I could with the information available to me at the time, and are traveling under strict orders to avoid any contact with the enemy until this matter is resolved. I don't think Raeder will have any difficulty with the Führer on this, and the Großadmiral has made it abundantly clear that there will be no involvement with the Americans at all. As an additional precaution, I further instructed the U-boat commanders that there is to be no involvement with any of the "Town Class" British or Canadian destroyers. You may remember those, Willi – they are the old four-stack flush deck ships of the American Clemson and Wickes classes that we encountered toward the end of the last war. Those were transferred from our "neutral" enemy to our active enemy last year, of course. But the Yanks still have a few on active service, and under anything but ideal conditions, it would be impossible to tell the nationality of one or the other at sea. And ideal conditions hardly ever occur where these boats will be operating, I'm afraid."

"All boats, save two, are now on station and patrolling in two lines, north to south. One is centering on the area surrounding

55N-25W, the other on a line radiating north and south from 55N at 35W. To plot that on your charts, Willi, that would enter at about grid AL61 and depart at AL47, or thereabouts. We've received very short "on station" signals from eight boats, and expect to hear from U-115 shortly. He has the longest transit to his operation area."

One boat, Gelhaus in the U-143, had to abort and return to Brest. On his last patrol, he was shaken up badly by a depth charge attack, and, while Flotilla I made all the necessary repairs, he had continued severe leakage along his forward torpedo doors and made the decision to return to port. He discovered this on his first night out in the Bay, so there was no real danger to the boat or crew, save from air attack on the way back in. He's now undergoing additional repair work, and I may yet bring him down to Lorient, where the facilities are somewhat more advanced. The other boat, U-115, is my last-chance boat, and, as the only type IX-B on the mission, has much longer time-on-station, especially since we stripped all unnecessary armaments and added about 200 kilos of additional provisions for the crew and their 'guests'. Himmler's hand-picked team of saboteurs/snipers is onboard now. I'll have Moll and his boat sitting just east of the Flemish Cap seamount at 47N-45W. He's about 300 miles or a day's sailing time east of Cape Race. That's a particularly good place to linger. It's somewhat south of the normal convoy and escort track, far enough east that it's outside the zone where the Americans are apt to venture on their own, and the convergence of the cold waters of the Labrador Current and warmer waters of the North Atlantic Current and Gulf Stream provide layers of water where underwater sounds are much confused. Sound ranging by the British and Canadians will prove of little use there, I think."

"Himmler's hand picked team of saboteurs, Karl? What do you know about them?"

"Not much at all. I am told that it's a three-man team, and they arrived on the dock at Lorient just as Moll was about to give up and sail without them. Two of the SS-men were reported by the Marine-stosstruppen (Naval shock troops who guarded the U-boat bases) as being falling-down drunk. And, heaven knows, the Marine-stosstruppen know a drunk when they see one. I wouldn't take any one of them on my boats."

"Well, in confidence, Karl, I don't think much of Himmler's private army myself, but that's another matter entirely. What kinds of communication do you have with the ten boats out on this mission now?"

"Willi, if we are speaking in confidence I must tell you what I told Großadmiral Raeder when last we met. I am convinced – absolutely convinced! – that one of two conditions is occurring. And, Willi, I mean no disrespect to you, or to the Abwehr, nor to the *B-dienst* nor to anyone, but I am convinced that the British somehow have broken our *Heimische Gewässer*, our *Hydra* codes. I know that everyone says that the Enigma machine is secure, and that the scientists tell us that the chances of anyone reading messages encoded with the Enigma machine are several million to one, but I am certain that it may still be happening. I have spent too many nights in the operations room watching convoys steaming right into the path of our boats – not only single boats, but complete Rudeltaktik groups (wolf packs) - only to turn aside and avoid us. Take Rudeltaktik Kurfürst (Elector) for example. We had five boats, operating together, with Schnee in U-201 on the tail of an inbound convoy from Freetown, which scattered just a score of miles or so before coming into the "trap." Of that large convoy, we were able to get one old Laker boat of 2700 tons, sunk by Lüth in the U-43. It has happened too often to be coincidence or bad fortune. I know that I have been accused of adding risk by engaging in too much communication with the boats at sea, and I take responsibility for that. But either this is happening, or, more sinister still, someone has penetrated our highest level of command and is privy to our most guarded secrets. I think that is the less likely of the two, and I've made arrangements that we begin to use a specially modified Enigma configuration, using four rotors rather three, but these will not be available until later this year or perhaps even early next year. Raeder dismisses the idea out of hand, but personally and confidentially, Willi, I think he is just reluctant to bring up either of these possibilities to the Führer. But it frightens me, not just because of the targets that get away, but from the idea that we're adding yet another level of risk to the men in the boats. It's not as if they don't have enough risk now."

Canaris sat silently for a long minute, considering Dönitz' heated outburst. It was not like Dönitz to make accusations without evidence, even if the evidence was, as in this case, highly circumstantial. Canaris, who by no means was a rabid party supporter – or, indeed, in his heart of hearts, a party supporter at all - knew how explosive a "witch hunt" would be, not only within the Navy, but within the entire Party establishment. The Night of the Long Knives was long past, but the knives remained in the laps of everyone sitting around the table at the Führer bunker. Finally, he spoke.

"What can we do to avoid even the most remote possibility of this happening on this mission, Karl? I give you my solemn pledge that the number of individuals who know of this plan are absolutely few, and all are most senior members of the Führer's inner circle. We can easily count on one hand those who know what we are about. And it goes without saying that you issued orders to your boats which were only to be opened when the boats were well away from land, yes? Himmler must have certainly done that with the small SS team he provided. In fact, I would wager that your captain –what was his name? Pell, Nolle – ah, yes, Moll – would be the first to inform him once the U-115 was on the open seas. So where do we take this from here, Karl?"

Dönitz chuckled. "We take a page from the book of the British, Willi. You know, of course, of how the BBC sends messages to the saboteurs in the occupied countries, yes?"

Canaris replied, "Of course. They read the 'news' in French three times each day, and the newsreader ends the broadcast with the same phrase '*Et voici quelques messages personnel*', (And here are some personal messages). We know those are intended for the Resistance in France, certainly. Are you going to try something similar?"

"Similar, but more complex. Raeder has arranged with the *Propagandaministerium* to broadcast certain music at specific times of day. I understand that Goebbels was quite happy to accommodate the Großadmiral's wishes. To confuse the enemy even more, the Reichsminister suggested that we encrypt the messages inside broadcasts of 'Charlie and his Orchestra', which enemy soldiers and sailors in the field are prohibited from listening to; mostly because it is designed to sow discontent among those who do listen. Raeder told me, privately, that Goebbels thinks that many enemy troops do listen in, although the Minister thinks that it's more successful as entertainment than as propaganda. Nevertheless, he is willing to go along with the plan."

"So here is what is going to happen, beginning tonight. At 0015, and at fifteen minutes past each hour until dawn, Reichtsender's Hamburg, Bremen, Luxembourg, Hilversum, Calais, Oslo and Zeesen will rotate transmission of shortwave station DXB in the 25,

41 and 49 meter wavelengths. The program they carry will originate here in Berlin, and will feature light music from a number of bands and orchestras. But one song at the fifteen minute mark exactly, will be selected from one of these American bandleaders recordings: Artie Shaw, Benny Goodman, Bing Crosby, Duke Ellington, Gene Krupa, Glenn Miller, Guy Lombardo, Harry James, Jimmy Dorsey or Kay Kyser. I have no idea what songs will be played, but that is immaterial. The message is in the band playing: A record by Crosby indicates we have no information; Goodman indicates that Churchill is on the seas, and each of the others indicates an approximate location, devolved either from observation or dead reckoning. Since the boats will most certainly be surfaced for ventilation and recharging batteries, and DXB has been heard throughout the North Atlantic by our boats for years, there is a high probability that those messages will get through. In addition, the announcer – most likely "Charlie" himself, will manage to work in the general coordinates immediately following the song, although I leave it to the inventiveness of the *Propagandaministerium* to figure that out."

"Well, they certainly have experience in hidden messages, don't they?" Canaris replied, without a trace of irony in his voice.

There was a knock at the door, and Canaris' adjutant entered when the door was unlocked. "Admiral Raeder has sent this message, with his complements and those of Reichsmarschall Göring. He handed Canaris a sealed envelope and departed. Opening the envelope, Canaris scanned the single message blank enclosed. Marked *Most Secret*, it said: "Morning reconnaissance over Target Siegfried at 1100 MET shows one battleship, believed to be pennant number 53 with heavy steam as if preparing to sortie. Several destroyers and tenders are shuttling between capital ship, pennant 41, who appears to be laying "cold iron" at anchor. Other small craft are moving in the vicinity of Flota, Fara and Cava Islands. Two small ships, perhaps destroyers or corvettes are approaching from southwest of the old head of Ronaldsay. Departed station at 1120 MET without incident."

Dönitz smiled. *Wenn der Berg nicht zum Propheten kommt, muss der Prophet zum Berg kommen, ja?* Canaris smiled, rose and took Dönitz by the hand. *Weidmannsheil. Kamerade!*

THE DUQUESNE SPY RING – NEW YORK CITY – 1941
(FBI)

14 THE FLEMISH CAP - I

05 August 1941
Aboard the U-115
47N-45W
East of the Flemish Cap
Northwest Atlantic Ocean
0805Z

It has been a long, slow transit across the North Atlantic. For two weeks the U-115 has crept slowly northwest, never exceeding 3 knots submerged during hours of daylight. From nautical twilight to nautical dawn, however, she had sped along at her top speed of nearly 18 knots, while recharging batteries and ventilating the boat. One extra lookout crowded the small bridge, and all other crewmen and passengers participated in a rota, allowing one man at a time a precious fifteen minute escape from the rank atmosphere inside the boat. At 0315Z the previous morning, Reichssender Hamburg, DXB had played Artie Shaw's "Stardust," which has spent the last eleven weeks at the top of the popular U.S. radio program *Your Hit Parade.* According to the top communication plan which had accompanied Moll's sealed orders, this indicated that Churchill was at sea and headed westbound on the North Atlantic. Everyone understood the meaning of that report.

Two weeks previously, as he had promised Fleischer, Strebel and Muller, he had waited until U-115 had completed the first night's surface transit and had submerged for the day before opening the sealed orders which Braun had delivered upon arrival. At 0930Z, he had the crew assemble in their respective berthing areas, and asked Obersturmführer Braun, as a courtesy, to come to the operations area and to be with him as he opened the packet. Allowing him a few minutes to read the materials, he asked Braun "Is this what you expected?" Moll, who found the Schutzstaffel distasteful in the extreme, had vowed not to refer to the SS men by their ranks, although he showed deference based on their general equivalent in the Kriegsmarine. Braun would be treated as an Oberleutnant zur See, while his two sleeping underlings were roughly equivalent to Petty Officer and Able Seaman.

Braun stiffened. "Yes, Herr Kapitänleutnant."

Moll frowned. "You'll soon find, Braun, that we are much less formal here than you may be accustomed to. When you spend six weeks within inches of your comrade's smelly armpits or feet, or watch him do those things which most men do in private, it tends to breakdown barriers of protocol and formality. Now, if you fully understand what we are about, it's time I let the rest of the crew in on our little secret. Do hand me that microphone hanging over your head, if you would." Moll's voice reverberated throughout the boat. "Officers and men, your attention to orders. I have just opened the packet given to me shortly before we left Lorient. I know that you have all been curious about what is afoot, and that the rumor factory has been working overtime." He could hear laughter coming from the various compartments.

"Well, fantastic as some of those rumors have been, truth is often stranger than fiction. We have learned of a meeting, planned for later this month, between Churchill and Roosevelt. That meeting is expected to take place somewhere in Newfoundland, most likely in Placentia Bay. There is the possibility that it may take place in the capital, St. John's, or even at some other place along the coast. All of that will sort itself out in good time. A few weeks ago, I attended a briefing at Chateau Kerneval. There were nine of us there – all U-boat commanders, and, of course, Admiral Dönitz and his staff. The very highest command, with the Führer's explicit authority, has ordered that the meeting between these two leaders can not take place. Eight of the other boats, mostly from the first and second flotillas will be arrayed in such a way as to maximize our chances of intercepting the ship carrying Churchill to the meeting. We'll do so in such a way that the possibility of interference by the Americans, which the Führer has expressly prohibited, is minimized. All of the boats, including ours, are operating under strict radio silence. We have other means of receiving messages from BdU. They are ingenious, and I think you will enjoy them, when we finally reach our holding point." Moll continued, "Men of the U-115: For the first time in my career, and I suspect in the career of each of you, we get to operate as true submarines. As well you know, most of the time we act as 'submersibles'; we dive only on those occasions when we need to creep up on our target, or, as all of you are painfully aware, during those frightening hours when he is creeping up on us. This time we will transit only at night, and will "sleep in" during daylight hours. We'll maintain just enough headway so as to not lose control of the boat, causing us to pop up like a cork at some most unfortunate moment. Speaking of corks, 'Onkel Karl' has included several cases of wine, as well as some extra beer, in the additional rations which were loaded right before we left."

"Bootsman Wulff! - I understand from a little birdie that you were questioning the sanity of everyone involved when you had to offload the torpedoes you had just spent two days loading! Well, Wulffie, if we had those big iron fish littering our tidy little boat, where would we stow the champagne and other good French wines, as well as your favorite beer, eh? See, my friend, how 'Onkel Karl' takes care of us all! So get comfortable if you can – we'll certainly eat well on this trip, and there is plenty of extra tobacco on board too, although the smoking lamp may well be darkened by our schedule. We have received an even greater honor; more perhaps than any boat since the war began. We have been selected as the "goalkeeper" – if by some evil chance Churchill's vessel slips past the patrol lines, we will be closest to the target, and will have the last opportunity to prevent our enemy from scoring a winning goal. If this meeting does take place, even in spite of our best efforts, the high command expects a declaration of war on the part of the Americans. I need not tell you what that will mean, and it must be prevented at all costs. If we succeed, the high command is certain that the British will sue for peace. I expect us to be at our holding-point sometime in the first days of August, and if we must attack, I expect that we'll get only one chance before all hell breaks loose above us. That's why we are carrying a limited number of 'fish' – if the first attack doesn't succeed, there will not be another.

"We are also carrying a special team of highly trained members of the Waffen-SS, who, if necessary, will go ashore and complete the mission by other means. I have here with me their commander, Lt. Braun, and you will give him the same respect that you give to your own officers. Later tonight, he will address you as a group as well. Assist his subordinates, and treat them as you would your own messmates. We're all in this together. I will be around the boat later, and will answer any specific questions you might have, if I can. Rest well–we have an historic mission before us."

As Moll replaced the microphone in its cradle, he could hear murmuring throughout the boat. Each of the messes – seamen, petty officers, chief petty officers, and officers – was quietly discussing what this might mean, each from their own perspective. The officers knew, of course, that he had been with Prien at Scapa Flow as a young cadet. And if a torpedo attack were necessary, they knew that the good fortune that brought Prien home to fame and adulation was not likely to happen twice. "Eat, Drink and Be Merry – for tomorrow we die" was becoming more than a motto which graced the stairs going upstairs at their favorite tavern and brothel, 'Les Trois Soeurs' in Lorient – this time the danger was very real.

During that first night's transit, First Watch Officer Fleischer had called the senior members of the seaman and petty officer's messes to the operations table. Obermaschinist Friedrich Unger, at age 44, was the oldest man on board, while Oberfunkmeister Helmut Amsel was the longest serving chief petty officer on the U-115. "I have a special mission for the two of you," Fleischer informed them without preamble. "We have those two commandos aboard – and I've berthed one in each of your messes. The younger one, with the broken nose and the scar on his chin, is an SS equivalent of a petty officer. The older one, although he ranks just above an Ordinary Seaman, is of an age where he'd be more comfortable among the chiefs – and, as you know, we detached one man from your mess so that he could get home to Berlin and see about his family, so space should not be a problem. I believe this fellow is not from the *Heimat* – the Skipper thinks he is Norwegian. Why he is here, I have no idea, but both of you must take special care of your 'guest' – and, for heaven's sake, don't let them touch anything! If one of them reaches up and asks 'Now, what does this valve or lever do?' just wallop them with a marlinspike, and let me sort it all out. If you keep them safe, you'll be keeping us safe, too."

The First Watch Officer had good reason to worry. Aside from their rather undignified arrival the evening before (and they were not the first crewmen to arrive in such a state, by any means), a U-boat is an incredibly dangerous place. Even in peacetime, when things went wrong on a U-boat, they went wrong quickly, and often with fatal results.

The U-115 was constructed of four major pressurized compartments, both welded and riveted to comprise the inner hull of the boat. In the rear of the boat, the after section held all the propulsion machinery, including compressors, electrical mains and one torpedo tube which could not be reloaded. Taking up nearly three fourths of the space were two 4400 h.p.diesel engines, which, at full power, allowed the U-115 to travel at nearly 12 knots while on the surface. In addition, two heavy-duty electrical motors were connected to an array of batteries, stowed beneath the deck plates of the center passageway.

Between the diesel compartment and the operations area was a tiny galley, where the sole cook ruled as an absolute monarch, assisted by men from the various divisions assigned by rota. There was a small head, which was piped to the sea, as well as the seaman's mess, which was frequently inaccessible if the electricians pulled the deck plates to inspect or perform maintenance on the aft battery array. The control room, the central nervous system of the U-115, was amidships. Crewmen taller than 5'8 inches learned to duck and bob their heads in the control room, the overhead of which was stacked with pipes, ductworks, valves, hand-operated wheels, and other mechanical obstacles. The ship's gyro-compass was also located in the control room, as were the pumps, desalination gear, chart closet and table, and rudder and hydroplane controls. Forward of the control room were the radio shack, and a special space for passive hydrophones which were vital in times of attack. Also forward were the seaman's mess, petty officer's and chief petty officer's messes, and the officer's "wardroom." All of these spaces were simply wide spots in the passageway: seamen and petty officers ate on benches which ran along side the three-high stack of bunks, while the chief petty officers and officers had tiny "alcoves" for their meals. Forward, at the very front of the ship were the four main torpedo tubes, each named after a wife, girl-friend or mother of one of the senior petty officers. There was also another head in the forward area, a great improvement over early type U-boats. The three pressure compartments were sub-divided into seven watertight spaces, which could be isolated by heavy watertight doors (the door jams of which were nicknamed "knee knockers" for obvious reasons), each of which could with-stand pressure equal to that at a depth of 120 meters. The fourth watertight section was welded and riveted atop the main hull. The conning tower contained the attack periscope, torpedo computer, and helm. It also supported the bridge, which could be reached by an aluminum ladder. It was considered lubberly to use the rungs of the ladder, and much more seamanlike to grasp the side rails, each of which was fabricated in a single unwelded piece, and slide from bridge to control room in one fluid motion. Crewmen of the U-115, like ever submariner, soon learned that fractions of a second saved could mean the difference between life and death.

There was, indeed, nothing ashore or float to compare to life on a U-boat. It was unlikely that the U-115, even if success-ful, would return to port before the end of August. During this time, no one would be able to bathe, shave or even change clothes. There was no masking the unpleasantness of living with nearly fifty shipmates, none of whom had taken a bath or put on a fresh set of clothing for the past six weeks.

U-boat crews were highly specialized, and the designers had made no accommodation for passengers. Every man had specific duties. The men with specialized training: radiomen, torpedo men and most especially the enginemen, were responsible for the daily operation and maintenance of equipment aboard the U-115. Men with lesser qualifications, although talented, loaded torpedoes, stood watch on the bridge, manned the deck gun when surfaced, and performed other general tasks throughout the boat. The seaman's mess operated on three watch sections of eight hours each, one for sleeping, one for their assigned duties and one for ship's work. Petty officers, such as the radiomen, rotated three four-hour shifts between 8am and 8pm, and two additional six-hour shifts during the night. Crew members used to sneak into the passageway outside the radio shack, and watch the operators copying Morse messages with their eyes closed, as if asleep. And, perhaps in many ways, they were.

For personal hygiene, the men of the U-115 were forced to rely only on saltwater sponge baths. Cheap perfume was frequently used to control the reek of unwashed bodies. Most of the crew obtained perfume as "favors" from some of the denizens of the various brothels which appeared like mushrooms wherever sailors congregated. Other "shower baths" were less desirable. Going topside during rough weather was detested by everyone, especially in the stormy Atlantic; near freezing waves constantly swept over the conning tower, completely submerging the boat and anyone exposed to the elements. Foul-weather gear did little to keep watchstanders dry, and clothing did not dry well in the steamy and humid atmosphere of the boat.

While Dönitz and other commanders did their best for their operational crews, exigencies of U-boat life made habitability a lower priority than strength of the hull or offensive capabilities. Fresh water was limited and strictly rationed for drinking and cooking; washing and showering were prohibited, and shaving was deferred, thus providing the crews with their traditional "post patrol" beards, some of which, when combed, were luxurious. Personal space was limited to a single locker for each man's personal items. The crew slept surrounded by, and often atop, torpedoes, and the offloading of all but the "ready" torpedoes was silently greeted with joy, particularly among the junior members of the crew. Even with guests aboard, every man would have his own bunk, and would not have to share his bunk with shipmates through out this mission.

No one, not even the officers, had any personal privacy. Three-high bunks lined both sides of the main passageway, and aside from those in the very forward part of the junior mess, located right behind the forward torpedo tubes, traffic in the passageway was constant: Not even Moll or his officers had any privacy. There was a curtain serving as a "door," but it did nothing to attenuate the noise of the foot traffic in the passageway. And, in any event, the Captain's personal space was adjacent to the control room and radio room, for quick access in case of emergency.

Even the use of the "head" was complicated and distasteful. While Type IX boats had two heads, the nearly fifty men had to plan for their use with some forethought. Indeed, rations were selected with some care, lest outbreaks of intestinal problems flowed over (literally!) and caused operational issues. The flush system was a marvel of German engineering, and the very first set of instructions to the SS "visitors" concerned the exact sequence of operation of the various valves to avoid backup, or, worse, backflow.

Although propagandists took pains to avoid reporting negative information about the boats, war cruises took their psychological toll on the crew. Aside from the famous "hours of boredom punctuated with moments of terror," weeks would pass in complete isolation from anything outside the steel walls. Moll always encouraged "periscope liberty," allowing various members of the crew a good look around through the attack 'scope when submerged in relatively safe waters. There was a gramophone provided as part of the communication equipment, and, during surface recharging during darkness, a general-coverage multi-wave wireless brought the latest news and music to the crew spaces. Moll, unlike some other commanders, did not permit the radiomen to tune to stations other than those in Germany or the occupied countries. While everyone knew that homeland broadcasts were heavily censored, life aboard was hard enough without unfiltered information reaching the crew. Card and domino games were constant, and phenomenal amounts of "money" – usually matchsticks or part of the cigarette ration, changed hands. All debts were immediately cancelled, however, the moment the first line went over the side when returning to port.

If nothing else, the crewmen of the U-115 were well fed. Admiral Dönitz made certain that the normal rations, which were a significant cut above that which other types of vessels in the Kriegsmarine served, were always top notch. It was his personal decision to use some of the space freed up by the torpedo offload to accommodate additional special rations for the men. The additional two hundred kilos of provisions included tinned beef, cooked hams, salami, tomato sauce, tinned salmon, cooking chocolate, tea, dried mixed fruit, and nuts as well as condensed milk in tins, plus ten bottles each of brandy, rum, and various liqueurs. An additional ration of 500 cigarettes for each man, and, most importantly, 50 kilos of almost unavailable "real" coffee, had been smuggled on a German-flagged merchant vessel which had broken interment on the coast of Brazil. Most of the additional provisions would not be subject to spoilage, giving the crew something to look forward to at each of their two daily meals.

Over the two-week transit between the Bay of Biscay and the Flemish Cap, everyone on the crew became acquainted with their unexpected, and as it turned out, involuntary, shipmates. They had expected to be transferred by surface ship from Spitzenbergen to the east coast of Greenland, as part of a force deployed to protect critical German weather stations north of Dansborg, but now found themselves aboard a U-boat, wallowing its way across the North Atlantic. Privately, Hirsch and Fiskdal blamed Obersturmführer Braun for the unwelcomed change of plans. Hirsch, in private conversation with his messmates, continually referred to his detachment leader as *Der Hitler Jugend,* or even more irreverently as Hitler's bastard child. Hirsch, a Freikorps veteran from Altona on the east bank of the Elbe, was a party member, a veteran street fighter and from time to time had served as a bodyguard for Karl Kaufmann, the Gauleiter of Hamburg. When not so employed, he told his new messmates, he was an independent "businessman" in the areas surrounding the Davidwache, an area of very tough sailors' dives in the St. Pauli district of Hamburg. "An independent businessman, indeed," remarked Petty Officer Unger, appointed by the First Watch officer to be Hirsch's 'sea daddy', – "pimp is more like it." Those of the mess who had frequented the Davidstraße and the Herbertstraße in the district knew exactly what he meant. To give Hirsch his due, though, when he awoke the first morning after coming aboard, it was as if he had been a lifelong teetotaler. There were no signs of a hangover, which impressed some of the older crewmen. "A real professional drunk," one remarked to the knowing smiles of the others.

Garrulous as Hirsch was with the men of the petty officer's mess, his comrade, Lars-Anders Fiskdal, was his complete opposite. A much older man, and taciturn, he answered most questions with a single word or short statement, and volunteered little information. A native of Strandebarm, in the forests east of Bergen, he had emigrated from Norway to North America shortly after the end of the first war, and had spent over a dozen years working in the lumbering woods near Badger and Botwood for the Anglo-Newfoundland Company. More importantly, he had traveled several times on the Newfoundland Railway, and had a good understanding of the geography of much of the island. He spoke English well – indeed, better than his German – and had joined Vidkun Quisling's Norwegian Nasjonal Samling, in part over his dissatisfaction with the economic situation in Norway when he returned in 1933. At the height of the depression, and of his own desperation, he found release and a certain level of remuneration, when the SS Norge was established after *Operation Weserübung*, the German invasion of Norway in April 1940. The general consensus among the small number of chief petty officers with whom he associated was that he was a decent fellow, caught up, as many were, by the events of the day.

None of the officers, nor anyone else who associated with him, felt the same about the detachment's leader, SS-Obersturmführer Fritz Braun. "Meaner than cat shit" was the pithy, and mostly accurate, evaluation provided by Strebel, the chief engineer, whose bunk was immediately adjacent to the third-officer's regular space, temporarily occupied by Braun. Born in Lehnitz, just south of the infamous concentration camp Sachsenhausen at Oranienburg, his father was a minor functionary in the Deutsche Reichsbahn, and his mother was an adult leader in the Bund Deutscher Mädel, the female component of the Hitler Jungen. Both were early and ardent party members. With a family structure such as his, it was no surprise that his elder brother Thedor and he became active in the HJ at early ages. Both joined the Deutsches Jungvolk (DJ), the "Cub Scouts" of the Hitler Youth movement at age 10, and migrated to the HJ itself at age fourteen. Both attended HJ training academies, and Fritz was invited to participate in the 1938 national rallies at Nürnberg . Thedor became a member of the SS in 1940, was later transferred as a company commander to the 12th SS Panzer Division (Hitlerjugend) and would die at Caen in 1944. But that was yet in the future. Frantz (called Fritz) followed his brother into the SS, and building upon his experiences in the Hitler Jungen, trained first as a sharpshooter, and later as a sniper. While he was by no means the top graduate of his class, his proficiency was enough to qualify him for independent duty, and it was in this capacity that he found himself on the U-115.

Braun had an opinion on every subject, no matter how obscure, and regardless of how much or how little experience he had in the area. His political views hewed sharply to the Party line, and he was astounded to see and hear the relaxed, indeed, cynical opinions of his erstwhile shipmates. It was not necessary for Moll to remind his officers or men that they had strangers in their midst, and that each should guard his tongue when the SS men were present. This was somewhat more difficult for those who shared their mess with Hirsch than for those who shared space with Lars-Anders Fiskdal; all had at least a grudging respect for the other's skill and bravery, but conversation with Fiskdal was painful because of his limited German. Fortunately, Fritz Braun's personality made it unlikely that anyone would want to enter into long heart-felt conversations with him anyway, and as the long transit continued, the ship settled into a routine which, if not particularly welcoming to their passengers, was at least tolerable.

15 NORTH ATLANTIC OCEAN

(Tactical Situation Charts Follow This Chapter) *(Charts A.R.E)*

05 August 1941
BdU Chart 3401
Grid Square AK+
North Atlantic Ocean
1800Z

Were you to ask a civilian to name the U-boat warrior's main enemy, most would reply "the British." Those better informed might reply "The Allies' Corvettes and Destroyers." Those of a more geopolitical inclination might say "The merchant vessels bringing war materials to Britain: aviation petrol, steel, foodstuffs, ammunition." Those who served in U-boats would have one answer, "Our chief enemy is the North Atlantic Ocean."

On a smooth summer evening, gazing into the luminescence of a cruise ship or transatlantic liner's wake, one could be forgiven for being lulled into a false sense of security. But even at the best of times, in the strongest and most seaworthy of vessels, the North Atlantic can be treacherous waters. A constant train of storms, moving west to east, can bedevil mariners in any season. The weather is particularly severe just north of the Tropic of Cancer, and just south of the Arctic Circle. It is there that various currents meet and stir the waters. For those on large ships: capital men-of-war, aircraft carriers, large bulk carriers or cruise ships, it can be an uncomfortable place. For those who go down to the sea in small boats: corvettes, destroyers, or submarines, it can be deadly. While winter brings freezing gales from the northeast, causing ice buildup on weather decks and bulkheads; mid-summer brings tropical depressions, gales and even hurricanes, traveling eastward from the coast of North America. Such was the case in August, 1941.

After leaving Dönitz' office, the nine commanders agreed to meet for dinner that evening at the club *Sechs Titten,* a favorite of Second Flotilla officers. By 1900 M.E.T. the wine and beer was flowing copiously. Sensing a momentary lull in the conversation about potential storms, Hans-Heinz Linder, the senior and most experienced commander in the group, rapped on the table to draw the attention of the others. As the group quieted, he spoke.

"Kameraden," he began, "while the intelligence provided by the Abwehr, and the strategic planning provided by Admiral Dönitz and his staff is fine, we are left with translating strategic intent into tactical action. It is best that we come to some agreement here, as all indications are that we are going to be busy once we reach our patrol stations. The first decision has to do with how we can most effectively organize the patrol lines of which Admiral Dönitz spoke. I suspect that when we receive our sealed orders, each of us will have assignments to specific positions along those two lines. While we'll be spit into two lines, the distance which needs to be covered is fairly large, and each of us will be responsible for an area nearly 500 km square. Does anyone have any ideas as to how we can best coordinate the patrol, since we will be operating under complete radio silence? We will certainly listen closely for each other's 'on station' report directed to BdU, but from that point on we'll risk being like blind men looking for a black cat in a darkened room. Any thoughts?"

"Well," responded Günther Krech, commander of the U-558. "I made an observation earlier this afternoon. I stopped for a haircut (the others murmured their appreciation for his now clean shaven appearance), and as I watched the barber, I had an inspiration. All of you have been to the barber at one time or another in your lives, right? I know, I know, it's been years for some of you and for a few of you, there's not much left to cut, in any event. But as I watched him prepare to cut my hair, I noticed how he rather rhythmically squeezed the levers of his hair clippers – perhaps it is a nervous habit of barbers – I can not say. But as I watched how the blades crossed each other, one set of blades going left, the other going right, I had an idea. Suppose each of the lines sets up, equidistant from the center longitude, with the boats equidistant from each other on a north-south axis. If we operate in a circular pattern – we can effectively cover a wide area with little fear of overlap or omission. One group will operate clockwise, the other counterclockwise, all staying within the limits that the BdU has set for us. I haven't a pen, or a piece of paper on which to draw it for you, but I think you may get the idea. What say?"

Krech was well regarded, and the others nodded, discussing the suggestion. Zimmerman of the U-112 gathered up the empty beer bottles on the table and arrayed them in two lines on the table. Since there were nine boats, and only five bottles, he called for another round for everyone. With beer bottles, both empty and full, Krech demonstrated his idea, and with much further discussion, and some modification, the plan was adopted. "I'm certain that our specific starting spots will be contained in our sealed orders, and since we're all Type VIIC boats, essentially similar, our capabilities should be well know to each other. As soon as one of us makes contact, I suspect our orders will permit us to break our silence, and we can communicate the attack just as if we were approaching a convoy of merchantmen." He left unsaid the very clear realization that this would be a much more closely guarded and heavier armed target, and the risks to each of the U-boats on the patrol line would be grave.

The party continued until the late evening hours, and avoiding the strict curfew and blackout in Lorient, those whose boats were undergoing maintenance returned to the billets established for them in the town, accompanied by the Brest-based officers, who would return north in the morning. The others returned to their boats to supervise last minute preparations before going back to the North Atlantic.

All boats departed on schedule, either Lorient or Brest, and all save Gelhaus in the U-143 arrived on station by midday on August 3. Each boat sent the required "on station" message to U-boat headquarters, and each message was copied by the other boats. Fortunately, there was a lull in the weather; it was relatively calm with westerly winds of less than 15 knots, and light seas through-out the patrol area. But weather broadcasts from stations at Basse Lande and Croix Dhins forecasted deteriorating conditions over the next several days. More importantly, the evening transmissions from DXB had begun broadcasting the coded messages that Churchill was at sea, although none of the patrol boats knew the details of the ship or ships now streaming toward them. And, since the boats were west of Kap Farvel, Greenland, the forecasts were less detailed than those to the east of the Denmark Straits, where German weather ships were operating. Several of the radio-men resorted to an old U-boatman's trick of listening to the inshore-waters weather broadcast along the U.S. coast, through stations WCC at Chatham, Mass. and WSC at Tuckerton, New Jersey. While the forecast was valid only to sixty miles from the shore, it did not take much experience to extrapolate the weather conditions farther out, so long as the rate of advance of the storm was known. Each captain knew that the fine weather would soon be overtaken by an oncoming gale, the remnants of a tropical storm which had begun in the very warm waters east of the Florida Coast. Conditions would quickly worsen, and a full gale could be expected in grid AK by late evening on Tuesday, 05 August.

As the day wore on, the weather did begin to worsen. Since the storm was still to the northwest of the patrol area, the boats began to encounter strong southwesterly winds as the storm rotated clockwise. In many respects, this was the worst position of all: aside from their "turn around" headings to run the reciprocal bearing of their patrol assignments, wind and waves were striking either on their port quarter when southbound, or just aft of their starboard beam when northbound. U-boats suffered four conditions in heavy seas; because their hull was designed for maximum efficiency underwater, when surfaced, they tended to yaw, pitch, roll and porpoise. Yaw – the side to side swing of the bow, was similar to that which happens to an automobile which suffers a flat tire at speed; it veers left or right, and the driver overcompensates, leaving a "wiggle worm" trail of skid marks behind. Pitch – the up and down motion of the vessel – could be extreme, particularly when, as in this storm, the wind direction conflicted with the normal climatic progression of wave trains from west to east. For the men in the forward compartments, it was both nauseating and dangerous – some boats had suffered sudden changes in angle related to the horizontal of greater than 60 degrees in seas such as these. Roll, of course, was well known, and, while this storm was not expected to reach levels where the conning tower or "sail" was in danger of submerging, 20 degree swings starboard to port were probable as the storm worsened as it crossed through the center of the patrol area. And finally, porpoising was the unfortunate habit of U-boats and other submersibles to change buoyancy quickly. A boat lying in wait for a convoy, barely submerged and with decks awash, might soon find itself popping 8 meters or more above the wave crests, ruining any attempt at stealth and making the vessel an easily spotted target. And, to make matters even more complex, Radio DXB transmitted the second of the coded messages shortly after local midnight. Charlie and his Orchestra – for some reason, a very popular musical program, featuring second rate musicians playing first rate songs – began playing Glenn Miller's "Chattanooga Choo Choo," which the U-boat's sealed orders indicated was a warning that *HMS Prince of Wales* had been identified as the capital ship carrying Churchill, and was expected in the general patrol area within twenty four hours. Several boats decided to remain surfaced after sunrise to improve their changes of a visible sighting of the enemy ship, while others decided to submerge and to rely on hydrophones to pick up the distinctive sound-signature of a capital warship. Georg Zimmermann in U-112, the northernmost boat of the eastern element of the patrol, submerged at 0400Z. Although he made due consideration of the comfort and safety of the crew, he exhibited good tactical reasoning for his decision.

Hydrophones (Gruppenhorchgerat or GHG) were simple but critical elements in a U-boat's arsenal of offensive and defensive weapons. Consisting of sets of underwater microphones, which listened for propeller noises, the third watch officer who was traditionally responsible for communications equipment measured the amount of time it took for sound to arrive at each microphone. He could then triangulate the bearing of the vessel from the U-boat. Good operators, when the engines were stopped and silence maintained on the boat, could distinguish between merchantman and warship, often, in the case of large conveys, up to 100 kilometers away.

Zimmermann was more fortunate than several other boats on this patrol. Beginning with U-111, boats constructed at

Aktien-Gesellschaft Weser in Bremen were outfitted with a much improved system of hydrophones, The "Balkon Great" (Balcony Apparatus) was an improved version of GHG. Consisting of an array of forty-eight hydrophones and improved electronics, it enabled much more accurate readings to be taken. And, as a final advantage, both the third officer, Wilhelm Wagner, and the chief Radioman, Hans Becker, had just completed a short course at Kiel on the tactical use of the new equipment. Becker, in particular, nick-named "Hasenohren" (rabbit ears) by his messmates, was particularly astute in separating the sound of cavitating propellers from the mating cries of krill, the "cricketing" of shrimp, or the fascinating, if bizarre, sounds of cetaceans copulating. They both settled in for a long watch as the ship settled into its underwater routine.

At 0715Z, Wagner asked Zimmermann if he could level the boat at 60 meters depth. He and Becker had learned at Kiel of newly discovered "channels" – generally where waters of various density, riding on deep undersea currents, met. That depth would also minimize the impact of wind-wave interface noises at the surface. The water was colder at that depth – other crew men quickly searched out their jerseys and jackets – but it was the optimum tactical solution to the problem at hand. As they settled at that depth, Becker made a complete 360 degree scan with the hydrophone array. As expected, there were no close targets, and he began to slowly rotate, concentrating for several minutes on each fifteen degree quadrant extending out from the boat.

There was a great deal of mixed engine noise to the north-north-east of the U-112, and Wagner and Becker quickly surmised that it was a convoy heading away from them, at a distance of some 90 kilometers or more. From the cavitations (the unique sound of bubbles bursting as water churned up by the propellers broke the surface), they deduced that it was a relatively fast convoy

189

westbound from Canada to Britain. (It was, in fact, convoy HX141, which – because of the preoccupation of so many U-boats, reached Liverpool on August 11 without losing a ship to enemy action).

Shortly after 1100Z, while scanning the quadrant to the south-east of their position at 54.2N-33.8W, Becker began to detect a faint, but strengthening indication that a large vessel might be moving from their northeast to southwest. He reported it immediately to Watch Officer Wagner, who listened through a second pair of earphones and detected the rhythmic "thumping" of a fast moving target. He delayed reporting this to Zimmermann for several minutes, since both he and the captain assumed that the *Prince of Wales* would be traveling in consort with protecting cruisers and destroyers. As the target signature became louder, he called the captain to the sound station and handed him his earphones. "We've held this target for several minutes, Kapitän." He reported. "It appears to be a large warship, and it's position indicates it will be crossing our bow in about twenty minutes if we continue on this southbound track. While we can't esti-mate the distance before us, all indications are that our closest point of approach will be at about 15 kilometers or more – out of range, even were we to surface now and actively pursue the target. Zimmermann continued to listen, as he contemplated his options. *Prince of Wales* was the second of the *King George V* class of battleships, and bore four propellers. Working closely with Bauer, he asked that the signal be "fine tuned" as closely as possible. Listening as the still unidentified target approached the U-112, Zimmerman felt certain that he could hear three dis-tinct, and slightly asynchronous beats within the overall signal. "I think it's a warship, Wagner," he said to the third officer standing at his left shoulder "Although I hear only three propeller notes in there. Are there any three-prop warships active in the British fleet?" Wagner reached up for a binder on the shelf above the apparatus, and quickly scanned the sound signatures of enemy capital warships. "None that I can see, Kapitän," he replied after several seconds.

"Well, then, there's the possibility that the captain of the *Prince of Wales* is operating on reduced power, but why in heaven's name would he do that? If that's him, he's carrying the most valuable cargo that he's ever likely to see, even in a long career at sea. Wagner, signal for absolute quiet throughout the boat, and have the Chief drop us to the minimum number of revolutions to keep us at this depth without blowing tubes or taking in additional ballast. Becker, unplug your earphones, and let the rest of the crew listen for about two minutes before this target gets too much closer and is a danger to us, even if it does "cross our T" by 15 kilometers or so."

They did as ordered, and, as the boat settled into neutral buoyancy, heard a sound not unlike a rushing Deutsche Reichsbahn express from Berlin to Munich. "Men of the U-112," he announced over the internal communication system, "listen closely. I know that none of you are ever so foolish to listen to our enemy's propaganda broadcasts. But listen closely, now. Do you hear that sound from our hydrophones? That's Winston Churchill, no doubt sitting down to his midday meal, thinking that he has outwitted the Kriegsmarine, as he goes off to meet with his crony, Roosevelt. Think again, Mr. Churchill, think again."

He turned to the chief radioman. "Well done, Becker, well done indeed. As soon as you hear the Doppler shift indicating that he has passed before us – and I damn the luck who placed him just outside our reach – signal BdU to contact all boats and transmit the current position of the target. There's no reason to maintain radio silence now. The captain and navigator of the *Prince of Wales*

191

certainly know where they are, and now so do we. It's time to let our Kameraden in on our little secret, don't you think?"

The message, encrypted in the Enigma system, and marked "Most Urgent" was dispatched within the next five minutes. Barely a minute long, it listed U-112's current grid location, the estimated distance and bearing to the target, estimated speed and the details of the three-screw signature detected by Zimmermann and his crew. It reached the BdU receiver sites immediately, and after decoding and re-coding was broadcast to the fleet within an additional twenty minutes.

Boats in the patrol group who had remained on the surface received the message immediately; others would receive it as they surfaced for recharging and extended their antennas for the constant U-boat broadcast from shore. One of the surfaced boats, Kapitänleutnant Paul Schröder in the U-114 was northbound at 52.5-35.8W. Schröder quickly plotted the reported position of the target and his own position, immediately recognizing that, with a bit of luck, he could intercept the British warship. He ordered a continual turn to port, coming around to a course of 195 degrees true, and ordered his chief engineer, Lieutenant zur see (I) Ernst Hoffmann, to make full revolutions driving the U-boat to a speed of 17 knots. Schröder and his officers, First Officer Friedrich Richter, Second Watch Officer Hermann Neumann and Third Watch Officer Melchior Schmitz, gathered around the attack plotting board in the operations compartment.

The boat, in the teeth of the still strengthening storm, rocked violently. Gripping the overhead piping for stability, they marked the plotting board with the information newly received. "We have a chance to get him," Schröder began. "If he stays on the course that Georg reported, he'll be at his closest point to us just before midnight. This storm will make it incredibly difficult for us to spot him. Neumann, if you can read the almanac with this blasted rolling, tell me the conditions for later this evening." With difficulty, Neumann read out, "Sunset occurs at 2203Z, and full darkness at 2248. I say full darkness, but the moon rises, full, at 2155Z, even before the sun is set. The moon will arise from our southeast, about 35 degrees above our horizon. Not that it will make much difference, I'm afraid: we'll have solid cloud cover throughout the evening and into the early hours of the morning, before this storm has moved off to our east."

"I'm not so certain of that," Schröder replied. "If we stay north of his predicted track, and he is making over 28 knots, which would be expected, we can have him on our port quarter a few minutes after 2200 this evening. We'll still have about forty five minutes of twilight, and, if we stay north he will be silhouetted by the rising moon. There are too many damn variables here – I assume he is zigzagging, and we have no real idea of his speed of advance, or if he's planning a change of course in the next ten hours, but we must work with what we have, and hope that the other boats are doing likewise. I would break radio silence myself, but the target is moving into our area, and I don't want to risk their HF-DF operators locking into our transmission. But we must be ready – Richter, have your best torpedomen check each of the four forward torpedoes. Have them take the strongest men on the boat with them, and pull the gratings from the deck plates so that, if we have to reload we can save a few minutes. In fact, get at least one torpedo onto the chain hoist, and then pull the men who berth in the forward torpedo room out and distribute them evenly around the ship. I don't want that torpedo to start swinging around – leave it in position, but fasten the hoist to the lifting brackets. If we want it, we will want it quickly, but there's no need placing men in harm's way if it starts swinging about. You all know what to do – this may be our only chance – or indeed, any boat's chance to strike a fatal blow at the British where it will hurt them most."

The torpedomen and their helpers went about their duties. Conditions were incredibly difficult. With the boat now headed south-southwest, the wind and waves were moving from stern to bow, causing the boat to pitch uncontrollably. Checking the loaded tubes was not a difficult task, per se, but the danger of being slammed by an inner torpedo tube door, swinging out of control, was acute. Nevertheless, after much struggle, and with continual prayer to the gods of profanity (without whom, sailors would not be sailors), the condition of each "hot" torpedo was verified, and reported to the captain. Lifting the deck plates provided an even more strenuous exercise; the difficulty came not from the size or weight of each plate, but from the fact that there was no convenient place to put the plate after it had been lifted from its place. About a quarter ton of provisions had to be moved to compartments behind the forward torpedo room, bunks tied up, and space provided to stand the plates on their side, along the bulkhead. All of this was accomplished, but not without injuries, albeit minor, caused by the instability of the platforms on which they had to stand to accomplish the work.

Schröder dispatched his second officer, and two additional lookouts to the bridge. Conditions there were horrific; in addition to the wild rolling of the surfaced U-boat, every time the boat pitched forward a deluge of cold water inundated the watchstanders, and flowed down the coning tower ladderway to the operations space below. The length of the watches was shortened significantly; to leave the same bridge crew to long operate under those circumstances would have been homicidal.

Shortly after the watch change at 1600, Schröder called his first officer, Friedrich Richter to the operations table. "I have to make a tactical decision, Fredi" Schröder began. "While we can make perhaps 15 knots at emergency flank speed while on surface, we're not making that much distance across the ground, with this wind and weather pushing us on our starboard beam. I'm going to take us down, and see if we can learn anything from the hydrophones. If the enemy is traveling at his flank speed of nearly 30 knots, we still have a chance to intercept, but if he zigzags, as he should, our odds are only 50-50 that he'll be anywhere near his base course when we finally make it to the intercept point. If we are lucky – and we'll have to be very lucky – we'll have him "crossing our T" at an oblique angle – perhaps from 50 or 55 degrees off to our starboard. In that case, we'll fire all four bow torpedoes, and hope to heaven that we can reload before his escorts turn after us. We'll surface again at sunset, and stay on the surface for as long as we can. Whatever happens, it is going to be a very long and difficult night for all of us."

"There's one thing that bothers me, Kapitän." Richter replied. "112 reports cavitations from the capital ship only. Where are his escorts? Surely he has not come through his air-protection gap unescorted; is there something we are not understanding about this target? Could this be a decoy? Are we moving into some sort of trap, Kapitän?"

"It worries me too, Fredi. I've been worried about that since Georg's message arrived right after noon. It's possible, I suppose, that the *Prince of Wales* sent the escorts back when she entered into this gale-front, although I can't imagine the commander of a ship of the line doing such a thing. A German captain would certainly not do that. Even Admiral Lütjens had *Prinz Eugen* and three destroyers: the *Lody*, the *Eckoldt*, and the *Z23*; a couple of our boats, and minesweepers – and he was just going raiding, and not carrying the Führer or any party bigwigs to a conference or anything. But to travel these waters unescorted – no, Fredi, I don't believe it either. But before long we're going to know, one way or another. Have everyone who can, grab something to eat. We'll be out of daylight soon, and there'll be no chance again for several hours."

By 2200, U-114 was at her closest point of approach to the projected track of the *Prince of Wales*. Even with the main periscope raised to its maximum height, the waves were so intense that the lenses were underwater half the time, and shedding water the rest of the time. Peering intensely to the southeast, he could not even discern the full moon. "It's like looking into a *Stroboskop* (Strobe light)," Schröder remarked to no one in particular. "These clouds are moving so quickly with the wind that it makes it difficult for me to focus my eyes against the disk of the moon. And, even on a clear night, the distance to the horizon from the bridge is less than 15 kilometers. Tonight it will be almost impossible to sight the target unless he is directly on top of us. Third officer, have your hydrophone operators monitor closely to the quadrants to our northwest and southwest – we'll stay down to the last possible moment, so that when we need a burst of speed we can surface, run in on the target, and then get as deep as we can go. Is that understood?"

Melchior Schmitz, a taciturn Bavarian, did as ordered. Even the hydrophones were of limited use; the wave noise made even the largest of ships difficult to hear. But at 2310, Schmitz reported a strong audible signature, although it was somewhat south of the anticipated track of the *Prince of Wales*. "Surface now," Schröder called out. "Chief, make maximum revolutions when we surface, Richter, have your best lookouts ready to get up the ladder. We're only going to get one shot at this one."

U-114 surfaced, and proceeded at flank speed in the direction of the target. The hydrophones were useless, and the continual motion of the boat on all axes of movement made visual sighting almost impossible. Nevertheless at 2326, lookout Dieter Krack rang out "Ship on the port bow, unknown type, distance estimated to be 2500 meters!" All eyes strained in the direction indicated by Krack's left hand, pointing in the direction to which he had made his observation. Richter called down the speaking tube to the skipper in the control room below, "Very large vessel, unknown type, appears to be moving parallel and away from us, at 2500!" It was clear that they had intercepted the *Prince of Wales* as the battleship was on a port-tack as part of her zigzag plan. If it continued, the best shot would be toward the stern, and not an oblique broadside, as Schröder had hoped. With the difference in speed between hunter and hunted, the best shot would have to be taken within the next ninety seconds, or the range would be too great for the Type 2 torpedoes loaded in the forward tubes. "Torpedo room, forward! Prepare to fire!" Richter locked his long range glasses into the target repeater, which automatically modified settings on all four torpedoes. "Ready One!. . . Fire! Two. . . Fire! Three. . . Fire! Four. . . Fire!"

"All torpedoes away!" came the reply from the forward torpedo room. Schröder had clicked his stopwatch at the command to fire, and watched as the seconds crept by: "Fifteen–Thirty–Forty-Five–Sixty–Eighty–One Hundred." There was no sound of impact. *Prince of Wales* sailed on, unaware of her near tryst with disaster, safely into the arms of three waiting Canadian destroyers who would meet her shortly after dawn, and escort her on the last leg of her most important mission of the war.

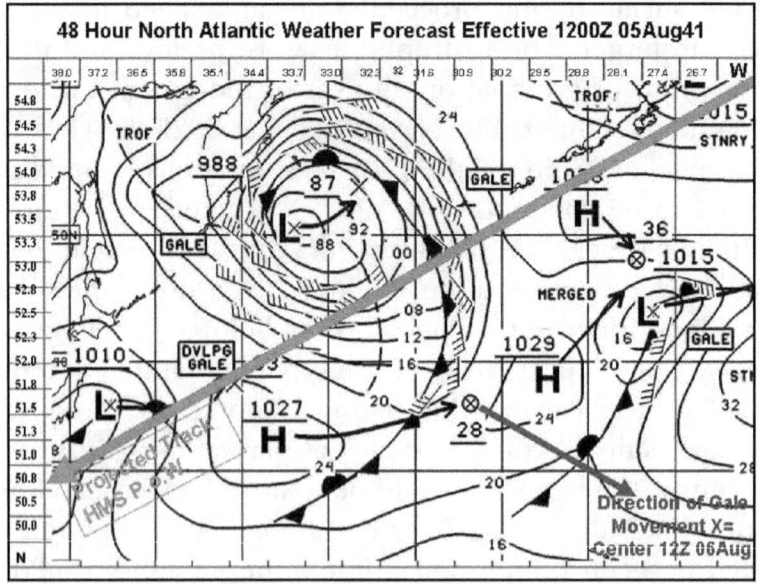

Track of HMS Prince of Wales, 04–08 August, 1941

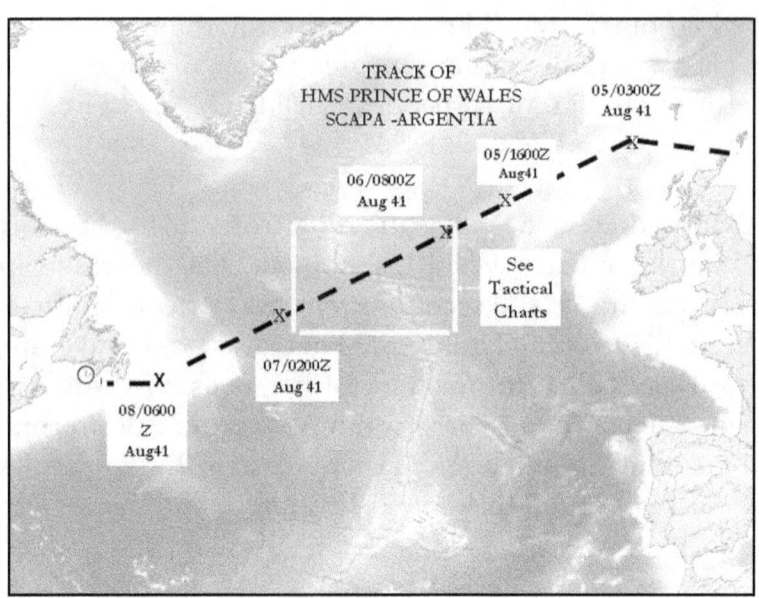

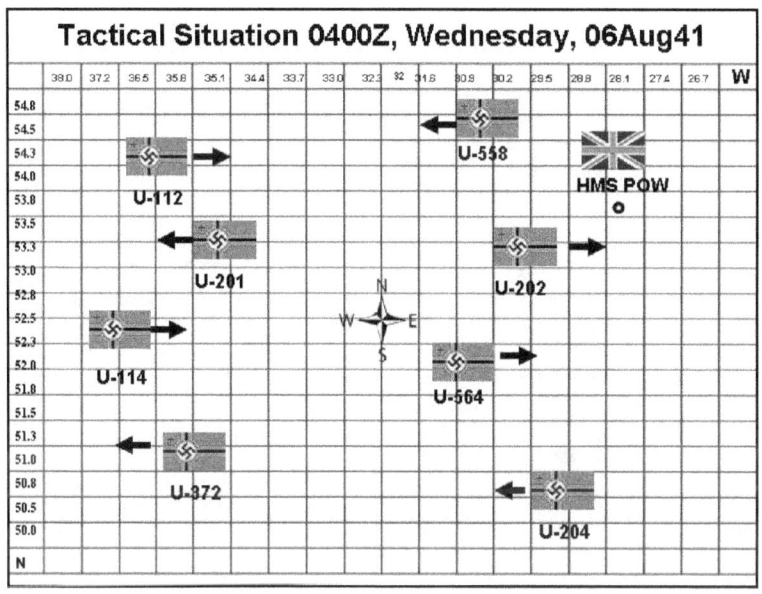

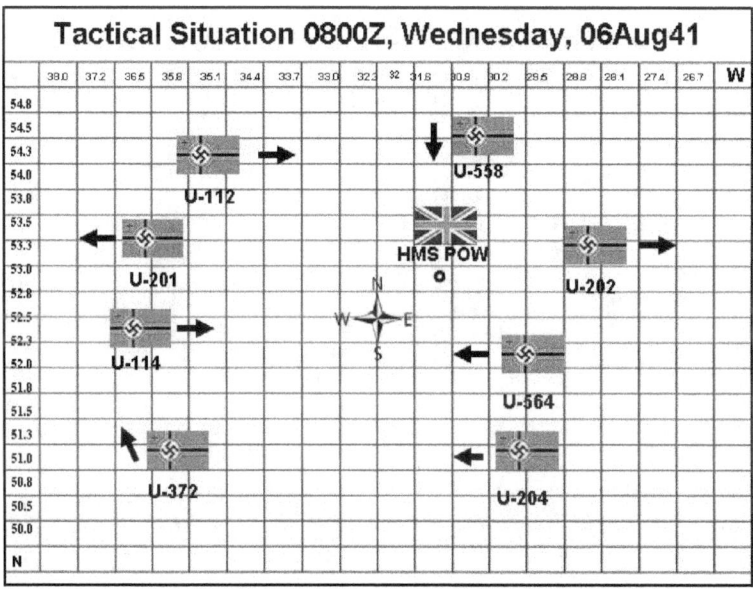

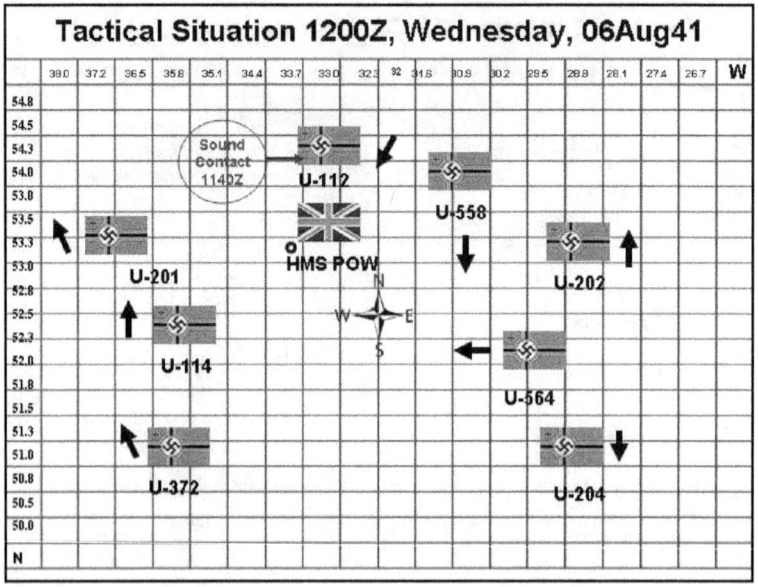

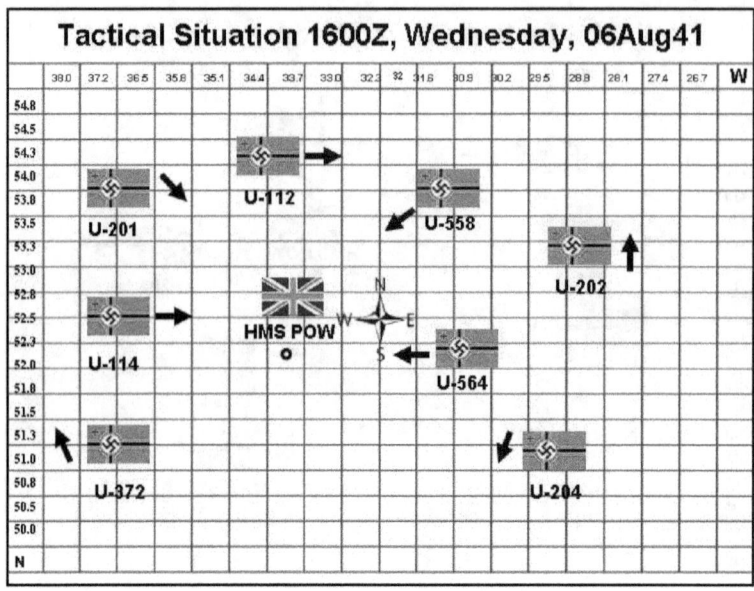

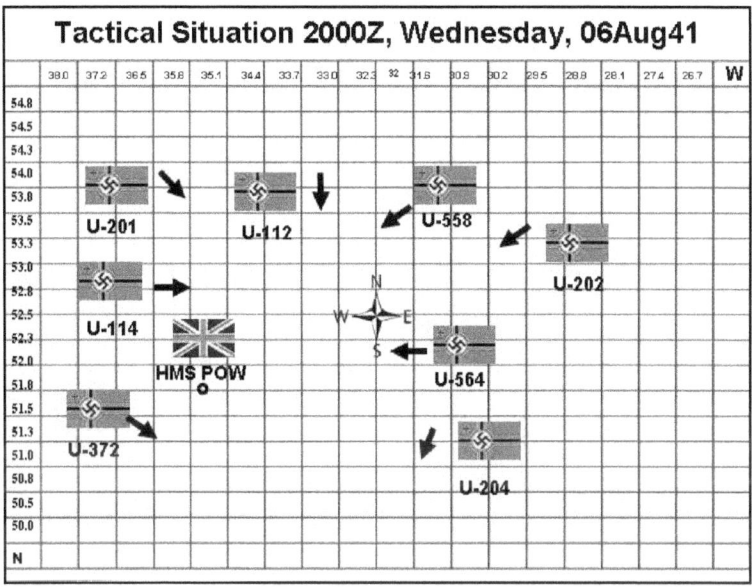

Tactical Situation 2000Z, Wednesday, 06Aug41

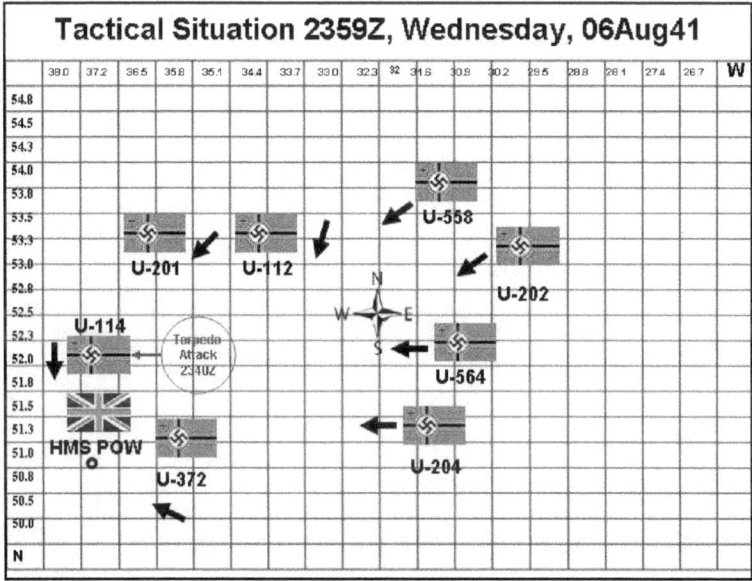

Tactical Situation 2359Z, Wednesday, 06Aug41

16 ABOARD USS ARKANSAS (bb-33)

04 August 1941
Naval Radio Station NWP
Argentia Newfoundland
0815 NST

Hannigan's status among his shipmates had risen sharply after word of his adventures in Freshwater had spread. "Didn't know the boy had it in him," seemed to be the general consensus. Boudreaux, with pride better fitting an elder brother, told everyone in the barracks about Hannigan and his "main squeeze," particularly how they managed to get together for several hours in an "honest ta gawd real house." Their barracks mates, more used to "romance" in a commercial establishment or standing in a doorway, were suitably impressed. No mention was made of ice cream, nor Hambone's fascination with the radio. The attitude of gentle derision was evolving, ever so slightly, to one of grudging admiration.

His admirers did not include Chief McCroy. After giving the matter some thought, Lt. Carpentier had asked Chief McCroy to temporarily assign Hannigan to a monitoring watch, tracking signals which might be of interest to the intelligence community. A division officer "asking" a Chief Petty Officer was simply a formality; protocol between junior officers and CPOs never mistook the officer who was nominally in charge with the man who really made things happen. Junior officers who got cross-wired with chief pretty officers who worked for them often found their

203

promising careers gone badly off track. And chief petty officers had long memories.

Hambone, who could always rescue defeat from the jaws of victory, didn't make things any better. He spent much of the mid-watch making himself a cozy monitoring station on the rear test bench. He acquired a second receiver, a typewriter and some reference materials for what was becoming, in all but name, his private nest. It never occurred to him to ask permission, and was surprised that Chief McCroy was not impressed by his weekend industry. Although off watch at 0730, he was back at the radio station by 0745, and much of his Monday morning was consumed with returning things to their proper places. By 0930 he was standing in the passageway outside the Chief's office, awaiting a summons from the great man himself.

Doyle motioned for him to enter, and then quickly left the office. It was going to be ugly, and ugly situations often spilled over upon innocent bystanders. Hannigan stood before the chief's desk, in something approaching a position of attention. McCroy looked him over for several long moments without saying a word. He shook his head.

"Hannigan, what part of 'This is the Navy and not your personal playpen' do you not understand? You are an RM3 – that's radioman third class, in case you missed that during your three days at radioman's school. And in my Navy – and my Navy is *your* Navy, sailor – an RM3 is lower than whale shit. In the short time since you appeared on my doorstep, you have managed to irritate your first LPO, RM1 Holden, and encouraged the next one, Boudreaux, to venture off the straight and narrow path for the umpteenth time. You've misused a Navy pickup truck under the guise of delivering cable which you do not have, to a ship which is not here. You took that truck off base by bribing the motor pool guys, and no doubt done other shit which I haven't heard about yet, but which I surely will. And that's on your good days, Hannigan. On your *bad* days, you've got the Lieutenant all worked up about spies, and secret codes, and decoder rings and I don't know what other kind of down right tomfoolery. And what's this I hear about you onboard a Canadian corvette, too? Boy – if you want to go to sea on a ship that rolls on a wet lawn, Hannigan, I can fix that for your real fast. And by the time you'd come back ashore, sailor, you will damn well know where an RM3 stands in this man's Navy. Am I making myself clear to you, sailor? Am I?"

Hannigan attempted to stammer out a simple "Yes, chief" but was interrupted again. "Don't answer me back, sailor. If I want your opinion, I'll tell you what your opinion is. Is that clear?" Hannigan wisely remained silent.

His vitriol expended, Chief McCroy looked skyward for a moment.

"Hannigan, I have no idea what you are hearing back on that SX-28 on the bench. There is, I suppose, the possibility that you are on to something, although I don't have the slightest idea what it might be. I'm about 99% convinced it has a logical explanation, and it's nothing that ought to concern us. Mr. Carpentier seems to think, though, that we ought to check it out, and let the rest of the fleet in on your little fantasy. The USS *Arkansas* (BB-33) just anchored at berth one on Friday, and you and I are going to get dressed up like good battleship sailors and escort Mr. Carpentier on a wardroom visit with their Communications Officer and several of his top radiomen. Take a good look around when you get there, Hannigan, because there are going to be a lot of good sailors in that room, and trust me on this, son, you ain't one of 'em.

Notice I didn't say 'good radiomen' because that's something all together different. But not till I get done with you, Hannigan, can you ever claim the title of 'sailor.' Is that clear, Hannigan?"

"Doyle! DOYLE! Damn it, you can never find a yeoman when you want one. Hannigan, get back down to the barracks and fetch Boudreaux and tell him to get his ass in here, ASAP. And you come back with him, is that clear? Go!"

Hannigan did as ordered. All in all he had heard worse from the Catholic brothers in the orphanage, and at least Chief McCroy didn't bust him back to seaman recruit, and take away his crow. He got the keys to the bread truck from Doyle, and hustled back to the barracks as ordered. Frenchy was still awake. He grabbed Frenchy and within a very few minutes they were both standing at attention in front of the chief's desk.

"Boudreaux, if you ever have any plans of making RM1, they're fading fast, shipmate. Rule one of being a good petty officer is looking after, and looking out for, your men. This sack-of-shit is beginning to tarnish your reputation, and if I hadn't spent my first tour on the *USS Louisiana,* I'd have your ass so far up Bayou Teche that it'd be snowing. And it never snows down in Cajun country – that's why your grandpappy left Canada in the first place. Now, this fine sailor (pointing to Hannigan) and Lt. Carpentier and I are going to take a little trip by launch out to the *Arkansas* at 1400 local. You ain't coming along, but don't think you are getting away easy on this thing, Frenchy. Because at 1315 this afternoon, RM3 Hannigan here is going to be standing in front of this desk, A-J-squared-away, from his flat hat to his spit shined dress shoes. I don't care what you have to do to him – scrub his gear with holystones for all I care, but he is going to be standing there, at attention, looking like he just came off the front of a Cracker Jack box. No gear adrift, no

Irish pennants, no stains, rips, tears or wrinkles on his uniform, his thirteen buttons all buttoned in the right holes, and so-help-me, if you need to get him to iron his socks too, then do it. You're an old battlewagon sailor, Boudreaux; you know where I'm coming from on this. Beg, borrow or steal whatever you need, but if this 'sailor' from your section comes in here looking like a refugee from the lucky bag; you, Boudreaux, as well as he, are going to become lifelong buddies working down in the scullery among the rats and roaches. I trust you get the idea, Boudreaux."

"And have that other idiot, Doyle, gather up all the logs and notes that Hannigan has made about his Captain Marvel magic decoder ring, or whatever the hell he is listening to, and set them up nicely in a folder for Mr. Carpentier to carry along." Chief McCroy reached into his desk drawer and retrieved a pad of request chits, the ubiquitous form used to communicate between divisions or commands on a base. He signed the chit, and handed it to Boudreaux. "And get him into the barber shop on the way back to the barracks. I've marked this chit 'urgent'. I want him high and tight and so squared away that those guys on the battle-wagon will think we shanghaied a jarhead and stuck him into a sailor suit. Now, MOVE!"

Boudreaux knew that there were times when leeway in carrying out orders was appropriate, and times when there was not. "That's why they call 'em orders and not suggestions, Hambone," he said, as they hustled across the base. The chit earned them front-of-the-line privileges. "I was gonna get one myself on Saturday," Frenchy commented, "but no use waiting behind twenty guys if I can get one right on the spot." They returned to the barracks, and Hannigan disappeared into the head – the combination toilets, showers and wash basins which served forty men or more. At this early hour, he had his choice of stalls.

Newly scrubbed, he returned to his rack to see Boudreaux, cross legged on his own rack, sewing a crescent shaped unit patch above the right sleeve of Hannigan's jumper. "Grab that iron, heat it up, and get started on your bell-bottoms. Didn't anybody ever tell you about folding your uniform inside-out and putting it under your mattress at night to body-press the creases? An iron will do, but any good battleship sailor is gonna spot you as a rookie from across the deck. And where's your flat hat? You ain't going over there in dress blues with a white hat on, boy. You'd look like a refugee from the Sea Scouts, Hambone."

As it turned out, Hannigan owned no flat hat. Somewhere, in whatever had passed for boot camp, he had forgotten to get one from the ship's store. They looked around the barracks; sailors may at times be dumb, but are never stupid, and everyone's gear was stowed in ditty boxes protected by thick Yale locks. In desperation, Frenchy retrieved his own flat-hat, size 6 7/8s, which was not a perfect fit by any means on Hannigan's size 7 3/8s head. "It looks like a bubble on a piss pot, Hambone, but I got the answer for that. As soon as you get onboard, take your hat and stuff it under your arm. Since you ain't wearing a duty belt, you can get away with going uncovered. It's drifty, but then again, so are you."

The two sailors, working as quickly as possible, split up Hannigan's only pair of dress shoes. Each one spit shined a single shoe; by 1300 both shoes were presentable, although the left, shined by Frenchy, definitely put the right shoe to shame. "Pull down your pants on the right side as soon as you get on board, Hambone; that's an old trick when one shoe looks worse than the other. Some day, boy, if you survive this afternoon, I'll teach you all the tricks that old Frenchy learned out on the China station. But we ain't got time for that now."

Hannigan was standing at attention, promptly at 1315, when Chief McCroy returned from noon chow (as well as the short siesta which was the unspoken privilege of all chief petty officers). He went over Hannigan's uniform with the practiced eye of a man who had spent way too many hours standing inspection himself. There were a few Irish pennants – stray threads at the seams of the uniform – but quick snips with finger nail clippers fixed that. McCroy grunted, which in other settings would have been taken as a deep complement. "OK Hannigan, listen up, because we've only got time to go over this once. We're going to get into the launch. You go first, I go second, and Lt. Carpentier brings up the rear. The senior always goes last – the theory is that his time is more important than anyone else's, but that's just a load of horseshit. You sit forward, I sit amidships, and Mr. C. sits in the stern sheets. When their OOD calls the launch to their landing stage, we reverse the procedure. You go last. When you get to the top of the gangway, turn aft, and salute the ensign hanging from the fantail. Seeing the confusion on Hannigan's face, McCroy exploded. "No, dip-shit, not an Ensign like Ensign Brockman in payroll – the *ensign*, the national flag. And no, they are not hanging junior officers off the stern this week, although they may hang an RM3 before the day is done. Then turn, salute the OOD and say, 'RM3 Hannigan requests permission to come aboard, sir.' Don't screw it up like you do when you change watches; you don't think that I miss that stuff, do you? When he gives you permission, drop the salute, and follow me. When we get to wherever we are going, you stand at attention, with the folder of papers under your left arm, until you are called into the wardroom. Hannigan, if you screw-up-one-little-thing, you are dead meat. Deader that that crap you are going to be serving up in the mess hall for the rest of your enlistment, boy. Now, go get your folder, and let's get moving. We need to be down at the landing not later than 1345 to catch their launch. The lieutenant will meet us there."

After one minor foul up (when getting the folder, he forgot the flat-hat, and had to run back while Chief McCroy stood by the side of the road, fuming), they embarked in good order, and reported aboard the thirty-year old Battleship. From the quality of the paint and the bright work, it might have been commissioned only yesterday. Compared to the battle-worn and scarred Canadian and British ships along the waterfront though, the old *Arkansas,* probably the most shopworn of the remaining WW-I battlewagons, was a painted lady, indeed.

The messenger of the watch led the small party to the staff officers' wardroom. Knocking and uncovering, he waited until he was bid to enter. Lt. Carpentier and Chief McCroy crossed the raised threshold, and exchanged greetings with the small group inside. Commander Koshue brought LCDR Wilson, Chief Warrant Officer Prichard and Chief Radioman Bowen to the meeting. Bowen and McCroy exchanged handshakes; they had been stationed together at Subic Bay several years before, and shared a mutual respect.

After a few minutes of pleasantries and a bit of naval gossip, the meeting got down to business. Lt. Carpentier explained, in general, the unusual events of the past two weeks. He alluded to Hannigan by name, and advised the others that he was waiting in the passageway should they have any questions. "What kind of guy is he, Jack?" Chief Bowen asked of Chief McCroy.

"One hell of a radioman, John," McCroy replied. " He's got tremendous hearing, a rock solid fist, both on a speed key and a J-38, and if this thing turns into a shooting war, he's going to be somebody's leading radioman in a year or two." Lt. Carpentier, although amazed, showed no emotion, though he was not certain that McCroy was describing the same RM3 Hannigan who had taken up so much of their time recently. He had yet to learn that wise Chief Petty Officers were masters of the concept of "Rebuke in private, praise in public."

"Well, let's look at the transcripts you've brought along," Lt. Commander Wilson suggested. "I've asked Mr. Prichard to join us; he finished up a tour in Washington with Op-20-G, the communication security folks a few months ago. He was also Chief Radioman at NSS Annapolis, as well as a half dozen ships since he first went to sea. That was back in the days of sail, wasn't it, Chief Warrant Officer?" The thin fit older man, with a thin pencil mustache, just smiled. "Bring in this fellow and let's see what he has."

The messenger of the watch opened the door and bid Hannigan enter. "Here's where we lose it," thought Lt. Carpentier, but watched in relief as Hannigan cleared the lip of the watertight door frame without landing on his face. He stood at attention, and for a moment at least, Chief McCroy thought he might pass for a real sailor, if the lighting were right. He crisply handed the file folder to Chief Bowen, and stood back at attention. "Damn near clicked his heels," thought McCroy. "So far, so good."

Chief Warrant Officer Prichard looked closely at the perfectly typed logs. "Did you copy this traffic yourself, Hannigan?" "Yes sir, at the times noted in the upper left hand side of the log sheets, sir." Prichard nodded, and continued reviewing the sheaf of papers. "Are you certain you copied this correctly? What was the signal like? Was it machine-sent code, or was it hand sent? Did the operator have any characteristics that would distinguish his fist?"

"It was hand sent, sir. He was running no faster than twelve or thirteen words per minute, probably a little slower than that. His keying was perfect; I don't recall him eight-dotting any of the letters in the group."

"Eight-dotting? You're a ham operator too, aren't you? So am I. Good work, Hannigan."

Prichard passed various transcripts around the table. McCroy noted with pleasure that Boudreaux had Hannigan use four-ply paper, so there were either top copies, or enough flimsies to go around. After the others had a chance to review the various transcripts, Prichard began again.

"I'm fairly certain – no, I am actually quite certain, that these are encrypted using one-time cipher pads, which the Germans call *Vernam* or *Vigenère* ciphers. Given that there are letters in the main body, I am also certain that they are built in modulo-25. For all intents and purposes, these can not be broken. Two identical copies of each page, which is used only once, are printed and distributed to sender and receiver. If the sender is operating in compromised territory, such as this side of the Atlantic, he probably received these on water-soluble paper, or, in rare instances, on paper which has been impregnated with sulfur and which will literally vanish when exposed to the heat of even a small light bulb. The number group, repeated in the first and second boxes of the matrix identifies the serial number of the sheet being used. This is a five-by-five matrix, which usually indicates a pro-forma message, and I'd suspect that this may be weather data, which lends itself to encryption in that format. What is interesting, and indicates that this may be higher level material, is the word in the last box on the lower right. You'll see that some have the words 'Anton' or 'Berta,' or 'Josef,' and, let's see. . .yes, there's one with 'Ypern' on it. These are standard Nordic phonetics for A, B, J and Y – just as we'd use Able, Baker, Jig and Yoke. So your mysterious sender is Nordic, although not necessarily German. I'll get back to that in a minute. But first, Lt. Carpentier, do you have any Huff-Duff gear at the station yet? For those of you not familiar with the equipment, that's High-Frequency Direction Finding, which uses much more sophisticated antennas and reception equipment than the simple loops we use at sea."

Carpentier shook his head. "We're brand new at this, CWO. We don't even have any rotational antennas yet. We've got a couple dipoles, a vertical sleeve or two and a number of good tall rhombics pointed back toward NSS and NAA on the east coast. My technicians tell me that both stations come in so strong that you could light a cigar at the ends of the rhombic antennas, though."

"Well, that won't help much. Even if you swapped out the Annapolis for the Washington antennas, the beam heading wouldn't be enough to tell you anything. Commander, do you want to get Op-20-G into this game? I'm not sure they'd be eager to pick up the extra target; they've got their plates full in both the Atlantic and the Pacific. But maybe the FCC monitoring station, part of their Radio Intercept Division at Chopmist Hill outside Providence, would be best suited to get a handle on this guy anyway. My personal estimate – and this is just an educated guess – is that this fellow may be a fair distance away from Newfoundland. Hannigan, what did his signal sound like? Not his keying, mind – but the signal itself."

"He was about RST 577, sir, to put it in ham terms. His signal was strong but watery, with just a little bit of a chirp. If you remember what a ground wave signal sounds like on 40 meters, this station on 9 Mcs, just up the band a little, sounds how an operator in, say, Washington might sound to an operator in Philadelphia. Or maybe a bit closer, sir."

Prichard laughed. "I used to sneak over to the ham shack at Navy Arlington when I was there in the late '30's, Hannigan, and

I know exactly what you are describing. But there's one big difference which may be outside your personal experience. As you go higher and higher in latitude, and we're at about 48N here, propagation affects signals differently than they do at lower latitudes. And with the short nights we have at this time of year, which favors the shorter wavelengths, if we get bearings on him my bet is he may be a Dane or a German somewhere in Greenland. He's most likely on the west coast, which is where you'd expect their weather guys to be operating. I'd expect his signal to sound watery, and maybe even chirp a little if he's battery powered. The hardest thing to calculate, and the scientists are working day and night on this now, is how to distinguish between a strong signal traveling long distances, and a weak signal coming from close by. If we ever get that figured out, I wouldn't give a damn for any of the German U-boat skipper's chances."

Commander Koshue spoke up. "So what do you recommend, CWO? What should we do with this information? I don't think we ought to sit on it, that's for certain."

"Nor do I, sir. I'd box these transcripts up, Commander, and send them by courier down to OP-20-G at Arlington Hall. They may not take them all that seriously, but, to give them their due, they're up to their necks with some really serious strategic problems, some of which may be critical to our survival if the Japs and the Germans ever gang up on us. I can't get the FCC involved, obviously, but OP-20-G can, and the FCC can shoot some really accurate bearings if they triangulate with their other stations. I don't know what the Canadians have on their side of the lakes, but I bet it's similar. But it's way above our pay grades to involve them into this just yet, in my opinion. We should get an answer in a couple days, maximum, and that seems to be enough for what this is likely to be. But I must say one thing, to you, Lieutenant, and to you, Chief McCroy. This young V3 you have here, RM3 Hannigan, has done us a great service by poking around the airwaves in his free time, and he'd make a proud addition to anyone's radio shack, I should imagine. There is one thing I can do to assist you in the interim, though. That is, with Commander Koshue's permission, sir?"

"What is it, CWO?"

"Well, the last time that Chief Bowen and I made a cumshaw run around the warehouses at Brooklyn Navy Yard, we came across an old APR-1 shipboard direction finder. It must track back to the early '30s – I remember seeing one at Pensacola in '35 or so, when I was with VN-1, an aircraft training squadron. It's in really bad shape, and weighs more than a battleship anchor, but Chief Bowen and I got it from the storekeeper for a carton of Luckies. But if you want it, and think it might be useful, I'll have the boatswain dig it out of the forward locker and load it into the launch for you. Do you think your RM3 can get it working again?"

"No doubt -There are very few like him, are there Mr. Carpentier?" Chief McCroy replied as they rose to depart. "Very few indeed." "For which," he said silently to himself, "I am eternally grateful."

17 THE FLEMISH CAP - II

06 August 1941
Aboard the U-115
47N-47W, West of the Flemish Cap
Northwest Atlantic Ocean
2300Z

As the gale-force winds continued to rock the U-115, Moll directed his watch officers to begin a slow "drift" westward. Proceeding submerged at less than five knots, he anticipated that the winds would die down as he got behind the center of the storm. He also suspected that, with eight patrolling U-boats actively seeking the *Prince of Wales,* and with the position report filed by Zimmerman in the U-112, any action would now likely be to the northwest of the Flemish Cap. At 2200Z he instructed First Officer Fleischer to place the boat on a heading of 277 degrees true, which would bring them to the south coast of Newfoundland west of Cape Race. They surfaced shortly after nautical twilight, and found the sea and wind much attenuated from the previous evening.

The first Officer had the watch, and Moll suggested that he allow two additional men to rotate topside, at five minute intervals. It would relieve the claustrophobia of confinement below decks, and allow all hands to taste a breath of the fresh sea air. He himself went topside, and invited Braun to join him. In time, Hirsch, Braun's "second in command" joined the rotating group of men invited to the bridge. He did not appear to be in a hurry to return below. Braun did not seem to notice. Moll scowled, but said nothing.

"So, Braun, are you sorry you are not a U-boat sailor, eh?" the captain asked, half in jest. Braun replied "No, not at all. I don't see how you fellows stand it, to be truthful. In the Waffen-SS, there are moments of great discomfort, and even fewer moments of great fear, but for you, every day is like that. Imagine, there are men queuing at the foot of the ladder, eager to come up to the bridge and to stare out into the fog and rain. Does the weather often get as bad as it had been for the last twenty- four hours?" "Often, Braun, often. There are evenings like this when it's not so bad, but, tomorrow, I promise you, the seas will be calm, and the winds light. Sounds wonderful, doesn't it?"

"It does, Herr Kapitän, it does. But why are you laughing? Are you mocking me, Kapitän?"

"Oh, I wouldn't think of it, Braun. It's just that when conditions are like that, one of two things is likely to happen. Either we will come under air attack, or the fog will be so thick that we could be right atop the Hartz Mountains, and we wouldn't know it. Do you see that deck gun out there? Tomorrow morning, I wager, you won't see half as far – perhaps even a quarter as far – as that. We're just south of the place called the 'Nose of the Bank,' and within several hours, we'll be passing abeam of the Virgin Rocks. This part of the Grand Banks has fog about ninety percent of the time. If the fog is heavy, I'll stay surfaced longer – most of the fishing fleet are local boats from Newfoundland, and they ran for shelter when they knew the gale was bearing down upon them. By the time they are back out here, we'll be long past. Clever men, those Newfoundlanders, though. Some of the best sailors in the world."

Watch Officer Strebel, who was acting as communication officer in the absence of the third officer, called up the voice tube.

"Kapitän, I think you ought to see these messages immediately. Schroder in U-114 has made contact with what he believes is the *Prince of Wales*, and has fired a spread of torpedoes."

"Coming down! Watchstanders, prepare to clear the bridge." Turning to the two SS visitors, he said, "Time to get below until we figure how we are going to play in this. Alarm, Alarm! Prepare to dive!"

He slid down the ladder to the operations area. Braun, lacking this essential U-boat skill, came down rung by rung. Hirsch, having spent much of his life in the sailor's dive bars and brothels of Hamburg thought he could manage the maneuver and impress his messmates, several of whom were standing behind him waiting to get below. He grasped the side rails, stepped over the coaming into the ladder-way, tottered and fell four meters to the deck plates below, narrowly missing Braun who had just stepped off the ladder. He landed in a heap at the foot of the ladder, his left leg in agony.

"Funkmaat to operations! Clear the passageway – Funkmaat to operations!" Strebel called for the off-duty radioman, Lothar Andreas, who had received perfunctory training as a first-aid man, as did most radio operators. Andreas, awakened from a deep sleep, arrived a few moments later. It was clear that the leg was broken, and, with the assistance of the lookouts, who had descended carefully, dogging the hatch cover on the way down, he removed Hirsch to the third officer's cabin. One of the watchstanders was sent for a bottle of Admiral Dönitz's gift brandy, and allowed Hirsch to drink deeply, as Andreas, as best he could, realigned the bones and improvised a cast from two operations manuals and small jute line. The captain stood in the background. "It will have to do, Herr Kapitän. I don't think it's all that serious, as injuries go, but we'll have to wrap it tightly in an hour or so, to prevent swelling and the possibility of infection. But there's no way he is going to walk on that, at least for several weeks, of that you can be certain."

Braun stood ashen-faced, cursing his luck. He had no idea what, if anything, their role would be over the next few days, but he needed Hirsch, of that he was certain. Accompanying the captain, he returned to the operations table, and waited until Moll had read the incoming messages, received when they had surfaced a short time before. "Schroeder took a long shot about an hour ago, but he was at the very limits of his range, and still in the teeth of the gale. He signaled Lorient that he was unsuccessful, gave the coordinates of the attempt, and the target's course. It appears that he is well to our north, and the last message from BdU directs me to request that you open the second part of your orders, and to place myself under your direction. Are you prepared to open those orders, Herr Obersturmführer?" Braun noted the new tone of respect, but made no comment. He turned, and returned to his berth, now occupied by Hirsch, then retrieved the second envelope from the small locker above. He returned to the operations table, and read the orders for several long moments before turning to Moll.

"We're directed to proceed to the French Islands of St. Pierre and Miquelon, off Fortune Bay on the south coast of Newfoundland. I have a small chart here which indicates where we should approach the coast. We'll be signaled by radio. The operator will key his transmitter twice, but say nothing. That will be our signal to look for two men in a small rowing boat. We are to bring them on board, and to follow the directions which they give us. Do you anticipate any difficulty, Kapitän?"

"I think not, Herr Obersturmführer. I calculate our transit time as less than 20 hours, and we may even arrive sooner if the heavy fog allows us to remain surfaced. What do you know about St. Pierre?"

"Nothing, I'm afraid. To tell you the truth, I never heard of the place until I opened the second envelope of orders. What do you know?"

"A bit. I heard talk of it when I was a schoolboy. The Pfälzerwald is quite close to the French border, as you well know. The islands are the only remaining French possession in the North Atlantic. There are a few small islands, and the population is but a handful of fishermen and traders. When the Americans outlawed strong drink back in the 1920's, it became a rendezvous place for smugglers running down to the east coast of the United States. When France fell to us last year, the local governor and his gendarmerie remained loyal to Marshal Philippe Pétain at Vichy. The gendarmerie, I believe, are all from metropolitan France, and are not islanders. They are quite close to the mouth of Placentia Bay, it appears." Checking his maneuvering chart, he continued, "Ah yes, while they are nearly 6500 kilometers from our base at Lorient, they are only 30 kilometers from the tip of the Burin Peninsula, which makes up the western shore of the Bay. Why are we headed that way, and where exactly in the group of islands are we going?"

"We're to meet a contact, named Le Corse (the Corsican) at 2300 tomorrow, Thursday, 07 August, at a point between Anse aux Soldats and Anse a Ross. He will signal us at 2100 by wireless – I have the frequency here in the orders – by clicking his microphone twice, one long and one short. When we have come to the meeting place, we are to shine a shaded lamp to the shoreline every two minutes. The man we are meeting will come to us in a rowboat, along with his son. He will greet us by asking '*Allez-vous acheter mon poisson?*' (Will you buy some of my fish ?) We are to reply *'Mais non! Mon poisson en fer sont très forts.'* (No, my iron fish are very strong). He will come aboard, with instructions and maps and the latest intelligence. Perhaps we can convince him to come ashore with us to take the place of that idiot, Hirsh. Do you think that is possible, Kapitän?"

"I think that unlikely, Braun. If we enter Placentia Bay, the likelihood of discovery is great. Prien was able to accomplish the impossible at Scapa Flow, but Scapa Flow has several entries and exits. Placentia Bay is a fjord, and although wide at the seaward end, it narrows down to a very small reach of water north of the new American base. If for some reason you and your comrade from the Germanske SS Norge, Fiskdal, need to go ashore and are successful in your mission, all hell will break loose along the entire coast of Newfoundland. I trust you have considered that, Herr Obersturmführer?"

"I have thought of little else since beginning this voyage, Kapitän. If I must die, well, *Ich Sterben für Führer und Vaterland. (I die for Führer and Fatherland), yes?"*

Moll looked at him for a long moment. "Well, Fritz, on my part, I don't have any intention to die for anyone on this mission, be it the Führer or the Fatherland. I'd just as soon that Churchill dies for his fatherland, thank you very much." Braun glared, but said nothing more.

"You might find it useful to open the three large crates which the Boatswain has stowed for you in the aft compartment, where they are secure and dry. When they arrived, we assumed that your 'conjurer's kit' contains some explosives, and we certainly didn't want those rattling around. I'll direct the members of the chief petty officers' mess to vacate their space for a while to give you and Fiskdal – and Hirsch, if you think he'll be of any help – some privacy to make the necessary adjustments."

"That won't be necessary, Kapitän. By now, your crew must surely understand why we are here, and what we have been ordered to do. We will use the CPO space, though, to sort things out, and I may ask the cooperation of your weapons petty officer and chief radioman to assist us in preparing. Shall we begin now?"

Moll directed that the three wooden crates be transported to the chief's mess, and that unnecessary personnel limit their presence or transit through the cramped space. In due course, Fiskdal reported to Braun that the crates had been opened, and they proceeded to the area. From the first crate, Braun retrieved three long items – obviously rifles, wrapped in olive-brown canvas. He turned to Moll, who had accompanied him.

"As perhaps you know, the Mauser Karabiner 98 Kurz (K98k) is now the most frequently used weapon in the Wehrmacht. As a short carbine, it has an effective range of about 500 meters when using the standard iron sights. It's a controlled-feed bolt-action rifle, loaded with five rounds of 7.92 x 57mm Mauser ammunition from a stripper clip, loaded into an internal magazine. We're carrying specially loaded cartridges, loaded with 12.8 g schweres Spitzgeschoß (heavy pointed bullet). With the long barrel, such as these, the range increases markedly. And we of the special ScharfschützeKorp (sniper corps) select from among the most accurate weapons from the factory, and add the Zeiss Zielvier 4x (ZF39) telescopic sight. Many men have hit a 500 mm target at 1000 meters distance. I myself have been very close to these results while at the Waffenakademie. Of course, I've been shooting military weapons since very early in my HJ days, Moll."

Moll, in spite of his deep distaste for his arrogant passenger, was impressed. In many ways it was the same with many of his colleagues: they had no stomach for destroying ships and killing their fellow seamen, but the country was at war, and the lives of their loved ones at home depended on their ruthlessness. He watched as Braun and Fiskdal examined each of the three weapons, mounted the sighting scopes, and applied a light coating of oil to the moving parts.

Stuffed in the far corner of the CPO mess, his knees almost folded to his ears as he wrapped the three weapons in the now grimy olive-brown canvas, Braun asked if the captain could store the weapons and ammunition under the bunk in his small cabin. Moll readily agreed; there was no sense in taking unnecessary chances; one round if fired aboard could easily damage critical components of the boat, or even penetrate the pressure hull. Turning to the second crate, Fiskdal began to lay out radio equipment on the small table.

"Kameraden, please clear the passageway, and allow your radio operators to have a good look at this," Braun continued. I am certain that you have perhaps never seen a battery-operated transmitter and receiver pair as compact as these. This is the latest design from Telefunken, the SE 92/3 sending and receiving set. You know that the greatest defect in portable radio equipment is the weight of the batteries – well, these 'Petrix' cells weigh less than a kilogram, and the entire station weighs less than three kilos! Even the sending key is modified so that it can be strapped to the leg above the knee, and used even while walking from place to place. I have several crystals to control the wavelength, and you can listen on your main receiver as we cross over to our destination during the hours of darkness. We'll select the crystal whose wavelength has the least interference. In the thirty to fifty meter wavelengths, we can generate about three watts of power from the transmitter, and the battery should last us about one hour of sending– more than enough for the task for which we may call upon to accomplish. But we'll learn more, I'm sure, when we meet with our 'visitor' later this evening."

The U-boat continued toward the French islands. Not surprisingly, most of the crew had never heard of St. Pierre and Miquelon. Of the few who did, most made the understandable mistake of confusing these French islands with the French-speaking Canadian populations of Quebec and parts of the Maritime provinces. Braun and Fiskdal continued to prepare the materials which they'd take ashore, including several grenades, limpet charges and two days of hard rations. By the time they had completed their preparations, they had three large rucksacks, each weighing about twenty kilos, and stowed for ready access in the chief petty officers' mess. While the chiefs grumbled, as chief petty officers often do, they knew that life for their uninvited and to a certain extent unwanted, passengers was about to become much more dangerous.

The heavy fog permitted the U-115 to remain on the surface for much of the daylight hours, and by 2000Z, Moll could easily see Pointe Plate lighthouse on the southwest tip of Île Langlade, which was connected to Miquelon island by a sandy, and often impassable natural causeway. At 48m in height, the lighthouse provided an excellent navigational fix for the low riding submarine.

Moll called all hands to their action stations at 2100. Although the dense fog had continued throughout the day, there was a chance of entrapment in the shallow and rock strewn waters surrounding northernmost island in the archipelago. More critically, he had no idea of the political sentiments of the inhabitants, nor any idea of what defensive measures might be available to them. He stayed in the deepest water offshore, and was prepared to dive at a moment's notice if attacked. By 2200, the junior radioman, Funkgast Gustav Zweig, reported to Second Officer Kalb that he had clearly heard the prearranged signal at 9.23 megacycles at the thirty-one meter wavelength. At 2247Z, Moll had the leading seaman, Matrosen-Obergefreiter Wolfgang Spahn, signal shoreward with a hand-held lamp, and they soon heard the muffled sound of oars in the water. The fog was so thick, and the night so dark, that they could not clearly deduce the direction from which the sound came, and the dory was almost abeam of the U-115 before they could see it clearly. The sign and counter sign were exchanged (in very elementary French by Spahn), and the short and very thin visitor was hauled aboard. The dory rowed back into the fog, but remained in close proximity to the U-boat. The captain and the visitor proceeded to the operations area.

"Bring us some Schnapps," Moll ordered Scherer, the cook. Downing the schnapps quickly, the visitor looked about the vessel in some wonderment. "You have come all the way from Brittany in this?" He asked, incredulously. "We have, indeed," Moll replied.

The man continued: "We have many Bretons among the islanders: Bretons, Normans, Basque; the name of this island 'Miquelon' is a rough form of Basque for 'St. Michael'. I and many of the gendarmerie are from Corsica. My name is Paulu Albertini, and I've been here since coming with the gendarmerie nearly twenty years ago. I married a woman from St. Pierre town, and now I fish with her brothers, but my loyalties are still first to Corsica, my homeland; then these islands, and lastly, to France. I have been asked by friends to transport these documents to you." He removed a waterproof wrapper from under his shirt, and sat back, eyeing the bottle of liquor. "Go on, Paulu, have another," Braun interjected. Moll spread the thin sheets of paper across the table. There was a complete chart of Placentia Bay, a chart of St. Mary's Bay to the east, and a Royal Ordinance Survey map of the thin peninsula separating the two. Moll and Braun studied the charts and maps for a few moments and Moll finally asked Albertini, "How well do you know this region?" "As well as any place on earth," he replied, not without pride. "For years, Pierreans have landed along the south coast of Newfoundland, bringing things the Newfoundlanders want and need, and taking things that our people need and want. I suppose you can call it smuggling, but how can it be that if both sides profit? No one else seems to care very much about the people in the outports; not the British about the Newfoundlanders, and certainly not the French about us. Even we gendarmerie took part in it, and proudly so; who better can hide from a *flic* than another *flic*, eh? We Corsicans have a saying '*Vali più un tontu à fattu soiu cà centu astuti à quiddi di l'altri'* A fool doing what he knows is better than a hundred wise men doing what they don't know. I assume you have good reason to want to reach the American base without being discovered, eh?"

"Quite so. But tell me, what are the chances of getting the U-boat into the bay, and close to the base?"

Albertini laughed dryly. "Impossible. Totally impossible. You would be detected not two miles into the bay, and there are a dozen or more destroyers or other small warships which would be in pursuit within minutes. They'd chase you all the way back to Brittany, if they didn't kill you before you rounded Cape Pine. It would be a fool's errand to even try."

Moll studied the chart again. "Suppose we entered St. Mary's Bay, off to the east. By the chart, it looks as if there's deep water on the western side of the bay. That would be the closest point to the base at Argentia, wouldn't it?"

"It would. I'd make it about 19 Kilometers – about 13 miles, as the Newfoundlanders measure it, and it's mostly scrub land between the bays. Many the days my friends and I have hunted sea birds there, as well as moose and the odd caribou. We don't have any large game on our islands, nor farmlands, either. For us, everything comes from the sea. It either swims to us, or we go in the dark of night and take it for ourselves."

"Well, you're quite honest about it, if nothing else. Things must be difficult there these days. Are you getting any help from the government at Vichy?"

zMoll sat for a long moment. "Is the bateau with your son still just off our port quarter?"

"I instructed him to wait there, and he is a good boy. He's there, for certain."

Moll called for his officers and leading petty officers. "Admiral Dönitz was kind enough to give us provisions for a two month voyage. It appears that, whatever happens, our mission will be much shorter. Scherer, our good old 'Smutje' – quickly go through the extra provisions and sort out about 150 kilos of the most nutritious food we have. Take the meat, and sausages, as well as some of the rice, flour and nuts and berries. Wulfie - take four of your strongest seamen and wrestle the provisions up to the deck. Signal the dory that is off the port quarter to return. M. Albertini, you may wish to go topside and tell your son that your plans have changed, and your return to the island will be delayed for a week or so. Have him distribute the food to whoever needs it most. It's not much, but it's all that we can do for you."

The working parties quickly accomplished their tasks, and the dory was loaded to the gunnels with food for the starving people of St. Pierre and Miquelon. Indeed, the 150 kilos had nearly doubled.

'Smutje' Scherer had smuggled in some additional pork, canned vegetables and even some of the precious real coffee, and Wulff the boatswain had grabbed extra cans and tossed them into the sacks when Scherer's back was turned. Albertini grasped his son, hugged him, and spoke quietly to him in the Corsican tongue.

Moll and Obersturmführer Braun stood on the conning tower deck, watching the provisions transferred below. "That was very clever of you, Herr Kapitän. I'm sure that, when the boy tells the story, the people of these islands will think more highly of the generosity of the German People and her Führer. I shall inform my superiors when we return that the extra provisions were put to good use, and I'm sure they will inform the BdU of the wisdom of your strategy."

Moll turned and glared at the SS officer. "Wisdom of the strategy, my ass. I just wanted to help the women and children caught up in this insanity. First Officer! Secure the deck for transit. Make your course 050 true, and strike for the Mouth of St. Mary Bay. Let's get the hell out of here."

U-115 OFF ISLE ST.PIERRE – AUGUST 1941

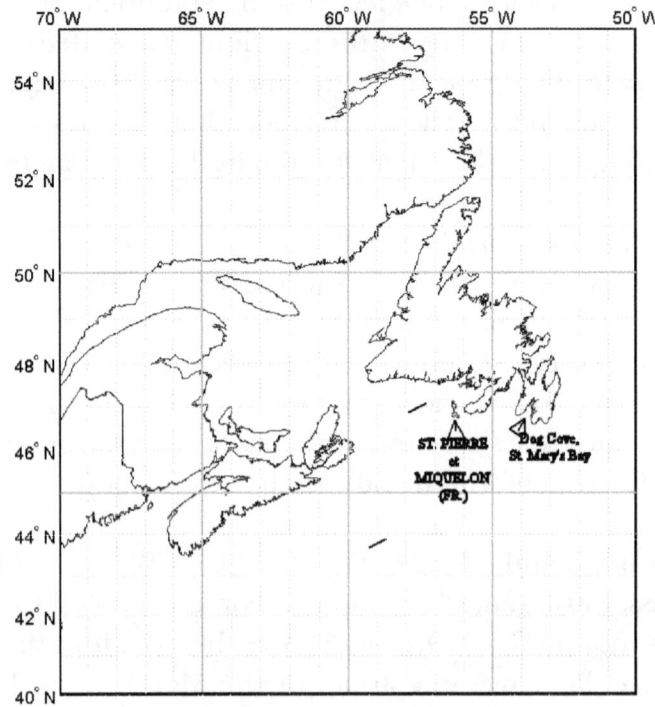

**U-115 OPERATIONAL AREA ALONG THE
SOUTH COAST OF NEWFOUNDLAND
AUGUST 7-10, 1941**
(chart A.R.E.)

18 - ISLE ST. PIERRE

08 August 1941
Aboard the U-115
46.77N 56.2W
Off Isle St. Pierre
0045 Local

Moll consulted the Admiralty charts provided by the Corsican. It appeared that the distance to Cape St. Mary, the western headland defining St. Mary's Bay, could be reached in fewer than 12 hours transit, as the distance from St. Pierre to the middle of the bay was only 115 nautical miles. Since the U-115 was able to make 17.2 knots at flank speed when on the surface, Moll hoped that he would be able to avoid submerging and travel under the cover of darkness and heavy fog until he reached the heavily trafficked shipping lanes along the south coast of Newfoundland. Again consulting the charts he looked for a likely place where he could launch a rubber dingy to deposit Braun and his companions on the western side of the bay. He called Braun, Fiskdal and Albertini to the chart table. Addressing the Corsican directly, he asked, "Where would you suggest that you should go ashore to begin your cross-country march to the American naval base?"

Albertini consulted the chart closely and pointed to an indentation about three quarters of the way up the bay. "I would suggest here, Kapitän." he replied. "As you can see there are a number of islands in St. Mary's Bay. The water in the bay is quite deep, especially along the western shore. There are two major islands of consequence to us, *Great Colinet Island* to the south, approximately one half the distance between Cape St. Mary and the head of the bay, and *Little Colinet Island,* just a bit farther north. At about the latitude of the northern tip of *Little Colinet*, there is a small deep-water bay, uninhabited, called by the Newfoundlanders *Dog Cove,* where the men of Isle St. Pierre often go ashore to hunt puffin and other sea birds which roost north of the cape. It is an isolated place, with good holding ground, and you have plenty of water within a mile or so where you can lay on the bottom to await our return. There are no houses within several miles, and it seems to me it would fit our purpose perfectly. The distance between Dog Cove and the new American base at Argentia is about 15 miles, mostly scrub forest, bogs and wetlands. The land is largely flat, but there are some small hills and a few streams and small rivers which we will have to navigate. While we do not know where Churchill's ship will anchor, I rather suspect it will be in the northern reaches of the naval station, where there is deep water sufficient for a battle cruiser or battleship. It would be very useful were we to know where and when his ship will anchor, Kapitän. It will allow us to determine the fastest route to our destination."

Moll explained to the Corsican and the others that he was in constant contact with U-boat headquarters both in Berlin and on the west coast of France, and that he had been informed that there was at least one agent ashore somewhere near the American military base. He was certain that when one of the coast watchers spotted a large British warship steaming north in Placentia Bay, that information would be relayed to Berlin and transmitted immediately to the U-115.

"Well, if that's the case, landing at Dog Cove would make as much sense as anywhere else in St. Mary's Bay," replied the Corsican. "The only difficulties we will face then are the number of fast moving streams which flow from north to south and which must be overcome for us to reach the target. Even now, can you determine when we will arrive on the west coast of St. Mary's Bay?"

Moll made some quick calculations on the side of the chart. "If the fog continues this thick during daylight hours, we can proceed on the surface for most of this incursion. I will however, submerge when we reach the shipping lanes along the south coast and will remain submerged until we round Cape St. Mary. If conditions are favorable, I will surface again and proceed up along the west coast of the bay. We will have extra lookouts on the bridge; in the event of any aircraft coming within view we will submerge yet again. But the fog which is our friend is the enemy of our enemies. Even if there are air patrols, as I expect there will be, visibility will be such that they would have to almost be on top of us for us to be discovered. Assuming that we can spend 85% of our time on the surface, we should arrive at Dog Cove sometime late tomorrow afternoon, Friday. At a very conservative pace, you should reach your target the following evening, right? What you do from that point onward will depend upon circumstances, but *Obersturmführer Braun* informs me that he will be in contact with our wireless operators throughout the entire transit across the peninsula between St. Mary's and Placentia Bays, so we can update you with any information we receive from U-boat headquarters. I will take your suggestion, and withdraw to the deep water of the bay outside the Cove, and will wait there as long as I can for your return. I need not remind you that conditions will become very difficult for us if you are successful in your mission. If you are discovered, I expect that every aircraft and ship in the area will be looking for a submarine that could not be very far away from the naval station. I will wait as long as I can do so without placing the U-115 and her crew in jeopardy."

"That is understandable, and very fair of you," Braun interjected for the first time. "Now, if we may impose upon your hospitality yet again, may I ask that we be given the use of your chief petty officer's mess once more, for the duration of our time aboard? With the unfortunate accident to Hirsch, there are some modifications to our original plan which we must discuss."

"There should be no problem, Herr Obersturmführer. The chief petty officers will be quite preoccupied during this dangerous transit, I'm afraid. Would you like the assistance of any members of my crew?"

Yes, Herr Kapitän –if you would ask your senior wireless operator to stop by, we can discuss our communication protocols for this excursion, which will be very important to both my team and to the U-115." Moll nodded, and directed the messenger of the watch to summons the leading radioman to join the group in the CPO mess in fifteen minutes time.

Hirsch's careless accident caused a number of difficulties for Braun and his team. The most important obstacle had to do with language. While Hirsch's main qualification was that of a street fighter, he was, at least, a German speaking thug. Fiskdal, although a Norwegian, spoke limited German as well as serviceable English, which he had learned during his years in Newfoundland. The Corsican, Paulu Albertini. spoke French and English in addition to his native language, but spoke no German. Braun himself spoke German and basic French. Effective communication without a common language was going to be difficult. The team members sitting around the table in the chief petty officer's mess decided to use simple hand signals whenever necessary to communicate once they had begun their mission. If necessary, commands or instructions would be translated first from German and then to French, so that at least a common mechanism was in place to communicate critical information.

A second issue confronting the team was that of clothing. Braun was well aware that being captured in enemy territory while not in a recognized military uniform would most certainly result in his immediate execution. Additionally, while Fiskdal was a member of the Norge SS, and thus would be considered a prisoner-of-war, Albertini had no military affiliation whatever and was at risk of capture as a *franc-tireur*, an irregular guerilla fighter. After considerable discussion, Braun decided that the best course of action was for Fiskdal and himself to wear standard SS battledress while on the march across the peninsula and to wear easily removed and nondescript civilian outer garments as a simple form of camouflage. Albertini felt that they could obtain suitable clothing from the many hunting cabins in the area, all of which would undoubtedly be found unlocked.

As directed by the captain, the leading wireless operator, Oberfunkmeister Helmut Amsel joined the group in the chief Petty Officer's mess. He had been present, of course, when Braun had demonstrated the light-weight portable wireless equipment to the officers and chief petty officers of the U-115. Braun opened a folder marked *Most Secret* and detached the top copy of each of ten one-time encryption sheets, keeping the second copy for himself.

"We shall take advantage of these single-use encryption forms so that we may maintain communication security while we undertake this mission," he stated. "Under no circumstances," he said, looking at his two mission colleagues, "can we ever allow the forms to fall into the hands of the enemy. Our very lives and the security of our fellow countrymen depend upon our absolute adherence to our communication security procedures. The flimsy copy which I retain is printed on special easily-dissolved paper. It is necessary only to wet the paper slightly to cause it to dissolve into an unreadable pulp. Oberfunkmeister, I depend upon you to destroy your copy after you have encrypted and transmitted the necessary information to us." Amsel, who had been a wireless operator and had handled encrypted messages since before the arrogant Obersturmführer was born, simply nodded.

Additional technical discussion between Braun and Amsel concerning frequencies and wavelengths to be used during the mission continued. Braun opened a small wooden box, and removed six small electronic components and passed them to Amsel. "These are the crystals which control our transmitting and receiving wavelength," he explained. "Each crystal is marked with a distinct frequency. I would ask you to return to your wireless position, and if you would, Oberfunkmeister, I would like you to tune to each of these frequencies, to investigate which is least susceptible to interference and would best be suited to our purposes. You may rejoin us here again when you've made your determination."

Amsel did as requested, and returned about twenty minutes later. "I have good news for you, Herr Obersturmführer. The crystals marked 9723 kcs and 9147 kcs seem to be on clear channels, at least when I used our best receiver and long wire-dipole antenna to listen. There is strong interference on the other four frequencies, I'm afraid, but we should be able to manage communication with those two channels, I believe. I'd propose that we utilize 9147 kcs as a primary link, and save 9723 for a back-up, if that is acceptable to you, Sir. And I'd recommend that we test our link frequently when you are ashore, perhaps as often as every two hours. That way we can be certain that any important developments can be reported to or from U-boat and SS headquarters quickly." Braun quickly agreed.

As he spoke, the diving alarm sounded throughout the boat. "We must be coming into the shipping lanes within a very few kilometers of the south coast of Newfoundland," Amsel remarked. "It would be wise of you to each return to your berthing areas until we have passed through the danger zone. Now if you will excuse me I must return to my duty station." The others returned to the various areas of the boat where they had resided since coming aboard and awaited the signal to resurface, at which time they expected to well inside St. Mary's Bay.

Oberfunkmeister Amsel was only partially correct in his assumption that the diving alarm was sounded because of proximity to the shipping lanes off Newfoundland. Moll had three conditions in his mind when he directed the alarm to be sounded.

The early rays of sunlight, marking the coming dawn began to appear through the fog to the east. Secondly, their track would soon take them across the mouth of Placentia Bay, arguably the most dangerous point in their transit. Thirdly, he recognized that at their current rate of advance they would arrive in the relatively narrow waters of St. Mary's Bay during the late morning or early afternoon, at a time least likely to provide heavy concealing fog. He determined that the safest course of action was to travel submerged, more slowly but much more safely, at least until later in the afternoon. While he did not consult with Obersturmführer Braun before making his decision, he recognized that the trade-off between additional time for the shore party to cross the peninsula on foot and the overall safety of the operation suggested this more prudent course of action.

The entire U-boat crew was on high alert during this critical phase of the transit. Periscope observations were made every five minutes, either by the captain or by his first officer. The passive underwater listening apparatus was fully manned by two train operators and would remain so until they surfaced. The forward and aft torpedo rooms were fully manned, in the possible event that it would be necessary to defend the boat from any allied warships overhead. The chief petty officers and leading petty officers issued strict orders that the boat be rigged for complete silence and any unnecessary movement be prohibited until the captain ordered normal activity to resume.

The second officer, who was the duty watchstander, started his stopwatch. "We're abeam of the headlands marking the western shore of Placentia Bay now, Kapitän. I estimate that we will be clear of the eastern shore of the bay in two hours and thirty-four minutes at our current rate of advance. At that time we will have only a short distance until we need to change course to 043 degrees northeast to enter the mouth of St. Mary's Bay. I will inform you when we are five minutes away from the optimum turning point." Moll acknowledged the report.

The U-boat continued silently and carefully across the mouth of the bay. About 50 minutes later, while abeam the midpoint of Placentia Bay, the sound operators reported weak to moderate pinging and propeller sounds characteristic of a Flower-Class Corvette, but after analyzing the signal for several minutes it was clear that the corvette was traveling away from the U-115, most likely enroute to the American base at Argentia. Other weaker signals, characteristic of large merchant ships or possibly capital warships were detected at the extreme limits of the sound detection systems. No enemy warship was detected within striking distance of the U-115. As they approached Cape St. Mary the second officer reported that the optimum position for the turn to the north was just a few minutes away. Consulting the chart provided by the Corsican, Moll issued orders to the navigator and first and second officers to steer for the southernmost point of Big Colinet Island, keeping to the center of the bay where the water was deepest.

"When we are within 3 km of the island's south shore, we will swing to the west keeping the islands abeam of us to the east until we reach the entrance of Dog Cove. The waters of the cove are shallow, and I have no desire to take the boat into the cove itself. Rather we shall launch our rubber boat with our visitors aboard at the mouth of the cove, and allow them to pick their own landing spot. We will do this within one hour of nautical twilight this evening. The coming darkness as well as whatever foggy conditions might then prevail will provide some level of safety to the landing party. After they have disembarked we will return to the deeper waters of the bay and submerge to a point where our decks are awash, yet our radio receiving and transmitting antennas are well above the water line. We will remain on high alert for the possibility of patrolling aircraft or enemy ships in our vicinity and will take it down to a safe depth if we are in danger of discovery. First officer, notify the landing party that they are to be ready to disembark not later than 1800 hours local time, although it is likely that they will not depart much before 2000 hours."

The rest of the transit proceeded without incident, and as planned, the U-115 arrived at the mouth of Dog Cove as dusk was falling. Moll shook hands with Obersturmführer Braun on the main deck of the submarine and watched as the rubber dingy was secured to the side of the U-boat. "I suggest, Braun, that you sink the dingy as soon as you reach the beach. Upon your return, we'll have our second boat standing offshore awaiting your signal to pick you up. Good luck and God speed your return." Braun returned these wishes with a perfunctory party salute. Moll looked on in some distain.

"Grüß Gott, Herr Obersturmführer, Und Es Grüße euch Gott," he replied softly as he gave the order to untie the dingy carrying the landing party and then ordered his ship to return to the safer depths of the bay.

**LOADING THE EXTRA RATIONS,
LATER DONATED TO THE STARVING
PEOPLE OF ST. PIERRE**
(DL Archiv)

19 SAINT MARY'S BAY

August 1941
Dog Cove, St Mary's Bay
Newfoundland
2100 Local

With muffled oars rowed by Rodefører Lars-Anders Fiskdal, the tallest and strongest of the landing party, the 3.2 meter rubber dingy cast off from the U-115, and steered northwest to the low gravel shoreline near the mouth of Dog Cove, some 400 meters distant. Taking advantage of the light of the nearly full moon, Albertini, seated at the bow, communicated directions to the Norge-SS corporal via hand signals, while Obersturmführer Fritz Braun, seated in the stern, scanned the water and horizon for threats.

Detection was unlikely; the weight of the three men and nearly eighty kilos of equipment forced the dingy deep in the water, and the black battledress of Fiskdal and Braun, as well as the oilskins worn by Albertini, blended with the black rubber of the inflatable boat. They were ashore within minutes, and pulled the dingy well above the water line. Albertini, speaking slowly in heavily accented French, whispered to Braun that a spit of land separated Dog Cove from a pond to the west, and that scrubland there would provide adequate camouflage for the boat after their departure inland. Albertini and Fiskdal lugged the boat about one hundred meters along the spit of land, while Braun followed, sweeping the tracks made by the boat with boughs of fir and pine. Within minutes there was no visible indication of their passage.

Squatting near the overturned and camouflaged dingy, the landing party again consulted the ordinance survey map which the Corsican had obtained at St. Pierre. Shielding Braun's electric torch close to his body, Albertini traced the best route to their first reporting point, the north bank of the Little Salmonier River, some five kilometers distant. "The river is at its narrowest some six kilometers east of Skin Cabin Pond and the north bank opens on to low scrubland, reaching farther to the northwest, which is the direction to the American base," he reported. "As we move inland, the sea fog will dissipate and we should be able to easily avoid boglands or thickets which would slow us down. When we reach and cross the river – really just a minor stream at that point - we can attempt to make contact with the submarine at 0400 hours, and learn if they have any new information for us. We may come across hunting and fishing camps enroute, where we can obtain additional clothing for you two fellows. As for me, my woolen shirt and moleskin trousers are identical to those worn daily by Newfoundlanders, and if we are discovered, I will speak to them in their own English dialect. If you two remain silent they'll think we are just Piereians engaged in smuggling in the area."

Braun and Fiskdal nodded their agreement with the plan, Albertini again took the lead, with Braun navigating, frequently consulting his SS-issued compass. The route to the Salmonier River took them over a number of hillocks and ridges, from which they had a view of the surrounding countryside. As they reached the top of each elevation, Braun signaled them to crouch down among the scrub bushes and trees, so as not to provide an easily identified target against the skyline. At the crest of each rise they waited for several minutes, although they felt it unlikely that anyone else would be in that desolate area in the hours after midnight. Detection by the enemy, however, was not their most pressing concern; the mosquitoes and deer flies which inhabited the area were well already aware of their presence. At their second halt, Braun reached into his rucksack and passed around a tube of anti-mosquito lotion, of a type developed by Bayer-AG for troops on the eastern front. The others nodded their appreciation and discovered that the ointment was as effective in the bog lands of Newfoundland as it was on the steppes of Ukraine or Russia. They reached their first waypoint on the southeastern banks of the river more quickly than they had anticipated and rested while Braun assembled the portable radio equipment. Promptly at 0400, Braun transmitted the agreed upon recognition signal and was greeted by a strong Morse code signal from the U-boat. He whispered each letter clearly to Fiskdal as received and the Norwegian fill in the blank boxes on the first single-use encryption pad. The signal was quite short and when it was completed Braun read the now clear language text transcribed by his colleague:

"TARGET ARRIVED 0900 FRIDAY, BERTHED 47° 20' 18" N - 53° 56' 12" W. 720 METERS OFF COOPER HEAD BEARING 78.5 STERN SHOREWARD. LARGE ASSEMBLY 1000 LOCAL SUNDAY 10 AUGUST."

Braun transmitted a quick acknowledgement message and secured the wireless equipment. He shared this new intelligence with the Corsican, who quickly located the coordinates on his ordinance survey map. "The good news," he replied, "seems to be that the ship is well within range of our weapons, and the headland will provide us with cover until we get into firing position. The bad news seems to be that reaching this position will require us to pass close by some inhabited areas and will require us to cross over the Northeast Arm of Placentia Bay, quite near the settlements of

Freshwater and Dunville. It would be best if we timed our approach for the hours of darkness, and limit our visibility here during daylight. The crossing will not be difficult, and we can actually skirt around the landward end of Northeast Arm, and still arrive well before 1000 tomorrow." Again consulting the map, he suggested that their next waypoint should be just south of a rough dirt track linking the tiny settlements of Colinet and Pointe Verde. He estimated that their travel time would be another four hours, and that there would be ample cover to rest during daylight.

As they crossed the stream – now not much wider than a rivulet – the landing party spotted a number of rough cabins used by local trout and salmon fishermen. After ascertaining that they were empty, they searched each, and removed caps and waterproof boots from the largest cabin. Smiling, Lars-Anders Fiskdal commented to the others. "I've always found it peculiar that a race of men who make their living from the sea would be so enamored of fishing as a pastime. When I worked in the logging woods on the north side of the island, each Sunday many of our native Newfoundland lumbermen would spend the afternoon fishing in the Humber River. These were the same man who spent their boyhood rowing dories out in the freezing ocean in pursuit of the cod fishery. We Norwegians are men of the sea too, but we prefer to spend our free time with our family and friends ashore. Very peculiar, these Newfoundlanders!"

"Peculiar or not," Braun replied, "We will find their rubber wading boots useful when we encounter more of this cursed bogland between here and the target. It's a good thing that I have brought several pairs of dry stockings, since my feet are now wet and frozen. But now we will be able to travel in style." The others, disgusted that Braun had kept the cache of dry clothing for his own use, glared but remained silent.

Braun signaled the party to move out. "If we take advantage of this last moonlight we can reach our next waypoint well before our 0800 scheduled radio check with the submarine. Albertini, what kind of terrain will we encounter before we come to the dirt track you mentioned?"

"We'll find open meadow or more wet ground for the first hour or so, I think. We may even encounter some wildlife over the next several hours. The area through which we are passing is one of the best hunting areas for moose or other large game in the region. Once we get further on, we will encounter small patches of forested land, with pine, spruce or other evergreens, although not of a great height. Nevertheless, it will provide us with cover during the dangerous hours immediately before and after dawn. If we are making good time we can rest there during the morning hours and observe whatever traffic may be passing across the peninsula. We also can expect to see aircraft, either in patrol or transit, as soon as the fog lifts after daybreak. If we see any unusual activity either on the ground or in the air it may be an indication that our mission has been compromised and that we can expect some resistance if we are spotted. I suspect that we will not have any difficulties in that area, but one can never be sure. Remember if we come across either a military or civilian party to allow me to speak for the group. Fiskdal, you can also answer if addressed, as you speak with the particular lilt of the Newfoundlanders."

They started out again and while the terrain was not much different than that which they encountered at the beginning of the trip, it was made more comfortable by the waterproof boots and warm woolen caps. It was not a difficult passage, and they arrived on the south side of the rural road well before 0800 hours. Braun spotted a large copes of trees about 100 meters south of the dirt road and directed the men to take cover in that area. Moving forward alone, he inspected the conditions of the dirt road and returned to report that it appeared to have been recently traveled by military or other heavy vehicles.

Working quietly, he configured the portable wireless set once again and precisely at 0800 transmitted the prearranged signals to the U-115. The return signal was clear but somewhat weaker than the signal four hours previously. Once again Fiskdal recorded each Morse character on the decryption pad as whispered loudly by Braun.

AGENT REPORTS NO UNUSUAL SECURITY ACTIVITY NEAR TARGET VESSEL. U.S DESTROYERS ARE SHUTTLING DIGNITARIES BETWEEN PRESIDENT'S SHIP USS AUGUSTA AND HMS PRINCE OF WALES AT POSITION PREVIOUSLY REPORTED. MORE LATER.

"It appears that the conference between the American president and the British prime minister has already begun." Braun commented. "I would like to complete this transit as quickly as possible, but I agree with our Corsican friend that it is foolish to risk detection when we are so close to our destination. How long will it take us to reach those coordinates?"

"Well if we rest here until afternoon, and cross this road carefully, we will look like a hunting party returning to the settlements to our north. We'll cross the Newfoundland Railway spur line just east of the hamlet of Dunville around dusk. If anyone spots us, we'll just look like a party of hunters from the capital, St. John's who have just come out by train for a weekend of hunting while the weather is pleasant. About an hour later we'll cross the main east-west rail line, so the deception ought to work at least to nightfall. Once we pass by the small settlement of Villa Marie, and skirt to the east of the village of Fox Harbor, we'll be within two hour's hike to Cooper Head, the anchorage mentioned in the first message."

The landing party retreated more deeply into the grove of trees, and using fallen branches and boughs constructed a lean-to for shelter from the open skies. Braun suggested that they take turns resting and since he had been awake for nearly 48 hours, he would be the first to nap. As the morning progressed, they heard the sounds of vehicles on the dirt track, and Fiskdal left their refuge to investigate further. He returned with a report of a large convoy of military vehicles heading westbound toward the American naval base. Clearly the road was more frequently utilized now since the Americans had arrived than it had been at the time of the ordinance survey.

"This appears to be important information" he commented, "and something that we might wish to report to the submarine. It's also good to know this since we will be returning in this direction after we have completed the mission." As the morning fog dissipated and the skies cleared there were also sounds of aircraft operating in the area. One past so closely to their hideout that they were clearly able to identify it as a US Navy PBY seaplane, and to read the markings on the aircraft. The airplane appeared to be in transit to an offshore patrol area.

Neither Fiskdal nor Albertini considered the risk of detection from these transiting aircraft to be a major danger. They remain alert however, for any indications of aircraft patrolling the peninsula or the area surrounding the naval station. While Braun slept, they conversed quietly. "Why are you here, Lars?" Albertini asked. "I can understand Braun fighting for his beliefs and homeland but you are not a German. Why would you as a Norwegian take sides in someone else's fight?"

Fiskdal sighed. "It's all very complicated," he said. "Norway is a very old nation but a very new country. We had hoped when Norway became free from Sweden that it would be a good place for working people, but that proved not to be so. Things in the country were so arranged in favor of the rich and the merchant classes that we were not even able to establish our own monarchy and had to import one from Denmark. While it's true the King swore an oath to the Norwegian people, his interpretation of who the people were was pretty much that of the merchants. Many of us had to leave our families and our homeland to seek work elsewhere, either as sailors in the merchant fleet or as emigrants to North America. For those of us of rural origin in the small villages of the interior life was very difficult. There were few doctors and the health of the people was poor; my own parents and one sister died of consumption while I was a young boy. While we remained neutral during the Great War it was clear that the British merchants controlled our fishing and sailing fleets and set the prices for fish and our woodland products to their own advantage. When I left Norway in 1922 the depression had already begun for our country, and when I arrived in Newfoundland, conditions here were even worse. We would work sometimes 20 hours a day during the summer in the logging camps along the Humber River. We were poorly paid and poorly fed, yet anyone could tell that the great quantities of pulp wood which we shipped from Botwood and other ports to Canada and the United States were immensely profitable to the merchants and the owners. I remember hearing the Newfoundlanders singing a folk song with the words *'oh dear me, the world is ill-divided; those who work the hardest are the least provided.'* Truer words were never spoken. Occasionally someone would try to organize a union to better our working conditions. That was usually a death sentence for the organizer. In a world where injury or death was commonplace it was easy to mask an intentional murder committed by company goons or anti-union sissorbills or finks. I finally got fed up with things and return to my native land in 1933. Little did I know how bad things would be then. There was no work, and the conditions of the people were, if anything, worse than they were before I left. I entered with a number of other young returnees into an organization which affil- iated with the Norwegian National Samling party. After 1935 we could see the changes happening in Germany and wanted some- thing similar to happen in our beloved Norway. Our organization worked closely with the German SS, and after the British forced Germany into war in 1939 many of us volunteered for active ser- vice with our brothers to the south. I was asked to volunteer for this mission because of my experience in Newfoundland. But why are *you* here, Albertini?" he asked.

"It's not dissimilar to your experience, Fiskdal. My homeland of Corsica has always been a battlefield. Sometimes the Genoans or Venetians won, and sometimes the French. From our boyhood we Corsicans learn to be fighters first and foremost, and many of us became mercenaries for whichever country would have us. I joined the French national police force, the gendarmerie, and was sent to the island of St. Pierre. At first I knew no one there but gradually made friends with the local population. I left the police at the end of my term of service, married an Islander, and set off fishing with her brothers. It was a good life and I was accepted by everyone in the community. But when war broke out in 1939 every- thing changed. We could no longer fish offshore, we received no support from the Metropolitan French who were busy with their own battles and the limited farmland and inshore fishery was not enough to support our people. Many migrated illegally to Québec and other parts of Canada. Some migrated here to Newfoundland but there were still some 5000 of us left on the island and condi- tions were impossible. I have seen babies die because their mothers could not provide them with nourishment. Many of us believe that our problems were made worse by the British, who established revenue barriers and neutrality patrols around our island. We could not get out and food could not come in. I had been asked by those who supported Marshal Pétain to simply deliver a message to a submarine which would approach our island from the sea. The skipper of the submarine was so kind as to provide hundreds of kilos of food from his own scarce resources to assist my people. How could I not agree to help him, particularly when the mission might well speed the end of this senseless war?"

Shortly before noon, Fiskdal woke Braun, who relieved him on watch, and who went forward and observed the road for several minutes. When he returned he reported that he saw another convoy, this one pulling large anti-aircraft guns headed west toward the naval station. Albertini reported their observations of earlier in the morning, and Braun agreed that this information should be forwarded via the submarine to the authorities in Berlin. He settled next to Albertini and they continued their conversations in basic French. "Do you think the assassination of Churchill will have any impact on the outcome of the war?" the Corsican asked.

"Yes I do, most certainly. There are a number of efforts afoot to change the attitude of the British toward the Führer and toward Germany, about which you perhaps are not aware. Just recently Rudolph Hess, Deputy to the Führer, flew on a secret mission to Britain to seek the intercession of the Duke of Hamilton, an influential member of the House of Lords. Sir Oswald Mosley and his Union of British Fascists have great influence among the members of Parliament, and as perhaps you know the Duke and Duchess of Windsor are great friends of Germany and of the progress made in the country. In the United States the famous aviator Charles Lindbergh and his many friends are active in keeping that country out of the war. Even so, Churchill has been conversing with Roosevelt, and if they enter into some accommodation while here in Newfoundland it will not be to our advantage. Already the Americans have violated their neutrality by providing the British with some fifty naval destroyers. If Churchill is removed from the scene chances are very strong that the British will soon come to their senses and sue for peace. That will allow the Führer to concentrate on our real enemies in the Soviet Union to our east. This may be the best chance to bring the war in the West to an early and satisfactory conclusion which will be to our advantage and to the advantage of governments such as the French at Vichy. I believe that will to permit normal relations and commercial activities to resume on your islands."

He continued, "You and I and our Norwegian colleague stand at a critical point in world history. If we succeed we will ensure the continuation of the thousand-year Reich for generations. But the Führer has issued strict orders that we do nothing to disturb the balance between the United States and Germany and that we take every effort to ensure that we do not harm the American president. Here, I have a number of photographs of Churchill in the different uniforms and clothing which he wears, and it would be good for you and for Fiskdal to study these, since one of you may be in a better position than I to fire on the Prime Minister when we reached our destination. I still plan to be in the best firing position though, and to use my extensive training with long range firearms to our advantage."

As the sun passed the meridian, and fog returned, Braun felt it would be wise to depart immediately in the event that they encountered unexpected obstacles during the remainder of the trip. The landing party was soon ready to continue, and Albertini took the lead, carefully observing the road for several minutes before crossing. His two colleagues followed and they continued north by northwest toward the coordinates provided by Moll.

Again consulting his ordinance map, Albertini remarked, "if we continue at our current pace without interruption we should cross the two railway lines within the next four or five hours and should be very close to our destination by midnight. This will allow us sufficient time for reconnaissance before the 1000 hours assembly mentioned in the message. I think that we should meet our 2000 hour wireless schedule and report the intelligence which we have uncovered regarding movements of equipment and personnel toward the Navy base. I will try to find an appropriate halting place for us at that time."

The landing party set out yet again, this time in a more northerly direction so as to avoid a number of large ponds in the area and to cross between Kelly's Pond and Lookout Pond over the narrow stream which linked the two. They moved slightly to the northeast so as to cross the branch line linking Argentia with the main Newfoundland Railway line about 5 km east of the village of Dunville. Albertini was surprised to find a large graveled road parallel to the railway tracks which appeared to connect with the main cross-island route farther north at the center of the Avalon peninsula. This road was recently constructed and was capable of carrying much more traffic than the smaller Colinet-Pointe Verde Road which they had passed earlier that morning. An additional easy hour's march brought them to the main Newfoundland Railway line. After midnight, they were in deep woods east of the village of Fox Harbour, where they stopped to complete their scheduled wireless transmission to the U-115.

This time Braun chose a different mode of operation, first encrypting the intelligence which they had gathered during the day on a single use pad and then transmitting the agreed-upon recognition signal. The return transmission from the submarine was quite weak because of the increased distance which they had traveled since their first communications. Braun received a go ahead signal from the submarine, and slowly transmitted each line of the message twice to ensure reception. The wireless operators on the U115 had some difficulty with the weak signal from the portable transmitter and frequently asked for repeat transmission until the message was successfully received.

The U-115 had no new information for the landing party but asked for an additional contact at 0600 the following morning. Braun expected to be well within range of Cooper Point at that time and agreed to the scheduled transmission. They remain in the heavily wooded area until shortly after midnight and then continued the additional 4 km until they reached the southern outskirts of Ship Harbour about 1.5 kilometers from Cooper Head. They agreed to nap in rotation until shortly after daybreak when they would begin their reconnaissance of the target area.

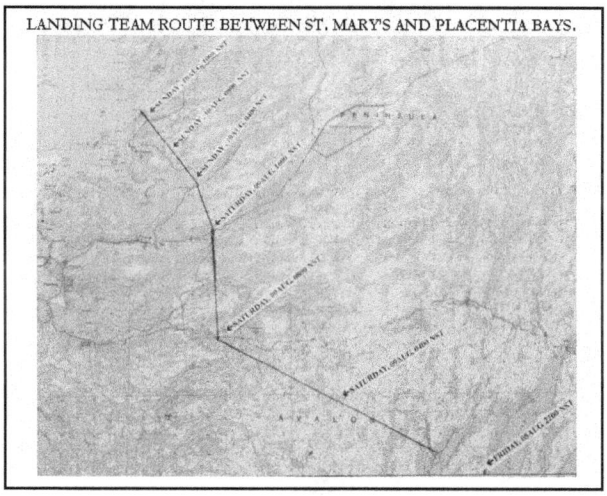

LANDING TEAM ROUTE BETWEEN ST. MARY'S AND PLACENTIA BAYS.

(Chart A.R.E)

**HMS PRINCE OF WALES AT BERTH TWO, N.O.B
ARGENTIA (NEAR SHIP HARBOUR)AUGUST 8. 1941**

**F.D.R. AND CHURCHILL CONFER AT
SHIP HARBOUR, NEWFOUNDLAND**
(official USN)

20 SHIP HARBOUR

10 August 1941
Aboard U-115
West of Colinet Island
St. Mary's Bay, Newfoundland
0030 Local Time

U-115 had remained submerged during the daylight hours of August 9th. Shortly after midnight, Moll had given the order to surface, and the ship rose into the blackness of St. Mary's Bay. Sheltered from the fishing village at Admiral's Cove by Colinet Island, the U-boat, lying in deep water and ready to dive at a second's notice, had little to fear.

Oberfunkmeister Amsel had tuned his receivers to Hamburg Naval Radio. Among the large number of messages for the wolf-packs in the North Sea and Atlantic, was a message addressed directly to Moll and the U-115. Unlike most messages, this was marked "Most Secret and Urgent," and Amsel watched as the skipper and his officers went behind the curtain to his cabin to decode the message.

The news was disturbing. The Abwehr had informed Dönitz that one of their informants had provided solid information that a Russian agent, or agents, was operating at Argentia, with orders to assassinate President Roosevelt. The logic behind the plan was clear – America would blame the Germans, who were known to have U-boats and saboteurs operating throughout North America, and the U.S. would be immediately be drawn into the war on the side of the Allies. "It wouldn't surprise me in the least if the British have a hand in this." Moll remarked to the First Officer. 'It's just the kind of thing that they are famous for doing."

The message, countersigned by Himmler, ordered Braun to abort the operation immediately, and to take evasive action to avoid implicating the Reich. Any attempt on Churchill while Roosevelt was at risk was now far too dangerous. Himmler knew that Roosevelt was not mobile – any kind of firefight might place the American's life in further danger, and that Hitler had issued firm orders that no action be taken that would encourage the Americans to come into the war. Moll directed Amsel to inform the landing party, using unencrypted voice if necessary, that their mission now was to prevent, rather than implement, a political assassination, and that the U-115 would remain off Dog Cove only so long as the submarine's presence was undetected.

No acknowledgement of the message was received from the landing party, and Moll ordered Oberfunkmeister Amsel to continue transmitting the message at ten minute intervals. The landing party, which was experiencing communication difficulties caused by the intervening hills and by the dwindling power remaining in their batteries, continued unaware for the next several hours towards their intended destination.

Braun was dismayed, and, indeed furious, when he finally transcribed the message from the U-115 shortly after daybreak, just before reaching the outskirts of Ship Harbour. He had finally received the order from the submarine when the landing party was within a kilometer of Cooper Head just south of the settlement. He keyed the transmitter once, but then decided that he would not acknowledge receipt of the message, which continued to be repeated throughout the morning. An ardent Nazi, the only thing he hated more than the British were the Russians. Disassembling the radio equipment, he withheld the content of the transmission from his two companions as they steadily completed the last stage of their journey.

Sunday, August 10, 1941
Naval Radio Station NWP
Naval Base, Argentia
0600 NST

After Hannigan had returned to the base from the *USS Arkansas,* lugging the old APR-1 direction finder in a wheelbarrow he had found on the dock, he had wasted no time in restoring it to full operation and installing it on the workbench next to the SX-28 receiver. He found that it was much less sensitive, and much less selective than the modern equipment, but the large loop antenna allowed him to pinpoint strong signals, at least on a single line of bearing. Although preoccupied with official radio traffic regarding the VIP visitors, and copying the Navy Fox broadcast for hours on end, he nevertheless did find odd moments to return to his listening post.

He was still learning to operate the APR-1 direction finder during the midwatch early Sunday morning. Because it was a broadband receiver he discovered that it was easiest first to locate a signal of interest using the original SX-28 receiver and then to use the direction finder to locate the signal independently. But because it was so insensitive, it usually would lock into only the strongest signals, making the task less complicated. Hannigan tuned randomly through all of the usual frequencies for about ninety minutes until one signal in particular aroused his interest. It was an unmodulated carrier signal similar to the signals he had heard when first he identified the mystery transmission. He eagerly turned the large directional loop antenna, and was mildly surprised to see the signal strongest *southeast* of his location, unlike the first signals which he had discovered on a bearing from the south or southwest. He had jotted the information in his log - it was shortly after 0100 local time - and continued to listen on that frequency.

His efforts were rewarded several minutes later by a stronger signal, also to the southeast, which began transmitting five letter encrypted groups, although much faster and cleaner than those of the previous mystery station to the southwest. He summoned the watch supervisor, and plugged in an additional set of headphones so that he might monitor the station as it was received. "What do you make of this, Frenchy?' he asked. "This guy is off to our southeast and it's not very far away according to the direction finder. He definitely sounds like a professional radioman and you'll notice the German words –there's Anton and later on there's Dora –which Mr. Pritchard told us were the mark of an enemy transmission."

"There are those strange characters you heard in the Köln transmission, too, aren't they 'bone? We ought to let the Chief know. I'll call over to the Goat Locker and wake him with the news as soon as it gets light." Hannigan did as ordered and continued to monitor the frequency for another hour or so but no additional transmissions were heard until shortly after 0600, when a very strong and very close unkeyed transmission was again received on the same 9147 Kcs. frequency. This was by far the strongest signal received over the past 48 hours, and showed a bearing of 075 degrees at a distance of about five miles northeast of the radio station. Frenchy again listened, but since there was no text, decided not to risk the wrath of an angry Chief by disturbing him before reveille.

"I don't know what else we can do, Hambone. It's all in the hands of the flagship now and if there is anything to be done, it will be done at their direction. I'll just keep the Chief in the loop under the theory that a surprised CPO ain't likely to be a happy CPO. Go ahead and secure your equipment, straighten up and help the rest of the crew get ready for turn-over to Holden's crew. Violet is working the day shift today, so I'm going to hit the sack when we get back. Do you want to use the truck?" Hannigan happily agreed.

When the section returned to the barracks Hannigan washed up, changed from his working dungarees to his clean summer uniform and drove the short distance from the main gate to the Duffy household, arriving shortly after 7:30 AM. As he drove up he saw Mrs. Duffy and the twins standing expectantly on the front porch.

"Hello there, Yank. We're just waiting for my sister to come by to drive us over to Mass; you're here for Kathy no doubt. She's inside - I can hear her fooling with the new wireless set. You've set a bad example for her, the last few weeks she can't seem to keep her hands off it!" Hambone smiled and entered in time to see Kathy switch off the set and quickly spin the tuning knob. "Oh hello there Tim, I didn't hear you drive up. I was just tuning around to see what I could hear. I've heard London and Paris and even Moscow on some evenings. It really is a fascinating set. But I hope you're not too keen on attending Mass this morning; I worked all night and am dead beat. Besides, I usually go with Violet and she volunteered to work the day shift, so that matron could celebrate her birthday. Let's just go for a ride in the truck."

Hannigan was struck with a brainwave, an always dangerous condition for him. "We've got some very special visitors on the base today, and I understand from reading their messages that they are going to meet at the north end of the anchorage. And we've been hearing some strange radio signals lately; let's take the radio with us and listen to what we can hear, OK?

"If you break Mr. Duffy's radio he'll kill you" she said. "He's terribly proud of that – Mr. Duffy is partial to the Boston Bruins and sometimes he can even hear the games directly from the States."

Hannigan continued to fiddle with the radio. He noticed that it had both medium wave and short wave capabilities, and, although not nearly as sophisticated as the Navy radios, was indeed quite capable of picking up distant broadcasts.

'Do you mind if we just take the radio outside for a while? There's this radio signal I've been hearing, and I'd like to see if I can figure from what direction it's coming. Ignoring Kathy's protests, he took the radio, and, with Kathy following, exited through the kitchen door. As he walked, he tried to explain the mysterious signals to Kathy, who listened intently, but with no real comprehension as to what Hannigan was trying to convey.

Hannigan trudged along the Dunville road, stopping from time to time at a convenient rock to rest the radio. The radio had an adjustable antenna, and Hannigan showed Kathy how signal strength could be read, and direction determined, by a meter on the face of the radio. Tilting the antenna broadside to the station made the signal strongest. He experimented with several stations, until, tuning around the nine megacycle mark, he heard the mysterious signal once again. This WAS a local signal. . . and close-by, too. He tuned the radio more accurately, and adjusted the antenna until the signal was at its peak. As it ended, they backtracked to the Duffy house, and Hannigan, waving to the Duffy family, jumped into the driver's side of the Navy pickup.

"If you want to see where the big ships are, last night one of the midwives mentioned that the biggest warships she had ever seen came into the bay on Friday and are just north of Fox Harbour," Kathy remarked. "Come on, I know the road that goes up that way, and maybe we can see the visitors from there." Hannigan, busy trying to keep the truck on the narrow track, continued a few hundred yards further, finally pulling off to the side of the road. He fiddled with the dials but did not hear the mystery signals again.

As they stood on the side of the road, Kathy nudged him and giggled in a fake gangster accent: "We'se in trouble now, buster. Cheese it, here comes the coppers!" It was Mr. Duffy in his Constabulary vehicle.

"And what the hell do you think you are doing with my radio, Yank?"

Startled, Hannigan turned, and was confronted by the angry policeman. "The missus told me that you took off out my back door with the radio in hand, and she's some upset. . .she wanted to listen to the women's programs on VONF from St. John's later this morning. Want to explain yourself, sailor?"

Hannigan stammered, and tried to explain, as best he could, what he was trying to accomplish. In a torrent of words he told about the Philadelphia Athletics, Morse signals with umlauts, Chief McCroy and the leading radioman who was picking on him...all of which made Duffy even more suspicious and doubtful. When Hannigan argued that the signal was coming from just north of Fox Harbour and was undoubtedly local, Duffy just laughed. "There's nothing up that way except a few fishermen – it's not likely one of them can afford a table to rest it on, let alone a radio transmitter," he said.

Hannigan fumbled with the dials again. Much to his great surprise, he heard an unmistakably German voice, loud and clear on a frequency very near the mysterious Morse signal, as U-115 transmitted the urgent message by unencrypted voice to increase the chance that it would be quickly picked up by the landing party. Duffy – who recognized German even if he could not speak it – listened more closely. Much to their amazement, they recognized several words in the jumble of whispered, hurried German – words like "Argentia," "Churchill' and "Placentia." This was clearly something of interest to the constabulary. He continued to interrogate Hannigan, and remained confused by his excited answers. Finally Hambone quickly rotated the antenna, demonstrating direction-finding by radio. The signal was close by, and this time the signal was north-northwest of their current location.

Duffy thought for a moment. "Kathy, get into my constabulary truck and drive back to Freshwater. Use the telephone at the house to call the police station. I don't know what this is all about, but I know a special train is due with bigwigs from St. John, and this may somehow be connected. Ask the sergeant to come along with our other fellows, and he may want to involve the Yanks from the base and the Ranger detachment at Whitbourne. And – if you can find your way back here – bring back my hunting rifle and ammunition. You know where it is; it's hanging by the back door, and the ammunition is in a locked drawer in the kitchen cabinet. He handed her a small ring of keys. "It's the small brass key. Be sure to lock it again; I don't want the babies getting in there. Whatever you do, though, stay on the road between here and town and don't go any farther to the north when you return."

Kathy did as directed and Duffy continued: "As for you and me, Yank, we'll head up to the top of Crow Cliff." he said. "It's only about a half-mile west of here, and, at about 700 feet it has a view for miles around. Bring that radio along: if there's anything out there you can get a better bearing on it from up there, and we'll be able to see anyone moving around in the flat scrublands below."

Duffy and Hannigan headed west to the rocky outcrop. It was an easy walk to the foot of the hill, and a simple climb to a north-facing clearing near the top, which gave a commanding view of the area toward the roadstead where the capital ships were anchored.

Hannigan again (gently!) placed Duffy's radio on a granite boulder, and tuned carefully through the wavelengths where he had last heard the mysterious signals.

He was not disappointed. He clearly heard the German voice signals again, this time coming from nearly due south. He rotated the directional antenna, and soon had a solid bearing on the blank carrier signal which answered. "Just sight down the top edge of this antenna, " he informed the Constable. "Whoever is transmitting is out there, and not at all far away, given the strength of the signal." Duffy walked a few feet away from the sheltering evergreens, and, protected by a small ridge on the west side of the hill, scanned the horizon.

Quickly he whispered to Hannigan. "Get down, now. I can see a group of three moving off toward our west. It looks like they are hunters – two of them are wearing flat caps, one has an old woolen shirt – but there's definitely something strange about them. Two seem to be in coveralls and carrying large backpacks. No hunter from around here would burden himself with so much equipment – not on a Sunday morning jaunt into the bush."

"From the direction they are heading they will come out of the woods at Ship Harbour. So we'll do this. We'll use your truck again and attempt to intercept them just south of Ship Harbour. We can cover the distance faster than they can, and stop them as they cross the Ship Harbour road. We'll soon sort out what this is all about."

Still undetected by Braun and the landing party, Duffy and Hannigan continued shadowing them throughout the early morning fog and mist. Again keeping between the coastal villages and the landing party, as they were approaching Ship Harbour, both kept awaiting the return of Kathy French with weapons, and news that reinforcements were on the way.

By the time they reached the easternmost houses of Ship Harbour, Duffy was worried. Kathy French had more than enough time to sound the alarm. Even if she had awakened others to bring back with her, she should have caught up to them by this time. Something seemed amiss.

Meanwhile, the Germans had turned toward Placentia Bay. Duffy and Hannigan climbed another small rise where they had a clear view all the way to Berth Two of the Argentia Base. They could clearly see the *HMS Prince of Wales*, and dozen or more other vessels lying there in the roadstead. "I'd better go down to the general store in Ship Harbour myself, and use the telephone there,' Duffy concluded. "Whatever you do – WHATEVER you do - I do not want you to leave this hill, do you understand? The Germans – or whoever they are – will cross the road about two or three hundred yards north of you if they keep on their current heading. Keep your head down, and I'll be back here within a half-hour at most." Hannigan agreed, and Duffy headed toward the village store.

Hannigan observed the scene. After several minutes, impetuously ignoring Duffy's instructions, he decided to circle around behind the landing party, and to follow it where ever it went. He knew that in the dense underbrush and trees behind Ship Harbour, he'd be safe from detection. He left the hill, and was soon tracking behind the German landing party.

As 0930 approached, all was being made ready aboard the *HMS Prince of Wales*. The ship lay in some thirty fathoms of water, bow seaward, with her stern anchors gripping the bottom of the bay just abaft the berthing dolphin marking Berth Two. Although her stern was less than six hundred feet from the shoreline, the depth of the water in Argentia harbor presented no problems for Captain Leach. He kept steam up in three boilers – in an emergency *Prince of Wales* could be underway and moving down the bay in a matter of a very few minutes.

Churchill had invited Roosevelt and his party to divine services aboard the battleship, and a mixed group from the ship's companies of *USS Augusta* and *HMS Prince of Wales* were gathered on the fantail. The ship's chaplain was making the final preparations, with comfortable chairs for the dignitaries at the very front of the congregation. The officer of the deck, standing on the quarterdeck had a fine view of the *USS Mayrant* – the executive officer of which was Franklin D. Roosevelt, Junior – as she laid aside *USS Augusta,* preparing to ferry the American President to the *Prince of Wales* for the church service.

Meanwhile, the German landing party continued its progress toward the water. By 0945 they were less than two hundred yards from the beach. Braun halted the party, and, looking around, spotted a small sea-cliff to their south. "That must be Cooper Head," he whispered to the others. From there, we should be able to see everything going on. And, thinking to himself, "From there I can get a good shot at Churchill, if he's going to be the center of attention of all those sailors on the aft deck of the battleship." Braun had hunted as a child – often alone since his contemporaries preferred not to have him in their company – and he knew that, with the calm winds prevailing, it would be an easy shot with the specially modified Mauser Karabiner 98 long-barrel sniper's rifles with telescopic sights carried by the landing party.

With the Corsican acting as a rear guard below the ridgeline of the small hill, Braun and Fiskdal crept slowly to the crest and started down the other side. The cliff-face was rocky, and there were numerous large boulders behind which to hide. The seaward face of the cliff was irregular – Braun signaled Fiskdal to move to his right, where there were a number of shallow cave-like openings in the face of the hill. As they began to move in that direction, their attention was distracted by the commotion in the bay, as *Mayrant* pulled along the port side of *HMS Prince of Wales* to deliver the American President. Strains of the American national anthem honoring his arrival were clearly audible across the short distance to the shore.

They moved swiftly but carefully across the steep and rock strewn cliff. A glint of sunlight off to their right caught Braun's eye. He waved Fiskdal down, and they crept slowly toward the rocky opening. They both saw the glint of reflected sunlight from within yet again, and heard the sounds of gravel shifting as someone moved inside. As the strains of the Star Spangled Banner rang out as the British greeted Roosevelt, Braun rose, and turned toward the opening. Approaching in stealth, in the morning light he clearly identified his target, and saw the shooter adjust the telescopic sights to better target the U.S. President, supported on the fantail by his two sons. Braun crept forward, and as he saw the assassin's finger move toward the trigger, aimed quickly, and fired a single shot. The glint of sunlight, reflecting off the scope of the assassin's weapon faded, as the rifle held by the assassin fell to the ground. The Russian, it appeared, had gotten there first.

Albertini, crouching behind the hill and hearing the premature shot, panicked. Braun and Fiskdal came scurrying back over the crest of the hill and gave the order to retreat. As they did, they retraced their steps back down the hill, and encountered Hannigan, desperately trying to obtain cover. A second shot rang out – this time fired by Fiskdal, and the Navy Radioman tumbled, dying, into a rocky ravine. He still had the portable radio cradled in his arms as he fell. The Germans retraced their steps as quickly as possible toward the St. Mary's Bay side of the peninsula.

Duffy, meanwhile, had returned to the hill where he had left Hannigan, but, finding neither Hannigan nor Kathy French there, headed directly toward Ship Harbour. Shortly after arriving, he was joined by two Newfoundland Rangers, who had responded to the repeated urgent telephone calls to Whitbourne. The remainder of the Constabulary detachment were not far behind. Hearing the gunshots, Duffy and the rangers ran west toward Cooper Head and thoroughly searched the area. They soon made grim and startling discoveries: the lifeless body of Hannigan in the ravine behind the hill, and the body of Kathy French, Duffy's Lee Enfield .303 rifle still at her feet in the rocky alcove facing the water. Neither gunshot had been heard over the Royal Marine band and sounds of the dignitaries arriving, nor by others ashore. As they looked down in confused shock upon lifeless body of the young nursing sister, the sounds of "Nearer My God to Thee" played by the Royal Marine bandsmen, could be heard clearly from the church service now concluding on the afterdeck of *HMS Prince of Wales*.

DIVINE SERVICES ABOARD HMS PRINCE OF WALES, SUNDAY AUGUST 10, 1941.
NOTE THE ATTENDANCE OF BOTH ROYAL NAVY AND U.S. NAVY SAILORS
AS THE BAND OF ROYAL MARINES PLAYS
'NEARER MY GOD TO THEE' AT THE CONCLUSION OF THE SERVICE.
(Official u.s.n.)

Epilogue

20 December 1999
Provincial Route 100
Freshwater, P.B. Newfoundland
1830 NST

Darkness comes early on winter nights in Newfoundland. Long shadows crept across the darkened parlor as John Duffy finished his story.

Father Cashin sat, silently. What he had just been told – and he had no doubt that every word was true – was incredible. As a priest, he had trained himself to show no emotion, regardless of how much turmoil he felt inside. But the story he had just heard was almost beyond belief.

"What happened next?" He asked. What became of the Nazi assassins?"

"It was fortunate that the car carrying the Newfoundland Rangers contained a radio transmitter as well as a receiver. They contacted their headquarters at Whitbourne, which immediately contacted the Shore Patrol at the base. Then, using their car and our Sergeant's truck, we split up and decided that the best place to intercept the Germans was along the railway branch west of Dunville.

The Americans agreed to search the entire peninsula with US Marines, and launched several aircraft to conduct surveillance between the bays. They soon discovered the black dingy, and focused their search around Dog Cove. We too were fortunate; the Rangers and we arrived on the Dunville road just as two of the landing-party members were attempting to cross, and they surrendered without a fight. Apparently, the team had decided to split up, and we found only the two military members still wearing battledress. Their colleague had decided that his chances were better on his own. Despite the best efforts of American and Canadian military he was never apprehended.

Braun and Fiskdal claimed prisoner of war status, since they were on a military operation while in uniform behind enemy lines. They were lodged temporarily at His Majesty's prison at Quidi Vidi near St. John's until things could be sorted out, and were later interned at a prisoner of war camp near Iroquois Falls, 700 kilometers north of Toronto. The Americans had wanted to take custody of the prisoners, but their status-of-forces agreement gave them no jurisdiction over foreign nationals off-base, and in any event they were still "neutral," so the government in St. John's prevailed upon the Canadians to assist. The Norwegian remained steadfast throughout interrogation, but Braun broke quickly and provided his interrogators with a wealth of valuable intelligence."

"We believe that the third member of the party, who Braun identified as the Corsican from St. Pierre, probably made contact with smugglers who operated all along the south coast and returned successfully to his island. Margaret and I were questioned extensively by senior officers from St. John's, but they finally came to understand that we had no involvement in the affair, and in fact had been prevailed upon by the Cottage Hospital staff to take the girl as a lodger. Her nursing companion from St. John's, who had lodged elsewhere, was shown to have no involvement either."

"But what, in the name of God, caused that young woman to want to shoot the American President? And for all these years you've kept this secret? Surely others must have known – at the very least the other policemen who came to your assistance. Why *would* a young girl – a trained nurse, no less – do something so absolutely...so absolutely bizarre?"

Duffy sighed. "Well, after several hours, and several hushed, frantic telephone calls, we were joined by a number of senior police officers from Fort Townshend and, soon after by other senior government officers from St. John's. As soon as the politicians arrived, of course, we police were shoved into the background. Now, in those days, most of the officials were British, you know – we had lost home rule during the depths of the depression and were being ruled directly from Whitehall during the war. At their suggestion – no, at their *insistence*– we wrapped the bodies and laid them in a disused fishing stage just south of Ship Harbour. The politicians sat and conferred, and one or two of them went back into town, and returned with a very senior official – you'd recognize his name immediately if I told you – who had been aboard *HMS Prince of Wales* as Churchill's guest that morning. It was pretty clear to everyone there that the whole affair was better hushed up. The British – who were hoping for a declaration of war on the part of the Americans – certainly had no interest in the Yanks finding out that their potential allies the Russians had just attempted to assassinate their President. The Newfoundlanders in the party were embarrassed that we'd let a party of German saboteurs get to within five hundred yards of two of the most important guests to ever visit the island. And, you have to remember too - most of us here on the bay had overcome our resentment at the Americans for having build their base at Argentia by this time. There's many a family in these fishing villages that owes its existence today to the jobs and prosperity that the base brought to Placentia Bay over the last fifty years. But it was still the depression back then, as far as we were concerned; no one was keen to kill the golden goose even before she'd laid all her eggs. I suppose it's what those fellows on the TV nowadays call a "cover up," but for us it was just looking out for our best interests, I suppose. You can't blame us for that, now, Father, can you?"

The priest shook his head. "I'm not here to judge, Mr. Duffy. Things happen in God's way, in God's own good time. But that still doesn't answer the question of why the young woman acted the way she did, does it? So, why the nurse?"

"Well, for one thing, we soon found out that her name wasn't Kathy French. Our superintendent in St. John's quietly contacted his opposite number in the RCMP, and they soon discovered her real name was Katrina Franczac. The rest of her story was true – she'd trained at the Grace Hospital at Winnipeg, but she'd changed her name when she came out here in 1941. Father Cashin thought for a moment. "Franczac, Franczac. . . Where have I heard that name before?" Wasn't that. . ."

"Yes, it was. Her father, Ivan Franczac was well known. He never worked in the CNR yards as the girl had told us; he was the head of the Communist Party of Canada before the war. He was an old Wobblie – one of those anarchists out there in the prairie provinces – and he led those strikes in Winnipeg all through the depression. The Canadians threw him into prison in '39, right after the war started, and he died in prison a year or so later. He had four kids – Katrina and three sons, – and all of them were devastated, I suppose. None of them were Reds themselves, at least not as far as anyone knew – but the communists used her to their advantage and they facilitated her wish to transfer to the Grace hospital at St. John's, and then, when the base opened, to the Cottage Hospital here in Placentia. I know that she was terrified that something would happen to her older brothers – when she lived with Maggie and me that's all she ever talked about. All three brothers had joined the Winnipeg Rifles and went overseas right around the time she came out here. I suppose, in her fear, she believed that if someone thought the Germans had assassinated Roosevelt, then the Yanks would immediately come in on our side, and it might make things easier for the British and Canadians, and maybe spare her brother's lives. Unfortunately, even that was a vain hope. One brother died in Normandy – and two made it almost through the war, dying with the First Canadian Army in the Ruhr. So it's fair to say that all four of them died at the hands of the Nazis, I suppose. No one ever learned if she had been instructed to attempt the assassination; personally I think she just saw it as a target of opportunity, and 'snapped'. Afterwards, we did learn that there were, in fact, Soviet agents active on the island at the time. Our fellows spotted a clandestine radio setup on the old Petty Harbour road just a few months later, and sailors from every allied nation could be found on the docks of St. John's. The Poles, especially, were ruthless in their hatred for the fascists, and some of them no doubt were sympathetic to the Russians. Were one or more of them here along the bay? There were certainly allied ships with crewmen from along the Eastern Front here at Argentia in those days. Remember too, that we had a terrible fire at the Knights of Columbus seaman's hostel in St. John's, and ninety-nine servicemen were killed. It was a brand new building, and well constructed; many felt then as I do now that the fire was deliberately set. I don't know for certain of course, but this I *do* know . . . I've blamed myself from that day to this for sending her for my weapon and giving her the key to unlock my ammunition. She'd be alive to this day, with kiddies and grandbabies perhaps. . ." his voice cracking, trailed off.

"But how could you keep something like this secret for so long? Didn't anyone miss the American and the nurse? I mean – it's not like this were a big city or something…didn't the Americans wonder where their sailor had gone?"

The old fellow sighed. "Ah, Father, it was easy, really. The Americans and the good folks from the Cottage Hospital were concerned when neither of the kids turned up for duty, of course. The Shore Patrol officer came to me – we had a good working relationship the whole time the Americans were at the base – and we, of course, made inquiries. Several folks were found who had "seen" a young couple fitting their description on the train to St. John's, and the skipper and mate of the Green Cross line that sailed between St. John's and Boston identified their pictures as a "Mr. And Mrs. Hanlon" who had left the island a few days later. A few dollars discretely distributed went a long way in those days, Father. And as for me – well, Maggie and I had two kids to feed – we later had six – and good steady work was hard to find in those times. The same went for the other fellows. They stayed with the Constabulary or the Rangers till after confederation, and then they and I and several other outport constables were quietly absorbed into the RCMP. Most Mounties have to serve outside their home province, but they made an exception for us, and I stayed on duty here in Placentia Bay until I retired in 1962.

"But what about the photographs? Why did Father McHugh keep them so long? Obviously, they meant something to him, didn't they?"

"I honestly don't know. One of the other constables and I quietly went to Father McHugh and told him that we had two youngsters lying dead at Ship Harbour. We led him to believe that it was a lover's tryst gone wrong – things like that happened often enough in those times, particularly if the young girl was expecting a baby. To avoid a scandal, they'd often bury the couple in another parish some distance away - and St. Colm's was just far enough down the bay so that it wouldn't attract attention. That night, after dark, we drove the bodies down there, and dug the grave the next morning. It was in a part of the cemetery that was just about filled up – we knew that there wouldn't be many folks traipsing around that area after we were done. Later, Father McHugh came to me and asked the names, and I told him. He knew that the girl had gone missing from the hospital, and I suspect he knew that it was her grave that he blessed that morning. He told me then that he'd mark the grave, but he'd do it in a way that kept the secret. He used what he called "Ogham" writing – some old way of writing that came from the west of Ireland in the old days. It has their names and the date of death – August 10, 1941 on it, if you can find someone around that can read the Old Irish writing. And there's one other thing that I suppose you're wondering, eh?" Father Cashin nodded.

The old fellow stopped and looked out across the darkening waters of Northeast Arm. For a long moment he sat silent. Sighing, he continued: "I went down to St. Colm's one afternoon in, oh, I suppose it was 1979 or 1980." he said. "It was the hundredth anniversary of the parish, and a few of us went down there to help spruce the place up a bit. Father McHugh was away – he was in hospital in St. John's, nothing serious – and Mickey McGrath and I went up into the steeple to replace the rope on the bells there. I got to looking around, and I found this."

Duffy went to a cabinet drawer and returned with a six inch round billet of porcelain. "I found this attached to a long piece of copper wire that ran down the inside of the bell tower. The wire was brittle and corroded with age – it had to have been there for years." He handed the porcelain insulator to Father Cashin. The priest looked at it closely. On one end was the faint impression of the manufacturer. "Siemens-AG 1938" Duffy nodded.

"Father McHugh was in contact with the Germans, I'm sure of it. He was Irish, and he hated the British, and he made no secret of it. He had grown up in Bombay Street, just off the Falls Road in West Belfast. His family were Republicans for years, though his father had been active in the church. He was the caretaker for St Gall's School off the Lower Falls, I believe. When Jerry McHugh was just a child, he saw the Black and Tans murder his father, a simple decent man just walking home from his work to his dinner. He must have been just a boy of six or seven, back then."

Tears filled his now clouded eyes. "A parent dies in prison, and a girl becomes an accomplice to assassination. A man dies at the hands of his nation's enemies, and his son burns with hatred and sells out his own people and his own convictions in retribution. A poor young sailor gets caught up in things he can never understand, and dies on the rocky foreshore of an island he didn't know existed a few months before. And we Newfoundlanders go on and on. That's the story of the place, Father. It's not like we don't have enough troubles of our own – sometimes they come from away."

APPENDIX I–WHERE ARE THEY NOW?

Albertini, Paulu (The Corsican) Evaded capture after 10 August 1941, believed to have successfully returned to Isle St. Pierre.

Boudreaux, Francis Xavier RM2 USN Remained on active duty until April 1947, retired as Chief Radioman after service in several warships.

Braun, SS-Obersturmführer Fritz Interned as POW by Canada, repatriated in August 1946. Settled in Berlin, upon establishment of German Democratic Republic joined STASI, the East German Secret Police. Implicated in the torture and death of scores of dissidents. Died by his own hand in 1978.

Canaris, Admiral Wilhelm Long suspected of disloyalty by Himmler and others, Canaris was arrested and executed at the Flossenburg concentration camp in April 1945, following the unsuccessful attempts on the life of Hitler the previous year.

Carpentier, Lt. Tom USNR Successfully completed tour of duty at Argentia, later commanded two Destroyer Escorts as Lt. Commander. Resigned commission in 1946, employed as Mate and Master on a variety of ships of the Lykes Brothers Line. In 1973 rescued nearly two hundred Vietnamese refugees from certain death in the Torres Strait.

Cashin, Rev. Michael, Returned to Cape Breton in 2004, hit and run fatality while jogging on NS Route 327 near Albertsbridge in 2007.

Charlie, and his Orchestra (nee Karl Schwedler) The band continued broadcasting on various German radio station until conditions deteriorated in 1944-45. Reputed to have become a businessman who retired at Tegernsee in mid 1950s.

Dönitz, Admiral Karl Shortly before his death, Hitler named Dönitz his successor as Head of State and Supreme Commander of the Armed Forces. Convicted at the Nürnberg trials. Dönitz was imprisoned for 10 years in Berlin. Died December 1980.

Fiskdal, SS-Rodefører Lars-Anders Interned as POW by Canada, refused repatriation in March 1946 to remain as a landed immigrant in Canada. Settled and farmed near Flin Flon, Manitoba.

Fleischer, Oberleutnant zur See Jürgen Left U-115 to take command of U-113, lost at sea in Denmark Straits, winter 1944.

Guidry, Jean Claude EO2 USN Successfully avoided sea duty, served with distinction in Mobile Construction Battalion One in the South Pacific.

Hirsch, SS-Unterscharführer Died on the Eastern Front 1942.

Holden, Ashford RM1 USN Promoted to Chief Radioman, served on *USS Iowa* before retiring in 1946.

Hopkins, Harry Continued in his role as one of Roosevelt's most trusted advisers and died in January 1946.

Kinna, Patrick Declined the opportunity to stay with Churchill after the war. He remained in government service, working in the Foreign Office, and died, aged 95 in 2009.

Leach, John (Jack) Captain RN Remained in service as the commanding officer *HMS Prince of Wales* until it was sunk by Japanese naval forces on December 10, 1941 near Singapore. Lost at sea.

McCroy, Jack D. Chief Radioman, USN Retired in 1947, after service in three additional ships. Became an instructor in H.S. Junior ROTC program in Texas, died in 1986.

McHugh, Rev. Jeremiah O'Donovan Continued as Pastor of St. Colm's until his death in 1999.

Moll, Kapitänleutnant Josef, transferred from U-115 after two additional successful war patrols. Remained in staff and training positions until war's end. Returned to Landau in der Pfälz where he opened a bed and breakfast/retreat center, popular with U-boat veterans. Died peacefully in his sleep, 1978.

Mueller, Leutnant zur See Theodor Lost at sea Summer 1943.

Oster, General Hans Along with his commander Canaris, Oster was executed at the Flossenburg concentration camp in April 1945, following the unsuccessful attempts on the life of Hitler the previous year

Prichard, Melvin CWO USN Retired 1946. Became one of the first communication security specialists at the National Security Agency, where he served with distinction until 1966.

Raeder, Großadmiral Eric sentenced to life imprisonment following the Nuremberg trials, he was released due to ill health in 1958 and died in February 1960

Schröder, Kapitänleutnant Paul (U114) Lost at sea with all hands of the U-114 off Cape Hatteras in 1942.

Maloney, Violet Continued duties as a trained nurse, and later became matron of the surgical wards of a number of small hospitals in the Toronto area. Very active in the Royal Canadian Legion Auxiliary.

Strebel, Oberleutnant zur See Ulf (Eng) continued serving in U-boat until the end of the war. Nothing further is recorded about his postwar activities.

Thompson, Inspector Walter Retired from the Metropolitan police force in 1945 and died of cancer in 1978.

U-115 When he had received no reply to several urgent transmissions, Moll ordered the U-115 to deeper water closer to the mouth of St. Mary's Bay. By noon on Sunday, August 10, lookouts spotted greatly enhanced air patrols in the region, and hydrophones indicated destroyers and other warships in the immediate vicinity. Moll exited the bay, and rounded Cape Pine, the Eastern headlands defining the bay. He then submerged deeply and awaited the cover of darkness before making good his escape. After an uneventful transit the boat reached Lorient, where all hands were sworn to strict secrecy about the mission. Moll conducted two additional patrols in the U-115 as noted above.

U-115 was reported lost off the coast of Gibraltar in the late 1943 and no additional information was made available.

Zimmermann Kapitänleutnant Georg Survived the war, settled in Bonn, employed as electrical contractor.

APPENDIX II–GLOSSARY

US Navy Usage

AF and RF gains-(USN): Front panel controls regulating the strength and volume of the signals on a communications receiver.

Aiguillettes-(USN): Gold braid, worn at the shoulder, identifying military aide to senior government or military officials.

Bainbridge-(USN): Located at Port Deposit, Maryland, the primary communications school for World War II sailors.

Belay-(USN): Navy jargon for "cease and desist immediately."

boondockers-(USN): Wellington-style, ankle length working boot, worn with the dungaree uniform.

Bread truck-(USN): A standard enclosed panel truck, with modified benches to transport sailors.

Bust-(USN): to reduce in rate or pay grade.

Butter-bar ensign-(USN): So called because the single gold bar worn by an officer in paygrade O-1 is said to resemble a bar of butter.

By Saam-(USN): Sportscaster Byrum Saam, a native of Texas, long the broadcast voice of Philadelphia baseball.

C+P-(USN): Chesapeake and Potomac Telephone Company. The local telephone provider for Washington DC and vicinity (until 1984).

Cartons of Lucky Strikes-(USN): A much desired unit of exchange in the Navy's bartering (cumshaw) economy.

China Station-(USN): squadrons of gunboats and other small ships stationed at Shanghai and vicinity in the 1930s. Reputedly, sailors on the China station were a cut above all others in the fleet.

cold cock-(USN): to knock unconscious, usually with a marlin-spike or other blunt instrument.

Crypto vault-(USN): highly secured room where classified messages were encrypted or decrypted.

Cumshaw-(USN): The Navy's long-standing and cherished method of barter. Often the most convenient or indeed only method of quickly obtaining mission critical supplies or material. In the author's experience always pronounced *commshaw*.

CW-(USN): continuous wave radio transmission. Interrupting the continuous wave by use of a telegraph key facilitated Morse code transmissions.

CWO-(USN): Chief Warrant Officer. Nominally ranked between the most senior enlisted Chief Petty Officer, and the most junior commissioned officer; serves as technical experts in a number of critical disciplines.

Dipshit-(USN): mild pejorative; frequently used by senior Petty officers when addressing lazy, inattentive, or incompetent juniors.

Ditty boxes-(USN): small wooden box, often intricately decorated, used by Navy enlisted personnel to store personal belongings.

Drifty-(USN): inattentive to detail. Comes from the concept "gear adrift" (material not in its proper place) a situation often caused by inattentive sailors.

Dufus-(USN): mild pejorative; frequently used by senior Petty officers when addressing oafish or dull-witted juniors.

Duty belt-(USN): white nylon webbed belt, worn by sailors in a duty status. Examples include messenger of the watch, duty master at arms etc.

Flat hat-(USN): traditional "Donald-Duck" headgear, worn in the 19th and early 20th centuries. The United States Navy has not been the same since this popular and flattering headgear has been discontinued.

Goatlocker-(USN) : Berthing and messing spaces reserved for Chief Petty Officers only. Derivation will be obvious to anyone privileged to associate with these fine sailors.

Hallicrafters SX-28 -(USN): high frequency radio receiver first manufactured in 1940 in Chicago. Arguably the best general coverage receiver available at the time.

Hamerlund BC779-(USN): high frequency radio receiver. Excellent sensitivity and selectivity, but provided less versatility than the SX-28.

HF-(USN): High Frequency. The radio spectrum between 1.5 megacycles and 30 megacycles (175 meter to 10 meter wavelength). Shortwave radio operates in the high frequency spectrum.

HF/DF-(USN): High Frequency Direction Finding. Technique using specialized equipment, including rotatable antennas, to identify direction, bearing, and often distance to the source of a targeted radio transmission.

Holystones-(USN): sandstone blocks, often used to scrub or scour the wooden decks of warships.

HW-6 Caesar-(USN): A semi automated encryption and decryption system bearing marked similarities to the German enigma system.

Irish pennants-(USN): stray threads, often found in this seams of Navy uniforms when first received from the manufacturer. Only drifty sailors would be seen in such uniforms.

Ixnay-the-amegay-(USN): Pig Latin for "turn off the ballgame."

J-38-(USN): Standard US Navy issue telegraph key used during the World War Two era.

Lagniappe-(USN): regional dialect (Cajun) for a small gift to facilitate business.

LCDR-(USN): Lieutenant Commander. Roughly equivalent to the rank of Major in other branches.

Lifer-(USN): Individual who has served or is serving with the expectation of a 20+ year career.

Lucky bag-(USN): Repository for lost, found or unwanted uniform items.

Messman-(USN): Unskilled assistant to a Navy cook or baker. Frequently washed dishes for months on end.

Midwatch-(USN): Navy equivalent of civilian's third shift operation.

Modulo-25-(USN): Cryptographic category of matrix 25 to the 25th power. Essentially unbreakable.

Navy's FOX.-(USN): Worldwide radio broadcast originating in Washington DC relayed through transmitters throughout the world.

Ninety-day wonders-(USN): Junior officers (reserve) who complete Officer Candidate School and not a military academy.

OOD-(USN): Officer of the Deck. Holds delegated command authority during his watch.

Op-20-g-(USN): Naval communications security headquarters during World War II.

Oscilloscope-(USN): Device used to visualize and analyze electronic signals.

QST-(USN): Monthly journal of the American Radio Relay League, an association of amateur radio operators.

RG8/U-(USN): A high capacity form of coaxial cable, used between radio transmitters and their associated antennas.

Request chits-(USN): small form used between commands to request a specific action or favor.

RM3, RM2, RM1, RMC -(USN): progression through the Petty Officer grades for Navy radioman. Roughly equivalent to corporal to master sergeant in the other branches.

Rope-yarn Sunday-(USN): time set aside to attend to small personal needs i.e. clothing repair etc.

Groundwave-(USN): component of a HF radio signal which is not reflected from the ionosphere.

Scuttlebutt-(USN): Navy jargon for rumor or unverified speculation.

Sea daddy-(USN): Experienced sailor who mentors newly arrived shipmates.

Sparks-(USN): Nickname sometimes applied to radioman, reflecting the four sparks on their rating badge.

Speed-key-(USN): Eectromechanical device produced by Vibroflex Corp. and others to facilitate much higher transmission speeds on CW circuits.

Squared away-(USN): Polar opposite to a drifty Dufus. (see above)

Strikers-(USN): non-rated personnel, engaged in on-the-job training in a specific rating.

Thirteen buttons-(USN): Navy dress blue uniform trousers use 13 buttons on a square flap in lieu of a zipper fly.

Trick-(USN): element of a Navy watch. Facilitates rotations among positions to deter boredom or fatigue.

V3 program-(USN): Naval Reserve program, established shortly before World War II, to directly procure experienced radio technicians and operators for the Petty Officer grades. Not universally admired by those who had spent years or decades reaching those levels in the fleet.

Watch-Quarter-and-Station bill-(USN): Document listing the assignment and duties for each individual in a division under a variety of circumstances i.e. fire, abandoned ship, boarding party, etc.

White hat.-(USN): The traditional Navy "Dixie Cup" worn by sailors in a variety of circumstances.

Winding the dog-watch-(USN): late afternoon watches are traditionally "dogged" (four hour watch divided into two two-hour watches) to facilitate the evening meal. New or inexperienced sailors are often directed by their seniors to "go wind the dog watch" as an initiation or a prank.

German Usage

Abwehr: -(German): Ausland/Abwehr im Oberkommando der Wehrmacht: the main German intelligence service in the early years of World War II.

BdU: -(German): Befehlshaber der U-Boote: the Central command element of the U-boat service

B-deinst: -(German): Beobachtunsdienst, the German wireless monitoring service in World War II.

Bootsman-(German): German equivalent to a boatswains mate in the US or British navies.

Chateau Kerneval-(German): Chateau in Lorient France confiscated for use as German U-boat control center during World War II.

Davidwache-(German): red light district in the St. Pauli area of Hamburg Germany.

Enigma-(German): electromechanical encryption system used extensively by all branches of the German military during World War II.

Focke-Wulf Condor-(German): Long Range bomber or reconnaissance aircraft operated by the Luftwaffe.

Freikorps-(German): independent militia which arose after WW-1.

Gestapo: -(German): Geheime Staatspolizei: German secret state police during World War II.

Germanske SS-Norge.-(German): Norwegian volunteers who served with the German SS during World War II.

Grüß Gott-(German): traditional Bavarian greeting or farewell; God bless you.

Heimat-(German): "the Homeland." Less political than "the Fatherland."

Kapitänleutnant-(German): Officer equivalent to a full commander in the British or American Navy.

Keroman 2-(German): the second of three U-boat protection structures established at Lorient France.

M.E.T-(German): Middle European time. GMT + 1 hour

Matrose-(German): equivalent to Ordinary Seaman.

Matrosen-efreiter-(German): equivalent to an Able Seaman.

Matrosen-Oberefreiter-(German): equivalent to a Leading Seaman.

Oberfunkmeister-(German): equivalent to a Chief Radioman.

OKW: -(German): Oberkommando der Wehrmacht. High command of the German army.

Oberleutnant zur See-(German): equivalent to a full lieutenant in the US Navy.

OKM-(German): (Kriesmarine) high command of the German Navy.

one-time cipher pads-(German): highly secure message encryption system used by all combatants in World War II.

Pfälzerwald -(German): A low-mountain forested region in southwestern Germany, located in the Palatinate in the state of Rhineland-Palatinate, near the current border with France.

Quadratkare Nr. 3401-(German): Main Atlantic Ocean chart used by U-boats in WW2. The area was divided into a grid containing 100 squares, each subdivided into 100 smaller units.

Rudeltaktik-(German): Wolfpack technique. Common tactical formation for German U-boats in World War II

SS-Obersturmführer-(German): SS grade roughly equivalent to the rank of lieutenant in the Allied services.

SS-Rodefører (German-Norge): Roughly equivalent to the rank of corporal in the Allied services.

SS-Unterscharführer (German): Roughly equivalent to the rank of sergeant in the Allied services.

umlauts-(German): Diaeresis (diacritic), a pair of dots (¨) above a vowel, used in German and many other languages.

British Usage: (including Cockney Rhyming Slang)

Andrew, the-(UK): Nickname of the Royal Navy. Origin obscure, may derive from one Andrew Miller, a zealous officer of the Impress Service during the French Revolutionary and Napoleonic Wars, who 'recruited' so many men to His Majesty's ships that the Navy was said to belong to him.

Coxswain-(UK): Petty Officer in charge of a ship's boats. Traditionally the senior coxswain is the leading petty officer for a British warship.

Graft China-(UK): [CRS] workmate. From Graft=work. China from china plate=mate.

Isle of Dogs-(UK): Area of docklands and working class lodgings on the south shore of the river Thames in eastern London.

Loaf-(UK): [CRS} Head From loaf of bread=head.

Lower decks-(UK): the traditional berthing and messing spaces of other ranks (i.e. enlisted sailors) in the Royal Navy.

Mince pies-(UK): [CRS] eyes From mince pies=eyes.

Ratcliffe Highway-(UK): particularly rough area frequented by sailors and others in southeast London.

Scapa Flow-(UK): the main anchorage for the Royal Navy in the Orkney Islands off of the north coast of mainland Scotland.

Siren suit-(UK): single piece coverall or jump suit, popular during World War II for ease of wear during air raids.

Squadie-(UK): popular slang for a soldier in the British forces during World War II.

The Smoke-(UK): London, the derivation of the nickname is obvious.

Newfoundland Usage

Bakeapples-(Nfld) Fruit of the Rubus chamaemorus a rhizomatous herb native to alpine and arctic tundra and boreal forest, producing amber-colored edible fruit similar to the raspberry or blackberry, delicious and beloved to Newfoundlanders. More fun to eat than to define!

Bayman-(Nfld) Resident of one of the many outport villages or settlements throughout the island of Newfoundland.

Cape Race-(Nfld) that point of land located at the southeastern extreme of the island of Newfoundland.

CNR-(Nfld) Canadian National Railway.

Come-From-Away-(Nfld) An individual, not island born, who as a visitor or resident, abides on the island of Newfoundland.

Flemish Cap-(Nfld) An area of shallow waters in the north Atlantic at 47° north, 45° west, 560 km east of St. John's, Newfoundland.

Foster Hewitt-(Nfld) Canadian radio broadcaster most famous for his play-by-play calls for Hockey Night in Canada for forty years. Died April, 1985.

Fox Harbour-(Nfld) A small community on the Avalon Peninsula of Newfoundland, north of Argentia and south of Ship Harbour.

Gibraltar Rock-(Nfld) A distinctive geological formation, similar in shape to its more famous namesake, 2.9 km southwest of Point Verde, Placentia Bay.

Lorne Greene-(Nfld) Principal newsreader for the CBC National News during WW2. Often called the *Voice of Canada*, he was the Walter Cronkite of the North. Later starred as family patriarch Ben Cartwright on the American TV western *Bonanza* (1959–1973).

Newfoundland Constabulary- (Nfld) Dating to 1729 when the first constables were appointed, the Newfoundland Constabulary may be considered the oldest law enforcement force in continuous service in North America. During World War II, the Constabulary pursued not only spies but also criminal elements within the foreign military stationed at St. John's and in the outports on the Avalon Peninsula. In 1979, Queen Elizabeth II conferred the designation *Royal* on this extraordinary "thin blue line between crime and society," in recognition of its long history of service to the people of Newfoundland and Labrador.

Newfoundland Rangers-(Nfld) A now disbanded police force of the pre-confederation Dominion of Newfoundland, which provided law enforcement and other government services to rural areas of the island.

NST-(Nfld) Newfoundland Standard Time. Because of its location in the North Atlantic, Newfoundland is one and a half hours ahead of Eastern Standard Time.

Ogham-(Nfld) an Early "Runic" alphabet used primarily to write the Old Irish language. Examples of the alphabet include:

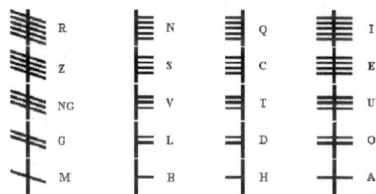

Outer Battery-(Nfld) One of the oldest inhabited areas of St. John's Newfoundland. Located on the slopes of Signal Hill facing the Narrows, the entrance to St. John's Harbour. Until recent years was home to active participants in the inshore fishery.

Scoff-(Nfld) an old-fashioned stick-to-the-ribs Newfoundland meal. One great example is Jigs Dinner; a feast of salt beef and boiled vegetables, usually served with pease pudding—yellow spilt peas boiled to a paste in a linen sack.

Screech-(Nfld) Potent beverage first created by traders when the same barrels were used to carry both molasses and rum, and were only occasionally cleaned. The barrels built up a deposit of strongly sweet sediment at the bottom, which was melted out with boiling water and either fermented or mixed with grain alcohol.

Joe Smallwood-(Nfld) The Hon. Joseph R. Smallwood, Newfoundland's Father of Confederation and first Premier. Successfully negotiated Confederation with Canada in 1949 and served as Premier until 1972.

Tomcod-(Nfld) the North Atlantic codfish, the staple of Newfoundland fisheries from 1600 to the very recent past. When the author asked an old fishing skipper why the cod fishery has failed, he sadly replied: "We've caught 'em all, my son, and there'll never be no more." An ecological disaster, and a warning to those who come after us.

Townie-(Nfld) A resident of the capital city of Newfoundland, St. John's.

Upalong-(Nfld) Newfoundland usage for those portions of Canada west of the Maritime Provinces, most commonly the province of Ontario.

OTHER READINGS

The reader may be interested in these works, which present the significant events of July and August 1941 without the overlay of fiction.

Blair C., (1996). **Hitler's U-Boat War.** 1st ed. New York: Random House.

Browne (M.O. M). G., (2008). **To Serve and Protect: The Newfoundland Constabulary on the Home Front World War Two.** 1st ed. St. John's NF: DRC Publishing

Hagan J. and Leahy J., (2006) **The Chief Petty Officer's Guide.** 1st ed. Annapolis, MD: Naval Institute Press

Henrichs, W., (1988). **Threshold of War: Franklin Roosevelt and American Entry into World War II.** 1st ed. Oxford U.K.: Oxford University Press

Leahy, J., (2004) **Ask the Chief, The Backbone of the Navy,** 1st ed. Annapolis, MD: Naval Institute Press

Mallmann Showell J.P., (2003). **German Naval Code Breakers.** 1st ed. Annapolis, MD: Naval Institute Press

Milner M., (1994). *The U-Boat Hunters: The Royal Canadian Navy and the Offensive against Germany's Submarines.* 1st ed. Toronto: University of Toronto Press.

Persico J, E., (2002). *Roosevelt's Secret War.* 1st ed. New York: Random House.

Wilson T.A., (1991). *The First Summit: Roosevelt and Churchill at Placentia Bay, 1941.* 2nd ed. Lawrence KS: University Press of Kansas.

ABOUT THE AUTHOR

J.F. (Jack) Leahy is a noted writer on naval topics, and is author of *Honor, Courage, Commitment – Navy Boot Camp*, (Naval Institute Press, Annapolis, Maryland, 2002); *Ask The Chief – Backbone of the Navy*, (Naval Institute Press, 2004) and co-author, with former Master Chief Petty of the Navy John Hagan, of *The Chief Petty Officer's Guide.* (Naval Institute Press, 2004). He also edited and mentored the author of *Lost at Sea–An Enlisted Woman's Journey* (with Rebecca Anne Freeman). A former Navy radioman, his active duty included a combat tour with Mobile Construction Battalion One at Phu Bai and Da Nang Vietnam in 1969-70. After completing his graduate education as a civilian, he spent over thirty years in the intelligence community and telecommunications industry. During 1972-75 he served as station manager at an intelligence gathering and processing detachment within the U.S. Naval Facility (NavFac) aboard Naval Station, Argentia Newfoundland. In 2001 he became a professor of business in the Ross School of Leadership and Management at Franklin University, and in 2006 was concurrently appointed Associate Vice President of the Pontifical College Josephinum, a Roman Catholic seminary, in Columbus, Ohio where he resides with his wife, Margaret. This is his first work of fiction.

ABOUT THE PUBLISHER

Established by a cadre of writers who first met through the Naval Institute at the Naval Academy, Annapolis in 2002, the Naval Writers Group is a specialized publishing imprint which provides a voice to "the sailor on the deck plates." No distinction is ever made based upon the author's rating or rank – be it seaman or admiral – for we strongly believe that each story deserves to be evaluated on its merit alone. You may learn more about the Naval Writers Group at www.navalwritersgroup.us or by contacting exdir@navalwritersgroup.us.

www.ingramcontent.com/pod-product-compliance
Lightning Source LLC
Chambersburg PA
CBHW072100020726
47501CB00003B/662